BLOOD & STEEL

AN EPIC ROMANTIC FANTASY

THE LEGENDS OF THEZMARR
BOOK I

HELEN SCHEUERER

First printing, 2023

Print paperback ISBN 978-1-922903-03-7

Print hardcover ISBN 978-1-922903-04-4

Ebook ISBN 978-1-922903-02-0

Cover design by Maria Spada

BLOOD & STEEL

For my partner in wine and crime, Gary.
With you, every day is an adventure.

Delmira

Dorinth

Thezmarr

The Mourner's Trail

The Bloodwoods

Hailford

Harenth

The Chained Islands

The Broken Isles

Ciraun

Naarva

The Scarlet Tower

The Veil

THE MIDREALMS

PROPHECY OF THE MIDREALMS

In the shadow of a fallen kingdom, in the eye of the storm
A daughter of darkness will wield a blade in one hand
And rule death with the other

When the skies are blackened, in the end of days
The Veil will fall.
The tide will turn when her blade is drawn.

A dawn of fire and blood.

CHAPTER ONE

A ltmea Zoltaire's death had been carved in stone since
she was a child. That was how she knew, as she crept
through a realm on the brink of darkness, that the world was
not ending. Not yet.

Lightning split the sky, chased by the crack of thunder.
Thea inched along the bluff, savouring the rich scent of the
incoming storm, revelling in the chaos it threatened to
unleash. She shouldn't be up here, but she had learnt long
ago to take destiny into her own hands.

Heart pounding, Thea scoured the rocks for a hiding
spot. The meet was due to happen at any moment, here on
the black cliffs, hemmed in by jagged mountains and savage
seas, where giant waves barrelled through the clouds. An
unnerving territory to most, the wild landscapes and the
cold, sharp lines of Thezmarr was the only home she'd ever
known. She had next to no memories of what had come
before she and her sister, Elwren, had been left beneath the
maw of the fortress portcullis.

Thea turned her attention back to the rendezvous point.

There was no sign of them, not a whisper in the wind. With an impatient sigh, she toyed with the fate stone around her neck, running her thumb over the number engraved there, the number she was bound by in this life.

Twenty-seven.

The age she would die. Just three more years until her death would come to pass; a future she didn't fear, but resented. For three short years was no time at all for a woman to become what she wanted.

A legend.

She squinted into the sky, searching for the watery orb of the sun amidst the grey. In a realm cloaked in darkness, it was often hard to tell the hour of the day, but if she was a betting woman, and she generally was, she'd say that the warriors were late. A bad sign to be sure.

The skies opened up and the downpour began, turning the ground into a muddy river beneath her boots and another bolt of lightning flashed, illuminating that which lay beyond the lashing waters: the Veil. An enormous wall of impenetrable white mist, reaching for the gods, wrapping the midrealms in its protective embrace. For hundreds of years it had shielded their realm from the monsters, until one day it hadn't.

The thought made Thea check that her most prized – and forbidden – possession, her dagger, was snug in her boot beneath the hem of her trousers as it always was.

Hooves suddenly sounded on the rocks and Thea threw herself behind a cluster of brambles, hiding herself in the shadows as two great stallions came into view.

Her pulse quickened; her source had been correct. Those gleaming black horses belonged to only one kind of rider.

Heavy boots hit the muddied ground with a splash, and low voices danced along the cliff.

They were here.

The Warswords of Thezmarr.

Thea peeked around the rocks, desperate to see the legendary warriors up close.

A pair of men strode into the clearing, armed to the teeth, clad in black armour with their totems displayed proudly on their armbands: a steel design of two crossed swords with a third cutting down the middle.

Thea's hand went to her own sleeve absent-mindedly, willing there to be a totem secured there.

A Warsword answered to no one but the guild master.

Ballads were sung about their power, about how upon completing the Great Rite, they became stronger, faster, more agile than the most formidable men. Some were much rumoured to be immortal. It was said they were not born, but forged with blood and steel. There were only three of them left.

Now, two of them stood mere feet away from Thea in the rain. She had been trying for over a year to get this close to them, to get a better sense of what was coming for the midrealms – for she would not be caught unawares when darkness came for them all.

She had seen the pair many times before in the Great Hall: Torj the Bear Slayer, the hammer-wielding hero with golden hair who had supposedly fought off two cursed bears in the forests of Tver; and Vernich the Bloodletter, the older warrior who had spilt *rivers* of enemy blood in the countless battles he'd led, chiefly at the fall of Delmira.

The latter looked around the cliff, a deep crease in his brow. 'He said he'd be here.'

'Probably got lost, it's been so long since he's been home,' Torj declared with a note of amusement.

'I'm too thirsty for your piss-poor jokes,' Vernich all but growled. 'I want to get out of this fucking rain. I haven't had dry boots for a week.'

'His letter said to wait here —'

'I *know* what it said,' Vernich snapped. 'Or I'd already be three ales deep by the fire.'

'Well, by all means, go pamper yourself. I can always fill you in,' Torj replied, a hand resting on the head of the war hammer at his belt.

Thea chewed her lip, her heart still pounding wildly.

Vernich paced. 'We haven't seen the bastard in years, as if I'd —'

Another set of hooves thundered against the mountain and a spray of water showered the clearing amidst the rain.

A thick silence fell as a third rider joined the others. Dismounting from his great stallion, subtle notes of rosewood and leather tangled with the scent of rain in his wake.

As he came into view, Thea didn't know what detail to take in first. His towering build was a wall of muscle wrapped in black armour, giant twin blades peeking out from behind him. Wet, dark hair was swept up in a knot at the back of his head, a neat beard lined his fierce jaw...

The nape of Thea's neck prickled. She knew *of* him, of course.

Although he had been gone for years, there were few who hadn't heard of Wilder Hawthorne, the youngest Warsword of Thezmarr, the last of his kind to have passed the Great Rite.

The one they called the Hand of Death.

Power rippled from him in waves.

Thea froze as it thrummed outward, the force of it strange, unexpected... She'd never been this close to *true* magic before, not many common folk had. Magic in the midrealms had become unpredictable over the centuries. It had faded from the people and was now a gift only possessed by those in the royal families and bestowed upon Warswords during the Great Rite. But it manifested in other ways, in places, in spells, in monsters.

Thea could only imagine what it was like to have that sort of force at one's fingertips, to revel in that kind of strength —

The Hand of Death's power pulsed from him now, calling out to her.

Hawthorne turned to his fellow warriors, surveying them critically.

Neither spoke.

'Good,' he said at last, his voice rich and deep. 'You're here.'

'Not that I appreciated the summons,' Vernich replied tersely.

Hawthorne ignored this. 'We have much to discuss.'

For the first time, Thea's gaze went to what he held in his right hand. A hessian sack. A sack that dripped red.

Torj noticed it too. 'Grim news?'

A muscle tensed in Hawthorne's jaw. 'It's always grim news.'

'Tell us then.'

'I've come from the Broken Isles,' he said, his voice low and deep. 'I slayed a new swarm of shadow wraiths there. I planned to return to the fortress immediately with the report, but a reef dweller stalked my ship all the way to our coast, so I led it further west, towards the Veil. Until...'

He thrust the bloodied sack at Torj. 'I came upon a wraith far too fucking close to Thezmarr for comfort.'

With a noise of disgust, Torj pulled something black and dripping from the bag.

Thea nearly gagged.

A heart.

'Where there is one, there are many.' Hawthorne warned. 'I have two more of those in another pack. There are more tears in the Veil. More breaches every day by this scum and worse.'

'Furies save us,' Torj murmured.

Hawthorne laughed darkly. 'The Furies don't save anyone.'

As the words left his lips, he looked up – a thrill raced down Thea's spine, a quiet bolt of lightning surging through her veins.

Through the brush, her celadon eyes met the silver gaze of the infamous Warsword.

Her heart seized, her entire body tensed.

His stare pierced her very soul.

Slowly, Hawthorne blinked and he turned back to his companions. 'There's more, but I won't discuss it here.'

'What do you mean, not here?' Vernich snapped. 'I thought that was the whole fucking point —'

'Not here.' Hawthorne snatched up his reins and without another glance in Thea's direction, led the others away into the black mountains.

Thea's legs went completely liquid, her hands trembling at her sides. He'd *seen* her. Hawthorne had seen her and hadn't said anything... *Why?*

Her mind still churning, she forced herself to her feet. When she was sure the Warswords were gone, she darted towards the narrow, rocky path that led back to the fortress. Her fate stone beat against her chest like a war drum as she scrambled across the cliffs and down the rugged mountainside, past the thick walls and the gatehouse, to the doors of the north tower. Panting, she threw herself inside, at last out of the wind and rain. Wringing the water from her bronze and gold-streaked hair, she gave herself a moment to process what had happened; what she'd seen and heard.

It was true.

After years of absence, Wilder Hawthorne had returned to Thezmarr, and he carried the hearts of monsters with him.

CHAPTER TWO

'You reckless fool,' her sister, Elwren, hissed as soon as Thea halted before her in the upstairs halls.

Thea met Wren's glower. She and her sister shared the same eye colour: an unusual shade of celadon; as well as similar dark, strong brows. Wren usually used hers for scowling at Thea. They also shared the same bronze tresses, though more gold threaded Thea's from more time spent outdoors. They were two sides of the same coin, but where Thea was all sharp lines and muscle, Wren was the softer, more beautiful of the two. Two decades of fortress life had only confirmed that fact; fortune looked upon those with pretty smiles and skirts, not broken fingernails and threadbare trousers.

But now, any semblance of Wren's gentle nature was long gone as she yanked Thea out of earshot from the others and pulled off Thea's sopping cloak, brushing away the larger chunks of dried mud.

Thea batted her hand away, already irritated. 'Will you stop? I'm the eldest, it should be —'

Wren snorted. 'Thea, you are one of the few cases that prove older is not always wiser.'

'Then you're lucky I'm here to make you look good. Stop complaining.'

Shaking her head, messy bun bobbing, Wren passed Thea several pieces of parchment, which she took with a grimace. More *women's work*. Poisons and potions, rather than blades and blood. Another reason to curse the laws, to resent the prophecy they'd been taught to fear:

In the shadow of a fallen kingdom, in the eye of the storm
A daughter of darkness will wield a blade in one hand
And rule death with the other

When the skies are blackened, in the end of days
The Veil will fall.
The tide will turn when her blade is drawn.

A dawn of fire and blood.

Twenty years ago, after that deadly prophecy had been uttered, women had been forced to surrender their blades. Thea, only four years of age at the time, had seen bits of it unfold from a grate in the cellar, had watched the women rage as they were stripped of their right to protect the midrealms.

It hadn't stopped Thea carrying her dagger.

Nothing could.

Her attention drifted down the hall to where the trophy

room was located. Even as an adult, she longed to visit, to gaze upon the names of champions. Talemir Starling, for one – the Warsword called the Prince of Hearts, who was undefeated in dual sword wielding and, who according to the tales, had carved out more monster hearts than one could count.

Another name had always fascinated Thea. Six years ago, she'd discovered the name of their warden, Audra, there too, under *Knife Throwing Champions of Thezmarr*. The stern-faced librarian had been the only woman warrior to surrender her weapons and stay on at the fortress.

'I covered for you with Farissa, told her you had one of your nosebleeds,' Wren was saying.

Thea grinned. 'Thanks.'

'There's only so many nosebleeds a woman can have before the masters ask harder questions.'

'Good thing you always have the answers then.' Thea slung an arm around her sister's neck. Wren was a revered alchemist of Thezmarr, whereas Thea was more of a drifter. While she worked alongside her sister in the workshop and in the library to earn her keep, her mind was always elsewhere, with the limited years she had left, with her dreams of damning the rules and wielding a blade of her own against the darkness.

Wren clicked her tongue in frustration and shook her off. 'I would sooner hit you than hug you right now.'

'Only because I taught you how.'

'Know when to shut up, Thee.'

Sensing that her sister's annoyance was indeed at its limits, Thea clamped down on the rest of her retorts.

The sharp ring of steel on steel echoed up from the

courtyard and she went to the window, nails digging into the damp sill as she looked down.

A new unit of shieldbearers, varying in age from teens to mid-twenties, were making their way towards the gatehouse, some sparring as they went.

The guild honed warriors from the very beginning, training shieldbearers in the art of war until they passed their initiation tests to become Guardians of the midrealms who bore the totem of a pair of crossed swords. From there they could stay faithful mid-level warriors of Thezmarr, or they could work their way up to commanders and masters of a particular field. Then, there were the Warswords.

To be a Warsword... was to be a legend incarnate.

But below, there was no sign of the elite warriors, nor could Thea see Esyllt, the weapons master. Thea's chest tightened as she watched them go, shields slung across their backs, no doubt on their way to drills she'd watched a hundred times before, hidden away in the Bloodwoods.

Her fingers itched to retrieve her dagger from her boot.

'Thea...' her sister warned.

Making up her mind, Thea snatched her cloak from Wren's grasp and thrust the papers back at her. 'I feel another nosebleed coming on.'

'Thea, no —'

Thea was already walking away. 'Oh it's going to be a bad one, I can tell. Transcribing Audra's fascinating tomes and re-shelving dusty books will have to wait, I wouldn't want to mar the pages...'

Wren attempted to block her. Her eyes, a near perfect match to Thea's, blazed with frustration. 'Gods, you're not a teenager anymore.' She glanced back at their friends.

'I've got a blinding headache, too, Wren.'

Her sister flung her hands up in exasperation, shaking her head once more in disbelief. 'You're a damn fool, Althea.'

Thea grinned; she knew exactly what she was. But she would rather live a hundred lives in three years than waste the little time she had left in these realms. She threw a little wave over her shoulder as she started back down the stairs and burst out into the rain once more.

Outside, true dark had fallen around the fortress and Thea passed unnoticed through the gatehouse as usual. She followed the unit of shieldbearers at a distance, knowing precisely where they were going. The Bloodwoods were a dense forest surrounding the territory of Thezmarr, where the trees bled the blood of warriors long dead and whispered ancient secrets with the rustle of their leaves.

Further south was a clearing that the weapons master, Esyllt, favoured for initial drills with smaller units. He would already be there waiting, but Thea kept off the main trail in case there were any late comers, though she doubted even the dimmest of shieldbearers would be that stupid. Esyllt's wrath was not to be trifled with.

Wonder who'd emerge victorious if he was pitted against Audra... Thea snorted. Audra could beat him over the head with one of her books easily enough, and she *had* been a knife throwing champion long ago.

Still amused at the thought, Thea delved deeper into the dark glades of the Bloodwoods, relishing the damp smell of the earth and the slide of the leaves beneath her boots. She was close enough to hear the unit bash their way through the forest, could even see the stragglers at the back. *A stealthy bunch to be sure*, she scoffed. Though, she couldn't help but eye the weapons that swung at their belts with envy.

On the night the prophecy had been triggered, the Master Alchemist, Farissa, had evacuated all the children of Thezmarr to a hidden cellar. But after the others had fallen asleep, Thea had found a grate in the stone, giving her a glimpse of the scorched courtyard above. She would never forget the sight of the women surrendering their blades in the dead of night. The steel had sung as the swords were thrown into a pile, their rage palpable.

'The prophecy has begun,' the Guild Master had called over the shouts of fury and the several brawls that broke out. 'We can no longer have women wielding blades. You will find other occupations, or henceforth leave the guild.'

'Osiris you bastard,' someone screamed. 'You would leave Thezmarr so weakened? You would turn your back on all those who have served loyally —'

'It is not how I wanted things to be. But it is the will of the gods,' he replied. 'Surrender your weapons, or they will be taken by force!'

Thea had been too young to understand then, but it had haunted her ever since. Except for Audra, the warrior women had left that very night, to where, no one knew, for it was a law not only of Thezmarr, but the midrealms in their entirety. No woman would brandish steel again.

For years Thea had tried to get her warden to talk about it, but the librarian refused. Various lessons and all the books Thea read had told her it had been a little girl holding a blade that triggered the prophecy, and the laws that followed were the Guild Master's attempt to protect the midrealms from further *daughters of darkness*.

He'd lost his shit at a child holding a small scythe. If he knew Thea had a weapon, well... He'd never find out.

She stopped at a clearing she frequented, well hidden from the training ground below, a perfect viewing platform, and crouched in the leaf litter, straining to hear the speech she'd heard Esyllt give a hundred times before, the speech that made her blood sing.

The lean weapons master paced before the group of bright-eyed recruits, resting his hand on the pommel of his longsword, his chest thrust out as he eyed them with a harsh expression.

Esyllt's voice carried across the clearing, full of authority. 'A month ago you were mere students, boys whose purpose did not extend beyond the ordinary... Today, you are shieldbearers of Thezmarr and you have come here to the Bloodwoods hoping to be something far greater.'

Goosebumps rushed across Thea's skin and she hung onto every word, as though they were an elixir she desperately needed.

'The months that follow will be the best and worst of your life,' he continued, letting his words fall upon his captivated audience. 'That's *if* you make it that far. Some of you will give up, a day, a week, or a month in. The rest of you will come to know pain and fear intimately, you will come to know what it means to fight tooth and nail for your place. You will come to know who to trust, and when to sleep with one eye open. Those who fail our tests will be shunned from our ranks. Those with special talents might become apprentices to the commanders. Some of you will be injured. Some of you will die.'

Esyllt paused again as he surveyed the faces before him, as though he could determine then and there who would make it, and who would fail. He cleared his throat. 'And a select few of you' – he gave pointed stares to his chosen shieldbearers – 'will be forged into what many only dream to be: Guardians of the midrealms, warriors of Thezmarr.'

Thea loosed a breath. Gods... It didn't matter how many times she had heard Esyllt's orientation, it hit her right in the chest every time. Rooted to the spot, she was as transfixed as the shieldbearers, wishing she could stand alongside them, wishing she could share this with someone, anyone. But she remained hidden, as always.

Esyllt cleared his throat. 'Right, get into your groups. I want to see what you've learnt so far.'

The shieldbearers hesitated.

'Drills,' Esyllt barked. *'Now.'*

The recruits burst into action, splitting up into several smaller groups and drawing their weapons, hoisting their shields up in defensive stances.

Thea watched on, noting those who held their shields too low, those whose footwork was too heavy, and those who might just interest her as opponents. She had studied the theory for years, practiced in privacy, but her fingers itched to hold a sword as theirs did and she found her hand creeping to the dagger in her boot.

Carefully, she stepped back, well out of sight, and started going through her own drills. Like all children of Thezmarr, she had gone through years of basic defence training, but that had never been enough for her. Since she was a child, she had spied on every training session she could, learning every scrap of information, every technique from afar. It was hard without a sword of her own. But her dagger was her pride and joy. Six years ago, she had seen it fall from the hand of an injured Warsword as he'd been escorted back to the fortress in a wagon. She'd made the mistake of showing Wren her prize. Her sister had told her it was made of Naarvian steel, before insisting that Thea turn it in. Naarvian steel was for Warswords and Warswords alone, a gift given upon the completion of the Great Rite.

The steel source in Naarva was created by the Furies themselves, who had struck the land with a star shower. The rare iron ore found there was the strongest in all the midrealms, and held the power of the gods. For a man to bear such a weapon without initiation was forbidden; an insult to the elite warriors who served the midrealms. But for a *woman* to wield a blade, let alone Naarvian steel? That was a unique form of treason.

Thea had refused to return the dagger at first, of course. But her sister had worn her down, spelling out a lengthy list of nasty consequences. Wren had been a pain in Thea's arse, and not long after, Thea had reluctantly trudged up to the infirmary to return it to its injured owner.

Thea had waited until the healers had left to attend other patients before she went to his bedside. He was the most enormous man that she had ever seen, a giant almost. His legs hung off the end of the bed and the mattress sagged beneath his weight. His head was wrapped in dozens of bloodied bandages, his face was so swollen and bruised that the whites of his eyes were red.

He was dying.

Thea had taken in the sight of him, her whole body screaming at her she shouldn't be there. But she dug deep for a sliver of the courage that warrior must have needed on the battlefield, and she held out the dagger to him.

'You dropped this,' she told him. 'Figured you might want it back.'

The man had gasped, his eyes widening with the effort, sounding as though a wagon full of stone bricks sat upon his chest. He'd murmured something that had made no sense to Thea, before his trembling hand rose from the bed, and pushed the dagger back towards her.

No words came when he opened and closed his mouth.

But she understood one thing: he wanted her to have the weapon.

She clutched it to her chest. 'I'll use it well,' she had told him.

Now, she guided herself through a range of movements, holding the dagger as a would-be sword. She knew she moved well, but how she longed to spar with a worthy opponent, someone who challenged her. Sometimes she could convince the odd alchemist to indulge her, or one of the kitchen hands, but it wasn't the same...

A gentle breeze rustled the foliage around Thea, and the faintest hint of leather and rosewood tickled her nostrils, stirring a strange yearning within. She sighed, relishing the shouts and clang of steel echoing from below. Still clutching her dagger, she peered over the ledge in the terrain again —

Something whistled through the air.

Thea threw herself to the side, a sharp sting slashed across her cheek.

An arrow embedded itself in the gnarled tree trunk beside her with a thud.

The fletching shivered in the breeze.

Trembling, Thea stared with wide eyes at the still quivering arrow and took one – two, steps back.

And then, she ran.

CHAPTER THREE

There was no time for stealth. Thea ran, a blur of shadow in the night, her boots pounding against the damp earth of the woods, a thin line of blood trickling down her cheek. The branches of the trees scratched at her exposed skin and tore at her clothes as she wove between them, the wind whipping through her braid.

Someone had *fired an arrow at her*, and she knew there had been no archery training taking place. It was no wayward shot. Had she been a half second slower, it would have hit her between the eyes. But that was not what destiny had in store for her. The comforting beat of her fate stone against her breast bone steadied her short, shallow gasps.

Made of jade and tied to a black leather string, it had been presented to her as an infant by a seer. Back then, they carved out destinies; sometimes the marker was a name, sometimes it was a symbol, or a number. All signifying a future that would come to pass in no uncertain terms. Rare as fate stones were, they were not sought after. Not by those who wished to live their lives in peace.

Twenty-seven. The black number was a promise from the god of death himself. At the age of twenty-seven, Enovius would come for Thea, but not before having his fun. For death could find her the minute the clock struck her name day, or it could wait until the full year, until the moment before she turned twenty-eight. Thea's fate stone offered her a window of time, no details – a curse she would wish upon no one.

On she ran, mud flicking up on the backs of her legs, fear spurring her on. Not for her life, no, she would not die today. Instead, she feared for her place in Thezmarr, her home. She had known the risks when she'd accepted the dagger and practiced with it time and time again, but the consequences had never felt so close as that arrow.

Lightning flashed, illuminating the Bloodwoods before her for a split second. There was nothing ahead but gnarled trunks and an eerie emptiness.

Soon, the torchlight glimmered before her. Keeping close to the base of the stone walls, Thea made for the staff entrance, her breathing ragged.

Thank the gods, Thea thought as the handle turned. Pausing at the larder, she brought her piece of jade to her lips.

'And so we test the fates again,' she murmured before ducking into the dimly lit room. Inside, the air was cool and meat hung from the ceiling on giant hooks. She moved past these, noting that the trap door to the cellar below was ajar.

Wincing as the kitchen door creaked, Thea peered within. The warmth of several stoves and the mouth-watering aromas of dinner in full swing hit her in the face. With no servants in sight, she crept past the work benches and bubbling pots, suppressing the urge to swipe a freshly baked roll from a basket on the side. Cook had likely counted every single one.

Just as she neared the door, Thea froze.

For in a tattered armchair before the blazing hearth sat a massive figure, a large dog at his feet.

Thea's gaze went from the dozing animal, to the half-braided leather belt in enormous hands, and to the grey eyes that met her own. 'Malik.'

The giant man who grinned back was the very same who had gifted her his dagger on his deathbed. Only, he hadn't died. His now smiling expression was one she'd come to love on what had once been a fierce, scarred face.

Malik was a retired Warsword. He had sustained a near-fatal blow to the head on the battlefield and hadn't spoken since. Amongst other details, Thea had heard Guardians and shieldbearers alike prattle about how the famous warrior had fallen from glory and was now a simpleton, but she knew better. Not long after the dagger gifting, she had been in the corner of the library, reading a difficult passage aloud to make sense of it. There, she met Malik for the second time. His hulking frame had appeared from behind a shelf, startling her out of her skin.

But he'd approached with a broad smile and sat down in a nearby chair, as though he wanted to listen to her. That interaction had shown her he loved the words, but perhaps could no longer understand them on the page. She had read to him ever since.

Now, he lit up with amusement as he surveyed her wet, dishevelled state and the scratch on her face.

'Can't stay,' she told him. 'You won't tell, will you?'

Malik just smiled and turned his attention back to the belt he was braiding.

'Thanks.' With a grateful squeeze of the gentle giant's shoulder, she made for the south-west tower.

By the time Thea had changed into a dry tunic and made herself presentable, the evening meal was underway. Crackling fires blazed in generous hearths on either end, while torches in sconces cast their flickering light across the thick pavers.

At the heart of the hall loomed the Furies - giant sculptures of the three mighty swords wielded by the first ever Warswords, those who were gods. The stone shapes rose from the ground up into the hall's ceiling, where the hilts broke through the rafters above and into the night's sky.

Beneath their shadows was a table that overlooked the rest, where the Guild Master, Osiris, sat in his high-backed chair like a king. On either side were the Warswords of Thezmarr, several commanders and the heads of the staff, including Audra who wore a severe expression, her eyes keen as a hawk.

A few steps below, two long oak tables ran the length of the hall, where warriors of every rank and fortress workers were already digging into the pots of stew and trays of roast potatoes.

Thea was careful not to make eye contact with anyone at the head table as she hurried to where her cohort sat.

Elwren reluctantly made room for her on the bench, spearing her with a furious gaze.

'Should I even ask?' she said between clenched teeth, eyeing the cut on Thea's cheek.

'Probably not.' Thea reached for an empty plate and the tray of potatoes.

'You could have at least covered up that scratch with the cosmetics I prepared for you. Doesn't exactly look like you were in bed with a nosebleed and a headache.'

Thea ignored her sister as she bit into her dinner, stifling a moan of delight.

'You missed a fascinating transcription shift, Althea,' Ida, one of their friends, said from across the table, tucking her dark cropped hair behind her ear.

'"Fascinating" and "transcription" aren't generally two terms I'd put together,' Thea replied around a mouthful of gravy-soaked bread.

'Shut up.' Wren thrust her chin to where Osiris was getting to his feet.

Thea straightened in her seat. It wasn't often that Osiris addressed the entire hall.

Osiris was a man of average height who was dwarfed by the warriors he surrounded himself with. His head was shaved and he wore the leathers and boots of the Thezmarrian commanders; the uniform suited him despite his lean build. He scanned the tables before him with sharp eyes, somehow able to pierce everyone in the crowd before he spoke.

'Tonight, we welcome home one of our most revered Warswords...' he began.

Whispers burst out and spread across the hall like wildfire, many people craning their necks to get a glimpse of the famous warrior seated to Osiris' right.

Thea's skin prickled as she recalled the silver eyes that had locked with hers on the clifftop.

The Guild Master cleared his throat. 'Wilder Hawthorne

has been abroad for several years defending the midrealms. Tales of victory and valour follow him everywhere he goes —'

The bloodied hessian sack flashed in Thea's mind.

'But above all else, he has wrought the justice of Thezmarr upon those who would see it crumble.'

Thea's gaze fell to the warrior in question.

Hawthorne's hood was pushed back off his face and in the candlelight's glow, she drank in his chiselled jaw, his slightly crooked nose, his dark brows and several faint scars marring his sun-kissed skin. His expression was just as fierce, just as unforgiving as it had been earlier.

It was said that the Warswords were chosen by the Furies themselves and imbued with their power. When they emerged from the Great Rite, the warriors were presented with gifts from the kingdoms: steel from Naarva, a stallion from Tver, a vial of healing springwater from Aveum, armour from Delmira and poison from Harenth.

Thea knew from the stories that Hawthorne had been the youngest to ever attempt the Great Rite, the youngest in history to become a Warsword, and that he'd been the last one to do it.

For now, she vowed silently.

But there was no spark of youth about him, only the cold, relentless brutality of a killer. He didn't get up or speak, he simply leaned back in his chair and cast his cutting stare across the hall. Despite his apparent savagery, the defiant gleam in his silver eyes sent a bolt of energy through Thea, warming her from within. She angled towards him, a featherlight shiver washing over her.

Osiris lifted his cup. 'To Hawthorne's return!'

There was a flurry of movement as the rest of the assembly rushed to echo the toast.

All the while, the Hand of Death watched on, enemy blood still staining his boots.

'How many monsters do you think he's slayed?' Thea didn't take her eyes off the warrior, the rancid wraith heart flashing in her mind.

'Who cares about monsters?' Samra snorted. 'What about women? Look at that jaw, those shoulders… Look at the *size* of him… He can slay me anytime.'

Ida laughed. 'Oh keep it in your pants, Sam.'

'Why should I? The men never do. And I'm surprised Hawthorne can at all, he must be hung like a —'

'Sam!' Thea snapped. 'Shut up. He's a Warsword of Thezmarr, show some respect.'

Samra rolled her eyes. 'Just because *you've* taken a ridiculous vow of celibacy, doesn't mean the rest of us have to ignore the feast in front of us.'

'I took no such vow,' Thea replied bitterly, her body tensing. 'I just —'

Wren's hand found her arm and squeezed it. 'It wasn't your fault Evander turned out to be a prick.'

'A complete moron,' Ida chimed in.

A guilty pause followed before Sam nodded. 'A world-class twat.'

Thea's chest warmed at their unified front when it came to the stable master's apprentice, but she waved them off. 'That was years ago now.'

Sam shrugged. 'He's still a twat.'

Thea forced a smile, but her shoulders sagged at the memory.

'I have no interest in warriors. You already conceal your

beauty with men's clothing and mud... I liked you as an alchemist. But if you're going to mess around with weapons and run around like a boy... Not to mention tempt the prophecy...' Evander had told her when she'd confided her dreams to him, the world slipping out from beneath her.

It had ended in a blur of anger and confusion. She had shed her tears on the clifftops with her sister and then put the experience behind her. The only vow she'd ever made had been to herself, one that had seen her dedicate herself to the way of the Warswords as best she could. As for lovers, there had been others since, fleeting moments in the dark, but they were all the same. Evander and the rest were nothing but scared fortress boys, not men, and as Wren had told her: *'A true man won't cut you down as you fight your battles, nor will he fight them for you. A true man will help sharpen your sword, guard your back and fight at your side, in the face of whatever darkness comes.'*

None of them had fit that bill yet.

All around Thea, her cohort talked excitedly. Hawthorne's return wasn't the only one being discussed. A popular unit of warriors had returned from dealing with a threat south of the winter kingdom of Aveum, and the women were eager to note the changes in them on the next table over.

'Raynor's chest has certainly broadened.' Samra smirked, wiggling her brows.

'You'd hope so,' Ida retorted. 'There wasn't much there to begin with.'

Wren laughed. 'Don't be unkind. He's barely twenty. A little young for Sam's tastes anyway,' she chimed in, pouring another cup of ale.

Sam flicked her cherry-red hair over her shoulder and

put a hand on her chest in mock pain. 'You wound me, Wren.'

'What about you, Althea Nine Lives? See anything you want on the menu?'

The dried blood on Thea's cheek itched as she narrowed her eyes at the nickname their friends had given her after years of recklessness and close calls with the guild's laws. Today not included.

Althea Nine Lives. She had always hated it. For one, it made it sound like she were the stupid youngster of the group... Two... She liked to think she had more than nine lives.

She helped herself to another serving of stew, not allowing her gaze to stray to the Warsword at the head table. 'No. Besides,' she said, lifting her chin. 'Why should I be interested in anything other than the brief physical benefits?'

Sam snorted. 'If they're brief, you're doing it wrong.'

'It's just a bullshit distraction. Amidst the work with Farissa and Audra, training and the rest, there's no room for some simpering boy, not even on the side. I have too much to do, too much I want to achieve...'

And little time to achieve it, Thea thought. While the others had a lifetime ahead, she had three years and by all the gods in the realms, she wouldn't squander them.

'My purpose is singular —'

'Ah yes, your *purpose*...' Wren shook her head and pinched the bridge of her nose like some long suffering elder. 'They'll never let you be one of them, Thea. Not in a million years. Isn't it time you dropped this and accepted your lot like the rest of us? It'll only land you in trouble or worse. We still contribute to protecting the realm. There is still honour in the work we do.'

Thea bit back a retort about alchemists and scribes and took her sister's cup, draining it. 'You can go back to talking about boys now,' she said. 'Or girls,' she added, with an apologetic nod to Ida.

'You're too kind,' Ida replied drily.

Wren snatched her drink back and refilled it.

But Thea's attention was already elsewhere... On the Warsword with silver eyes at the head table.

Thea swore at the chill as the young women returned to their sleeping quarters, the hearth cold. With complaints from the others growing louder by the minute, Thea and Wren worked to light the kindling and build up a roaring fire. Thea sighed as warmth spread to her fingers. She stretched out her hands only to pull back sharply as something shot through the air towards her —

A small blade used for opening bottles embedded itself in the timber floor by her foot.

'What in the realms —'

Another came flying at her.

Thea dodged. 'Sam!' she shrieked. 'Enough!'

But she knew better than to stand idle. On her feet now, she leapt from one spot to another as more sharp projectiles rained down, hitting the wall and floor with rhythmic thuds. It was a game they had adapted as children from watching the boys in the courtyard; a Thezmarrian contest to develop quick reflexes. Of course, it was forbidden for girls to play, but Samra had always argued that because they were using alchemy tools rather than the traditional steel stars or daggers, no rules were being broken.

'I also just like throwing things at Althea,' she had said time and time again.

When the girls had hit their teenage years, they had also added an element of dance. Ida insisted that some day, they might need to attend a ball, or a wedding and none of them knew how to be light on their feet. Thea had never had the heart to tell her the unlikelihood of such events, thus, the game, 'Dancing Alchemists' was born.

Their sleeping quarters, and the girls themselves, bore the scars of the contest from over the years, though it had been some time since they had played. Work and the drudgery of every day had a way of robbing the quiet joys from life.

'Fuck.' Thea narrowly avoided a severed toe. 'What are you playing at, Sam?'

Samra shrugged and threw another pointed tool. 'You were chomping at the bit for some action, Althea Nine Lives... Thought I'd oblige you.'

'Don't test me... You know what will happen. You'll regret it.'

'Come on... I've got three left,' her friend said, brandishing the knives.

With a frustrated noise at the back of her throat, Wren tried to snatch the remaining projectiles from Sam. 'Farissa was looking for those!'

But Samra paid her no heed, instead, she flung the blades at Thea, one after the other in quick succession.

A thrill raced through Thea and she *danced.* It was the most natural feeling in the world. She spun gracefully, ducking and weaving, moving her body like water, all the while swiftly collecting the weapons. It was a skill she had honed deliberately, knowing that against bigger opponents, she'd need to leverage her speed and agility against their strength.

When the last of them left Sam's hand, Thea gave her a wolfish grin.

'My turn.' She flicked her wrist with masterful precision and the small blade was a blur through the air before —

'Thea!' Sam shrieked as the knife sliced through the lower half of her cherry-red ponytail, embedding the chunk of hair in the wall behind her.

'Furies save us,' Ida muttered, head in hands.

'What?' Thea said innocently. 'You've been harping on about how you needed a haircut.'

'I'm going to kill you…' Sam threatened through gritted teeth as she yanked the blade and her hunk of hair from the stone.

'I'd like to see you try.'

Sam stared at the severed tresses and then fingered the end of her now cropped ponytail, shaking her head. 'You're insane.'

'Or incredibly skilled.'

'Or both,' Ida offered.

'Definitely both.' Wren confiscated Farissa's tools from her.

'You should have known better than to challenge me at Dancing Alchemists,' Thea argued.

Sam was still shaking her head, but her anger had softened. 'Classic Thea,' she muttered. 'Doesn't want to be a woman, but she dances better than all of us.'

With the excitement dying down, Thea's hand went to the thin scabbed-over cut on her cheek, the sound of the arrow whistling through the air echoing in her mind. She had the feeling that Dancing Alchemists had saved her life earlier.

Wren caught her gaze, her eyes full of questions.

Thea shrugged, what Wren didn't know wouldn't hurt her, and all in all, it hadn't been a *terrible* day.

It wasn't until she reached for her nightgown and kicked off her boots that the realisation hit her. Thea's hands froze at the buttons of her tunic, her dinner turning to lead in her stomach, cold suddenly washing over her despite the glow of the fire.

Her dagger was missing.

And she knew exactly where she had left it.

CHAPTER FOUR

Althea dreamt of the seer again.

'*Remember me,*' the magic wielder whispered into the night as she carved the promise of death into the piece of jade. She had no face. No distinct features. But her voice was a song like a cyren's call. How many had come before Thea? How many had she handed over to Enovius?

The cold surface of the fate stone pressed into Thea's palm and she jerked awake with a ragged gasp.

Wren was watching from the bed beside hers.

'What is it?' her sister asked, brow furrowed in concern.

Panting, Thea allowed herself a moment to adjust to the dawn light filtering in through the windows and the chill of the crisp morning against her heated skin. The others were still fast asleep.

'It was nothing,' she mumbled, her heart still hammering as she released her fate stone, tucking it down the front of her nightgown.

But Wren had seen. 'You had another nightmare.'

There was no point in arguing. Thea gave a stiff nod, mopping the sweat from her hairline with her sleeve.

'I really think you should talk to Farissa. She could give you something —'

'I'm not taking some potion to wipe my mind for sleep,' Thea snapped. 'I need to be alert.'

'Forget I mentioned it,' Wren replied with a sigh. 'I just wish you'd confide in someone about it.'

'You know about it. That's enough.'

'Is it? To wear a fate stone... It's a heavy burden to bear.'

But Thea was done. 'It's no burden, but a gift,' she insisted as she swung her legs from the bed, wincing at the iciness of the floor. 'To know when you die, is to know how to live, sister.'

'Well, just remember, it's not fate until you actually die.'

Thea tugged on her pants and tunic. 'Noted.'

A groan sounded from the other side of the room. 'Don't tell me you two are at each other's throats already?' Ida muttered from beneath her pillow.

'Nothing but sisterly love over here,' Wren groused as she, too, dragged herself from her bed.

'Good gods, the world must truly be ending then.'

Thea winked at Wren and tapped the hidden fate stone. 'Not today.'

If there was one place Thea didn't want to be that morning, it was the alchemy workshop. The tasks were tedious and she usually ended up with a fresh burn or cut to her hands. She felt naked without her dagger in her boot and she was restless, desperate to scour the Bloodwoods for it before it rusted beneath the damp leaves or some nosy shieldbearer discovered it.

'Shit.' She drew her hand back from the bunch of wild lavender she was cutting, skin stinging from where the knife had slipped.

'You don't pay any attention.' Wren tossed her a clean cloth to stem the bleeding on her index finger.

'Because the job is thankless,' Thea retorted.

Wren's hands flew to her hips. 'Do you even know what we're making right now?'

'Some sort of potion?' But Thea said it quietly because, by the looks of things, her sister was about to burst.

'It's a tincture for blinding headaches —'

Thea opened her mouth, but Wren's hand flew up to silence her.

'Blinding headaches exactly like the ones your library friend gets.'

Malik.

Wren wasn't done. 'So you're telling me this work is *thankless*, too lowly for the likes of *you*, even though it eases the suffering of those who made unimaginable sacrifices protecting our realms?'

Thea flushed. 'No.'

'Good. Now shut up and don't cut off any of your fingers.'

A huff of laughter sounded from behind them and Thea was mortified to find Farissa, the Alchemist Master looking over their shoulders, her arms crossed at her chest.

'I couldn't have said it better myself.' She smiled pleasantly. 'You'd do well to listen to your sister, Thea.'

Thea's teeth clenched. 'Yes, Farissa.'

'I see you are much recovered from yet another bout of nosebleeds... How fortunate.'

Thea shifted from foot to foot, training her gaze once more on the lavender. 'Yes, very fortunate.'

The Master Alchemist shook her head before turning to Wren. 'I'd like to see those designs again when you have a moment, Elwren. I trust you brought them?'

Wren nodded. 'Of course.'

'I'd ask you to leave your sister to finish the tincture, but we don't want to poison anyone, do we?'

Wren laughed at this. 'Definitely not. I'll see you after.'

'Gods, you're a kiss arse,' Thea muttered as Farissa walked off to one of the other workstations.

'And you're as bad as a spoilt child,' Wren bit back. She gave a sigh. 'If you weren't such a pain, I'd show you what I've designed. It's something... Well, it's something you'd appreciate.'

Thea recognised the note of deviousness in her sister's voice and when her sister was in that mood, Furies help them all. Though she was loath to admit it aloud, Wren's mind was nothing short of brilliant. She was a born inventor and the spark in her eye told Thea that whatever she'd created was something that was bound to change fates somewhere in the realms.

'Alright then.' Thea folded her arms. 'Let's have it.'

Wren's answering grin was villainous. Their spat forgotten, she rummaged through her satchel and pulled out several sheets of parchment, smoothing them out on the workspace before them.

'Here,' she said proudly.

Thea frowned, scanning the sketches. 'A teapot?' It was artfully drawn; perfectly symmetrical, but then again, her younger sister was exceedingly good at nearly everything she tried. She was infuriating like that.

'It's no ordinary teapot...' Wren smirked. 'I'm calling it the Ladies' Luncheon Teapot.'

'I see,' Thea replied, though she didn't. She had no interest in ladies' luncheons.

But it didn't dissuade Wren, instead she turned to the next page, which featured a more detailed sketch of the interior.

Thea's eyes narrowed. 'Two chambers... Why?'

'One for tea,' Wren replied, celadon eyes bright. 'One for poison.'

'What?' Thea scoffed. Of all the things she expected to come out of her sister's mouth, 'poison' wasn't one of them.

'I've been working with Farissa on several minor projects while you're off having your nosebleeds,' Wren explained. 'This was one of my ideas. Each chamber has a hidden hole near the teapot's handle.' Wren pointed to the place on her drawing. 'To pour a specific drink out, you need to keep the hole connected to the chamber uncovered.'

'But —'

'Think about it, Thea. If you were already suspicious of your host, would you not want to see them drink the same drink as you before you took the risk?'

'Yes...'

'The drink in each chamber needs to look identical. And the server needs to remember which is which. From there, they need to keep their finger over the spot with the unpoisoned drink in order to poison their foe and over the hole with the poisoned drink if they wish to pour for themselves. But to the guest... It appears to be the same, coming from the same place. Do you see?'

Thea stared at the pages in disbelief. 'How?'

'I'm starting a working model this afternoon to show the theory. It's quite simple: the surface tension and pressure prevent the liquids from pouring out. By covering the hole, the server prevents air from entering the chamber.' Wren touched her hand to the sketch again. 'This should decrease the surface area of the liquid and prevent it from exiting through the spout. When the server covers the hole with their finger like so, it allows the air's pressure to hold the liquid in place.'

Thea gave a slow, disbelieving shake of her head. 'Impressive, Wren,' she managed, as she continued to stare at the illustrations.

'Thank you.'

'You know... It's quite a deplorable contraption.'

'Well, you can't have every drop of wickedness in the family.'

Thea laughed, finding her sister's passion infectious. 'I'm relieved to hear it.'

They worked in amiable quiet for the rest of the hour, making a range of tinctures for the healers and some more nefarious tonics for whom they didn't know and didn't ask. Thus was the work of Thezmarr's women. Mostly, Thea listened to Wren's instructions, still marvelling at her sister's cleverness, and imagining the stealthy missions the Ladies' Luncheon Teapot would be needed for.

All the while Thea chopped and ground ingredients, she missed the press of her dagger at her ankle, unable to believe she'd been so careless. Over the course of their shift, she tried to find an opportunity to slip out, but Farissa was watching her like a hawk. A damn good imitation of Audra, as though she knew Thea had one foot out the door.

. . .

To Thea's dismay, midmeal was brief and again provided no window for escape to duck away to the Bloodwoods. Feeling bitter, she made her way through the ground floor corridors with Wren, defeat chasing her with every step. Farissa had gone easy on her for missing the previous day's shift, but she doubted she would enjoy the same leniency from Audra. She touched her hand to the scab on her cheek, wishing she'd had the foresight to cover it with Wren's cosmetics.

Just as they reached the steps to the east tower, harsh laughter rang out from nearby. Thea flexed her fingers, recognising who it belonged to. Where that amusement sounded, no good ever followed. She took a step in its direction.

'Thea, leave it.' Wren's hand was already poised to grab Thea's arm.

Despite the squirming sensation in her gut, Thea acquiesced. 'Fine,' she muttered, making for the stairs.

Six years ago, during one of the defence classes, Thea had requested a more challenging opponent after sparring with a rather unenthused Wren. Sebastos Barlowe had volunteered to show her what a worthy adversary he would make. Only, she had landed a blow against him in front of the whole cohort, and sent him staggering sideways. Although he ended up winning the round, Seb had taken the hit personally. Thea had tried to make it right, offering to shake his hand at the end, but he'd refused.

You think I'm shaking the hand of some dirty stray?' he had said with a sneer.

Wren had warned her that she'd made an enemy of him.

As usual, her sister had been right. Whenever Sebastos Barlowe was near, a fight was never far away.

Now, the laughter sounded again, louder this time. Followed by the sneering voice that never failed to make her skin crawl.

' — look at the blithering idiot. Can't even walk in a straight line —'

Thea didn't think, she moved.

Shrugging off her sister's grip and protests, she rounded the corner.

There, Malik's giant form was surrounded by a group of shieldbearers, who were prodding him with their training swords. Malik was backing away from them, stumbling over his feet, his huge hands raised before him, trying to block them out.

Blood roared in Thea's ears. 'Seb!' Her voice echoed down the passageway as she planted her boots wide apart, her body tense.

She heard Wren's groan from behind her.

The shieldbearer in question whirled around. 'What do you want, stray?'

Thea took a step towards Seb, her cheeks flushing in anger. 'Still haven't come up with a more imaginative or relevant insult?' She fought to keep her voice even as she noted the cuts on Malik's arms and the confusion in his grey eyes. 'Half the population of Thezmarr are orphans.'

'But you're the dirtiest and most unwanted. Look at the state of you,' he said, his nose wrinkling in disgust as he surveyed her pants, tunic, and muddied boots. 'I can't tell if you're more like a dog or your monstrous friend here. Or are you trying to look like a man?'

She could feel the fury rippling from Wren behind her,

but Thea didn't glance back. Instead, her fingers flexed again, itching to grasp the dagger she no longer had. No matter, she'd kill him with her bare hands if she had to.

Seb continued to sneer at her. 'What'd you want?'

Thea took another step towards him, ignoring the shieldbearer's lackeys, who had turned away from Malik to jeer at her, gripping their training swords menacingly.

'Leave him be,' she told them.

Seb snorted. 'Or what?'

Fists clenched, Thea didn't reply. She had no weapon, and they outnumbered her, but there was no part of her that could have ignored what they were doing to Malik, no matter what it cost her.

She took a deep, trembling breath. 'Leave him be,' she repeated. 'He is a former Warsword. He deserves your respect. Your behaviour is an insult to Thezmarr.'

'You'd know all about insults to Thezmarr, being one yourself.' Chest puffed out, he approached, ensuring that he loomed over her.

Thea didn't yield a step, despite what she saw in his eyes.

His lackeys closed in as well, shoulders pushed back.

'I'd get away from my sister, if I were you,' Wren's voice sounded.

'Like we have anything to fear from this scrappy mess,' Seb retorted.

'I didn't say she was the one to fear.'

A puff of air blew past Thea's ear. A cloud of violet dust billowed and then settled over the shieldbearers.

Someone coughed.

And Seb looked down at his powder-covered tunic, annoyed. 'What's this, some witch's trick?' He brushed the dust from his shoulder, glaring at Wren —

His eyes bulged and his hand flew to his neck.

An angry rash appeared instantly on his exposed skin and suddenly he was scratching wildly. 'What have you done, bitch?'

Behind him, his followers were red-faced and clawing at their own flesh.

'I suggest you get yourselves to the infirmary,' Wren said, coming to stand beside Thea and survey her handiwork. 'I'd hate for that to get anywhere delicate. You wouldn't want your dick to fall off. You seem to enjoy swinging it around.'

Seb's eyes bulged again. 'Bitch!' he shrieked, before staggering away from them, his friends close behind.

Thea turned to her sister, her own eyes wide.

Wren raised her brows. 'Let's have it then,' she said. 'Let's hear all about how you didn't need help, how you had it all handled.'

'I…' Thea struggled for words. 'That… That was brilliant.'

'Oh.'

'Remind me not to piss you off too much.' Thea caught a streak of violet dust on her own skin. 'Why am I not —'

'Not affected?' Wren interjected. 'You're immune to Widow's Ash.'

'What? How?'

'Because I made it so.'

'What do you mean?'

'I've been sprinkling it in your bedsheets for the last few months. Building up your tolerance.'

'So that's why I woke up itching a bunch of times… Gods, Wren. You've got to be joking.'

'I don't joke about Widow's Ash.'

'You're mad…'

'Am I? Or am I just prepared for the inevitable moment

where my reckless sister bites off more than she can chew with a group of small-pricked shieldbearers?'

Rubbing her temples, Thea shook her head. 'Both.'

Wren laughed. 'Come on,' she said. 'We're late for Audra.'

But Thea's attention was on Malik, who now stood a few yards away, his face red and sweat beading at his brow.

'I have to take him back to his quarters,' Thea told her sister.

Wren followed her gaze, taking in the sight of the former warrior as he paced, blinking rapidly, his chest heaving. 'I think you're right. I'll tell Audra.'

'Never mind Audra, don't worry about making excuses. You'll be in enough shit already.'

'I'll come with you —'

But Thea waved her off. 'It'll overwhelm him. Just go, we'll be fine.'

With a tight nod, Wren made for the stairs and disappeared through the door.

Thea approached Malik, trying not to startle him.

'You're lost again, aren't you, friend?' she whispered.

Malik looked up at the sound of her voice, his eyes wide. He opened and closed his mouth several times before his posture loosened.

'Good thing I know the way,' Thea prompted. 'Come on.'

Although she wanted to take his arm to lead him through the corridors, she didn't. The injury to his brain was a web of complexities she knew she would never understand, but she had known him long enough now to recognise that sometimes he suffered from sensory overwhelm, particularly after a trying event or ordeal.

She crept through the fortress, noting that Malik's balance was suffering today.

'You just need some quiet,' she reassured him as she held a door open and waited for him to shuffle through.

Audra had shown her the way once before when this had happened. The sharp-tongued librarian had been gentle and kind with Malik – familiar. It wasn't until much later that Thea realised Audra had probably known him as a Warsword, they could have even trained together.

When they reached Malik's quarters, the door was unlocked and, once opened, Malik's dog, Dax, greeted them anxiously.

'He's alright,' Thea told the mongrel as his wagging tail threatened to bruise her legs.

She waited in the doorway until Malik had eased himself into his chair before the cold hearth.

'Do you want me to light a fire?' she asked.

Malik stared at the black coals.

'Alright,' Thea said, more to herself than to the former warrior. 'I'll leave you to it.'

As she turned to go, a rasping sound came from Malik.

She waited, knowing he was trying to get the words out, knowing she could never understand that torment. Her own throat tightened, wishing there was something she could do.

Malik shook his head, as though he had read her thoughts.

Thea pushed the loose hair off her face and sighed, her own words tumbling out of her. 'I lost it,' she confessed, tapping her ankle where Malik knew she kept his dagger. 'I lost it in the Bloodwoods and I'm sorry,' she told him.

Of all the things, *this* Malik smiled at? But with an unsteady hand, he motioned for her to leave.

Regret left a bitter taste in Thea's mouth. She had lost the only remnant of who Malik had been before his injury, the thing he had trusted her to keep and keep well. He had survived all that he had, only to have her lose the blade he had earned with his own blood and sweat and sacrifice.

No, she wouldn't stand for it. Closing the former Warsword's door behind her, Thea set out, not towards Audra's waiting orders, but back to the Bloodwoods.

Outside, the day was grey, but not dark enough to move freely through the fortress and beyond the walls. Still, Thea had her ways. During her short-lived fling with Evander, she had learned some of the least guarded spots of Thezmarr, some of the lesser known paths through the outerwoods. In that regard, the relationship hadn't been a *complete* waste of her time.

It wasn't long before she was once more surrounded by the bleeding trees of the forest, the rich, damp scent of looming rain heavy in the air. She found her trail from the night before and was sure to cover her tracks. The last thing she needed was some curious shieldbearer on her heels. She also wouldn't put it past Seb to send out some lackeys seeking revenge on his behalf. She hoped he was still in the infirmary, scratching his balls like some flea-ridden animal.

Soon Thea reached the clearing from yesterday. She'd know the place in her sleep, but with the arrow embedded in the tree, there was no mistaking it. Distracted, she ran her scarred fingers through its fletching, the feathers soft against her skin, in such contrast to the deadly tip buried in the trunk.

Whoever had shot it had almost impeccable aim; were it not for her quick reflexes, thanks to a lifetime of Dancing Alchemists, it would have found its mark.

But that was not why she was here.

Where did I drop it? Thea crouched in the leaves and

skimmed her palms across the ground. She retraced her movements... She knew she had been holding it right until the arrow came flying at her. She berated herself. Dropping things when surprised was not the trait of a formidable warrior.

Thea circled the entire arrow-speared tree, sifting through the leaf litter, convinced that the dagger had to be somewhere nearby, even if she had kicked it during her getaway. It couldn't have gone far.

But as she searched, a roiling sensation built in her stomach.

She scoured the forest floor more frantically, tracing her steps further back than she truly thought realistic. Her chest grew heavy and at last she fell to her knees on the damp earth.

'Fuck,' she murmured, staring at her empty hands.

A chill crept along her skin and her scalp prickled, forcing her to look up.

Her throat seized.

For leaning against a tree, clad in his black warrior leathers, was Wilder Hawthorne, twirling her dagger between his long, tattooed fingers.

'Looking for this?' he said.

CHAPTER FIVE

E very part of Thea shrieked at her to flee, but she was
rooted to the spot, still on her knees in the dirt.

Hawthorne's silver gaze pierced hers and he took a
powerful step towards her, a towering wall of muscle. 'Not
going to deny it?' His voice was deep and husky, his words
seeming to reverberate along her bones.

Thea scrambled to her feet, her heart racing to the point
of pain, her mouth welded shut.

'Do you even know what this is? What it means?' He
twirled the dagger again. His tone gave away nothing, but
Thea didn't miss the muscle twitch in his jaw. Up close, he
appeared even fiercer than he had up on the cliffs and in the
hall. His face was all unforgiving lines and the promise of
violence, his square jaw sharpened by his dark beard and his
eyes brimmed with an unbroken storm beneath long black
lashes.

Again, she chose not to speak. For what could she say
that he would believe, that he would understand? She was an
alchemist, a poor one at that. She had broken the guild's laws

and, as Seb had put it, she was an insult to Thezmarr. She had no business with any dagger, let alone... She glanced around them at the empty forest, and for a split second, considered —

'You can try to run if you like,' he said, a cruel glimmer of amusement in his eyes, almost a dare. 'But you forget what I am.'

Thea struggled to swallow the lump in her throat, her fingers numb at her sides. No matter how hard she had trained in secret, no matter how well she had learned the mysteries of the Bloodwoods, before her stood a Warsword of Thezmarr. There was no way out.

Hawthorne sheathed her dagger at his belt, watching each realisation as they dawned on her face. 'Are you going to come to the fortress willingly? Or would you prefer to suffer the indignity of me throwing you over my shoulder and carrying you?'

At that, Thea lifted her chin, resenting the subtle note of enjoyment in his tone. 'I'll walk.'

'Good.'

They didn't speak as they trekked through the Bloodwoods, but Thea kept glancing at her dagger in his belt, cursing herself for her own stupidity. Her prized possession had been taken from her and she was on her way to face the punishment she had long feared but never imagined would come to pass. Had she been that naïve? As reckless and foolish as Wren so often told her?

Apparently so.

As she walked at the Warsword's side, his commanding figure cast long shadows before them across the ground. Effortless power thrummed from him and she couldn't help the charged energy that simmered in her veins, or the fluttering sensation in her chest when she looked at him. As cold and unflinching as he appeared, swords strapped to his back and jaw set, something about him heated her blood, even now.

His silver eyes slid to her, as though he could sense her body's traitorous response to him.

'Is there something you need to say?' he growled.

Thea cursed herself. Her future at Thezmarr was at stake and she was ogling the very Warsword who might end it all?

'No,' she told him, eyeing her dagger now sheathed at his waist.

'Good,' he said again.

And so, in the shadow of a mighty Warsword, Althea Zoltaire walked to her doom.

They reached the Guild Master's residences and, as Hawthorne's fist closed and pounded on the door, Thea realised just how terrified she was. Her tunic was damp with sweat and it was taking all her willpower to keep her breathing even. She tensed as she heard the footsteps on the other side, her legs weak beneath her.

The door was thrown open and Thea stared into the discerning face of Osiris.

'Hawthorne, what is it?' he said, frowning at the Warsword looming over the pitiful sight of a dishevelled alchemist.

'Found her with a weapon, amongst other offences,' Hawthorne replied, not even looking at her.

'A weapon?' Osiris blinked.

'A dagger, out in the Bloodwoods. Of *Naarvian steel*.' Hawthorne's voice was clipped, as though he were impatient to get to the heart of the matter and be on his way, as though deciding Thea's fate was beneath him.

But Osiris' gaze pierced her, his mouth twisting into an ugly expression, his contempt almost palpable. He didn't deign to address her.

'Take her to the council room and wait for me.'

An icy shiver crept down Thea's spine as the door closed in their faces, and Hawthorne motioned for her to keep moving down the corridor.

The council room. Was there to be some sort of trial? Thea glanced up at the Warsword to her right, trying to gauge any clues as to what awaited her.

But Hawthorne's expression was unreadable. The only tiny detail Thea noticed was that his hand kept drifting to her dagger at his belt and a muscle beneath his dark stubble jumped.

The dagger means something to him, she decided. *But what?* It had been in her possession for the last six years and before that, it had belonged to Malik. She knew for a fact that Hawthorne hadn't even been in the territory when she'd found it.

At the council room doors Thea suppressed the urge to dig her heels into the ground and refuse to enter.

'What's going to happen?' she asked.

The Warsword didn't even look at her, just pushed the doors open and waited for her to go inside, anger rolling off him.

The room was a dimly lit, narrow rectangle with a rich mahogany table running down its centre, six high-backed chairs surrounding it. Hawthorne moved to gather several maps that were spread out, rolling them up and placing them on a nearby shelf that was otherwise rammed with

books. Heavy crimson curtains covered what Thea guessed to be a window, and a trolley of decanters stood in the far corner.

'You'll be wanting to sit for this.' Hawthorne's deep voice startled her.

'I'll stand.' Thea rubbed her arms as a draught swept through the room. She looked around for the hearth, but there was none.

The Warsword was watching her, noting her every movement.

She didn't like being assessed. 'What are you going to do with my dagger?' she ventured.

'It's not *your* dagger.'

'It is.'

'Let's forget for a moment that it's forbidden for a woman to wield a weapon...' he said, drawing the dagger from his belt and testing its sharpness with a tattooed finger. 'Where would an alchemist get a Naarvian blade such as this?'

'I didn't steal it.' Thea ground her teeth at his tone. 'It was a gift.'

Hawthorne blinked. 'A gift.'

Thea opened her mouth to defend herself, but the door flew open and, in that moment, she did indeed need the support of the table.

It was not only the Guild Master who joined them, but the other Warswords: Torj the Bear Slayer and Vernich the Bloodletter. Between them and Hawthorne, they seemed to take up the whole council room.

'Sit,' Osiris ordered.

And this time, Thea obeyed, taking the chair closest to her and sliding into it, clasping her trembling hands in her lap. She didn't know where to look. Had it only been yesterday that she'd watched the mighty warriors return to Thezmarr, never imagining she might be face to face with them so soon?

'What's the meaning of this, Osiris?' Vernich demanded, his voice gravelly. 'I was about to ride out to Harenth.'

'It appears we have a law breaker on our hands.' The Guild Master motioned toward Thea.

Despite her racing heart, Thea refused to lower her gaze.

Vernich's lip curled. 'I see.'

'She was in possession of Naarvian steel.' Osiris braced himself against the table and shook his head. 'Stupid girl. Do you not realise these laws are in place to protect you? To protect us all?'

'As I told him,' she jutted her chin towards Hawthorne. 'The dagger was a *gift*. The Warsword *insisted —*'

'No Warsword would ever give up his blade. Especially not to some scrap of a girl. And you know the laws. You know what you risked.'

Thea's shoulders sagged. They didn't believe her. And even if they did, she'd broken the rules. Dread sank to the pit of her stomach and she waited.

'Well, she's out then. Send her away,' Vernich stated.

'Agreed,' Hawthorne added, folding his arms over his broad chest.

Torj Elderbrock shot them a look of surprise. 'Don't tell me of all the things in the realms, this is what you two choose to agree on?'

'You know I have little patience for the shieldbearers,' Hawthorne continued. 'Let alone thieves who sneak through the Bloodwoods with our sacred blades.'

'Hear hear,' Vernich grunted. 'So why are we here about it —'

The door banged open again.

Audra, the librarian, strode in, her eyes fiery behind her spectacles, her silver hair pulled back into a tight bun that made her expression all the more severe. Despite her small stature, Audra had as much presence as the towering Warswords, more so, considering she was *not* happy.

'Why was I not informed you were questioning one of my charges?' the librarian asked.

Osiris grimaced. 'How did you know we were here?'

'Nothing happens in this fortress that I don't know about. I'll assume the lack of communication was an innocent oversight, shall I?'

Thea gaped at her warden.

'There is only one thing to be done here.' Osiris' face reddened. 'Therefore, your presence was not required. I will not have some *girl* compromise all the guild stands and fights for. Do you not know the state of the realm?'

'You think one *girl* can compromise all that?'

Was Thea hearing correctly? Was Audra *defending* her?

'You tell me,' Osiris countered. 'That was exactly how it happened the last time.'

'Furies save us, Osiris. Now is not the time for prophecies —'

'Which is what you said time and time again, before a little girl brought the darkness down upon Thezmarr twenty years ago.'

'And what was your brilliant solution? To strip half your warriors of their weapons and throw them out?'

'I had no choice —'

'There is always a choice. And Thezmarr is weaker for yours.'

'Enough about the past,' Vernich interjected. 'This girl here broke our laws. She must face the consequences.'

Girl. Always girl. Like she was an unruly child to be disciplined, not a woman who had *survived.* Anger crackled in Thea's veins.

Audra stiffened, as though the insult landed upon her shoulders as well. She seemed to draw herself up. 'Need I remind you,' she said between clenched teeth, 'that the original Warswords were women. The Three Furies were what our entire culture was based upon, what everything the guild stands for started with them.'

'Don't bring your books into this,' Osiris snapped.

'Don't bring your prejudices from decades ago into this,' Audra bit back. 'Rather than punish Althea for what she is, ask her *why* she breaks the rules.'

'I don't care why.'

'You *should.* She has wanted nothing more than to train since she was old enough to walk. All the while we have less and less recruits. Our shieldbearers are failing the initiation test more than ever before, some of them not even reaching the point where they can undertake it. Perhaps it's time to try something *new.* Althea is no scholar, that's for sure.'

Thea suppressed a wince at that last comment.

Osiris' eyes narrowed and adopted a dangerous glint. 'This is your fault,' he told Audra, his focus honing in on the small daggers at her waist. 'You encourage this sort of behaviour with your blatant disregard for our ways. You allow your past to cloud your judgement, to interfere with your duties.'

'You mean my past as a former Guardian of the midrealms? As a former warrior of this very guild?'

Air whistled between Thea's teeth. The librarian had never uttered those words aloud before.

But Audra didn't miss a beat, her voice icy. 'I have nothing but respect for the Thezmarrian ways, Osiris, as you well know. My very purpose here is to uphold its spirit, its vision and its place in the midrealms. That's why I stayed, even after your abhorrent law changing.' She gestured to the miniature weapons at her belt. 'And these are ceremonial, as I've told you before. A tribute to the Furies.'

'How can you expect your charges to follow the laws when you yourself —'

'They look like letter openers to me,' Wilder Hawthorne cut in, as though Osiris hadn't been speaking. 'A fitting tool for a librarian, Guild Master. Surely, we would not rob Audra of their uses. And surely, Thezmarrian warriors would not be threatened by such insignificant blades.'

He posed seemingly polite questions, but Wilder Hawthorne had swiftly ended the debate regarding Audra's *letter openers*.

'However, regarding your... charge,' Hawthorne said it with disdain.

Thea's fists clenched in her lap, her pulse spiking.

'She broke one of our most important laws, and now it seems you're suggesting that not only she be granted leniency, but what? A place in the shieldbearers' ranks?'

In that moment Thea didn't care if Hawthorne was the most celebrated Warsword of all time, or that she'd briefly admired his figure in the hall. He was an unfeeling bastard through and through.

But Audra spoke calmly as she faced him. 'In short, yes.'

Hawthorne laughed darkly. 'Warriors of Thezmarr are forged with blood and steel, not plucked from the shadows of the Bloodwoods, or the alchemy workshop.' His words were harsh, unforgiving, as was his gaze upon Thea.

Thea shifted in her seat. She had spoken no word in her own defence, but aware that her fate was hanging in the balance before her, she felt compelled to say something.

'I'm good,' she blurted. 'Better than good. As Audra said, I've been training all my life. I'd be an asset to Thezmarr, to the midrealms —'

Hawthorne's nostrils flared, his knuckles paling as he gripped the hilt of *her* dagger.

'Twirling sticks around in the dark is no warrior training.'

Thea blanched.

Osiris spoke again. 'The prophecy was clear then, and it is clear now: *A daughter of darkness will wield a blade in one hand, And rule death with the other...* You know it as well as I do.'

Audra snorted. 'Death comes for the midrealms, whether a woman holds a sword or not.'

'Althea risked an attack on us all by wielding a blade, one of Naarvian steel, no less. And now you beg a concession to the laws?'

'Yes.'

Hawthorne made a noise at the back of his throat. 'The system is already broken, a pathetic mess of would-be mentors and weak fools. The last thing Thezmarr needs is another shieldbearer's hand to hold like a child —'

'I'm not a child,' Thea objected. 'I'm twenty-four years of age.'

'Then perhaps you're too old —'

'Silence!' Osiris pinched the bridge of his nose. 'Wilder, I'm well aware of your opinions. You've made no secret of them over the years. And Audra, even if I wished to permit the girl to train, it's against the laws of the three remaining kingdoms. A law that was put in place for our own protection.'

The girl. The girl. The girl. That same fury from before sparked anew, coursing through Thea like a formidable current.

Silver eyes fell upon her once more and she stilled.

Audra paced at the head of the table. 'No,' she agreed. 'You cannot permit her that.'

Thea's heart fell.

'However…' Audra continued. 'As Hawthorne articulated *so well*, the system is broken and so something must be done. There is to be a feast in Hailford in three days' time, honouring the end of King Artos' mourning period for the queen. There will be an open court beforehand where all the kings and queens of the midrealms will be present. Althea can make her case there.'

Thea hadn't realised she'd stood, her heart daring to swell as Audra's words sank in.

The Guild Master spoke again, a curious lilt to his tone. 'I have never known you to fight the causes of underlings. Why?'

Without tearing her gaze from Osiris', Audra's hand went to one of the daggers at her belt. 'Because of this.'

There was a flash of silver as the dagger cut through the air.

Thea twisted, swerving from its path.

Suddenly, the dagger was in her hand, having caught it midair by its jewelled hilt.

WILDER HAWTHORNE

Wilder's whole body tensed, his hand shooting to the grip of his own blade. But the alchemist had caught the flying dagger. *Midair.* And she'd done it without flinching, without a flicker of fear.

He wasn't the only one staring.

'Holy shit,' Torj said with a low whistle.

The Guild Master's mouth had fallen open and he now slid from where he stood into the nearest chair, not taking his eyes off the alchemist.

Vernich said nothing, but his clenched jaw betrayed his shock.

The young woman's expression now gleamed with challenge as she flicked the weapon, catching it by the tip between her fingers before returning it wordlessly to the librarian, hilt first.

She was no novice, that was for certain.

He had a strange feeling about her the moment he'd spotted her hidden on the clifftops, spying on their meet.

Something had stopped him from hauling her out of the brush and demanding answers then and there.

Now, Wilder took in her slight build, the gold-streaked side braid framing her determined face and the scars littering her otherwise dainty hands. Unlike the other alchemists, she wore pants that clung to her curves as she moved, her sleeves rolled up to the elbows revealing sun-kissed skin and an array of freckles —

Something unwelcome stirred within Wilder, but he clasped his hands together and steeled himself. This girl was trouble. She went against everything that Thezmarr stood for and no pretty face made up for that.

As if sensing his scrutiny, the alchemist met his gaze with round, celadon eyes and she lifted her chin in defiance, as though she had won.

It was Audra who broke the silence that pulsed through the council room. 'For years I have listened to your concerns about the lowering intake of shieldbearers. For years I have stood alongside you as we've watched the darkness encroach further into the midrealms, cursing our lands, cursing our *people*.'

The librarian's voice was cold and factual. 'Less and less of our shieldbearers graduate to the rank of Guardian, and I don't even recall the last time one of our warriors even *attempted* the Warswords' Great Rite. There hasn't been a new Warsword since Hawthorne. It gets darker every day, the Veil shudders with the threat of more monsters... And you want to turn away a promising warrior?'

'We don't *want* to turn away anyone,' Osiris countered. 'But the laws are unbreakable.'

'Unbreakable, perhaps...' Audra allowed. 'But not unchangeable.'

The alchemist was biting her lower lip, fidgeting. It was more evidence of her lack of suitability. She was raw, untrained and undisciplined.

But Audra was not through. The stern-faced woman whirled to face Torj. 'Elderbrock, how many Veil breaches this month?'

'Ah...' Torj managed. 'That information isn't for civilians, Audra,' he said apologetically.

'I'm hardly a mere civilian, Torj Elderbrock. I trained in this fortress before the likes of you were even born.' The older woman shot him a glare. 'What about in the last year?'

'Again, not knowledge I can divulge...'

Audra whirled around to face Osiris, whose face looked more weathered than before. 'Do you want me to go on?' she demanded. 'We both know I don't need your warrior brutes to *divulge* anything.'

Osiris threw his hands up in frustration. 'What exactly do you want me to do, Audra?'

'That depends,' she said.

'On?'

'Do you consider these dark times? Do you consider the midrealms to be under immediate threat?'

A vein pulsed in the Guild Master's temple. 'Yes.'

'Then we should allow Althea to train as a shieldbearer.'

Osiris' whole body heaved in frustration. '*I told you*, the rules are unbreakable. My hands are tied.'

'Not as tightly as you might think,' the librarian replied, striding to the bookshelf on the far side of the room. There, she slid a thick volume from its place and dropped it onto the table with a loud thud.

Begrudgingly fascinated, Wilder caught the title before

she opened it and started scanning its pages: *The Constitution of the Founding Furies.*

He scoffed. *Of course Audra would bring books and the Furies into this.* She had been forced to give up her blades, but she would always be a warrior of Thezmarr. She could turn anything into a weapon.

'Here,' she declared, voice dripping with triumph as she read: '*In times of dire need, as declared by the Guild Master, all those capable may take up arms in the name of Thezmarr, as protectors of the midrealms.*'

'Audra, that's hardly enough to renounce a decades-old law.'

'No, but it's enough to petition the rulers.'

Wilder folded his arms over his chest, his eyes darting from the librarian to the alchemist. It was clear from the younger woman's raised brows she had no prior knowledge of such a clause, however he knew Audra well enough to know that this was not some impassioned defence of her charge. This was part of a plan she'd had in the works for a long time. When Audra had thrown the blade, her aim had been true, her faith in her charge had been unwavering. Audra was a sly old fox and whatever was occurring here and now in this room was just scratching the surface of her agenda.

'This is an unprecedented request, Audra...' Osiris warned.

'Unprecedented times call for such requests,' she shot back. 'As does unprecedented talent. How many of your warriors can pluck a knife from the air? Bring me one man from your ranks who can do that.'

Though Wilder was loath to admit it, Audra had a point.

The alchemist watched on in silence, blinking at her

warden, as though she couldn't quite believe what was happening. Wilder wasn't sure he believed it either, because from where he was standing, it looked like Audra was winning this battle.

The librarian seemed to share a silent exchange with the Guild Master. 'Good,' she said. 'So it's settled.'

'Settled?' Wilder echoed, clenching his fists at his sides.

It was the alchemist who addressed him, her voice cutting through the tension. 'What exactly is your issue with me? This has no bearing on you.'

'No bearing on me? You mean besides the fact you stole a sacred blade and put the midrealms at risk?' he snapped. It wasn't just because of a blade, but *the* blade. Though, the truth was, ever since the fall of Naarva all those years ago, he'd taken issue with a lot of things. It was one of the reasons he was barely stationed at the fortress. He took his simmering rage and scars with him wherever he went, the same rage that rippled off him now.

But the young woman folded her arms over her chest, the set of her jaw fierce. 'Yes.'

Wilder restrained himself from closing the space between them and shaking her by the shoulders. The alchemist had courage, of that he was sure, but courage alone couldn't face the darkness descending on the midrealms. A dagger-wielding girl was no match for the festering creatures from beyond the Veil.

Instead, Wilder fought against his rising aggravation and looked at Osiris, grinding his teeth. 'You're going to add this to your list of mistakes as Guild Master, then?' he asked, voice low.

Shock rippled through the room as Osiris' head jerked up, his eyes bulging. 'What did you just say?'

Wilder's pulse raced. 'You heard, Osiris. You've got quite the tally so far —'

'Hawthorne...' Torj cautioned.

'If we're done with the theatrics,' he growled, stalking towards the door, his patience thinning. 'I need a drink.'

'Your disrespect of the guild knows no bounds, Warsword...' Osiris said.

'Disrespect?' Wilder spat, his blood boiling. 'You think *I* disrespect Thezmarr?'

Vernich shifted, an eager gleam in his gaze. Wilder knew he relished any dressing down of his fellow warriors.

Wilder's gaze fell to the young woman again and he clenched his jaw, the muscles there beginning to ache as those celadon eyes pierced him. He had to admire her spirit, but it didn't stop the fury surging through him. 'She's going to be more trouble than she's worth.'

Torj, as always, begged reason. 'Walk away, Wilder,' he murmured.

'With pleasure.' And with that, Wilder threw the door open and stormed out, leaving Audra to her games and the alchemist to her fate.

CHAPTER SIX

A ltera Zoltaire had been instructed to return to her
room and pack a bag... not for banishment from
Thezmarr, but for the ride to Harenth, where she would
petition the kings and queens of the midrealms for her right
to train as a shieldbearer.

It had been *Audra's* idea. It had been *Audra* who had
fought tooth and nail for her. For once the librarian's
severity had been wielded not against her, but for her... And
despite the objections of the silver-eyed Warsword, the
Guild Master himself had relented.

Thea felt lightheaded.

It wasn't until she was being dragged into her quarters by
the arm that she realised she must have paused outside in
her bewilderment.

'Where have you been?' Wren half-shouted, peering into
her face worriedly.

'I...' But Thea couldn't get the words out.

'Oh gods, what have you done now? You've been kicked
out, haven't you?'

There was a blur of movement at the door as Sam and Ida burst in.

Sam, her freshly chopped red hair swaying, grabbed her by the shoulders. 'We just heard! Is it true?'

'Is *what* true?' Wren demanded, her expression tight with concern.

'Thea got caught in the Bloodwoods *by a Warsword*,' Ida supplied, the kohl around her eyes smudged. 'But then... if that was the case, you wouldn't be here, would you?'

'I...' Thea tried again and failed.

'Althea, so help me if you don't tell us what's going on right now...'

Thea swallowed the lump in her throat and allowed her sister to lead her to her bed. There she sat and took a minute to gather herself before looking at Wren and her friends.

'It's true,' she said.

'*What?!*'

Thea met her sister's celadon gaze and told her everything.

When she was done, to her disbelief, a whisper of a laugh escaped Wren.

'What is it?'

But Wren shook her head, still laughing. She rummaged through the trunk of belongings at the end of her bed and produced a small traveller's pack.

Sam and Ida were laughing, too.

Thea rounded on them. 'Will someone tell me —'

It was Wren who answered, amusement bright in her eyes as she shook her head again. 'You're going to petition the rulers... You truly are Althea Nine Lives, aren't you?'

. . .

It was still dark and icy when Thea arrived at the stables, pulling her cloak tight around her and adjusting the pack on her shoulder. She had hardly slept, tossing and turning into the early hours of the morning, wondering what Harenth would be like, wondering if she'd packed the right things. Wondering what the royals would make of her petition, or if she'd be laughed out of the palace.

But regardless of the uncertainty squirming in her gut, there was a much stronger feeling coursing through her: hope. She had been given the chance she'd always dreamt of, the chance to fight for what she wanted so desperately. She wouldn't squander it.

Audra was in the tack room, dressed for riding, hauling a heavy saddle blanket from its hook with surprising strength. Thea watched from the doorway, thinking back to their time together over the years... Audra had always kept her at arm's length, had always been impatient and easy to anger. But that fire had come to Thea's defence, had given her a chance at greatness.

Her warden spotted her. 'Well, don't just stand there. No one's saddling your horse for you.'

Ignoring the sharp words, Thea followed the librarian to one of the stalls. 'Audra?'

'What?' she snapped, looking up from where she was adjusting the length of her stirrup.

Thea couldn't help smiling as she peered inside. 'Thank you.'

Audra's gaze briefly softened, before she made an impatient noise at the back of her throat. 'You've got the grey mare in stall five. Be quick about it. We need to leave within the quarter hour. Don't dawdle.'

Soon, both women rode through the gatehouse, the

guards staring after them. It was an unusual sight to be sure: the librarian and an alchemist on horseback bound for Harenth.

Thea's chest swelled as they left the fortress. It had been an age since she'd escaped the grounds in the light of day, with nothing to hide, and even longer still since she'd ridden. All Thezmarrians were taught the basics from a young age, but rare was the opportunity for women to develop and nurture those skills later on. Those fleeting months with Evander had seen her brush up on her horsemanship, but she'd avoided the stables since his cruel words. Now, she relished the rhythmic trot of her mare beneath her.

For a moment, Thea dared to hope what her days might entail should the rulers grant her request.

'Pick up the pace,' Audra commanded. 'It's three days to the capital of Harenth.'

The words were music to Thea's ears, and she urged her mare into a canter, passing the outer stone walls of the fortress and the gates that opened up onto the Mourner's Trail, the only way in and out of Thezmarr. It was a narrow, rocky path that cut through the Bloodwoods, known for its deadly traps and magic wards. The name alone sent a small shiver down Thea's spine. Just how many mourners had it greeted? In the watery light of early morning, it seemed unthreatening... Nothing horrific sprang out at them, nothing dared to stop them leaving. But Thea knew Thezmarr and its masters better than to take things at face value.

Thea had only travelled it once, or so she'd been told – the day her parents had abandoned her and Wren. She wondered how they'd navigated the dangers, or if, because of what they offered the guild, they'd been given safe passage to the gates. It wasn't often she allowed herself to think about her family. Wren had always discouraged it, insisting that the fact they'd been forsaken said enough. Thea was inclined to agree, though sometimes she wondered if fighting was in their blood.

Thea and Audra rode in silence, cantering along the infamous trail, the crisp morning air stinging Thea's cheeks. She didn't know how much time had passed and she didn't care. She simply revelled in the freedom of the ride, and the unobstructed view of the Mourner's Trail, the grey sky peeking between the canopy of leaves that arched overhead.

But after a time, Thea could stand the silence no longer. 'Audra?'

'I knew the peace wouldn't last,' the older woman muttered.

Thea persisted. 'Will you ever tell me about it?'

Audra gave her a blank look.

'What happened the night they took your swords?'

Audra stiffened in her saddle. 'You know what happened that night. You've been taught about it. You've no doubt read all the books about it.'

'But you saw everything. You were actually there.'

'I wish I hadn't been,' her warden replied bitterly. But she relented, slowing her horse. 'The prophecy had been foretold only a few months before and the Guild Master had always been uneasy about it,' Audra began. 'But I was persuasive, told him that words couldn't fell the great fortress of Thezmarr, and certainly not the midrealms when they had our protection. He was twitchy... Still, I convinced him otherwise. Until that night. There was a girl, Anya. She was perhaps six or so? A prim and proper little thing, copper hair, very sweet. None of us know how she got her hands on a scythe of Naarvian steel, but she did... I sensed something was wrong moments before it happened, ordered Farissa to hide you and the other children away. I came into the courtyard just in time to see it. Shadows rippling off the curved blade, wraiths descending upon the fortress. Seven Thezmarrians were killed.'

Thea's throat constricted, recalling the smell that had lingered for days. Blood and heather.

'I told Osiris that there was an explanation, that it had been an accident. I tried to tell him that to strip women of their right to bear arms would only weaken the guild and stir dissent. But he saw nothing beyond the bodies at his doorstep and the words of the prophecy. The rest of the midrealms felt the same. After that, barely any children were sent to us. That's why there are no more families among us, why there are so few women, why there have been so few recruits to the warrior ranks over the years. Thezmarr is bleeding, has been, since that day.'

'What happened to the women warriors?'

'They left.'

'To go where?'

Audra sniffed. 'Far away from this place. No one knows exactly. Nowhere in these realms.'

'You didn't want to go with them?' Thea asked.

'"Want" doesn't come into it. Someone had to stay the course.'

Thea straightened. 'Am I part of that course?'

The librarian gave a soft laugh. 'I have been watching you for a long time, Althea Zoltaire. Your secret training, your Dancing Alchemists —' She paused to give Thea a pointed look. 'I've known since the very beginning. I always thought you might need some help with the guild.'

Thea choked. 'Why play this card now?'

Another laugh. 'Well, I was waiting until you were ready.'

'You think I'm ready?' Her fingers crept to her fate stone.

'No,' Audra said bluntly. 'But we're out of time. Everything I said in the council room was true. Whispers tell me that the Veil is weakening, that the threat to the midrealms is closer than we imagine.'

'You don't believe the prophecy?'

Audra scoffed. 'I believe that like all prophecies, it's up for interpretation and that the fears of men can distort those interpretations... After all, how long had you carried that blade? We're still standing, aren't we?'

Thea cleared her throat. 'Do you think I have a chance?'

'No idea. But the next initiation test for shieldbearers is in three months and you need more practice, more challenges than batting a stick against a tree. Of the most recent intake, it's a real mix. Some are castle staff no longer content with their lot, there are a few orphans from around the midrealms, and then of course those from Tver, Aveum and Harenth seeking glory as a Thezmarrian Guardian. You're already leagues behind the rest in terms of training, endurance, and everything else.'

Thea's stomach plummeted.

'But let's not get ahead of ourselves until this meeting with the rulers.'

More questions on her lips, Thea twisted in her saddle to see Audra's eyes still upon her, where Thea's fingers encased the jade pendant. She hurriedly tucked it back down the front of her tunic, but it was too late.

'You think I don't know what that is?' Audra said. 'You

forget who found you and your sister beneath the portcullis that night.'

'It's nothing.'

'Don't insult me. I know exactly what it is. I've known your obsession with it since the moment you arrived at Thezmarr.'

Thea shifted uncomfortably. Audra had known about her fate stone all this time? And had said nothing? Had spoken no words of comfort to the child grappling with her impending death? Had said nothing to the teenager who had convinced herself it meant liberation? And nothing again, to the young woman who raced against death's hourglass to leave a legacy?

Audra spoke. 'You will come to learn that most things to be feared exist in life, not in death.'

Thea's heart stuttered at those words. But by the time she'd gathered the courage to look at her warden, the older woman had pressed her horse into another canter.

Forcing herself to unclench her jaw, Thea adjusted her grip on her reins and followed, focusing on the route ahead.

The Mourner's Trail stretched on through the seemingly endless Bloodwoods, but at last the bleeding forest opened up, revealing a vast tapestry of land. From their position on the high ground Thea could see sprawling farmlands and hillsides, and cracks in the earth where rivers sliced through the terrain.

But rather than taking in the rich expanse of territory to the east, Thea noticed Audra's gaze drifting northward, to the glimmer of a great lake and the land beyond.

'What are you looking at?'

Audra's shoulders sagged. 'The ruins of Delmira are up that way…' She didn't tear her eyes away from the horizon.

'If you squint, you can see some of the lone watchtowers,' she pointed. 'Just behind the lake...'

The so-called watchtowers were all but shadows in the distance to Thea, and yet her scalp prickled as she surveyed the lands kissed by darkness. Delmira had fallen first, long ago, and Naarva, the kingdom of gardens, had followed only six years ago. The stain of monsters on the midrealms was undeniable.

She felt Audra's eyes on her. 'What?'

The librarian seemed to consider her, mulling over her words before she spoke. 'Tell me I chose well, Althea,' she said. 'That you will do me and the Furies proud.'

Thea blanched. Audra asking for reassurance was unheard of. Slowly, she nodded. 'I will, Audra. You have my word.'

'Good.' The older woman shortened her reins. 'Then know this... If you seek power in a world of men and monsters, there is nothing more powerful than knowledge and the ability to wield it. Remember that, would-be shieldbearer.'

Thea's throat closed up and all she could do was incline her head in acknowledgement, the weight of it all settling on her shoulders.

Seeking to lighten the mood, Thea looked to her warden again. 'Audra?'

'What now?'

'Back in the council room...' Thea ventured. 'That was a damn fine throw.'

The lines around Audra's mouth wrinkled as she smiled. 'The smallest blade can make the biggest difference.'

They continued riding until the Mourner's Trail became the Wesford Road, the route that passed through the three remaining kingdoms of the midrealms. There, at the edge of Thezmarrian territory, Audra brought them to a halt.

'This is where I leave you,' the librarian told her, holding out a satchel of what appeared to be rations.

Thea frowned, taking it. 'I didn't think I was allowed to ride alone?'

Hoofbeats sounded nearby.

'You're not,' came a now familiar deep, husky voice.

Astride a black stallion, twin swords strapped to his back, Wilder Hawthorne emerged from the Bloodwoods.

CHAPTER SEVEN

Thea stared at the Warsword, realising too late that Audra had already cantered off back in the direction of the fortress.

'Why you?' She tried to keep the rising anger from her voice. Of all the escorts she might have had, she was stuck with the one who had opposed her the loudest? The one who had stolen her dagger and tried to have her kicked out of Thezmarr? To her frustration, she noticed that when he wasn't scowling, the lines of his face softened and there was no denying that he was handsome.

But her appreciation was fleeting because his scowl returned with a vengeance. 'The Guild Master likes to remind me of my place from time to time.'

Thea's brow furrowed. 'What does that mean?'

But Hawthorne pinned her with a glare and turned his horse towards the rolling hillside, not deigning to respond.

'Why aren't we taking the Wesford Road?' Thea squeezed her mare's sides with her heels and followed, clenching and unclenching her teeth.

'Because, *Alchemist*, there are faster ways to Harenth and I, for one, don't want to waste more time than necessary on this tedious escort.'

'My name is *Thea*,' she bit out before she could think the better of it.

'Like I said,' the Warsword eyed her warily. 'I don't want to waste time.'

But before Thea even had a moment to process his disdain, he was off.

Cursing him, Thea followed.

The sun rose high above the midrealms as they rode hard through the outer lands of Harenth, leaving the moody skies of Thezmarr far behind. Despite the surly company, Thea drank in the sights like a parched vagabond. The dipping hills and valleys were carpeted in luscious, long grasses, a different world from the jagged edge upon which the fortress sat.

For a time, they followed one of the many rushing rivers that carved through the verdant lands, heading east, and Thea realised with a start that this was the furthest from the fortress she'd ever travelled. She wished Wren was here to see it.

The hilts of the Warsword's twin blades glinted in the sun and she found herself staring at his broad, armoured shoulders with heated resentment, his harsh words from the council room echoing in her mind. What had she ever done to him? His refusal to speak made her all the more aggravated, stewing in the silence. That he was *ever-so-slightly* attractive only made matters worse. A tapered back of defined muscles or not, the man himself was a barbarian.

By late afternoon, they still hadn't stopped to rest, and Thea's entire lower body was throbbing. Her back ached, her tailbone felt bruised, and her inner thighs were burning. Not that she'd complain. Not in a million years. Though, she was concerned she might not be able to walk when she eventually did dismount... Her stomach gurgled; she hadn't eaten anything all day except a chunk of bread she'd swiped from the kitchens on her way to meet Audra.

It wasn't until the sun dipped behind the hills that Hawthorne brought them to a halt by the edge of a river.

'We'll camp here for tonight,' he said, the first words he had spoken in hours, jumping down from his stallion in one graceful motion.

'Right,' Thea replied, her voice croaky from disuse. She waited until his back was turned before she attempted to slide from her saddle. When her boots hit the ground, her legs buckled and suddenly she was falling.

Large, warm hands encircled her waist, drawing her upright and steadying her. Heat radiated from Hawthorne, his fingers brushing her hips, his towering body only inches from her own.

Thea's pulse quickened, and a thrill stirred beneath her skin, as did her awareness of every point at which they touched, at which they *might* touch.

Hawthorne peered down at her, his gaze firm and intense, as though assessing her.

Flushing, Thea drew back, praying that her legs would cooperate. 'Thank you.'

The Warsword's hands fell away from her in an instant and he shouldered a quiver of arrows and a bow, turning towards the nearby woods. 'I'll hunt,' he told her. 'You rub the horses down and start a fire.'

'So in other words, women's work.' The remark flew out of her mouth before she could think.

To her surprise, a fleeting glint of amusement shone in Hawthorne's eyes and he held out his bow to her. 'By all means, you catch the dinner.'

Thea's cheeks reddened.

'That's what I thought,' Hawthorne scoffed.

Thea took a bold step towards him. 'Show me how.'

'I'm not here to be your teacher or hold your hand. Tend to the horses. Start the fire.' He stalked off into the woods.

Thea swore.

'I heard that,' his reply sounded from the trees.

Thea inhaled the crisp air, allowing herself two minutes to let her anger subside, along with her curses about the insufferable man before she set about her tasks. She ignored her screaming muscles as she removed the heavy saddles and tack from the horses and rubbed them down. Hawthorne's stallion was enormous and she had to stand on a boulder to reach certain parts of his back. The beast was gentler than she expected, even nuzzling her shoulder as she led him and her mare to the river to drink their fill.

Thea watched, longing to throw herself into the water and scrub her sticky body clean. She could feel the grime of the day's ride caked onto her skin, and she knew she smelt like horse and sweat. But there was work to be done and she refused to rest until Hawthorne did. If he didn't believe she had what it took to be a warrior of Thezmarr, she'd damn well show him.

She left the horses to graze in a nearby clearing and started gathering kindling for the fire. Part of her still couldn't believe where she was, let alone who rode with her. And then there was her destination to consider, the Heart of Harenth - King Artos' palace, where she would petition to join the shieldbearers.

Thea searched for the best spot to build their fire, settling on a position near the edge of the woods, but close enough to the river. She took rocks from the riverbank and created a rim around the base layer of sticks she'd collected, and placed the kindling on top before scouring the ground for stones to light it with.

The last of the daylight was fading and with the right rocks in hand, Thea crouched by her handiwork and hit them together. Her whole body ached and she wanted nothing more than to lie down in the dirt and sleep, but her persistence was rewarded with sparks shooting down into the kindling. She blew air into the lit embers and, finally, it caught alight.

She stoked the fire, feeding it larger logs, ensuring it would continue to burn.

'Who taught you how to make a fire?' came Hawthorne's voice as he strode into view, his bow and quivers over his shoulder, two dead hares hanging from his hand.

'You thought I couldn't?'

'Why would an alchemist know how to camp in the wilderness?'

'So you were setting me up to fail?'

Hawthorne shrugged. 'Who taught you?'

'None of your business.'

Evander had taught her, but Thea would have sooner walked barefoot on the hot coals than tell the Warsword as much. She watched as he skinned the hares and speared them on two long sticks, balancing them over the flames. Soon, the aroma of roasting game had Thea's mouth watering.

'I'm going to wash,' Hawthorne announced, lighting a torch and leaving her to rotate the meat.

Soon, Thea heard splashes from the riverbank, warmth flooding her at the thought of seeing those broad shoulders stripped bare, at imagining the formidable Warsword without his armour. She licked her lips, her chest tightening. Nearby, the Hand of Death was undressed and dripping wet.

Her traitorous eyes glanced towards the river, where she saw a flash of tattooed skin beneath the moonlight. Even from afar, she could see that every inch of him was corded with hard muscle —

Idiot, she berated herself, forcing her attention back to the meal and turning the roasting hares with more vigour than necessary. Whatever physical reaction she was having to the Warsword was just that: *physical*, and she was more than capable of separating her mind from the rest. There was a certain beauty to his brutality and that was all, she told herself. Though her reasoning didn't stop her imagining that powerful body carving through the water, nor did it stop her recalling the imprint of his hands on her waist.

Hawthorne returned to the camp, the ends of his hair dripping as he swept it up and tied it back in a knot. 'The meat will keep a little longer on the fire if you want to freshen up.'

Thea nodded, hoping he didn't notice her flushed cheeks. She took the torch he offered and fled, utterly mortified by her own thoughts.

The water was icy and Thea bit back a yelp as she dipped her bare foot in. But there was nothing for it, she was filthy and she doubted she'd be able to sleep smelling as bad as she did. She made quick work of peeling off her pants and shirt, already regretting that she'd have to put them back on over clean skin. She only had two changes of clothes and she needed to be presentable for the king's feast in a few days' time.

Naked, she waded in the shallows, shivering as she rubbed away the dust and sweat from the road. She wished she had thought to bring a bar of soap, but water would have to do for now.

The hair on her nape stood up, goosebumps rushing over her skin. She glanced back to camp, where she could see the flicker of the campfire. Hawthorne was there, staring into the flames. But almost immediately, he seemed to sense her eyes on him and his head snapped up, his attention locking onto her across the distance.

Face flaming, Thea turned away, wrestling her clothes over her wet, tingling skin and muttering a string of curses to herself. She needed to pull herself together.

When she trudged back to camp, Hawthorne handed her a portion of roast hare.

'Thank you,' she said.

It was the best thing she'd ever tasted. The meat was rich and succulent, and she had to suppress the urge to moan in satisfaction as she bit into it.

She stole glances at the Warsword as she ate, unable to shake the feeling that sharing a meal before a campfire with him was something few experienced. His gaze slid to hers, sensing her attention.

'What?' he said.

'What's it like?' Thea heard herself ask.

'You'll have to be more specific.'

'Being a Warsword. Being the youngest Warsword in history? What's it like?'

Hawthorne wiped his mouth on the back of his hand and took a long swig from his flask.

'Full of adventure?' Thea prompted. 'Glory?'

He gave a dark laugh. 'There's a lot more adventure and glory when you're not on escort duty.'

Thea drew a sharp breath, anger bubbling. 'We have two more days' ride ahead, and then another three on our return.'

'I can count.'

'So why not be civil? We could pass the time more easily.'

'I'm not usually civil to thieves.'

'What?' But then Thea saw his hand move to her dagger. 'I told you, that was a gift. The dying wish of a Warsword, in fact. And actually, I'd like it back.'

Hawthorne scoffed again. 'Not a chance.'

'What's it to you?' she snapped. 'It's no more yours than it is mine —'

'I'll hear no more about it,' he cut her off. 'It's Naarvian steel, Alchemist. You know what that means. Besides, you've no right to a weapon.'

'Yet.'

His eyes narrowed. 'Tell me then, why are you so desperate to be a shieldbearer?'

'Not just a shieldbearer,' Thea snapped. 'I am far more ambitious than that.'

'A Guardian of the midrealms, then.'

'Try again. And no,' she added. 'Not a commander, not a master of weapons. Something more.'

After a pause, Hawthorne's brows shot up. 'You think you'll make it through the Great Rite? You think...'

'Why don't you tell me what it is, and I'll tell you if I'd pass.'

'I wouldn't tell you if Enovius himself had a blade to my heart.'

'You despise me that much?'

'The Great Rite is sacred, and known to only those who would dare undertake it and emerge victorious. It would betray my vows as a Warsword to tell you what it entails.'

'I *will* emerge victorious,' Thea replied. 'Although they have not given me the same opportunities as others, I will face it and triumph. With the right mentor, I could —'

'Mentors are overrated,' Hawthorne cut in. 'If you want someone to hold your hand through the trials of becoming a warrior of Thezmarr, then you'll be disappointed. You're better off staying an alchemist if a teacher is what you're after.' His voice was laced with bitterness.

Thea cracked her knuckles in frustration. 'I don't need someone holding my hand,' she ground out. 'All I ask for is the same guidance.'

'A word of advice, Alchemist,' he said, voice low. 'If you want to achieve anything in these realms, do it yourself. Rely on no one.'

'Is that what *you* did?' she bit back.

He shook his head in disbelief. 'Go to sleep. We ride hard again tomorrow.'

'Can't wait,' Thea muttered.

Anger still simmering, she went to her saddlebags and retrieved her bedroll, setting herself up a few feet away from the fire, silently cursing her resentful escort.

He might be one of the most powerful warriors in the realm, and his presence might stir a certain physical response... she allowed. *But Hawthorne is also an arse.*

· · ·

81

Dawn came all too soon, and Thea felt as though a herd of cattle had trampled her as she staggered to her feet. Everything hurt.

Hawthorne's sleeping mat was already rolled up and placed neatly by his saddlebag, but there was no sign of where he'd gone.

Good, Thea thought. She didn't feel like talking to him. If it was to be a Warsword to accompany her, why not the golden-haired one? He seemed friendlier. Perhaps he would have told her the story of how he'd fought off not one, but two cursed bears. *That* she would have liked to hear.

Bracing herself against the early morning chill, Thea eased into some stretches, whimpering at the pain lancing through muscles she didn't even know existed. If she was ever going to train as a shieldbearer and graduate to a Thezmarrian warrior, she'd need to harden up.

As she ate an apple, she set about readying the horses for departure. Splitting the core between the two beasts, they withstood her clumsily cinching their girths and securing their bridles. Another lesson learnt from Evander. At least he had been good for something. Now, she remembered their time together with sinking embarrassment. Her eighteen-year-old self had thought the stable master's apprentice handsome and knowledgeable, but in hindsight, he'd been nothing more than a narrow-minded prat. She still carried a piece of hurt with her, not hurt that it had ended, but that her dreams somehow made her a pariah: unwanted, ugly and ridiculous —

'You're awake.' Hawthorne was striding towards her, one of his swords unsheathed in his hand.

'Observant of you,' Thea replied before nodding to his gleaming blade. 'A little early to be slaying monsters, isn't it?'

'I was training,' he said, voice clipped. 'A discipline you're unfamiliar with.'

Thea finished attaching her saddlebags to her mare. 'I train.'

'Fumbling in the Bloodwoods while you spy on the shieldbearers is hardly training.'

Thea whirled around. 'I don't fumble, and how do you know about that?'

'Not much goes on in the Bloodwoods that I don't know about, Alchemist. Your pitiful excuse for a sparring session being the least of it.'

'Why didn't you tell anyone?'

'Not worth my time.'

'But reporting me for my dagger was?'

The edge to his voice returned when he spoke again. 'That was different. That dagger didn't belong to you. You insult and risk all of Thezmarr by wielding it. Not to mention —'

'Who else saw me in the Bloodwoods?' Thea asked, changing tact.

'No one.'

Realisation dawned. 'Then it was you... You shot the arrow at me!'

Hawthorne mounted his horse in one effortless motion. 'Figured you needed a warning.'

Thea gaped at him, outraged. 'You could have killed me.'

'Not with my aim,' he said and started forward, his stallion's tail swishing.

Thea scrambled to mount her mare, muscles protesting. 'You're unbelievable,' she said to him when she caught up.

Hawthorne simply raised a brow at her. 'You have no idea.'

CHAPTER EIGHT

The day was already long and Thea watched her escort with the same resentful fascination as before. The two great swords sheathed across his back were enormous and, like all Warsword weaponry, forged with Naarvian steel. But since the fall of that kingdom, no new warriors had passed the Great Rite and thus, no new blades had been presented. Was that why Hawthorne had called her dagger sacred?

Thea studied the way he sat in his saddle, how with a subtle movement of his knees, he could steer his horse as though it were an extension of him.

'Who taught you to ride?' she asked, deciding that it was an innocent question in the face of all she truly wanted to know.

He actually groaned.

'This would be a lot less painful if you got over yourself and just answered.'

'I don't owe you answers, Alchemist. My only task is to get you to Harenth in one piece, though with the rate you pry, I make no promises on the latter.'

'Is that a threat?'

'Is that another question?'

Thea swore.

'You curse like an alchemist.'

'And you act like a prick.'

'Perhaps I am,' he muttered.

'On that I have no doubt.'

A muscle twitched in his jaw. 'Sorry to shatter your illusions about the legendary Warswords.'

'No, you're not.'

'You're right, I'm not.'

'Are you this obnoxious with everyone? Or have you saved that just for me?'

'Obnoxious?' Hawthorne bit out. 'I'm obeying the orders of the Guild Master. I owe no one small talk, especially a woman who put the midrealms at risk by wielding a blade.'

It was Thea's turn to laugh. 'I've been carrying that blade *for six years*,' she snapped. 'And I didn't see a swarm of shadow wraiths invading Thezmarr.'

'Six years…?' Hawthorne chewed on the words.

'Yes. Six years.' Thea realised she was grinding her teeth. 'Perhaps you had it right from the start. It's best if we don't talk for a while.'

'Finally, something we agree on,' he retorted before surging forward on his stallion.

This time, Thea didn't race to catch up; she needed the fresh air without his smouldering presence.

They travelled through the gold and green farmlands, where workers paused in the fields to stare at them. Well, to stare at Hawthorne, the Hand of Death. Thea supposed it wasn't often they had a legendary Warsword in their midst. Some of them even bowed as they passed, their reverence only serving as fuel to Thea's burning curiosity.

At what point in his life had he changed from the man to the legend? Was there a moment? A particular battle? Was it years of culminating a bloody reputation? As her earlier anger ebbed away, several times she turned to the warrior, a question on her lips, but he shook his head, a look in his eye that said, *don't you dare.*

They had been riding for hours when the Warsword brought them to a stop just before the fields of a vast crop.

'The horses need to rest,' he said by way of explanation.

After hours in the saddle, Thea was grateful for the opportunity to stretch her legs. On the crest of the hill, she surveyed the farmlands beyond.

'Who owns it all?' she asked, forgetting the present company for a moment.

To her surprise, Hawthorne answered. 'King Artos.'

'He owns everything?'

'The Fairmoore family owns all the land in Harenth. That's why the people pay such high taxes.'

'Have you met him before? King Artos?'

'Many times.'

'And?'

'And what?'

'What's he like? What should I expect when I make my case to him and the other rulers?'

'The unexpected.'

Thea wished Wren was there to roll her eyes at. 'Gods, you're a terrible conversationalist.'

'I don't do pleasantries.'

'Clearly.' She sighed. 'But this isn't about pleasantries to me. This is important. It's *everything*.'

After hours of travel, he looked at her, *really* looked at her. 'King Artos is a hard man to predict,' he allowed. 'A trait you'll find common among the kings and queens of the midrealms.'

Thea paced, trying to rid herself of the unease that churned within. 'You think it's a waste of time, don't you?'

'I never said that.'

'But you think it.'

'What I think shouldn't matter.'

Thea stopped short. 'But it does,' she admitted. 'You're a Warsword of Thezmarr, the very thing I aspire to be. How could it not matter to me?'

For the first time since they'd met, Hawthorne's expression softened. The harsh lines of his face faded and he offered a tentative smile. 'You need thicker skin than that if you mean to succeed.'

The small kindness caught Thea off-guard and, for a moment, she struggled to tear her focus away from the soft curve of his lips.

'Thicker skin,' she managed. 'Got it. Anything else?'

'Try not to piss off your superiors.'

Thea blinked in disbelief. 'Was that a joke?'

'No idea what you're talking about.'

A sudden icy wind swept through the lands below, stinging Thea's cheeks. She pulled her cloak tight, though it made little difference.

'Winter winds from Aveum,' Hawthorne explained. 'This valley bears the brunt of it and we won't reach the end by sundown. We've got a cold night ahead of us.'

Thea's teeth were already chattering, the golden rays of sun doing nothing to warm her when she was back on her horse. 'Is it always like this in these parts?' she asked.

'No. The winds have come sooner than expected.'

'Why is that?'

Hawthorne gazed out into the distance and shifted in his saddle. 'The midrealms respond to unrest.'

When night fell, the winds howled in earnest, but there was nowhere to take shelter. They had no choice but to make camp in an empty paddock as the icy gale carved through the surrounding valley, sharp as a blade.

Both she and Hawthorne attempted the same duties as the night before, but not with all the skill in the world could Thea light a fire in those conditions. Nor was there any game to be found.

'We'll have to make do with rations,' Hawthorne said, returning his bow to the rest of his belongings.

Thea nodded numbly from where she sat in a ball on the ground and reached for her pack with frozen fingers.

Hawthorne still towered above. 'If we stack our saddles and bags and sleep behind them, we can create a bit of a barrier between us and the wind,' he said, already moving towards his stallion.

Though Thea wanted nothing more than to curl up beneath her blanket, she forced herself to follow suit. She wouldn't have him thinking she was weak or lazy. Together, they crafted a makeshift wall against the icy blast and took shelter behind it, shivering side by side.

Thea's focus went straight to where their arms grazed

one another. With Hawthorne being so huge, there was no way they *couldn't* touch in such a confined space. He noted her gaze.

'I can make do elsewhere if you're uncomfortable,' he said.

For a moment Thea imagined his hulking frame out in the open, exposed to the bite of the cold. Despite her misgivings about the brute, it didn't sit well with her. She shook her head. 'It's fine,' she told him, her stomach fluttering. 'Makes sense to stay close and make the most of what little body heat we have.'

'If you're sure...'

'I'm sure.'

In the end, they didn't bother with the rations, nor try to talk over the screeching gale. Hawthorne remained upright against the saddles, as though determined to keep some semblance of space between them. But Thea was too exhausted to care. She longed for the reprieve of sleep and, thankfully, she drifted off the moment she curled up on her bedroll.

Strong arms encased Thea, wrapping her in a delicious warmth while deep breaths tickled the crook of her neck. As she woke to the rose and lilac clouds above, no sign of the howling winds from the night before, she realised whose heart it was that beat steadily against her back...

Hawthorne was holding her to his chest, every inch of him flush against her, the heat of him soaking through the thin layers between them.

When did this happen? How? A Warsword held her in his

arms. *The* Warsword. And in the depths of slumber, he pulled her closer still, creating a hot friction between them that Thea, still groggy with sleep herself, arched into without thinking.

To find him hard against her.

Her breathing hitched, an ache building between her thighs. Tipping her head back, the scent of his soap was intoxicating, and a flush of warmth spread through her whole body.

Hawthorne stirred, slowly, every movement only heightening Thea's awareness of exactly where they touched.

A low hum of pleasure sounded against her skin and then —

'Fuck!'

The contact vanished and the chill of the dawn air swept in.

'Fuck,' Hawthorne said again, leaping up, a rare blush gracing the tops of his cheeks. 'I'm sorry, I —' he stammered, turning away from her and adjusting his clothes.

Thea was on her feet, holding her arms across her chest, trying to rub the warmth back into her limbs, trying to erase the memory of his imprint against her.

'It's fine,' she said, though her voice betrayed a tremble. Gods, she'd moved against him, she'd *sought* his touch...

'Truly, Alchemist, I never meant —' He ran his fingers through his hair. 'I must have... reached out in my sleep.'

Somehow, his mortification eased the throbbing in her own body and the confusion that came with it. A laugh bubbled out of her.

'You think this is funny?' he demanded, incredulous.

'A little.' She gave his pants a pointed glance where there was no hiding the unmistakable bulge.

'Gods,' he muttered, adjusting the fall of his shirt again. 'You'll be the end of me.' He snatched his swords from the ground and walked off. Thea soon heard a curse, and the distinct sound of water being tipped over his head.

WILDER HAWTHORNE

'F uck,' Wilder muttered again as he put as much space as possible between him and the infuriating alchemist. He left their camp behind, his cheeks aflame and his erection still straining against his pants. The sensation of her backside pressed against him was seared into his mind, as was the feel of her arching into his embrace.

'Furies save me,' he groaned, tipping an entire canteen of cold water over his head, hoping it would cool the inferno within.

It didn't.

His whole body was trembling, longing for contact, for release and – against his better judgement – for *her*.

I sought her warmth in the night, he told himself. *That's all.*

Wilder glanced back at their camp, spotting her tending to the horses. He had to hand it to her: she moved like a warrior of Thezmarr already. Her steps were light, her motions controlled and fluid. All her supposed training had paid off in that respect.

He tried to ignore the swell of her breasts, the swing of

her hips and how she flicked her braid out of the way as she went about her tasks.

He had sprung away from her as though burned, but in truth it was all he could do not to pull her closer, and by the Furies had she fitted him perfectly.

Gods, he needed to do something about his cock. Desire pulsed so fiercely he had half a mind to tend to himself, just to get it out of his system, just to take the rock-hard edge off.

He muttered another curse. That would hardly help. It might even make the problem worse. Instead, Wilder inhaled through his nose and unsheathed his swords. He swung them with unyielding strength, revelling in the comforting weight of the steel.

He'd burn off his frustrations the Warsword way.

Shedding his outer layers and planting his feet wide, Wilder started taking himself through his usual set of drills. Relishing the kiss of the wind as he swept his blades through the air, he tried to lose himself in physical exertion. It was a relief not to be training in his armour. The breastplate, in particular, bothered him, rubbing against his shoulder. Armour was one of the gifts a Warsword received upon completion of the Great Rite, but by the time Wilder had passed, the kingdom of its origin, Delmira, had fallen. As such, his armour was a poor imitation of Vernich's and Torj's, the latter receiving the last supplies from the famous armoury. Wilder made do with what he'd been given over the years, but it irked him nonetheless.

Squaring his shoulders, he attacked, slashing his swords in a flurry of movement, striking and retreating into a dance he knew all too well. But no matter how many times he sliced and carved his imaginary opponent, his thoughts kept coming back to her, and it wasn't long before he sensed her gaze on him.

He ignored her presence, not nearly finished with trying to blow off steam. And yet he was drawn to her. Her persistence, her innate questioning, the way she now studied his movements, as though committing them to memory. Regardless of the outcome at Harenth, he knew deep in his bones that the alchemist wouldn't give up, and he begrudgingly admired that.

Wilder looped both blades around, delivering a would-be deadly blow before twisting his hips and bringing both swords across, beheading the invisible enemy.

Only then did he glance up at the alchemist, who watched on with intense eyes.

The sooner she got what she wanted, the sooner he could be rid of her, and he could go back to hunting monsters in the darkness.

CHAPTER NINE

Thea paused at the crest on the land. There was nowhere to hide and so she simply sat on the damp grass and watched him in full view.

The Warsword had shucked off his outer layers and wore a sweat-drenched undershirt as he trained, powerful muscles bunching beneath the wet fabric. The black ink on his right hand trailed up his forearm and bicep, disappearing under his shirt.

He slashed his two mighty swords through the air in a blur of steel, cutting down imaginary opponents.

Thea had seen *no one* move like he did. Each strike, each parry, each feint was a step in a deadly dance, each movement blended with lethal grace, discipline and strength beyond her comprehension.

Not even Esyllt, the weapons master, can fight like that. Again, Thea wondered who had schooled the warrior in the art of combat, for it *was* an art when he did it. As arrogant as he was, there was no denying Hawthorne's predatory prowess, his unparalleled skill. Someone more than a weapons master had honed those abilities – and the Furies themselves had gifted him power upon completion of the Great Rite.

Clouds formed before Thea's face as she exhaled, wondering what it would be like to see Hawthorne in the heart of a proper battle. She could almost picture it: the warrior clad in his black armour, blood spattered across his handsome face as he carved through enemy after enemy —

'Do you think it wise, spying on a Warsword, Alchemist?' He didn't break his focus from his sparring.

'Here I was thinking we'd started getting along,' she said, unable to suppress her grin as a fresh blush tipped his cheeks. 'Besides, it's not spying if I'm in plain sight. Why don't you teach me some of your drills?'

'No.' It came out as a growl. 'Haven't I made myself clear?'

'Haven't I?' Thea countered. 'I want to learn, and who better to learn from than you?'

'I wasn't offering.'

'What do you have to lose?'

'You mean besides my time?'

'Didn't seem like you minded spending time with me this morning.'

He glowered. 'Not another word.'

But his irritation only fuelled Thea's amusement. 'Come now, we've shared so much already,' she teased. 'Why not share a few of your tricks? After all, Warswords used to have apprentices —'

'*Used to*,' he snapped. 'A tradition that has thankfully been dropped.'

She could feel the tension rolling off him in waves as he went through another set of movements. She tried to commit each twirl of the blade to memory, wishing she'd brought parchment and a pen to take notes. This was like no other training session she'd witnessed. There was a fluidity to every strike, every shift from foot to foot. He was a master in every respect of the word.

'Vernich would have killed you by now.' Hawthorne dropped into a powerful lunge, following through with a well-placed thrust of his second blade.

Thea found the words did not surprise her. *Vernich the Bloodletter...* The name said it all. 'You're not Vernich.'

'Good of you to notice.'

'What about the other, Torj the Bear Slayer? Would he tolerate me?'

'Only if he wanted to bed you.'

'Surely that's frowned upon? Aren't there rules?'

Hawthorne made a noise at the back of his throat. 'That's rich, coming from you.'

'Well, he's a Warsword though.'

'Perhaps alchemists aren't the only ones with a penchant for rule breaking.'

Hawthorne worked his way through a final round of sparring, his momentum increasing with every spin, every block.

'What are they like? The others?' Thea pressed.

At last, the Warsword came to a stop and mopped his brow on a scrap of fabric. 'I just told you,' he said, sheathing his blades in their scabbards. The warrior passed her on the ridge and made for a nearby stream.

Without thinking, Thea made to follow.

Hawthorne stopped in his tracks and turned to her with a piercing gaze. 'Do you mean to watch me bathe as well?'

Thea's cheeks heated, but she lifted her chin, recalling the press of his hard length against her backside. 'I'm sure it's nothing I haven't seen before.'

The corner of his mouth moved, betraying the hint of a dimple. 'I doubt that, Alchemist. I doubt that very much.'

By mid-afternoon, the capital city, Hailford, and the grand palace, the Heart of Harenth, were on the horizon. Even from afar, it was an incredible sight, as though the unnatural darkness at the edge of the midrealms didn't dare touch its shimmering soul. The palace sat atop a great hill at the centre, the city sprawling beneath it, its buildings in neat layered rows, like adoring admirers before a stage, surrounded by thick stone walls.

Before Thea knew it, they were at the towering iron gates tipped with spikes, though the imposing structure had been draped in banners and flowers in honour of the royal guests from the neighbouring kingdoms.

Hawthorne slowed his stallion upon approach and addressed one of the armed guards.

'The celebrations are well underway, then?'

The guard bowed his head in respect before he answered. 'Yes, Sir. The rulers from Tver and Aveum arrived two days ago. The main feast will begin by sundown.'

Hawthorne nodded. 'We're just in time. Thank you.'

Lowering his head once more, the guard pressed three fingers to his left shoulder, the utmost sign of reverence to a Warsword. His companion on the other side of the gateway did the same.

'Always an honour to host one of your kind in our city, Sir. Welcome to Hailford.'

Hawthorne nodded in thanks and urged his horse through the open gate, Thea close behind, her eyes widening at what lay beyond the walls.

The gates opened up to a paved square, an elaborate fountain at the centre with a mountain drake atop a jagged peak, streams of water shooting from the spikes on its back, the detailing so fine that Thea could see its individual scales. But there was no chance to study it, as Hawthorne urged them into a trot down the main thoroughfare.

Thea didn't know where to look first. Shops opened up onto the street, some selling wares from small stalls right on the cobblestones, goods spilling out from baskets, merchants calling out to those tempted to browse. More flowers and banners draped across the streets, petals lining the gutters. Celebration was thick in the air, people were drunk and cheerful, and the whole of Harenth pulsed with life and joyful abandon. Thea drank it all in, wishing she could leap from her horse and take part in the festivities.

A particularly colourful stall caught Thea's eye, and she longed for Wren to see the array of spices on display in little stone bowls and the range of herbs hanging from a thin rope across the width of the table. Sure enough, behind the stall was a fully stocked apothecary, likely where Farissa and the fortress cook got their supplies from, for potions and stews alike.

'Keep up,' Hawthorne called back to her.

Thea reluctantly squeezed her mare's sides, increasing her pace.

At the sight of the mighty black stallion and its rider, the crowded streets parted before them, some people making the three-fingered salute to the Warsword in their midst.

The street curled around the base of the hill and inclined, the celebrations and opulence growing with each step closer to the palace. The clothing of the onlookers became more colourful and lavish; instead of plain wool dresses and jackets, silk gowns trailed the cobblestones and velvet tunics with family crests and emblems emblazoned on the front lined the streets.

Thea and Hawthorne passed more shops, taverns and vibrant stalls, and eventually, the sight of the swinging wooden sign with crossed axes etched into it yanked Thea from her state of wonder. It was the great forge of Harenth, where she knew the Thezmarrian warrior weapons were made. It was a good opening to ask about the forging of the Naarvian blades and where that took place, but she wouldn't risk another verbal sparring match so close to the palace.

Thea's chest grew tight and nerves squirmed in her gut. She became increasingly aware of her worn and dirty travelling clothes amidst all the finery. The fresh shirt she'd changed into earlier that morning was dusty and smelt of horse. She knew that she would be afforded no opportunity to clean up before she was presented to the king, and the injustice of that fact nagged at her mind.

Towards the palace, the shops became more and more specialised: a gallery, a fine jeweller, a silk merchant and —

A plump man in a red velvet tunic waved so enthusiastically at Hawthorne, Thea thought his arm might pop out of its socket. He stood amidst a collection of massive oak barrels outside what appeared to be a wine shop.

'Hawthorne, my old friend!' he called, still waving, a wide grin splitting his face.

'Like you have any friends,' she muttered.

But to Thea's surprise, the Warsword slowed and when he turned to the man, she was even more shocked to find a genuine smile on his lips. It made him look younger.

'Hello Marise.'

'You must stop by today,' Marise gushed. 'I've received

several new vintages. There is one I know you will love especially!'

It was all Thea could do not to stare with her mouth agape. *Hawthorne likes fancy aged liquor...?* The Warsword and the wine merchant... It was an odd friendship pairing, to be sure. Also, it proved that Hawthorne was capable of manners and camaraderie, just not with her.

Brash bastard, Thea thought.

'Perhaps another time,' Hawthorne replied. 'I have business at the palace.'

'Business is thirsty work...'

'You're not wrong.'

Marise craned his neck, seeming to notice Thea at last. He made no effort to hide his blatant curiosity.

'And who is this intense creature? A new friend of yours?' he asked.

Hawthorne actually *laughed.* 'No.'

But Marise paid his rudeness no heed and waved to Thea. 'You must be the business, then. Pleasure to meet you, good lady.'

Thea nearly fell off her saddle. Never in her life had she been called a lady. But then, he was a wine merchant, wasn't he? He was likely drunk. He had also called her an *intense creature...* whatever that meant.

'You too, sir,' she managed.

'Sir?' He tipped his head back and chuckled deeply. 'You must call me Marise, like your friend here.' He gestured to Hawthorne.

Both Thea and Hawthorne ignored this.

Baffled by the man's enthusiasm, Thea nodded. 'I'm Thea.'

Marise beamed. 'You must come by for a tasting, my dear

Thea!'

'I...'

People had paused in the street to watch the exchange and she felt their stares boring into her.

Marise seemed to notice the unwanted attention and, with sudden seriousness, approached the Warsword's stallion. In a hurried whisper, he said: 'There is to be a dead red event soon. I shall send further details to the fortress.'

Thea blinked. *Dead red event? That sounds ominous.*

The Warsword bowed his head. 'Much obliged.'

They rode on, Thea's nerves well and truly kicking in as they moved through the residence quarter of Hailford, each townhouse more stately than the previous. It appeared that proximity to wealth created wealth.

At long last, the palace walls loomed before them and they came to a halt at the golden gates.

'You are most welcome, Warsword,' one guard said, making the three-fingered gesture to his left shoulder.

'Thank you,' Hawthorne replied, dismounting but still towering over the guards. 'My charge wishes to attend the open court. We have a letter from the Guild Master of Thezmarr.' Hawthorne produced a piece of folded parchment and handed it over.

The man scanned its contents, surveying Thea with an air of disbelief. Nevertheless, he gave the letter back to Hawthorne, addressing him, not Thea. 'The open court is taking place now. I believe it's nearly at an end.'

'At an end?' Thea started, jumping down from her mare. '*Now?* I thought we had until —'

'The royals and nobles are eager to start the feast and festivities,' the guard told her. 'If you wish this matter to be heard by the rulers, you must go now. Even then, you may be too late.'

Blood roared in Thea's ears, panic seizing her limbs. 'But —'

Hawthorne faced her, nodding towards the grand palace entrance and pushing the Guild Master's letter into her hands. 'I suggest you hurry.'

'You're not coming?'

'I have other matters to attend to.'

Thea gaped at him.

'What are you waiting for?' he prompted.

With her heart hammering and despair lurching in her gut, Thea turned on her heel, bracing to race for the stairs.

'Don't run,' Hawthorne added casually. 'They'll put an arrow through your throat.'

Cursing the Warsword, Thea walked as quickly as she could towards the entrance, taking two steps at a time. No one stopped her, no one shot an arrow through her throat. The palace was the most glorious place she had ever seen, but she couldn't stop to admire its opulent details. Instead, she asked the nearest guard where the court was being held and darted off, repeating his directions in her head.

Thea forgot about her dirty, dishevelled state. She forgot about the surly Warsword. She thought of only one thing: becoming a shieldbearer, and then, a legend of Thezmarr. This was the moment she had dreamed of her whole life. This was the opportunity that would make all her training, all her spying, and the many other risks she'd taken worth it.

When she reached the ornate pair of gold filigree doors, a herald greeted her.

'I'm afraid court is just finishing,' he said, eyeing her travel worn clothes with distaste.

Still clutching the now crumpled Guild Master's letter, Thea's heart plummeted to her stomach. 'Please, I've come a long way.'

The herald studied her for a moment longer, before spotting the Guild Master's wax seal on the parchment in her hands. 'One moment,' he said eventually, before ducking inside the room beyond.

Thea's heart was about to burst, and there was a real possibility that she might throw up all over the pristine marble floor.

A minute later, the herald reappeared. 'You were just in time,' he said. His earlier expression of distaste was gone, in its place was one of pity. 'They'll see you now.'

There was no time for shock, no time for panic. Thea straightened and brushed off her clothes as best she could before nodding to the herald.

He opened the doors.

The sight within took Thea's breath away.

The throne room.

Arched vaulted ceilings soared above her, punctuated with crystal chandeliers that sent light dancing around the room and the crowd of nobles that filled it. All eyes went to Thea, but she kept her gaze ahead. The marble floor continued beneath her muddy boots leading to the apex of the chamber, where three gilded thrones sat on a wide, carpeted dais, a ruler seated in each.

Thea had never felt so exposed in all her life. But if this was the path she had to walk, then she would walk it with her head held high. Reaching the foot of the dais, she stopped before the royals and bowed low.

The hair on the back of her neck stood up as something

strange reached out to her, wrapping around her senses, toying with the warring feelings in her chest.

Magic, she realised. She was in the presence of magic, and not the forged power of a Warsword, but magic born of the rulers of the midrealms – *royal magic*.

Here it was, almost visible as a spectrum of colours before her.

'Rise,' said a warm, rich voice.

Thea straightened, her eyes locking with those of King Artos Fairmoore, the ruler of Harenth. Though she had never seen the king in the flesh before, she knew it was him from the tales of his bright green eyes and handsome face. To his right was a man with a rearing stallion embroidered on his doublet, marking him as King Leiko Stallard of Tver. On the other side was a beautiful woman who could only have been Queen Reyna Dufort of Aveum, a crown of frosted jewels atop her head. An attractive man with a matching crown stood behind her, resting his hand on her shoulder; King Elkan, then.

Thea couldn't help but stare at the power gathered before her.

From her basic lessons, Thea knew that the Fairmoore family, King Artos' line, was known for mind magic. Over the generations, they had produced mind whisperers, dream wielders and empaths; King Artos was the latter. The Stallard royals had been fire wielders for centuries, though it was rumoured that King Leiko possessed but a drop of his ancestors' power, while the Dufort royals of Aveum were known for their seers of varying strengths —

'Tell us, child of Thezmarr,' King Artos said, bringing Thea out of her reverie with a start. 'What brings you to our halls today?'

A wave of whispers washed over the crowd at Thea's back.

A lump had formed in her throat and she struggled to swallow it, perhaps her thundering heart had lodged itself there. Thea bowed again, buying herself another moment. 'Your Majesties,' she said at last, her words croaky. 'I seek a concession to the no-women-in-arms law.'

This time, the noise that burst from the crowd was not hushed behind fans and silk gloves. It was outright shock, not to be contained with low voices and subtle glances.

King Artos raised a finger on the arm of his throne and the nobles fell silent at once.

Thea met his green-eyed gaze. 'I have a message from the Guild Master outlining the matter at hand, Your Grace.'

The King of Harenth nodded to a servant, who came forward and took the parchment from Thea, passing it to the king with a low bow.

Thea clasped her hands in front of her to hide the trembling and she watched as the king scanned Osiris' message, his brow furrowed, before handing it to Queen Reyna.

'Your Majesties, all my life I have wanted one thing: to wield a blade in the defence of the midrealms and its people,' Thea began. 'I was born to fight, to be trained by the best in our mighty guild, to join the warriors of Thezmarr and keep the looming darkness at bay. I come here today to ask you for that chance, for the opportunity to protect your kingdoms.'

Queen Reyna peered over the parchment. 'You wish to train as a shieldbearer? To take the initiation test in the next season and become a Guardian of the midrealms, is that correct?'

Magic crackled through the throne room, but there was no telling to whom it belonged or what form it might take. The rest of the court seemed unfazed, but then again, they must be used to its casual display.

Thea bowed her head. 'That is correct, Your Majesty. It would be a great honour to be a protector of the realm.'

The rulers of the three kingdoms exchanged looks and unspoken words. Her fate was in their hands. It was their ruling that would determine how she would spend the final years of her life... As a poor excuse for an alchemist, or as a warrior of Thezmarr.

King Artos cleared his throat, looking down at her with kindness. 'I do not doubt your courage —'

Thea's heart was already sinking, her knees buckled.

'Or your honourable intentions,' he continued. 'However, the past has shown us the way forward. Twenty years ago, a dark day in history altered the course of all our paths. It was proven then that for a woman to hold a blade was to risk peace in our realms. The prophecy spoke, the law was changed. And thus it must remain so.'

Thea bit back a broken sob.

The king rested a hand on his heart. 'I wish I could allow it, child. But to change the law now would be to endanger the midrealms. It has taken a long time to reforge our strength and power to hold the darkness at bay. Therefore the answer, I'm afraid, is no.'

Thea opened her mouth, but closed it at the widening eyes of the servants.

She was no longer in Thezmarr. There would be no arguing here.

Her fate, it seemed, was sealed.

CHAPTER TEN

King Artos was all sympathy and kindness, and Thea could hardly stand it. His apologies sounded sincere and the magic that surrounded her was warm and comforting, but apologies were not what she'd dreamt of all these years. Her vision blurred as her future crashed around her.

'I do hope you stay for the feast after your long journey,' the king was saying. 'You are welcome at my table. Do not think your current role in Thezmarr is not one of honour as well.'

'Thank you,' she croaked out and with a final hurried bow, she rushed from the throne room.

For a moment, it was as though time had stopped and the king's words spun over and over in Thea's mind.

For a woman to hold a blade in that place, was to risk peace in our realms. The prophecy spoke, the law was changed. And thus it must remain so.'

Thea's hands shook as she blinked back tears.

'And thus it must remain so.'

All she wanted was to be one of them, to give what little of her life remained some purpose. To become... something *more*. She wasn't usually one to cry, but this... This hurt in a way she hadn't dared to imagine.

'Well?' Hawthorne leaned against the shining tiled wall outside the doors, his arms folded over his chest.

She didn't allow her tears to fall. 'Well, what?'

'What did they say?' the Warsword pressed.

'They said no,' she told him coldly. 'Just as you hoped.' She made to push past him. Gods, the last thing she wanted was to be in his presence right now, to deal with his smugness, his satisfaction at her failure.

'I see.'

'*See?* You see nothing.' All her rage surged forth, vibrating through her like a furious current, a worthy outlet in her sights. It was all Thea could do not to snatch her dagger from his belt and put it to his throat. 'How could you possibly see? As if you'd know what this is like, what this means.' Her dreams had been within her grasp after years of secrecy and dreaming, only to be wrenched away by some stupid prophecy and law.

'Did they say anything else?'

Of course he wouldn't acknowledge her fury, the injustice of it all. 'No.'

'Nothing?'

Thea bit back an array of profanities. 'Only that I should stay for the feast. That I was welcome at King Artos' table.'

Hawthorne blinked. 'So we must find accommodations for the night.'

'What? I'm not going. The last thing I want to do is sit and dine with a bunch of people who —'

'If the king invites you to sit at his table, you sit at his table.' Hawthorne's gaze locked on hers, no compromise there.

Infuriated anew, Thea realised he was right. It would be an insult to not attend at the king's invitation, but she looked down at her filthy appearance. 'I can't go like this. It's one thing to address the king in muddied clothes, but to sit and dine with nobles when you smell like a sweaty horse...?'

'You may have a point.'

Thea threw her hands up. 'Well, what can I do? Do you know somewhere I can —' she gestured down her front dramatically, words no longer powerful enough to express her anguish.

Hawthorne gave a frustrated sigh. 'There's a place a few streets away. You can fix yourself up there.'

In the damp washroom of a boarding house, Thea scrubbed angrily at her skin with a rough cloth. Judging from the way the matron had batted her eyelashes at Hawthorne and used any excuse to touch his muscular arms, Thea wasn't sure she wanted to know how he'd discovered this place.

She stood naked and shivering as she sloshed the cold water over her body and washed her hair, praying that her efforts would make her even a modicum more respectable than before.

A fist pounded the door and she jumped.

'You done in there?' came Hawthorne's deep voice.

'No!' she half-shouted, leaping to grab the threadbare towel the matron had given her to cover herself.

Acutely aware of her bare skin, Thea rushed to pull on her undergarments and trousers, only to grimace at the state of her shirt. It was grubby, to say the least... with a giant stain down the left side - *when did that happen?* Her spare was worse.

The door creaked open and Thea's hands flew to cover her breasts, her heart seizing.

A tattooed hand slid between the crack, holding out a fresh, white linen shirt. 'Here,' said the muffled, gruff voice of the Warsword.

Trembling, from the cold or from anticipation, Thea took it, her icy fingers brushing the warmth of Hawthorne's hand. The shock of contact sent a bolt of lightning through her and a rush of goosebumps across her bare skin. She shoved the sensation aside.

Pity, that's what this was from him. After all his insults and bickering, the Warsword *pitied* her.

But who was she to complain? A nobody.

'Thank you,' she said quietly, and the door closed once more.

The shirt was crisp and clean and it felt amazing after days of wearing damp and dirty garments. Thea slipped her arms into the sleeves and buttoned it.

It was enormous.

His shirt, she realised. He'd given her his last clean shirt...

She did her best to tuck the billowing material into her belt before working her hair into a quick side braid, the end still dripping. She shoved her soiled clothes into her satchel and threw the door open.

Hawthorne stood there with his arms folded over his sculpted chest and surveyed her, his gaze lingering on the wet trail of her hair and the seemingly endless yards of fabric.

'Hmm,' he grunted.

'You're not even using words now? Do I not look alright?'

To her surprise, Hawthorne laughed, the sound rich and deep. 'Here.' He reached for her sleeves.

Against her better judgement, Thea leaned in.

She stared as the Warsword bent down and gently rolled the material to each of her elbows, his fingers brushing her skin ever so lightly, sending a delicious rush of warmth through her.

He caught his lower lip between his teeth in concentration while he secured the fabric in place with a tight tuck, before stepping back to scan her up and down once more, his eyes at last meeting hers. 'That's better.'

Thea exhaled. 'Thank you.'

The Warsword shrugged. 'You represent Thezmarr, we can't have you looking...'

The tingling sensation that had started to build within Thea dissipated. 'Like shit?' she supplied.

'Not what I was going to say.'

Thea forced her voice into a casual tone. 'Doesn't matter. Thanks for the shirt.'

Hawthorne hesitated for a second, but then he turned towards the exit. 'You need to get back to the palace.'

Upon her return to the Heart of Harenth, Thea and Hawthorne were shown to where the feast had begun. The Great Hall was resplendent in draped silks, hundreds of candles, ribbons and flowers, while two hundred or more nobles sat at long tables covered in elegant linens. The ache in Thea's chest would not relent, nor did the shame burning her cheeks as she moved further into the hall. She would return to Thezmarr as she'd left it: an alchemist and nothing more. What would become of her then? Her spying and secret training days were over, and she wasn't fool enough to think that they would be sufficient for her now anyway. Not after the time spent in a Warsword's company, however prickly it had been. Was she destined to mix potions and grind herbs until her fate caught up with her at the ripe old age of twenty-seven?

Hawthorne broke away from her, taking up a post by the far wall, watching the festivities like a hawk. Her Warsword escort; everything she'd now never be. The man who had been against her from the start of this cursed venture. But... He'd held her in his sleep... He'd given her *his* shirt... The man might be an arrogant bastard, but... there was an element of humanity in there... wasn't there?

Tucking her fate stone down the front of the billowing shirt, Thea started towards the king's table. King Artos sat beside King Leiko of Tver, with the Queen of Aveum opposite him. Their magic once more roiled towards her and she wished she could understand it, wished she could see it take their individual forms, untangled and free.

But that was not the most pressing matter at hand. Gods, she hated being so unsure of the correct etiquette and the warring emotions within. Did she truly have to acknowledge the man who, in a handful of sentences, had brought her dream crashing down around her, all the while forcing her to attend a party she had no interest in? Did she thank him for the invitation? Should she approach him at all? In Thezmarr she knew where she stood and what was expected of her, and what rules she wanted to break, but here... This was a new world.

However, she needn't have worried, King Artos spotted her and motioned for her to approach. Gratitude surged, there was a thoughtfulness to the monarch that she hadn't anticipated.

'Ah, Althea…' he greeted her with a broad smile. 'I'm pleased you accepted my invitation,' he said, smiling.

'Of course, Sire,' Thea bowed. 'You honour me.'

'Not at all, not at all,' he replied. 'My daughter, Princess Jasira, is eager to meet you. Your boldness impressed her today.' He motioned for a servant to make room a few seats down on the opposite side.

Thea couldn't find the words, so she said none as she tried not to glance in the Warsword's direction.

'The Guild Master's letter mentioned you were an alchemist of sorts. I thought you might like to share some of your tales with my daughter. She has always been fascinated by all manner of teachings.'

Thea's cheeks flushed. 'It would be a pleasure to speak with her, Your Majesty.'

And that was how Thea found herself seated next to the Crown Princess of Harenth. The young woman was Wren's age or a little younger, and her gaze was bright as it landed on Thea.

Thea bowed her head. 'Your Highness.'

The princess gave a wry smile. 'I'm sure this isn't where you had hoped to end up this evening.'

Thea blanched. 'It's a great priv —'

'Don't worry yourself.' Princess Jasira sipped from her goblet. 'If I had any choice in the matter, I'd be elsewhere as well.'

A servant placed a plate before Thea, the food upon it piled high. Thea murmured her thanks but the server was already gone.

'I would ask you of your work for the guild, but judging from your earlier request, I'd guess it interests you little?' Princess Jasira asked.

'I'd happily speak of it with you, Your Highness.'

'Not if you're going to harp on with formalities all evening. Please, call me Jasi, the titles are tedious.'

Thea chewed the inside of her cheek, unable to quite believe she was addressing the Princess of Harenth. 'Alright... Jasi.'

The princess seemed pleased. 'So tell me of your work for the guild. What is it you do there?'

'I work in the alchemy workshop mostly, Your — Jasi.' Thea corrected herself. 'Though I also transcribe texts from time to time, too.'

'And you dislike such work?'

'My sister is the true master of alchemy,' Thea admitted, glancing down at the burns on her hands. 'I specialised in the same at her insistence, though I suspect she only did so to keep a closer eye on me.'

'Those scars are from your work?' Princess Jasira asked, following Thea's gaze.

'Some are from work. Most are from my own carelessness.'

To Thea's surprise, the princess laughed. It was a beautiful, light sound. 'So your sister does not wish to be a shieldbearer as you do?'

Thea shook her head, sifting through the options of what she could possibly ask a princess without impropriety.

Princess Jasira saved her the effort. 'What is it you alchemists do then?'

'We make tinctures for the healers and potions for various uses; the more skilled carry out experiments and such.'

'Fascinating,' Jasira said.

'You sound like my sister,' Thea laughed.

Jasira offered a genuine smile. 'I shall take that as a compliment then.'

'You should, Highness — Jasi.' Thea's attention wandered back to the kings and queen, finding herself leaning into the magic that pulsed around them. 'It's incredible,' she murmured, more to herself than to the princess.

But Princess Jasira heard her, her brows furrowed. 'What is?'

'Their magic,' Thea replied in wonder.

Jasira gave her an odd look then.

'My apologies, Highness,' Thea bowed her head. 'I'm unsure of the... etiquette when it comes to such things. Is it best not spoken of?'

The princess seemed to have masked her expression. 'It's quite alright. I... I suppose I'm used to it, I hardly notice it.'

'Then, do you have magic yet? It's something you are born with as a Fairmoore royal isn't it?'

'It is...' Jasira said carefully. 'Though I admit, my abilities are not at full strength yet. Father says they will come through.'

'I'm sure he's right,' Thea replied. If anyone were to know about magic, it would be King Artos.

The crease between the princess' brows deepened as she looked from Thea to the rulers of the midrealms. 'So, you're telling me you can feel —'

'A toast!' someone shouted. 'To the late Queen Maelyn, may she rest well with Enovius!'

The princess stiffened in her seat and Thea felt a pang of sympathy for her. She knew the feast was in celebration of the king's mourning period ending, and she couldn't recall how long ago the Queen of Harenth had passed, but queen or no, she had been Princess Jasira's mother. She doubted very much that the pain ceased because a feast dictated so.

'To the late queen!' the hall echoed.

The princess flinched.

Without thinking, Thea leaned closer to her, forgetting royal etiquette. 'I'm sorry about your mother,' she whispered.

Princess Jasira's gaze was on the king, who was sniffing his wine. 'Thank you,' she replied.

Wine sloshed over King Artos' goblet as he swirled the drink within, inhaling the aroma appreciatively. 'I do say, this vintage has a hint of lilac to it... Wouldn't you agree, King Elkan?'

Thea watched the exchange, her own nose tickling with another scent lingering in the air... Was it ash she could smell? It was not the ash of a hearth fire, but something far subtler, with a tinge of sweetness to it...

King Elkan seemed surprised to be called upon, but dutifully sniffed his own goblet. 'I must have an underdeveloped nose for these things, Artos. It smells like wine to me.'

King Artos laughed. 'Yes, yes, of course. But there are subtleties to each barrel.' he sniffed again. 'Yes, I do detect lilac...'

Thea's skin prickled and she sat up a little straighter in her seat, searching for her Warsword escort. He was where she had left him, on the outskirts of the hall, watching everything with that discerning scowl of his.

Someone called out from further down the table, snatching her attention back. 'Marise the merchant says that often a wine can take on the smells of whatever is planted around it. Your Majesty must have a very keen nose indeed.'

Something wasn't right. Thea knew lilacs weren't native

to Harenth. Of course, the wine could have come from anywhere but... The added hint of strange ash in the air made her uneasy. She scanned the table, for what she didn't know.

Until she saw it.

Traces of a fine blue powder by the king's personal decanter.

King Artos at last raised his goblet to his lips —

'Stop!' Without thinking, Thea launched her knife.

It speared towards the king.

Shouts rang out down the table and then the wider hall.

Thea's knife hit King Artos' goblet and it fell, crashing to the floor, crimson wine spilling across the marble like blood.

Guards were on her in an instant, hauling her from her seat, roughly wrenching her arms behind her back.

'It was poison!' she shouted, kicking against the guards. 'It would have killed him.'

The king was on his feet, his face flushed as he looked from his wine soaked silk sleeve to Thea, shocked.

'Your Majesty, please,' she implored. 'It was poison.'

The guards started to haul her away, their grips bruising.

Thea's heart hammered. Was she to be executed then and there? No, that was impossible, given the stone that rested against her heaving breast.

Audra's words echoed in her mind then. *'You will come to learn that most things to be feared exist in life, not in death...'*

Bile rose in Thea's throat. She wouldn't die. Not until she was twenty-seven, but... There were worse fates than death. *Years of torture. Imprisonment...* She'd hurled a knife at the king for gods' sake. They'd think she was an *assassin*. But there hadn't been *time* – she'd used whatever she had to save him.

The guards were brutal, yanking her arms back so hard they nearly tore from their sockets —

'Wait,' the king commanded.

The guards froze in place, but did not loosen their hold on her.

The king motioned to a wiry man who had been lingering near the curtains behind him.

'Did you try the wine?' the king asked, his voice deadly soft.

The king's cupbearer, Thea realised with a start. She hadn't even considered that there would be someone to test the king's food and drink. She'd made a mistake.

'Yes, of course, Your Majesty.'

'When?' the king asked.

'When the wine was served, Your Grace.'

Thea's heart sank. The fate that awaited her now was not one that had been carved in stone, but one borne of her rash actions, her recklessness.

'Try it again.' The king's voice was hard.

'Sire?' The cupbearer blinked, wide-eyed at the monarch.

'Try it again.'

Thea tensed, watching the cupbearer's trembling hands reach for the decanter.

'Use my goblet,' King Artos instructed.

Face paling, the cupbearer bent down to retrieve it from the floor. With all eyes upon him, he poured the rich, garnet liquid into the goblet, his lips moving in prayer as he did. He looked to the king a final time.

King Artos merely waited.

The cupbearer took a deep breath and closed his eyes, raising the goblet to his lips. He drank deeply, as was required.

The entire hall was transfixed, Thea almost forgotten amidst the theatrics, though her arms throbbed from where the guards gripped her.

The cupbearer lowered the goblet, his shoulders sagging with relief.

A silent cry caught in Thea's throat, her heart seizing as she realised that she'd made a harrowing mistake, she'd condemned herself —

The cupbearer spluttered, his brow furrowing in confusion as he clapped a hand over his mouth, embarrassed.

Thea didn't dare move.

'I apologise, my king —' He coughed again, a ragged rasping sound before he swayed on his feet, his eyes red-rimmed.

The cupbearer staggered, clenching the table linens in his fists as he choked, spittle foaming at the swollen corners of his mouth.

He vomited blood, collapsing face-first onto the king's table.

More guards rushed forward, surrounding the king, while others hauled the cupbearer back to examine him, recoiling at what they found.

His parted lips were blue.

And he was dead.

CHAPTER ELEVEN

S ilence settled over the hall like dust motes.

'Bar the doors,' someone shouted. 'The assassin may still be in our midst!'

Several guards and attendants spurred into action, with the royal guards of each kingdom surrounding their monarchs protectively.

But Thea remained rooted to the spot, her eyes falling to King Artos, whose mouth was slack as he gazed upon his dead cupbearer.

After what felt like a lifetime, he looked to his men restraining her. 'Release her,' he ordered, his voice raw.

As soon as their hold loosened, Thea jerked out of their grip, rubbing her bruised arms with a wince.

'How did you know?' King Artos asked.

'You said the wine smelt of lilac, Your Grace. And then I smelt something similar to ash... The combination of aromas put me on edge, for there is a particular mixture that can have adverse effects. Then I saw the blue powder near your decanter... I have seen it before, Sire.'

'What is it?'

'Crushed Naarvian Nightshade, Majesty. With the added deadly blend of lilac and Widow's Ash.'

'And how do you know of such a poison?'

Thea swallowed the lump in her throat. 'Alchemy is a vast and varied arena, Sire.' Thea left out the fact that it was poisons that had always interested her the most when it came to the bubbling potions and strange herbs of the workshop.

The king nodded, clearly still unnerved.

The hall was tense, guards blocking every entrance and stationed all along the tables, while Hawthorne watched on from his position on the far wall, his expression unreadable.

Thea's mind whirred and she dared to take a step – two steps, towards King Artos, scanning the mess the cupbearer had caused when he fell.

A guard made to stop her, but the king raised his hand and Thea understood the opportunity she was being given.

Now, she stalked freely down the length of the table, studying not the array of food and drink, but the guests themselves. Some stared back at her, oblivious of her intentions, others looked defiant, offended, and some twitched in their seats, not guilty of poisoning, but other misdeeds at the forefront of their minds.

Thea slowed towards the end of the table, revelling in the power she felt. 'One thing I learned about Naarvian Nightshade, Your Majesty,' she said. 'Is that it stains...'

'Oh?'

She stopped before an immaculately dressed man, his hair slicked back with oil, his tunic embellished with gold thread. And at the tips of his fingers, were the faintest hints of blue.

'Him,' she stated.

Several people gasped aloud.

The noble in question paled but forced a laugh. 'These are but ink stains, girl.'

'I find it unusual that a man of your status, status high enough to be seated on the king's own table, would carry out his own correspondence. A man of your position would have a scribe, surely?'

Quiet followed.

'And surely were they ink stains, you'd have scrubbed your hands before dining with the king?' Thea pressed.

The man leapt out of his seat, his chair falling back with a crash. He surged from the table, ducking through the guards' attempts to grab him, darting for an exit Thea couldn't see.

She threw herself after him, determined not to let a royal assassin escape in her presence.

Something whistled through the air – a spear, which hurtled towards the culprit, lancing through his cloak and pinning him to the step of the dais.

The guards leapt upon him, all the while, the spear still wobbled with the force with which it had been thrown. Thea sought its point of origin, suspicion already curdling in her gut. Wilder Hawthorne leaned against a pillar as though he had barely lifted a finger. The awed expressions of the nobles around him and the precision of the throw confirmed Thea's hunch.

Hawthorne had apprehended the king's poisoner.

It took five men to dislodge the spear.

The noble protested, shouting curses in Thea's direction and straining against the guards' grasp. But when his eyes landed on the king at last, he fell silent.

Thea pointed to his hands. 'See the blue stains there,

Sire? Beneath his fingernails? Those are from the Naarvian Nightshade. It was this man who tried to take your life, who claimed the life of your cupbearer.'

The king looked from the colour marking the man's skin, to his wide-eyed expression. 'Well, Aemund... You have a choice.'

'Your Majesty, please —'

'You can choose death,' King Artos continued. 'Or, you can choose the Scarlet Tower.'

Thea's stomach roiled. She had heard only rumours of the Scarlet Tower, the prison close to the Veil, south of what used to be the kingdom of Naarva. Those rumours had been enough to make her blood run cold. The worst of humanity was sent there; those who had committed unforgivable crimes, those who deserved worse than execution, and those who had conspired against the rightful rulers. All forced onto a pitiful boat that sailed past the Broken Isles, past Naarva, to a tiny spit of land home to the worst place in all the midrealms.

'Your Majesty, no, I —'

The king stared him down. 'Death or the Scarlet Tower. Choose.'

Thea had seen a drawing of it once; a single column of stone on an uninhabitable island.

'Death,' the man called Aemund choked out. 'I choose death.'

King Artos studied him for a moment, his gaze lingering on the patches of blue at the man's fingertips. Then, he turned to his guards. 'Take him to the dungeons. Interrogate him. We need to know who he is working with. Then, he goes to the Scarlet Tower.'

'No!' shrieked the man. 'Your Majesty, I beg you —'

'The time for begging has long passed, Aemund.' And with that final dismissal, the guards dragged him away.

It was then that King Artos' eyes fell to Thea once more. 'I owe you a great debt,' he said.

Thea's hands tingled at her sides and a jolt shot through her veins. 'It was an honour to serve, Majesty.'

But the king shook his head, dissatisfied. 'Usually I would bestow lands and knighthood for such a deed...' he told her, his voice increasing in volume as he walked around the table to face her. 'But I know to such a woman that riches would mean little.'

'I need no repayment, Sire,' Thea insisted, bowing. 'I am only sorry for the alarm my actions caused.'

King Artos considered her, glancing at the other rulers and back to her. 'I wish to re-address your earlier request, Althea Zoltaire.'

Thea froze. *What?*

'It appears I was too hasty in my decision.' He turned to the other kings and queen. 'Althea wished to be admitted to Thezmarr as a shieldbearer,' he said. 'With your blessings, I now hope to grant that request.'

For the first time since Thea had thrown the dagger, chatter broke out around the hall. Hundreds of hushed voices filled the room, vibrating across Thea's skin, their stares boring into her back. But Thea didn't move, didn't dare to hope.

'It is not your decision alone,' King Leiko stated, standing, resting his hand on the hilt of his sword.

'You are quite right,' King Artos allowed. 'Which is why I turn to you, my fellow rulers. This young woman has the support of the Guild Master and now me, the King of Harenth in her petition to join the Thezmarrian ranks. What say you?'

King Leiko cleared his throat. 'What of all you said before? About the stability of Thezmarr and all it stands for?'

'Our law from two decades ago forbade women to wield blades, but were it not for a woman wielding a blade today, my life would be forfeit,' King Artos projected his voice to the far reaches of the hall. 'Were it not for this woman, the kingdom of Harenth would be kingless, my conspirators on the rise to power and this great territory might have descended into chaos and war. It's my belief that we have found an exception to the laws forged in the past. The courage and skill Althea demonstrated just now in saving my life surely proves that?'

'I do not deny the girl's bravery —'

The girl. The girl. The words bounced around in Thea's mind like a persistent headache, but she remained quiet.

'However,' King Leiko continued. 'You cannot vouch for her alone. It would mean you have a vested interest in Thezmarr, and Thezmarr was and always will be, an independent territory from the kingdoms of the midrealms.'

Thea watched on, as yet again she was talked about and not *to*. As yet again, men decided her future. As she fiddled with her sleeve, she remembered the Warsword whose shirt she wore... He was where he had been the whole time, stationed by the exit at the far end of the room, his hand on the hilt of *her* dagger, watching on without a hint of emotion on his harsh face.

'You do not think it reasonable for me to reward the woman who saved my life?' Artos argued.

'Not if it interferes with Thezmarr,' King Leiko bit back.

It was Queen Reyna of Aveum who spoke next, gracefully rising from her chair and turning to address both rulers. 'I vote with King Artos. The young woman has proven her worth. She would make a fine addition to the guild's recruits.'

Thea's chest was about to burst. She hardly dared to look from one ruler to the next, so sure that she had misheard the words she had spoken, that this was all some elaborate figment of her desperate imagination.

'As do I,' Queen Reyna's husband, the quiet King Elkan voiced from her side.

King Leiko of Tver's gaze fell to her. The pause seemed to last forever before he spoke again. 'So be it.'

King Artos beamed as he turned to Thea. 'Congratulations, Althea Zoltaire,' he said. 'You've just become the newest shieldbearer of Thezmarr.'

Thea's legs buckled so badly she had to steady herself on the back of a chair.

'You have all the rights a shieldbearer has. You may train, bear arms and partake in the initiation test to become a Guardian of the midrealms upon the next season.'

Slowly, he began to clap and soon, the entire great hall was on its feet, applauding her. At the king's signal, fresh wine was brought in, as were new cupbearers for the royals. Upon confirmation that the liquor was indeed safe to drink, King Artos raised his goblet to Thea, who found a cup pressed into her own hand.

'To Althea Zoltaire,' the king toasted.

Althea could not contain the grin that split across her face. Never in her twenty-four years had she ever imagined hearing her name being echoed back to her in salute through royal halls. Warmth radiated through her body, along with the hum of her racing heart. She wished Wren and the others were here to see this.

Althea Nine Lives, she laughed silently, raising her own goblet to her lips.

No sooner had the delicious wine hit her tongue, a heavy hand grasped her shoulder, gentle but firm, its heat penetrating the thin fabric of her shirt.

'Well, *shieldbearer*,' that familiar deep voice rumbled in the shell of her ear. 'We need to get back to the fortress.'

'Now?' Thea turned to face the Warsword. 'I thought you said we were staying in Hailford for the night?'

'That was before.'

'Before I became a shieldbearer of Thezmarr?' Thea grinned.

A muscle twitched in Hawthorne's jaw.

'Wilder,' King Artos greeted the Warsword. 'Please, join us!'

But to Thea's disbelief, Hawthorne was already shaking his head. 'My thanks, Sire. But duty calls us back to Thezmarr.'

If the king was surprised, he did not show it. Instead, he raised his goblet again, this time to Hawthorne. 'We are honoured to host you, even so briefly, Warsword. And I thank you for your role in my assassin's capture.'

Hawthorne bowed and made for the doors.

'Thank you, Your Majesties,' Thea blurted, bowing low before chasing after the warrior.

When they were out in the foyer, Thea turned to Hawthorne. 'I thought you said "if the king invites you to sit at his table, you sit at his table"?'

Hawthorne kept walking. 'That's true enough, *for you*. I, however, answer to no king.'

The sheer arrogance in that statement heated Thea's blood in more ways than one. But she unclenched her fists at her sides, vowing that one day, she would be able to say the same.

And just for a second, she pictured herself wielding her own twin blades of Naarvian steel.

The royal stables were immaculate and ten times the size of Thezmarr's. The building was alive with stableboys tending to the horses and servants polishing tack. It smelt of sweet hay, manure and leather.

'You have ten minutes,' Hawthorne told her. 'Be ready.'

'We're to ride through the night?'

'Does the dark scare you, Alchemist?'

Thea's eyes narrowed. 'I'm a *shieldbearer* now. And no. Nothing scares me.'

'Then you're even more of a fool than I thought.'

'I'm no fool.'

'No?' Hawthorne rounded on her. 'I have never seen such *reckless* behaviour in all my life. Do you have any semblance of a brain in that thick skull of yours?'

'I —'

'That was a rhetorical question,' he snapped, his mask of stone slipping. 'You threw *a knife* at the King of Harenth. What would you have done if you'd been mistaken about the poison?'

'But I wasn't.'

'You didn't know that. I saw your face.'

'I *saved the king's life* tonight!'

'You risked your own on a whim.'

'I saved a ruler of the midrealms. Isn't that *your* job?' she yelled. 'I protected one of the last remaining magic wielders to exist. Didn't you feel how strong he is? Imagine if it was gone? Another royal wiped from this realm, their magic with him?'

Hawthorne baulked. 'You felt it?'

Fury blinded Thea. 'Of course I felt it. I know I'm just an alchemist to you, but I'm not a moron. Their magic came alive in that throne room! And as for my own life, why do you care?'

Hawthorne hesitated a moment before he started on her again. 'By the gods, I *don't*,' his deep voice grew louder, the flickering torchlight making his eyes molten silver. 'There is nothing I want more than to be *rid of you*. You're a danger to yourself *and to others*.'

That familiar current of anger surged in Thea's veins. 'So *why* are you here?'

'Orders,' he ground out. 'You know that. You were placed under my protection. I didn't ask for it. I certainly didn't *want* this, but I am responsible for you. I hope to never be so again.'

'On that, we agree,' Thea retorted.

'At last, some common ground.' Fury laced every word, and the Warsword shook his head as he walked into the stables.

But Thea wasn't done. She charged after him. 'I presume you heard King Artos give me express permission to train *and* to bear arms. I want my dagger back.'

'Gods, you must have a death wish,' Hawthorne muttered in disbelief.

'It's mine,' Thea argued. 'I want it back.'

'I want a hot bath and a naked beauty to feed me grapes,' he snapped. 'Alas, we don't always get what we want.'

Thea didn't think, she swung her fist.

Only to have it swallowed by his hand. In a blur of movement, faster than she could process, the Warsword spun her around, trapping both her hands behind her and shoving her to the wall. The stone was cold against her face, against her heaving breasts beneath the thin shirt.

Hawthorne didn't release her. The pressure behind her increased as he pushed her harder into the wall, his chest now flush with her back, his voice hot in her ear.

'You're going to have to try a lot harder than that to hit me,' he growled.

Thea couldn't budge an inch, couldn't so much as squirm. His strength was *that* formidable. He had moved her like she weighed little more than a feather, and held her in place as though he could do so with a single finger.

Resentment rolled off her in waves as at last he let her go and disappeared to tend to his stallion.

After years of training in secret, of spying on ungrateful recruits, of harbouring a weapon against the rules and dreaming of the moment when she could wield it, she finally had what she had always wanted. And now the moody bastard was robbing her of her victory.

'Five minutes,' he called out sharply from one of the stalls.

Grinding her teeth, Thea found her mare and saddled her in a hurry. She had no doubt that if she wasn't ready in time, the surly warrior would gladly leave her behind, despite any supposed notion of responsibility.

The moon was high in the inky night when they departed the royal stables. Thea could still hear the festivities carrying on within the castle, but an icy shiver washed over her as they passed through the gates. Tonight, her actions had seen an innocent cupbearer die, and another man condemned to the Scarlet Tower. And she'd thought nothing of it until the rhythmic steps of her horse had lulled her into a state of reflection. Right now, she could be riding over the dungeons where that same man was in chains, awaiting a fate worse than death.

The cupbearer would have died anyway if he'd done his job in the first place, she told herself. *As for the other... Well, he'd committed treason of the highest order. He deserved what he got.* And yet still the sour taste lingered in her mouth.

Despite the angry words they'd exchanged, Thea twisted in her saddle and addressed the Warsword. 'What do you know of the Scarlet Tower?'

Hawthorne kept his eyes straight ahead. 'Enough.'

'Which is?'

'Enough to know that I, too, would have chosen death.' He silenced her with a fierce look and Thea tensed. Long gone was the glimpse of the man who'd given her his own shirt. The warrior who rode beside her was harsh, unforgiving and brutal in his manner. Once again she wondered what he had seen, and what he had done, in his years of service.

It surprised her to hear him speak again so soon.

'The first lesson of being a warrior of Thezmarr,' he told her, 'is this: *know that your actions have consequences.* Some more than others. And you will carry those with you for the rest of your life. Do you understand me?'

The arrow stinging her cheek flashed in Thea's mind. As did the sight of Hawthorne twirling her dagger between his fingers in the Bloodwoods. Then, it was Audra arguing her case to the Guild Master and her sister's initial fear upon discovering her intentions to petition the king. Then, a pair of trembling hands and the blue-lipped cupbearer, and finally, the treasonous noble... She found herself wrenched into the present, where she now rode alongside a Warsword, on her way to live and train as a shieldbearer. Her actions had set in motion every single one of those events.

'I understand,' she replied softly, hardly daring to wonder where they would take her next.

They rode in silence as they navigated the steep, cobblestoned descent from the palace and into the city proper. By night, the streets of Hailford were brimming with debauchery and Thea found herself curious as to what she might find in some of the raucous taverns and silk-draped pleasure houses. But they left the laughter and flickering candlelight behind and soon, the darkness beyond the capital swallowed them whole.

Thea didn't know how long they'd been riding for, only that the moon was still high and the stars that littered the velvet night were infinite. Her stomach gurgled in hunger. She'd scarcely managed two mouthfuls at the feast before the chaos had broken out. And before that...? She had no idea. Her vision swam for a moment and she righted herself in the saddle, her movements sluggish, muscles weak.

It had been a long few days – emotional, too – so it was no wonder she was a little out of sorts, she told herself. Despite the pangs of hunger in her gut, she decided none of it mattered. However it had come to pass, she'd achieved her goal at Harenth. She was returning to Thezmarr not as a poor excuse for an alchemist, but as a shieldbearer of the guild.

Althea Nine Lives was one step closer to becoming a legend.

It was this she thought of as her head dropped to her chest and she slipped from her saddle.

CHAPTER TWELVE

Thea woke to a hard wall of muscle at her back and a strong, but surprisingly gentle arm around her waist, fingers wrapping above the curve of her hip. Despite the chill of the night, solid heat enveloped her, reassuring and sturdy. Instinctively, she leaned into it, relishing the warmth, the contact and the subtle scent of rosewood soap and leather. The arm around her waist tightened and Thea went rigid.

Head throbbing, her eyes flew open, the stars above blurring together in one vibrant streak. Slowly, her vision sharpened and by the moonlight, she began to make sense of her surroundings and the fact that she now shared a saddle with a Warsword.

Still groggy, Thea raised a weak hand to her temple, but Hawthorne's fingers wrapped around hers and brought her arm back down.

'It's only just stopped bleeding,' he growled. 'Don't touch it.' His words were hot on the nape of her neck. He was so close, too close – his body rocked against hers, and as she shifted, his arm grazed the underside of her breasts, sending a hazy pulse of desire through her. She fought the urge to lean into him and forced herself to take a breath. Clearly she'd hit her head hard. Why else would her legs be involuntarily parting? Why else would her fingers ache with the need to reach out and caress him?

'What happened?' she asked, keeping her voice steady and glancing across at her mare trekking beside them, the lead rope wrapped around the saddle horn in front of her.

Hawthorne pressed a canteen into her weak grip. 'Drink this.'

Dazed, Thea obeyed, the cool water tasting divine on her swollen tongue.

'You passed out.' Hawthorne told her. 'Hit the ground pretty hard by the sound of it.'

The side of her head was throbbing. 'Feels like it too.'

She wasn't sure if she was imagining it, but had his arms tightened around her? She swallowed the lump in her throat, trying to distract herself from the press of his chest against her, the brush of his muscular inner thighs cradling her sides.

Their earlier argument came back to her, a flush creeping across her cheeks. They'd yelled at each other, she'd tried to hit him... and now this?

'I can ride my own horse.' She reached for the reins.

'Recent events say otherwise,' Hawthorne replied, and his deep voice shivered along her bones.

'I'm fine.'

'There's a good spot to camp a little further ahead. You ride with me until then.'

'But —'

'You're in no state to ride if you pass out in the saddle.'

Thea clenched her jaw. Gods, she hated it when he was right. 'I suppose you think this proves your point, that I shouldn't or couldn't be a warrior.'

'I never said that, not once.'

'You said —'

'Several things,' he cut her off. 'All still true, but not that. If anything, your fierce stupidity and need to prove yourself —'

Thea drew herself up, ready to explode.

'Means you'd fit right in with those idiots.'

'Oh.'

Somewhere in the near distance, something rustled in the undergrowth. It was hard to determine the detail of the surrounding landscape, but before she had fallen, they'd been in the middle of nowhere, nothing but plains of grass stretching on before them.

'You heard it too…' Hawthorne said quietly.

'What is it?'

'I don't know yet. But when we set up camp, I'm going to find out.'

By the time Hawthorne brought his stallion to a halt, Thea's head was spinning. It was bad enough that when the Warsword dismounted and reached for her, she didn't object to those large hands encircling her waist and helping her down. Wordlessly, he set her on one of the saddle blankets and handed her more water.

There was no arguing with the Warsword and Thea didn't try to. She couldn't tell if he was more angry at her, or himself. He didn't speak as he went about tending to the horses and building a small fire. He passed her some dried meat to chew on, and she found she felt better as she ate.

Thea suspected the warrior was creating tasks for

himself about the camp to avoid her. Perhaps she'd pushed him over the edge.

'There is nothing I want more than to be rid of you,' he had shouted earlier.

Well, he nearly got his wish, she mused, still chewing on her piece of meat.

Thea must have dozed off not long after, because she woke up to someone shaking her gently by the shoulders.

She started, pain blooming in her head once again. 'What?' Blinking rapidly, she followed the Warsword's gaze into the near distance.

A pair of vibrant yellow eyes stared at them through the grass. A monster?

Hawthorne placed himself between her and the beast, drawing her dagger from his belt. 'You've noticed we've got company,' he murmured, moving like a graceful shadow.

'I have,' Thea managed, squinting into the night.

In a crouch, the warrior was a born predator, readying himself for attack. 'It's been following us since we left the Bloodwoods,' he whispered. 'Strange that it seemed to wait for our return. Stranger still to see a lone wolf in these parts...'

Thea frowned, leaning forward, her hand reaching for Hawthorne's, forcing his weapon down. 'It's not a wolf.'

'What?' he asked, his gaze shooting to where she touched him.

'It's not a wolf,' she repeated, unwilling to let him advance on the creature with the blade. 'It's Dax, the former Warsword Malik's dog.'

Hawthorne stiffened. He seemed to stare harder into the night, and then, he loosed a tight breath. 'You know...' he trailed off.

'Dax? Malik?' Thea asked. 'It's hard to know one without the other.'

'How do you know them?'

When Thea was satisfied the warrior wasn't about to slice into Dax, she sat back against the boulder once more. 'Malik is my friend.'

At his master's name, the lanky mongrel came padding towards them. He sat at Thea's side and she wrinkled her nose.

'You smell terrible,' she told him.

Hawthorne watched them, transfixed. 'Your friend?' he prompted, looking more intense than usual.

Thea lifted her chin defiantly. 'Yes.'

'And how did an alchemist become friends with a Warsword of Thezmarr? How did you meet him?'

Thea's skin prickled at his sudden interest, her fingers coiling in Dax's fur. 'Why?' she demanded. 'Why do you want to know?'

'It's not a common occurrence.' He gave the space between them a pointed look. 'Clearly.'

'True,' Thea had to admit.

'So how did you become friends with Malik?' Hawthorne's voice was different, gentler, as though his interest was genuine, as though he truly cared. Thea didn't understand why he wanted to know, or how this subject of all things seemed to be the catalyst for the subtle change in him, but she much preferred this version of the Warsword to the growling, impatient escort she'd had before.

'Slowly, I suppose,' she answered, the pain in her head fading. 'I saw him when they first brought him back to the infirmary. I found his dagger on the Mourner's Trail and, believe it or not, went to return it.' She glanced at the blade now sheathed at Hawthorne's belt. 'I didn't know who he was. Back then there were more than three Warswords...' She hadn't thought about those days in some time.

'There used to be many of us. But over the years, things have changed. Some relinquished their totems and Naarvian steel for a quieter life, some retired from fighting to honorary positions among the royal courts... And many left the midrealms the only way they knew how.'

'You mean in battle?'

Hawthorne nodded. 'It's something that's instilled in us long before we undertake the Great Rite, that there is glory in death. But I was asking about Malik, Alchemist.'

Thea considered him. She supposed if she wished to question the Warsword, he had the right to answers as well. 'He didn't want the dagger. When I brought it to the infirmary, I mean. Malik didn't want it.'

'He spoke to you?'

'Well, yes... But not about that.'

'What did he say?'

Thea chewed the inside of her cheek as she searched for the words. 'His head was badly wounded. It didn't make any sense.'

'Tell me anyway.'

'He said... "Beware the fury of a patient Delmirian"... Does that mean something?'

Hawthorne's lips parted, his brows furrowing. 'I don't know...' His voice was distant. 'He didn't speak again after that?'

Thea shook her head. 'Not with words, but just as clearly. When I tried to give him his dagger, he pushed it back to me. He wanted me to have it. It was like...'

'Like what?'

'Like he saw me. Not just a scrap of a girl training to be an alchemist, but... me. Or who I wanted to be.' Thea laughed. 'Sounds stupid, doesn't it?'

'No,' Hawthorne said firmly. 'It doesn't.'

Thea smiled then. 'From there, I don't know... I saw him around a lot when he recovered. He was always so alone. I guess I felt alone too. Neither of us could be what we wanted. It wasn't long after that he found me in the library. He... He wasn't alright. His injury still affects him now. Sometimes there's too much for him to process, sometimes he can't remember things. Listening to me read seemed to help, so I've been doing it ever since.'

Hawthorne was silent. Thea could see the muscle working in his jaw, his hands fidgeting.

'You read to him?' he asked eventually.

'Yes. What's wrong with that? He likes it.'

'Nothing is wrong with it.'

Still frowning, Thea went on. 'I wondered if he'd once had a wife or a family. Maybe someone else used to read to him.'

'Warswords take no wives. It's one of the vows we make upon the Great Rite.'

'Oh.'

Hawthorne hesitated a moment before he spoke again. 'He's lucky to have you,' he said quietly.

His words caught Thea off-guard and she glanced across at him in surprise. He was a medley of contradictions, this Warsword. Rigid where he sat, jaw clenched, but those silver eyes... sadness brimmed there.

'How do you know Malik?' she asked, curiosity getting the better of her.

'All Warswords know one another,' he replied.

143

'Does that mean you'll tell me about them all? You could start with who trained you.'

A smile softened the harsh lines of his face for a moment. 'A fair effort, Alchemist.'

A quiet laugh escaped Thea. 'Can't blame a girl for trying.'

'I suppose not.' Hawthorne stretched out and stoked the fire. 'You should get some rest,' he told her.

For once, Thea did as the Warsword said.

WILDER HAWTHORNE

Wilder warmed his hands by the fire as the alchemist slept, his brother's dog standing guard at her side.

He had recognised Malik's dagger at once and there was no way he believed it was a gift, not for a second. Warswords gave their weapons to no one, least of all Malik, but... perhaps that had been *then*.

Wilder met Dax's yellow stare. The mongrel had appeared shortly after Malik's return to Thezmarr and had barely left his side. He had stayed with the injured Warsword as he learned to walk again, as he learned to feed himself. The dog seemed permanently attached to his brother. Which was why Wilder hadn't realised it was him in the outer lands of Harenth. For years the beast hadn't travelled further than the fortress walls, and yet... Here he was, by the alchemist's side, apparently with as much loyalty to her as he showed Malik.

'Who is she?' Wilder asked quietly, for there was no doubt in his mind that if Dax was here, she was *someone*.

A friend, she'd declared.

Wilder pinched the bridge of his nose and sipped from his flask, the fiery liquid warming his throat. Malik's friends had abandoned him over the years, unable to recognise him as the man he'd once been – a legend amongst their kind, one of the best, who'd met a fate worse than death in their eyes. Worst of all had been Talemir Starling, who'd left Malik's side at the lowest time, leaving Wilder to pick up the broken pieces.

Friends, they had once been, but no longer. And yet the alchemist had claimed Malik as hers, fiercely, openly, all the while clenching her fists as though she meant to spring to his defence.

Wilder's hand drifted to the dagger. He had assumed it had been lost in the battle that had nearly claimed his brother's life, trampled into the bloodied moors of Naarva. Unsheathing the weapon, he ran a finger along the flat of the blade where, in the flickering light of the fire, the words engraved in the ancient tongue of the Furies shone.

Glory in death, immortality in legend.

Malik had been known for whispering those words as he slayed his enemies.

A quiet cry sounded from the sky and Wilder looked up to see a familiar hawk circling above them in the moonlight. The creature swooped down and landed gracefully, offering his leg, where a scroll was tied.

'Terrence,' Wilder greeted him and reached for the message, hoping he didn't shred Wilder's fingers bloody. 'It's been a long time…'

Terrence ruffled his feathers and eyed Dax suspiciously.

'He's not stupid enough to think you're dinner.' Wilder raised a brow at the hawk.

Terrence continued to glare.

Wilder made quick work of the tie and turned his attention to the message, recognising the messy scrawl. Over the many years away from Thezmarr hunting monsters throughout the kingdoms, he'd developed a network of sources who sent him reports. The most regular were those from the fallen kingdom of Naarva, where unbeknownst to many, a small group of survivors remained.

'What do you have to say for yourself, Dratos...?' Wilder muttered, scanning the words in the fire's light.

H,

A tear in the Veil south of the Scarlet Tower appeared some days ago. A swarm of shadow wraiths managed to get through. Our brotherhood dealt with two, but three escaped and headed north. Several sea serpents came through the same breach, though we've not seen signs of them since. It's unclear if they are cursed or if they are natural creatures of the deep.

The Veil grows more unstable each day. Our rangers have reported strange sounds echoing from beyond its mist, and tremors wracking the outskirts of our lands.

What news from Thezmarr?

Best,

D.

Wilder sighed heavily. He gave Terrence a scrap of leftover meat before scratching a hasty reply on the back of the parchment, explaining his own recent findings. There was no doubt that things were getting worse, that the darkness encroached day by day, and as much as he hated to admit it,

Audra was right. Thezmarr, and therefore the midrealms, were weak.

He re-tied the scroll to the hawk's leg, marvelling at how the creature managed to find him wherever his Warsword duties took him, though he hoped it would be some time until he saw the temperamental creature again – no news was good news after all.

'For Dratos,' he told the bird.

Terrence made an insulted noise, as though he knew very well who the recipient was.

'Off you go then,' Wilder said with a note of amusement.

The hawk launched himself skyward and disappeared into the night.

Wilder refused to think about who else might be there with Dratos upon the bird's return to Naarva. He'd cut those ties long ago.

Instead, he focused on the alchemist across the campfire. In her sleep, she threw an arm over Dax, who didn't so much as flinch. Another oddity. While Dax had always been friendly with Malik and by extension, Wilder, the dog was not known for his gentle nature around the fortress. Most Thezmarrians avoided him if they could, knowing that he didn't like to be touched. Which made his tolerance and protectiveness of the young woman all the more intriguing.

Wilder glanced at Dax again. 'You and Malik and your secrets,' he muttered.

The glow of the fire illuminated long dark lashes kissing the tops of the alchemist's pink-tipped cheeks. Her lips were slightly parted and her small build rose and fell with each steady breath. Strands of bronze gold hair had come loose from her braid, framing her face. She was beautiful, he realised. Infuriating, yes, but beautiful; the type of beauty that was rare in its fierceness. Wilder found himself smiling, for even in the depths of sleep, her scar-littered hands clenched, as though itching to grip a blade.

Taking another sip from his flask, he leaned across to stoke the flames, and after a moment's pause, pulled a blanket over her.

'I'm beginning to think you are more than you seem, Alchemist,' he murmured.

CHAPTER THIRTEEN

As dawn kissed the sky, Thea woke to find the Warsword waiting for her, bow and quiver in hand. 'Today, I'll teach you how to hunt,' he said.

Thea didn't ask him what had changed his mind, she simply leapt at the opportunity, knowing that another might never come along. She drew no attention to the fact that the lesson would delay their return to Thezmarr, nor did she ask further questions. Thea just listened, and listened gladly, the Warsword's voice low and melodic as he described the finer details of hunting game by the arrow.

Dax remained, his ears forward, as though he were listening to every word as keenly as she was.

The light of day had revealed a small forest to the east, the morning was still early and a cool breeze rustled the thick green leaves of the trees. Once more, Thea was reminded just how different the realms were inland compared to the darkening horizons beyond Thezmarr's cliffs. While the air was crisp on her skin, her nose tipped pink with the cold, it felt like it could have been the beginning of a spring day. Though she knew autumn was upon them, a biting winter at its heels, it was nice to pretend for a moment.

When they reached the edge of the forest, Hawthorne carved a rough circle into the trunk of a tree and turned to her. 'I want you to watch me first,' he said. 'Take note of the movements I described and watch how I implement each action.'

Thea nodded. It was a request she was only too happy to meet. It also helped that when he wasn't shattering her dreams, Wilder Hawthorne was easy on the eyes.

She found herself fixated on him as his tattooed hand crept to his quiver, soundlessly drawing an arrow and nocking it to his longbow. His feet were planted apart and his whole body seemed to expand as he drew the bowstring back with his powerful arms.

He moved slowly, for her benefit, she knew, and still the sheer force of him had her mesmerised. She could feel the forged Warsword magic humming around him.

He released the arrow. It went flying towards the target he'd carved. Although he'd made no mark for the middle, that was exactly where it hit. Dead centre.

The soft thud of the arrow in the tree and the subtle vibrating sound of the drawstring were music to Thea's ears.

The Warsword shot again, and again, in a succession of smooth and practiced motions. The almost gentle drift of his hand to the quiver, the drawing of another arrow, nocking it, aiming and releasing… It was a beautiful dance to Thea.

She and Dax watched as Hawthorne strode to the tree and wrenched the arrows one by one from its flesh. She hadn't realised how deeply they were embedded into the trunk until she saw the force with which he had to remove them. Another arrow flashed in her mind then, the one that had nearly struck her between the eyes, the one he'd fired in supposed warning at her. She said nothing of it though, not wanting to remind the Warsword, not when she was so close to getting her hands on a weapon.

When he reached her, he held the longbow out to her. 'Let's see what you can do, Alchemist.' This time when he smiled, she appreciated the tug of his dimple fully. It made him look younger, less brutal for a moment.

Her fingers curled around the bow. It was bigger and heavier than she anticipated, though she supposed that was to be expected. She'd only seen it from a distance, or in the context of the warrior's hulking frame, whereas she was much slighter. She didn't care.

Thea planted her feet apart, just as Hawthorne had stood. There, she nocked her first arrow to the bow, her chest swelling as she did. She drew the string.

'Hold it higher,' came Hawthorne's voice, closer than she had realised. A hand touched her elbow, lifting it gently. 'There,' he said. His breath was warm against her ear.

'You need to give it more power than that,' he told her. 'Pull back.'

She did, trying to ignore the heat of his body so close to hers and the shock of that initial touch, almost familiar, yet still so new. But as fast as the touch had come, it was gone again and Thea quietly mourned its loss.

What's wrong with me? she chastised herself. *Here I am with a Warsword at my disposal for training and I'm thinking about batting my eyelashes? Has it been so long since I've —*

'More,' he instructed, pulling her from her thoughts. 'If I haven't snapped it, you won't.'

Her cheeks flushing now, Thea obliged.

'Here.' He stood behind her, his frame enveloping hers. He nudged her feet further apart with his and Thea spread her legs wider, face flaming as a pulse of desire coursed through her.

He placed his hand over hers on the bow, and his other over hers on the string. He made no mention of the scars that marred her skin, instead, gripping the bow in place, he drew her arm back, further, and further.

Good gods, she cursed, the hair on her nape rising. She was suddenly all too aware of the thundering of her own heart.

Focus, Thea, she told herself, returning her attention to her grip and her target in the distance, muscles trembling with the effort.

'That's it,' he whispered. '*Now.*'

A shiver washed over her as his words tickled her neck and she released the arrow.

It soared through the air, the fletching but a blur as it shot towards her mark.

A soft thud sounded as it hit the tree. Not the targeted tree, but two over.

Thea swore.

The Warsword at her back laughed, the sound like music. 'A touch wide there, Alchemist.'

Thea threw a hand up as she whirled around to face him. 'You distracted me!' she said without thinking.

A slow smile tugged at the corner of Hawthorne's mouth. *That damn dimple...*

'Distracted you?' Genuine amusement gleamed in his

silver eyes, though they looked more grey when he wasn't raging at her, like Malik's. 'I was teaching you,' he argued. 'Exactly what you've been harassing me to do since we stepped foot out of Thezmarr.'

Thea's body flooded with warmth, but she refused to yield. 'Is that how you mentor all the guild's shieldbearers?' she countered.

Hawthorne considered this, folding his arms over that impossibly broad chest of his. 'I don't *mentor* anyone.'

His gaze was firm, intense on hers, enough to make Thea want to squirm. She was the first one to break their eye contact, clearing her throat and turning back to the target.

'You want to try again,' came his voice, now further away.

'You didn't think I'd give up after one go, did you?' she said, widening her stance as he'd shown her and nocking another arrow.

'No...' Hawthorne replied quietly. 'I didn't think that for a second.'

This time, he instructed her from a distance, and Thea warred between regret and gratitude.

His criticisms of her form were firm but not unkind, his rich voice not breaking her focus, but rather honing it as she fitted the next arrow to the bowstring. Soon, Thea lost herself in the rhythm of the target practice and though her hands and shoulders started to ache, she was more content than she could remember being in a long while. She loved the vibration of the string as she released the arrow; she loved the moment where all time suspended, just before the projectile hit its mark. Upon impact, the arrow seemed to sing and Thea felt deep in her bones that this was what she was born to do.

'Not bad, Alchemist,' Hawthorne said from afar. 'Again.'

Her fate stone grew warm beneath her shirt and for the first time, she felt grateful. Grateful for the knowledge it had given her, grateful for the catalyst it had become in her life, urging her through the trials and tribulations to fulfil her dreams.

'You're a quick study.' Hawthorne removed her arrows one by one from the tree, each closer to the target than the last.

'I've watched enough practice,' she heard herself say. 'And Esyllt is loud when he gets a subject he's passionate about. Archery is one of those, but...'

'It's different when you're holding the weapon,' Hawthorne finished for her.

'Exactly,' Thea nodded. 'There's only so much you can learn in theory before you need to be the one drawing the string back.'

'My mentor used to say something to that effect,' the Warsword said thoughtfully.

Thea desperately wanted to ask who exactly that mentor had been, where they were now. She wanted to know everything about the man who had shaped the warrior before her, but... Hawthorne's gaze had grown distant and she sensed not to push.

'It's time we got moving.' He shielded his eyes as he judged the height of the sun.

Despite the tightness in her chest, Thea didn't argue. She was under no illusions as to what a gift the morning had been, so she nodded. 'Thank you,' she said, as she handed the longbow back to him. 'Thank you for teaching me.'

Hawthorne's lips pressed together, as though he were about to say something but was stopping himself. Instead, he merely nodded and turned away.

Saying no more, she went to her mare and hauled herself up in the saddle. Dax, who had been sprawled in a patch of sun, leapt to his feet, eager to resume the long journey home.

Together, Thea and the Warsword started back towards Thezmarr, the mongrel at their heels.

CHAPTER FOURTEEN

I n the blue tinted haze of the afternoon, it was
Hawthorne who sought conversation as they rode
across the plains.

'How long have you been spying on the guild's training
sessions?'

Thea shrugged. 'Since I could walk.'

'Why? What's so fascinating about early morning drills
and Esyllt yelling at the hopeless cases?'

Thea grinned at this. 'He yells at everyone.'

'True.'

For a moment, Thea looked inward. It had been a long
time since someone had asked her that question sincerely.
She couldn't tell the Warsword of her fate stone, he'd only
just warmed to her, she didn't want him to think she was a
waste of his time. So she searched beyond that. 'I don't like
staying still,' she admitted slowly. 'I have always felt a
restlessness within, and whenever I have fought or wielded a
blade I've felt more at home in my own skin than any other
time.'

'I can see that about you,' he replied. 'You crave freedom, adventure...'

'Who doesn't crave those things?' Thea asked.

'Everyone is different.'

'What about you? Why did you want to be a warrior? A Warsword?'

The Warsword in question adjusted his grip on the reins, seeming to mull his answer over before speaking. 'My brother,' he said eventually. 'My brother was a Warsword. And I wanted to be just like him.'

Was. The word echoed painfully between them and Thea's heart fractured for him. She couldn't imagine what it would be like to lose a sibling, couldn't imagine life without Wren. She didn't push the topic further. If Hawthorne wanted to talk about his brother, he would in his own time.

After that, they rode in companionable silence and Thea found that unlike the initial leg of the journey, this part was moving too quickly. Time was fickle like that, something she knew all too well.

When the second dusk fell on their return journey, Hawthorne didn't leave her to look after the horses and the fire – he took her with him, deep into the nearby woods and showed her how to track hares through the undergrowth.

'Usually you'd start with much larger game,' he explained. 'But we wouldn't manage to use an entire deer, and I've never been one to kill more than I need. So we're starting with the harder targets.'

'Good,' Thea said. 'I like a challenge.'

In the fading light, he showed her how to move without snapping twigs and rustling the leaves, an invaluable skill not only for a hunter but for a warrior, for a future Warsword. She watched him with a ferocious intensity, drinking in every kernel of knowledge he offered. How many monsters had he slayed in the name of the midrealms? How much dark magic had been wielded against him? What marks had it left on that warrior's body of his?

Thea had sought out tale after tale about Thezmarr's elite over the years. She knew most of the stories by heart. She knew of Thezmarr's resilience, of its Warswords' duty-bound code, but she had never spoken to one, had never ridden alongside one, and here she was... hunting game with the Hand of Death himself.

'You're staring,' Hawthorne said pointedly.

Thea started, cheeks flushing. She *had* been staring. 'I'm studying,' she replied, making a point to mimic his last step.

'You truly care about this, don't you?'

'Have I, for one moment, acted in a way that's made you think otherwise?' she countered.

Hawthorne's head tilted. 'No. It's just... been a long while since I've seen this level of dedication, and stubbornness,' he added. 'A long while.'

She was about to question him further when he raised a tattooed finger to his lips.

Thea followed his gaze to the small clearing up ahead, where a large hare stood on its hind legs, munching on some foliage.

Ever so slowly, the Warsword's hand went to his quiver. There was no sound as he nocked an arrow to the longbow and drew the string back, his muscles shifting beneath his creaking leathers.

The arrow flew.

The hare hadn't stood a chance.

It was impaled through the eye to the tree behind it.

'You always want to aim for the eye with smaller game,' Hawthorne told her as he went to retrieve his kill. 'It's a swifter death and doesn't make a mess of what little meat there is.' He passed her the bow and quiver. 'Your turn, Alchemist.'

They took cover in the bushes and waited. Crouching beneath the branches, Hawthorne was close enough that Thea could feel the warmth radiating from his body and she could smell a faint hint of his rosewood soap.

She glanced at him and gripped the bow tighter.

The Warsword was still as stone, but his silver gaze slid to hers, a glimmer of amusement there.

Movement caught Thea's eye, and she shifted silently on her toes as Hawthorne had taught her. In the clearing was another hare.

A thrill rushed through Thea and she drew an arrow from the quiver, nocking it to the bow. As she breathed in, she pulled the string back, allowing her chest to expand with the movement, feeling the muscles in her arm and shoulders burn —

'You're going to miss.' That voice vibrated in her bones.

Ignoring him, she loosed the arrow.

And cursed him, as the shot went wide.

A deep laugh burst from the warrior, and she looked at him in disbelief.

'Well, you didn't expect to become a master hunter in one day, did you?' he said.

Thea swore colourfully, and he laughed again.

Her frustration dissipating, Thea savoured the sound.

He took the bow and quiver from her. 'I'd best take it from here, or we'll go hungry.'

Before long, the warrior had two more hares and they were on their way back to their camp, Dax leaping about their ankles, overjoyed at the prospect of dinner.

Thea made quick work of the fire as the Warsword skinned the game with brutal efficiency.

'Will they teach us all this as shieldbearers?' she asked, feeding the flames more kindling. 'How to survive on the road, I mean?'

'Perhaps,' he allowed.

'You paint a vivid picture,' Thea said drily.

The corner of Hawthorne's mouth twitched. 'Truth be told, I don't know. It has been a long while since I was stationed at Thezmarr. Many things have changed during my absence.'

'Did they teach you those things back then?'

'Back then? Just how old do you think I am?'

Thea laughed. 'You're the one that said it had been a long time! How old are you then?'

'Old enough.'

'Cryptic, as usual, thanks.'

'You're welcome, Alchemist. As for the ranger skills... My mentor taught me. I went everywhere he went and most of our time together was spent travelling between the kingdoms. There was much to learn.'

Hawthorne set the game on sticks and balanced them over the fire to roast. Then, he sat back on his heels and looked at her, the flickering flames casting shadows across his face.

Dax padded out of the darkness and curled up at Thea's feet, drawing a bewildered look from Hawthorne.

'What?' she asked.

The Warsword nodded to the hound. 'He's not normally known for his friendly nature.'

'Not surprised,' Thea retorted. 'There are a lot of pricks in the fortress.'

Hawthorne coughed out half his drink. 'Is that so?'

'You clearly don't spend enough time at home,' she remarked, Seb's smug face flashing before her.

'Home...' He seemed to mull the word over. 'Is that what Thezmarr is to you?'

'What else would it be?'

Hawthorne shrugged. 'I guess we'll see how you feel about it once you start training.'

'I started training long ago.'

'Not like this,' he warned.

'I can handle it,' Thea told him, reaching for the delicate flowers she'd noticed rooted at her side. Suddenly needing to busy her hands, she plucked several from the earth, keeping the stems long. Slowly, she started braiding them together. It was something she had a blurred memory of doing with Wren when they were little, but where she couldn't say. There were certainly no flower fields in Thezmarr.

'Where have you been all this time, anyway?' Thea asked Hawthorne while she crafted a necklace.

'It's not something I like to talk about...'

Thea continued to plait the little flowers together. It surprised her when Hawthorne spoke again.

'You heard everything Audra said about the threats to the midrealms?'

'Of course. The world out there is chaotic, like it's waiting for something. The storms are brewing, the clouds are gathering. I've seen as much from the cliffs myself.'

'Ah yes, another rule you've been breaking.' Amusement laced his voice.

'It's best not to keep count,' she advised.

'I'll remember that.' He turned the meat over the fire, seeming to mull over his next words. 'I've been travelling the midrealms, chasing whispers up and down the coasts, following the Veil along the seas... There are forces at work we do not understand,' he told her quietly. 'Things that threaten the peace the three kingdoms have fought so hard for.'

'Like what? The shadow wraiths?'

Hawthorne stared into the heart of the flames, and for a moment, he spoke to himself. 'Not just wraiths. I have seen things, many things... So much suffering, so much fear that brings out the worst in humanity. It creeps across the lands like a poison.'

Goosebumps rushed over Thea's arms. There were always threats to the kingdoms, but this felt different. Bigger, darker... 'What are people scared of?'

'A scourge of sorts, breaking through the Veil.'

'How —'

'I've already said too much, Alchemist,' his words were firm but not unkind, and Thea knew the time for questions was over.

'I only mention it because you are a shieldbearer now. And I feel that the era of peace is once more at an end. Thezmarrians need to be ready.'

Thea nodded, the sombre mood settling over her like a heavy blanket. 'Thank you,' she said. 'For telling me.'

There was a brief pause.

'You need all the help you can get.'

The seriousness vanished.

And Thea threw her necklace of flowers at him.

Hawthorne looped it around his neck with a roguish smile. The man who shared her campfire was different to the one she'd started her journey with. As the night wore on, and he sharpened his blades on a whetstone, he spoke softly and thoughtfully. Thea got the sense that he hadn't done so for some time.

They talked quietly of fortress life, and for someone who had travelled so vastly and for so long, it still sounded as though Thezmarr had Hawthorne's heart. The Warsword's voice was a song, one that Thea didn't want to end.

To her delight, the warrior had offered her a pouch of dried tea leaves from his own saddlebag and she now cupped a steaming tin of peppermint tea between her hands.

'Peppermint's my favourite,' she told him, giving a hum of satisfaction.

'Is that so?'

'Mmm hmm…' She inhaled the rich scent, content. 'We could have talked like this all the way to Hailford, you know,' she ventured, looking up at him from across the fire.

Hawthorne was toying with the necklace of flowers resting against his chest. 'I thought you were a brat then.'

'No more than you.'

The Warsword shot her a look of disbelief and Thea laughed. Dax huffed at her side as though he were infinitely bored with them.

'What changed your mind?' Thea asked.

'Who said I changed my mind?' His gaze lingered on her hands as they threaded more flowers together, no – on her scars.

Flushing, she instinctively tucked them in her pockets.

'No need to hide scars from me, Alchemist. I'm well acquainted with them,' he told her.

Thea peered at him in the firelight. Sure enough, several scars cut through the grain of his dark stubble, another through his left eyebrow. His hands were littered with them as well.

Thea shifted. 'Mine are not scars from heroic deeds...' she ventured. 'Merely my own stupidity for the most part.'

The Warsword pointed to the scar on his eyebrow. 'This? I assure you, this wasn't from slaying a mountain drake,' he said. 'I got it walking, or rather, falling, out of Marise's cellar after too many bottles of a "special" vintage. Sliced it open on the gutter.'

Thea beamed at the thought. 'You? Drunk?'

'Annihilated more like.'

'I can't imagine it,' she said, shaking her head, her eyes still on the faint white line that cut through his brow. 'In fact, I'd pay to see it.'

'It was a long time ago,' he murmured, as though he were drifting back to the moment it happened.

'You don't have fun anymore?'

He met her eyes across the fire. 'There are many types of "fun", Alchemist...'

There was something about the way he said it, with the audacity to wear an arrogant half-grin that made Thea's toes curl in her boots.

'And how do the alchemists of Thezmarr have fun then?' he asked, his scarred brow lifting.

Thea plucked a frond of grass and began to wrap it around her finger. 'I don't know really... Many read and talk, some go for walks around the fortress and when they can, tend to the horses. My sister likes to invent things.'

'You have a sister at Thezmarr?'

'Yes. She's the most talented of our cohort. She'll be the master alchemist when Farissa retires.'

'She's that good?'

'The best,' Thea said proudly.

Hawthorne's gaze turned contemplative. 'It's good you have each other.'

'I know.' Thea hesitated. 'Were you and your brother together at Thezmarr for long?'

Hawthorne's expression changed, his fingers touching the flower necklace. 'Yes and no,' he said at last. 'My brother...'

Thea waited, she could tell how hard it was for him to speak of it.

The warrior sighed heavily. 'Malik is my brother, Alchemist.'

Thea froze, shock rippling through her. 'Malik? *My* Malik?'

Hawthorne's gaze glistened in the firelight, a sad smile on his lips. 'Yes, that Malik. I'm sure he'd find your claim to him endlessly amusing.'

Thea gaped at the Warsword. 'How can I not know something like that?'

'Hardly anyone left at Thezmarr knows. When I was a shieldbearer, I took my mother's family name. I wanted to make it on my own, without living in the shadow of Malik's reputation.'

'It seems you were successful.'

'All the glory in the world means nothing when you fail to save your brother from a terrible fate.'

Thea's throat constricted. 'What happened?'

'The fall of Naarva...' The words seemed to tumble from

Hawthorne now, as though this was the first time he was speaking them. 'A swarm of shadow wraiths and their masters attacked, Malik and my mentor were caught in the fray. These creatures were the largest of their kind I'd ever seen. Against them, even Malik looked small.'

Thea stared, unable to imagine her giant friend looking anything other than larger than life.

'Malik was cornered, thrown around like a child's toy, slammed into the rock again and again. I was too far away to do anything...'

'It wasn't your fault,' Thea murmured.

'I should have been at my brother's side.'

'If Malik couldn't stop them, you had no chance,' she told him, finding herself reaching for his arm. Her hand closed over the warm skin there. 'He wouldn't have wanted you to get hurt.'

'Malik the Shieldbreaker, they once called him. No one ever made a shield Malik couldn't break. He was also known for breaking the shieldbearers in.' As though remembering himself, Hawthorne looked at where she touched him. 'It's getting late,' he said. Her hand fell away as he got to his feet and rummaged for his bedroll. 'We should get some rest before tomorrow.'

Thea tried not to let her disappointment show. 'Of course.'

But then the Warsword paused. 'You never said what you did.'

'What do you mean?'

'For fun.'

'Oh...' Thea struggled for a moment then. Wren had her inventions, Sam had her dalliances, Ida loved helping out in the stables and riding when she could. But Thea... What *did* she do for fun? Fun had never been the purpose, had never been the driving force for her actions, but that didn't mean she didn't experience joy...

Slowly, Thea met Hawthorne's gaze once more. 'I train,' she said.

'Just as well.' Hawthorne nodded. 'You're already behind the rest of the shieldbearers.'

'Like I said, I like a challenge.'

Hawthorne lay down on his bedroll, resting his hands behind his head and looking up to the stars. 'So I've gathered.'

Thea woke with a jolt. The night stared down at her, a black vastness that made her feel small and insignificant. Something nudged her boot and she started, reaching for the dagger she no longer had.

It was only Dax. The embers of the fire were still glowing, enough that she could make out his elongated frame and ragged coat.

A few feet away, movement caught her eye.

Hawthorne. He was thrashing about on his bedroll, murmuring incoherently, a sheen of sweat on his brow.

Thea froze. He wouldn't want her seeing this, that much she knew. Anguish spilled from his lips in a language she didn't recognise, his face pained.

Thea understood the force of inner horrors all too well, and she wasn't about to let them drag him under. She went to him and laced her fingers through his. He was cold as ice.

'Hawthorne,' she said, as gently as she could. 'Hawthorne, wake up...'

His grip tightened around her hand and he quaked. 'No, don't!' The words were both a command and a plea. 'No...'

'Hawthorne,' Thea shook his shoulder with more force. 'Wake up. It's a dream, it's just a dream.'

He jerked beneath her touch and she leaned over him, this time shaking him harder. 'It's a dream,' she said again. 'You need to —'

With a ragged gasp, his eyes flew open, molten silver and savage.

And then suddenly Thea was on her back, the full weight of him pressed against her as he pinned her to the ground, panting.

'Hawthorne,' she said. 'It's Thea. It's me, the Alchemist.'

But his gaze was feral, as though he had no sense of who she was or where they were.

'Wilder,' she said his given name softly, but as a command. '*Wilder*. It's Thea.'

Slowly, the Warsword blinked. The glaze over his eyes faded. 'Thea...?' he breathed.

She swallowed the lump in her throat and nodded. *He's never said my name before*, she realised, suddenly more keenly aware of his body against hers.

He seemed to realise at the same time and jolted back as if burned.

The cold swept in where he'd touched her.

'I'm... I'm sorry,' he murmured, his shoulders sagging. 'I don't know what happened.'

'You were having a nightmare,' Thea told him, sitting up. 'It's my fault, I tried to wake you. Probably not a good idea —'

'No,' he cut her off. 'I needed to... I... Thank you,' he finished, not looking at her, but staring at the ground as though ashamed, his chest rising and falling as he fought to steady himself.

She waited, knowing there was a pocket of time between nightmare and reality where the two were still blurred, where skin still crawled and hearts refused to slow.

'I have them too,' Thea said quietly.

At last, he met her gaze, silver spearing celadon.

'What about?' he managed.

'The past. At least, I think it's the past,' she told him.

Nodding, his eyes met hers before trailing over her, assessing. 'Did I hurt you?'

'No.'

His broad shoulders sagged, and he started to nod, but then froze, his attention drawn to her chest. 'What's that.'

Taken aback, Thea looked down. One of the buttons of her shirt – *his shirt* – had come loose and her fate stone had slipped free. It rested between her breasts; the jade catching the light of the embers. Her hand went to it, hastily trying to tuck it back beneath the fabric, but Hawthorne was faster.

He closed the gap between them in a second, his fingers curling around the stone, turning it over in his grasp. 'I haven't seen one of these in a very long time.' His breath tickled Thea's face.

'Then you do know what it is.'

He traced the number engraved there, the rest of him deathly still. 'I spent a good deal of my apprenticeship travelling to and from the winter kingdom of Aveum...' he told her slowly. 'The royal family, the Duforts, come from a long line of powerful seers. During my time with them I learnt enough about these stones to know the havoc they wreak on people's lives.'

Thea was quiet. Besides Wren and the comments Audra

had made on their ride, she had never heard anyone talk of fate stones.

'What does *twenty-seven* mean?' Hawthorne asked, still uncomfortably close.

Twenty-seven. The number that had haunted Thea for longer than she could remember. The number she thought she had made her peace with time and time again, only to have it laugh in her face. A number that only gave her a single piece of a much larger puzzle – roughly when she would die, but now how, not why. She fought the urge to snatch the stone from his hands and step back. The physicality of his presence was nearly overwhelming, the scent of rosewood soap and leather everywhere at once.

'Althea?' He said her name, and she realised with a heart-pounding start that she liked the sound of it on his lips. 'I know no two fate stones are the same, so what does this one mean?'

'I don't know,' she lied, reaching for the stone gently. 'I don't know what it means. It belonged to a friend.'

'You're telling me this isn't your fate carved here?'

She shook her head, stomach lurching. 'No.'

'Whose is it, then?'

Thea fought to keep the lie steady on her tongue, hoping that it was an answer that dissuaded more questions. 'Someone long gone.'

'I'm sorry for your loss,' he said earnestly. 'But thank the gods that thing doesn't belong to you.'

The hair lifted at the back of Thea's neck. 'Why do you say that?'

Hawthorne's attention was on the fate stone he held in his open palm, where her hand now touched his. 'Because,' he replied quietly. 'Those things are more trouble than they're worth.'

Thea's hand lingered, and she found herself leaning into his scent, a current passing through her where their fingers met.

'But that doesn't matter, because it's not yours.'

Thea slowly pulled the fate stone from his grasp, tucking it into the front of her shirt.

'No,' she assured him. 'It's not mine.'

CHAPTER FIFTEEN

Thea woke to find her hand engulfed by Hawthorne's. He lay on his bedroll less than a foot away, his arm stretched out between them. She didn't move, instead, she watched the rise and fall of his broad chest and studied his face, its harsh lines softened by sleep. Long, dark lashes rested against high cheekbones and she had to stop herself reaching across and tracing the gentle curve of his lips. She didn't know who had sought whom in the early hours of the morning, but she was glad for the touch of his skin – if only to ward away the guilt from the lie she'd told. Even now, her fate stone dug into her sternum, a cruel reminder.

'*It's not mine...*' she'd said. But what good would the truth have done? At best it would have earned her pity, at worse, it might have jeopardised her newfound place as a shieldbearer. For what good was an investment that expired after three years?

Thea dared to run her thumb across the back of Hawthorne's hand, the skin there soft, littered with tiny scars like her own.

No, she wouldn't feel guilty. Not now. She pushed the thought to that dark crevice of her mind where she kept such things. The fate stone might rule her death, but it would not rule her life.

Hawthorne stirred, and Thea closed her eyes, letting her face relax, the picture of sleep. She had already decided that she'd save him from any embarrassment this time around.

Slowly, she felt the Warsword wake beside her and his hesitation upon discovering their joined hands. There was a long pause and Thea wondered if he now studied her as she had studied him. Then, he slipped his fingers ever so gently from hers. A few moments later, a blanket was laid carefully over her and the quiet crunch of grass told her he'd left.

Thea waited some time before palming the sleep from her eyes and sitting up, smiling to herself. She set about tidying the campsite and making sure Dax had some water and food. When she was sure Hawthorne was decent, she sought him out.

He was a few yards away, working through his morning exercises. But this time, Thea didn't sit and watch. She snatched two decent sized sticks from the ground and went to take a position nearby.

Surprisingly, the Warsword didn't growl at her. Nor did he laugh or reprimand her. Instead, he continued as though she wasn't there.

Thea followed his movements, clumsily at first, but slowly finding the rhythm in each strike, each parry. Her sticks carved through the air as his blades did, her sticks flew when his swords swung. She knew from Esyllt's shouting at the shieldbearers that footwork was half the battle with swordplay, so she watched Hawthorne's feet. Each step was crisp and clean, there was no dragging, no shuffling to be seen. He struck powerfully at his imaginary opponent as he moved, keeping his torso and shoulders squared to the line of engagement, allowing both swords equal opportunity to rain down blows.

It was a dance, a glorious dance.

Thea mimicked the steps, but felt clumsy despite her small size. The massive warrior moved with a graceful agility she couldn't match. But Thea persisted. How many more opportunities would she have like this?

Thea lost herself in the patterns, revelling in every step and every thrust of her makeshift weapons. She only wished she could feel the true weight of the steel in her hands, knowing that her upper body strength was something she would need to work on as soon as possible in order to wield a longsword herself.

When she stumbled over her feet for a fourth time, Hawthorne actually changed positions and slowed his movements, so she could better see what he was doing. And when she next faltered, he was suddenly beside her.

'You're thinking too much,' he told her, his voice low. 'You have your own natural rhythm, trust it and it will serve you well. Try again.'

Thea planted her feet as he did and followed his guidance through the range of motions, her sticks sweeping alongside his blades.

'That's it,' he murmured. 'Again.'

And so they ran through the drill again. Step, swing, parry, thrust, block.

Thea, who had never attended a ball in all her life, imagined that with Hawthorne moving in time at her side, it must have looked like the most beautiful of waltzes. And more than just looking beautiful, it felt *right*.

Step, swing, parry, thrust, block.

They repeated the dance across the plains until their shirts were damp with sweat and the sun had risen well and truly into morning.

Thea couldn't remember the last time she'd felt this... *Alive.*

Not just careening towards a fated death, but *alive* and in the moment.

Grinning widely, she turned to Hawthorne, who looked oddly pleased with himself as well.

'How about I try with your swords,' she asked boldly, offering the warrior her sticks in exchange.

'Not a chance. You know damn well Naarvian steel is reserved for Warswords.'

'Another stupid tradition.'

'You'd best get used to them. A warrior's life is full of stupid traditions.'

Thea chuckled good-naturedly and turned to camp.

Hawthorne sheathed his blades across his shoulders and followed, his arm brushing hers as they made their way back to their horses.

'Time to go?' she asked, trying to keep the disappointment from her voice.

He nodded, his stare lingering on her a beat longer than usual and Thea was brought back to the morning she'd woken in his arms. She could almost still feel the imprint of his body on hers.

He looked away. 'We ride hard today,' he called over his shoulder.

. . .

They rode hard indeed, with Dax running joyfully ahead through the grass. Thea's thoughts kept returning to those sleepy moments beneath the dawn; the Warsword's hand in hers. The memory was only soured by the lie she'd told about the fate stone and the relief in Hawthorne's voice upon hearing it. Guilt curdled in her gut, but she shoved the feeling down. It was none of his business. Whatever friendly truce had formed between them was nice... more than nice. But she was no starry-eyed fool. She knew that upon their return to the fortress, they'd likely never cross paths again, so what was the point?

As they rode, Thea glanced across at the warrior, who was deep in thought. She had no idea what he was thinking, only that she wished it was the same as her: that all of a sudden, a journey that seemed painfully never-ending to start, was ending all too soon.

Tomorrow they would be back in Thezmarr. Tomorrow, everything would change. Thea would be a shieldbearer and Hawthorne... Hawthorne would be sent away to protect the midrealms again.

Thea steeled herself against the tightness in her chest. From now on, her focus would be to earn a Guardian totem of her own.

Thea started recognising some of the fields and villages she knew to be south of Thezmarr. She had travelled through them as an alchemist, now she rode through with her head high as a shieldbearer. She imagined what Wren would say.

Althea Nine Lives, she'd likely scoff along with the others. The thought brought a fond smile to Thea's face – perhaps the name wasn't so bad after all.

She watched Dax bound through the fields ahead with bewildered amusement. She had always seen him as an old mangy creature, but out here one could mistake him for a puppy, his long legs flailing about, huge paws kicking up mud with unbridled joy.

For the briefest of seconds, Thea wondered what it felt like, to run without a care, just because one could. She wondered what life would offer, were the end of it not so near on the horizon. She shook her head. It wasn't often she indulged such thoughts, but this journey... It had unlocked something in her.

'Why don't you tell me about your mentor?' she asked Hawthorne, nudging her horse up alongside his.

Hawthorne made a noise at the back of his throat. 'You don't give up, do you?'

'Certainly not.'

To her surprise, the Warsword gave a resigned laugh. 'His name was Talemir Starling.'

'*Talemir Starling?* Your mentor was the *Prince of Hearts?*'

'So you've heard of him.'

'*Heard of him?* I've seen his records in the trophy room. I've heard the tales about how many monsters he slayed in Naarva. And once...' she trailed off, trying to bring the memory to the forefront of her mind. It had been the day Malik had given her the dagger, she'd been in the infirmary.

'Once?' Hawthorne prompted.

'Years ago I saw him in the flesh. Heard him talking to the Guild Master...' she said slowly, sifting through the recollection. 'Actually, they were talking about you.'

Hawthorne raised a brow. 'I imagine they had a lot to say.'

'Oh? What makes you think that?'

'Call it a hunch,' he replied with a grim note. 'But I also fought at Talemir's side for a long time before he left the guild. We were inseparable for years.'

'Was he as good as they say?'

Hawthorne smiled at that. 'Better.'

'What happened to him? Why did he leave?' Thea asked.

The Warsword was silent for a moment, seeming to mull his words over. 'After the official fall of Naarva, there were unresolved issues, and another conflict followed shortly after.'

'And he went back to fight?'

Hawthorne nodded. 'We both did. It was... unexpected.'

'There you are painting a vivid picture again.'

'I'm not used to talking about these things. It's not easy.'

Thea felt a pang low in her gut and her hand drifted to her fate stone. She knew that better than anyone. How many times had she yearned to express how she felt about the hourglass she raced against? How panicked she was at not having achieved what she wanted? How she wasn't ready to leave the midrealms behind? But once she opened those gates, who knew what else might come spilling out...

'I understand,' she said, waiting until he met her eyes again. 'But... Well, if you want to talk about it, I'll listen.'

Hawthorne's harsh face softened. 'It has been a long while since I've had an offer like that.'

Those words splintered Thea's heart. 'Hawthorne...'

He took a measured breath. 'Talemir was more than just a mentor to me,' he told her. 'Even long after I passed the Great Rite and became a Warsword. He was my family. Malik's family, too. And he taught me everything I know. He was the greatest Warsword the midrealms had ever seen...'

Bitter admiration laced the warrior's words and Thea noted how his hands gripped his reins tighter.

'That's what they say about you.'

'Only because of him.' Hawthorne replied. 'But after that second conflict at Naarva, he left the guild for reasons I didn't agree with, didn't understand. Still don't. Malik was badly injured, still recovering. Talemir was his closest friend, and he wasn't there. He didn't come back, didn't… Well, after everything we had been through together, after everything with Malik… Talemir and I… We didn't part on good terms.'

'I'm sorry,' Thea said, feeling the weight of his grief on her own chest. 'Is he still alive?'

'Somewhere out there, yes.'

Thea nodded. 'Maybe one day you'll meet again and mend the rift between you.'

'Maybe.' Hawthorne offered a sad smile. 'Maybe.'

A few moments of silence passed between them. There was still so much Thea wanted to know about the man who rode beside her.

It was Hawthorne who broke the quiet. 'Since you've so expertly wrangled my secrets from me, why don't you tell me yours?'

'You want to know my deepest, darkest desires do you, Warsword?'

There was a pause as his gaze intensified, became hooded. 'One of many things I'm surprised to find myself wanting.'

Heat flooded between Thea's legs and the rocking of the saddle against her did *nothing* to quell the sudden wave of arousal.

She cleared her throat and looked away, praying he

hadn't noticed the change in her. 'You already know,' she told him. 'I want to fight for Thezmarr, I want to be a warrior, I want to be a Warsword one day.'

Hawthorne smiled.

'What? You think it's stupid?'

'I thought we'd moved past that.' He shook his head. 'No, it's just that you remind me of someone...'

The way he said it made Thea pause, an ugly feeling rearing its head deep within.

'A woman?'

'Yes.'

'Was she beautiful?' The words tumbled out of her before she could stop them and her cheeks immediately heated. Where had *that* come from?

But Hawthorne considered this. 'Yes... She was – *is* – beautiful.'

Thea's gut twisted.

'Talemir married her,' Hawthorne added, his dimple showing beneath his beard.

'Married her?' Thea blurted. 'I thought Warswords don't take wives?'

'Talemir is no longer a Warsword.' There was an edge to his voice. But then his gaze slid to hers and lingered. 'You're beautiful, you know.' The words came quietly, cautiously.

Thea made a sound that was midway between a scoff and a snort. She had never been told that, not by anyone, bar Wren. 'You mean if I wore dresses and acted more like a girl?'

Hawthorne leaned over to draw her reins up short, bringing them both to a stop. 'No,' he said firmly. 'You're beautiful as you are. And I'd wager even more so with steel in your hand and the blood of your enemies splattered across your face.'

Her breath caught.

'Althea.' Her name sounded like a melody and he leaned across the gap between their horses, his gaze dropping to her lips, his voice low. 'There is nothing more attractive than a woman who knows what she wants.'

Her body went taut.

Hawthorne hesistated, before pulling away. 'Remember that.'

They cantered across the remaining fields and grasslands heading northwest to the fortress. Thea could see the haze of the black mountains on the horizon and could almost smell the pine and rich sap of the Bloodwoods. Thea glanced at the Warsword riding stoically beside her. His dark hair was swept up into a messy bun at the back of his head, his gaze trained on the path before him. Thea didn't know if she was imagining it or not, but it seemed to her that the tension had returned to the set of his shoulders. He'd been quiet for a while, even by his standards, and she found herself craving his conversation.

But the lines of Hawthorne's face became harder, his back straighter, as though he were steeling himself, against what she didn't know.

It was late afternoon when at last the Mourner's Trail came into view. The sun was hidden behind the mountains and the air was cool; the forest tinged with the blue hue of impending dusk. As they rode onto the trail, Thea heard Hawthorne inhale sharply.

Thea opened her mouth to talk to him, but to say what

she wasn't sure. The ease, and whatever else there had been between them, had vanished.

Up ahead, Dax disappeared into the trees, and with him went any remaining inkling of the Warsword she'd glimpsed. He was cold and unflinching once more. Tension rolled off him, but Thea couldn't make sense of it. Was it directed towards her? Towards the fortress?

Thea was sure she wouldn't hear him speak again, but as the gates to Thezmarr appeared ahead, Hawthorne's voice rumbled.

'You're already years behind some of them. The next initiation test will be in three months, then not for another year, perhaps longer.' He seemed to mull over his next choice of words. 'You need to be ready.'

Thea squared her shoulders. 'I will be,' she said, her voice hard.

The gates opened for them, and the Warsword and shieldbearer rode through.

CHAPTER SIXTEEN

Hawthorne led them past the stables and through the courtyard, past the southern end of the fortress.

'Where are we going?' Thea frowned, urging her mare to keep pace.

But the Warsword didn't respond.

Then, it became clear. He had told her he'd take her straight to Esyllt. What he'd failed to mention was that a sparring session would be in full swing.

When they arrived at the armoury where the weapons master was indeed shouting at a trio of shieldbearers, it took all of Thea's willpower not to baulk.

Twenty or so young men's eyes snapped up to Hawthorne in awe and then slid to her suspiciously. To Thea's dismay, she spotted Seb in the crowd, his knuckles turning white as his gaze fell upon her and he gripped his practice sword menacingly.

Thea tensed. If he'd disliked her because of that one self-defence lesson all those years ago, his hatred would know no bounds now that she was infiltrating his shieldbearer cohort.

'Hawthorne,' Esyllt ceased his reprimanding and bowed his head to the Warsword. 'What can I do for you?'

Hawthorne jutted his chin in Thea's direction. 'New recruit.'

Everyone stared openly. Seb was seething.

'What's that?' Esyllt said, cupping a hand to his ear as though he'd misheard.

'New recruit,' Hawthorne repeated. 'The rulers approved her petition, and she now has permission to train as a shieldbearer.'

'I see.'

'I'll leave her with you then, Esyllt.'

'As you wish,' the weapons master replied, frowning slightly.

Hawthorne nodded and turned his horse back towards the fortress, facing Thea. He glanced pointedly over his shoulder, surveying the now angry looking men.

'Well, Alchemist,' he spoke quietly.

The reversion to her former title didn't go unnoticed, nor did it sit well with Thea.

But the Warsword seemed determined to be cold. 'This will not be easy.'

Thea dismounted her mare and passed the reins up to him. She ignored her flushing cheeks, pushing her shoulders back. 'Who said I wanted easy?'

Hawthorne's callused fingers brushed hers, sending a bolt of energy through her as his intense silver gaze lingered on her for a moment. Then, he rode off without another word, her horse in tow. Thea stared after him, her chest tight, wondering when she'd see him again, wondering if the quiet moments they had shared together would simply fall away for him, if he'd remember her at all.

To his credit, Esyllt did not miss a beat. He threw Thea a wooden practice sword, which thankfully she caught, and waved her towards one of the younger looking shieldbearers.

'You're with Kipp,' he told her.

'My name's Thea, Sir —'

'I don't care,' he said bluntly, facing the group once more.

Refusing to blush, Thea gripped her own wooden weapon and went to stand by the young man Esyllt had pointed to. He was long-limbed with a wiry build, his auburn hair flopping into his eyes and he offered a sheepish grin as she approached.

'I'm Kipp. Kipp Snowden,' he added unnecessarily.

Thea had already noticed he was holding his sword incorrectly. She gave him a polite nod and turned her attention back to Esyllt, but not before sensing the biting resentment rippling off the shieldbearers around her. Angry scowls were aimed her way, many of the recruits muttering bitterly, others greeted her with twisted mouths and unkind smiles, while some openly shook their heads in disapproval at her presence.

Thea trained her gaze on Esyllt, ignoring the impulse to flee.

'I want fifteen minutes of sparring,' Esyllt told them sharply. 'Consider it a warm-up. And no broken bones today, Sebastos.'

A sour taste filled Thea's mouth. So, Seb was a bastard to everyone.

'Fifteen minutes, starting now.'

Noise broke out across the courtyard, wooden swords clapping together and shouts of frustration.

Seb took no time at all to seek her out, as though her

presence were a personal insult to him. 'How many people did you have to fuck to get in here, stray?' he taunted, circling her.

Thea's chest tightened, but she didn't answer.

Her silence only seemed to provoke him further. He closed in, surveying her travel-worn pants and cloak, the messy state of her braid and the man's shirt rolled to her elbows. 'Dressing like a man doesn't make you one of us,' he spat.

Thea's grip tightened on her training sword. 'You're no man.'

'Wanna bet?' Seb snarled, face reddening.

'Barlowe!' Esyllt yelled, spittle flying. 'Did I say measure your dick or did I say spar?'

Seb's ears now matched the crimson shade of his face, and thankfully with a muttered curse, he skulked away.

'You ready?' Kipp turned to her, grinning.

Thea gave him a slow smile, the tension easing from her body. 'Do your worst,' she replied, taking up her fighting stance.

Without another word of warning, Kipp lunged forward. But Thea was ready. From the way the shieldbearer held his sword, she knew the strike would be sloppy. And it was. Seb's cruel words forgotten, she batted it away and parried, revelling in the vibration the contact had sent up her arm. Circling him, she thrust her blade at his middle. Kipp only just managed to block her attack, stumbling back. Thea whirled around, bringing her sword down on his left side.

The shieldbearer let out a yelp of surprise.

But Thea gave him no chance for reprieve. She attacked, hard and fast, lunging, dodging and striking with as much precision and strength as she could muster.

Heated thoughts and feelings about Wilder Hawthorne retreated. Thea was glad he was gone, she told herself. She didn't need or want the distraction, or his moodiness, not now with her dreams at last within reach. She was *here*. She was *training*. *With the shieldbearers*. As she sparred with Kipp, knocking another blow away from her torso easily, she tried not to let it go to her head. She was *good*. She was holding her own —

'Messy,' came a voice. 'Very messy. Undisciplined.'

Thea turned, confident she was going to find the weapons master staring at Kipp, who was indeed all those things, but she found herself face to face with him herself.

He must have caught the look of surprise on her face. 'Oh yes,' he said. '*You*. We all know Kipp is as useless as the sky is blue and the seas are wet. But *you*... You are *messy*, there is no discipline to your movements.'

Heat flushed Thea's cheeks.

'And I said fifteen minutes. Have you not wondered what else this lesson has in store for you? Or are you so eager to prove yourself that you would expend all your strength and energy in one burst?'

Thea opened her mouth but words failed her.

Esyllt shook his head. 'By all means, carry on. If you drop dead from exhaustion, it will save the other shieldbearers the effort of hazing you.'

Thea's grip on her sword tightened, but Esyllt was already walking away, berating the next pair in line.

'Don't worry about him,' Kipp told her. 'He's like that with everyone.'

'I don't need your pity.'

'Nor do you have it. I save all my pity for myself, you see,'

Kipp replied, straight-faced. 'You heard him, *"Kipp's useless"*... It's only the twentieth time he's said it today.'

The tension drained once more from Thea's shoulders and she failed to suppress her smile.

'You'd best wallop me again or he'll accuse you of being lazy next,' Kipp warned.

He didn't need to tell Thea twice. This time however, she moved with conserving energy in mind. She kept her strikes strong and relentless, but she did less whirling, ensured all her footwork was concise and necessary. She thought about her style, what about it was undisciplined?

'Now you're thinking too much,' came Esyllt's voice, taunting.

Thea clenched her teeth. *Heard that before.* She suppressed the urge to tell the weapons master that there wasn't much teaching happening in the courtyard. How was she meant to learn if he merely critiqued and didn't instruct?

'Good gods, Kipp. It's a wonder you haven't fallen over your enormous feet yet,' he shouted, loud enough for the whole cohort to hear.

Laughter sounded around them and Thea could make out Seb's jeers from the crowd. Had they all stopped to watch?

The hair rising on the back of her neck told her they had. But Thea was too focused on Kipp's movements to worry about the others. His footwork was clumsy, like a newborn foal that wasn't used to its own legs, and even after only a short time of sparring, she knew his weakness was his left side – he left it open far too often.

Esyllt's words had stung her ego to be sure, but poor Kipp seemed to be the brunt of every criticism, every joke. Thea's mind churned as she blocked and feinted. She had two options before her: the first, she could take advantage of Kipp's open left side and end it, or —

She stepped into the path of Kipp's flailing blade and hissed in pain as the wooden sword came down on her shoulder.

'Your point,' she said.

Kipp gave her a baffled look.

Then, that familiar jeering laughter rang out across the stones. 'Guess we've finally found someone worse than Kipples,' Seb snorted. 'They make a fine pair don't they?'

Several of the bastard's lackeys sniggered, but for once, Seb's insults didn't land.

Let him underestimate me, Thea thought. And if it took some heat off poor Kipp in the meantime, that was fine with her.

Seb looked ready to continue his taunting, but the weapons master silenced them with a raised hand.

'I'm going to take this riveting recess as a sign that you're all sufficiently warmed up. Get your shields.'

While Thea wasn't exactly overjoyed at Esyllt's teaching methods so far, she had to admire the sheer command in his voice and the fact that even pricks like Seb followed his instructions without question.

As she went after Kipp towards a shed where the shields hung, the weapons master pulled her back by the elbow.

'Interesting choice there...' he murmured.

'I —'

But he had already pushed her towards Kipp.

So he knew she had feigned her defeat.

'Here,' Kipp said, passing her a shield.

Her arm buckled beneath its weight. 'Gods,' she muttered.

'Heavy aren't they?' Kipp replied, fitting his own shield to his forearm. 'The cavalry ones are much lighter, not that it makes a difference to me. I'm more of a strategist myself.'

Esyllt cleared his throat. 'As you all know, combat is as much about endurance as it is about skill with a blade. You need to not only be able to wield a sword, but a shield as well. There will come a time where you are on horseback having to do both, or a time where you need to run the length of a battlefield to serve one of our own.'

Thea grit her teeth and hoisted her shield up, her muscles already straining.

'Spar!' barked Esyllt.

Kipp's false victory must have instilled a sense of confidence within him because he attacked Thea harder this time, though with no improvement to his form. She lifted her shield against his blows, once, twice, and a third time before she parried to one side and struck with her own blade.

If the weapons master thought her messy before, she was a disaster now. The shield had her off balance and her movements lagging. While Kipp wasn't much better, he was at least more practiced than she was and could keep the shield upright for the duration of their match.

Gods, she'd been so cocky. How could she have thought that spying on training sessions, doing drills by herself in the dark and spending a few days with a Warsword would amount to anything resembling the type of skill one needed to become a great warrior of Thezmarr?

The shouts and clashing of practice swords from the rest of the shieldbearers faded into the background as Thea focused on raising her shield to meet each blow. Now, it seemed, Kipp was taking it easy on her. The blows of his practice sword landed softly, the impact still setting her teeth on edge as she fought to maintain her grip.

Sweat beaded at her hairline and the back of her shirt grew damp as she attempted to lunge again at Kipp. He evaded her strike easily, which only served to infuriate her. Had she underestimated him? Or was it simply the shield she struggled with?

Thea rolled her neck, trying to stretch out the tension there. Had it truly only been an hour or so ago that she had been riding alongside one of Thezmarr's Warswords, intent on this very destination, eager to hold these very things in her hands? She made to lunge again —

'Enough,' roared Esyllt and the sparring ceased at once. 'I've never seen a more sorry excuse for shieldbearers in all my life.'

'It's not our fault they let a girl in,' someone called from the back.

'Have you seen her? She's no girl.'

'Who said I was talking about a girl?' Esyllt snapped. 'Worry about your own abilities, Lachin. Or lack thereof.'

Thea couldn't help exchanging a grin with Kipp.

'That will be all for today,' Esyllt said sharply. 'I can only stand the sight for so long. Kipp, Thea and Callahan, you're on clean-up duty.'

The grin vanished from Kipp's face. 'But —'

'If that is anything other than gratitude on your lips, Kipp Snowden, I would think again.'

Kipp bowed his head. 'Yes, Sir.'

As the other shieldbearers staggered away, sweaty and dishevelled, Thea waited with Kipp by the shed.

'What is it we have to do?' she asked.

'Clean up the armoury. Polish the weapons. Make sure

everything is in order so we can mess it all up again tomorrow,' he replied.

'That's the spirit, Kipp,' came another voice. A young man strode towards them, lean and muscular, chestnut hair pulled back into a short tail.

'You know me, ever the optimist.'

'Ever the fool, more like,' the man clapped him on the shoulder with a laugh. He turned to Thea. 'I'm Callahan Whitlock – Cal,' he told her, offering a hand.

She took it firmly in her own. 'Thea,' she said.

He nodded. 'Nice to meet you under such happy circumstances, Thea. We'd best get started if we want to eat any time this century.'

Somewhat baffled, Thea followed their lead. It turned out the task at hand was exactly as Kipp had described and Thea found herself ordering the shields from largest to smallest along the wall and wiping them down with a wet cloth.

'Was there a reason Esyllt picked us?' she asked, wringing out the square of fabric.

'Well, Cal suspects he always picks the worst performing shieldbearers of the day...' Kipp answered as he rolled a large shield into its place. 'But personally I think it's because he only knows a few people's names.'

'Really?'

'That's what Kipp tells himself,' Cal said.

'Well, I don't know why you're objecting. It would at least mean you're not as terrible as you think.'

'You know my strengths lie in the long-range weapons. I'm never on clean-up duty after those sessions.'

'Whatever you say,' Kipp replied with a shrug.

'How long have you both been training for?' Thea asked, listening to the ease between them with increasing curiosity.

'Nine months for me,' Cal told her. 'Ten years for poor old Kipp. He needs a lot of repetition.'

'Ease off,' Kipp argued before turning to Thea. 'It hasn't been ten years, I swear. I'm useless but I'm not *that* useless.'

Cal snorted.

Shooting him a filthy look, Kipp continued. 'I've been here since I was ten. But I only started training as a shieldbearer... a few years ago.'

'Try five,' Cal quipped.

'Have you tried the initiation test then?' Thea pressed.

But Kipp shook his head. 'Weapons master insisted I give it more time. Said I'd wind up dead if I attempted in my first year. In my fourth year he said, "what's one more year of training?"...'

'Wonder what he'll say this year,' Cal laughed.

To Thea's surprise, Kipp just shrugged good-naturedly. 'Who knows, Callahan... Who knows.'

'You're not bothered then?'

'Depends what day you ask me,' Kipp replied. 'But personally I've never really seen myself as a Guardian of the midrealms.'

'Then why the training? Why not stay on as fortress staff?' Thea couldn't believe that there were people in the training program who didn't wish to be there, while she had fought tooth and nail for her place. She kept that thought to herself.

'Dwindling numbers, isn't it? The intake of shieldbearers each year gets less and less. So they take who they can.'

Thea had heard as much, but it was another thing entirely to have it confirmed directly from the source. The conversation dwindled, and they finished up with the shields, moving into the armoury.

'What now?' Thea asked.

Cal tossed her a clean rag. 'Esyllt likes things really shiny,' he said.

Thea groaned. 'This is turning into a very long day…'

They set about cleaning the countless blades in the armoury, and the questioning turned to her.

'So… You went to Harenth…? With a Warsword?' Kipp prompted.

'To petition the rulers of the midrealms?' Cal added, impressed.

Hawthorne's dimple, the scar through his brow, and then his scowl flashed before Thea in a blur.

'Uh… yes,' she managed. 'With Wilder Hawthorne.'

Cal let out a low whistle. 'Some say he's worse than the Bloodletter.'

Paying far too much attention to polishing a mark from a blade, Thea shrugged. 'He wasn't so bad,' she said defensively. And then, 'Perhaps I'll tell you about it another time.'

'Fair enough.'

And she was grateful to them for not pushing her.

'We should tell her about the code…' Kipp was saying.

'Code?'

Cal nodded. 'You know, the usual shit… What happens between shieldbearers, stays between shieldbearers.'

'You mean, don't tell the commanders when someone is hazing you?' Thea said.

'Pretty much,' Kipp sighed. 'There's a lawless side to Thezmarr's regime and it lies within the shieldbearer training.'

'Good to know,' Thea replied. 'Though I can't say it would have been my first instinct to go running to Esyllt.'

'Perhaps not now,' Cal said seriously. 'But I've certainly found myself in a situation or two where a commander's interference would have been welcome.'

'I'll say,' Kipp agreed.

The warning left a hollow pit in Thea's stomach.

It took forever to clean the weapons in the armoury to a standard that Cal and Kipp thought Esyllt would find acceptable. By the time they finished, not only was Thea starving, but she was dead on her feet. She'd been up since sunrise and had journeyed a long way, only to be completely battered by the sparring session.

When they reached the fortress and entered the lively Great Hall, Thea turned towards her usual table. She could see the messy knot of her sister's bronze hair from here.

Gods, she wanted to talk to Wren, to tell her about... well, everything.

'Where are you going?' Kipp asked.

'To my place at the —'

But Cal was shaking his head. 'You're a shieldbearer now, Thea. You eat with the shieldbearers.'

A sinking feeling settled in Thea's stomach as she craned her neck to see if she could catch her sister's eye. How had she not realised this sooner?

'Come on, people are starting to stare,' Kipp muttered, nudging Thea towards the table.

Reluctantly she tore her gaze away from where the alchemists sat. She would have to wait until the whole bloody fortress retired to speak with Wren.

'Thea...' Kipp whispered in warning, pointedly glancing at the crowds whose eyes bored into her.

But the inhabitants of the fortress weren't staring because they were late.

They were staring because a *woman* was with the shieldbearers.

Whispers broke out across the hall and Thea wished she could melt away into the background. But that was not the way of things. Between Cal and Kipp, they managed to make room for her on one of the benches, much to the disdain of the other shieldbearers. There was considerable shoving and swearing before Thea was settled between her two new companions.

The staring didn't stop.

Suddenly she felt more like an intruder here than she had amidst the nobles in the palace.

As Thea reached for the food, someone snatched it away.

As she reached for the mead, someone grabbed it to fill their own tankard.

Her ravenous appetite abruptly vanished.

Across the table she met scowls, pinched mouths and arms crossed over chests. Then there were the barely concealed whispers and soured expressions. Thea kept her shoulders squared and her chin high.

Though her appetite was well and truly gone, she reached again for the food, this time, a bowl of greens - the least popular dish on the table, only to have it yanked out of reach.

'Really?' she muttered.

'Here,' Kipp said, scraping half his plate onto hers.

'You don't have to –' she started to object.

But Kipp just shrugged. 'Usually they do it to me,' he said. 'Thick bastards get bored, eventually.'

'Thank you,' she said quietly, touched by his kindness.

She ate quickly, daring to glance around the hall as she did. The first thing she noticed was that Hawthorne was not at the head table. The seat he'd occupied before they'd left was empty. Audra however, was at her usual place and locked eyes with Thea from across the room. Though she didn't smile, there was a gleam to her eyes that Thea caught before the stern-faced librarian looked away.

Chatter had resumed at her table, but it wasn't pleasant.

'Three gold coins say she's done by the end of the week,' someone – the one Esyllt had called Lachin said, slamming a palm down on the surface.

'Five coins say she's done by the end of tomorrow. And that she cries,' said another.

'You don't have five gold coins you stupid git,' Cal retorted.

'I'll wager ten gold,' Seb's voice sounded, drowning out the rest, 'that the stray will spread her legs just to stay in the program.'

Thea was on her feet in an instant, a fistful of Seb's shirt bunched in her hand. 'You —'

But Kipp and Cal were already hauling her back.

'Not a good idea,' Kipp muttered. '*Definitely* not a good idea.'

'Leave him, Thea.' Cal forced her back down onto the bench. 'This is exactly what he wants.'

'What's going on down there?' Esyllt demanded from his seat at the head table.

'Nothing, Sir! Nothing at all,' Kipp called back.

'A likely tale,' Esyllt said, shaking his head. 'If I see a hint of trouble again down there, so help you all, I'll let the commanders use you for archery practice.'

Esyllt's threats were enough to cool the blood boiling in Thea's veins, and thankfully, Seb and the other idiots seemed to decide that the weapon master's wrath was not worth the joy of aggravating Thea further.

All Thea wanted now was for the meal to end so she no longer had to look at Seb's ugly, smug face. Gods, she never thought she would long for the confines of her sleeping quarters with Wren and the others, but that was not to be.

When the bell sounded, Wren approached her with a hessian sack of her belongings. There was no time to talk, other than Wren's hushed words of warning.

'I was told you're staying with the men now. May the Furies keep you safe, Thea,' Wren hugged her tightly. 'Sleep with one eye open.'

Thea squeezed her back, dazed. 'I'll be fine,' she said, though she wasn't sure if it was for Wren's sake or for hers. She patted her chest, where her sister knew her fate stone rested. 'Time to test the fates again, isn't it?'

Wren's face paled. 'You're running out of lives, Althea.'

Suddenly finding her sister's fear suffocating, Thea pulled back, gathering herself. 'I'll be fine,' she said again. 'See you around, Wren.'

But as Thea peeled away from the cohort and made her way towards the shieldbearer dormitories, she started to come apart at the seams. If the evening meal represented the general attitude towards her, then... Well, she didn't like her chances. Any notion of a safe space had been stripped away from her, there was nowhere to go where she could breathe. From now on, she was to be on her guard at all times.

'You wanted to be a shieldbearer, Althea Nine Lives,' she muttered to herself, rallying her courage. 'You got what you wished for. Now you live as one.'

When she reached the door, hearing the raucous laughter and shouts from within, she paused and squared her shoulders, digging deep for any comfort that might see her through the night.

Audra's voice filled her mind then. '*The original Warswords were women. The Three Furies were what our whole culture was based upon, what everything the guild stands for started with them...*'

And with those words echoing, Thea pushed open the door and stepped into the drake's den.

CHAPTER SEVENTEEN

The room beyond fell silent as Thea stepped inside, clutching her meagre belongings to her chest. There were at least twelve beds, maybe more and men in various states of undress as she walked in.

'What's she doing here?' someone shouted.

'You've got to be joking,' said another.

'I didn't ask for this either,' Thea replied tersely. 'Is there a spare bed?'

A man she didn't recognise pointed to the far end of the room, where a narrow bed sat beneath a large window.

No doubt the coldest corner of the dormitory. 'Great,' she muttered.

'You know, love… Maybe you should rethink what you want.' The shieldbearer was an older one, his attitude hardly surprising.

'To be a warrior is all I've ever wanted,' Thea replied, her chin raised.

'You'll never get that far.'

Thea hoisted her belongings up and turned to make her way to her corner. 'There's only one way to find out.'

Behind her, the man sighed. 'You don't belong here.'

Ignoring the angry stares of the others, she crossed the room and claimed the bed, cursing the guild master for his cruelty. Sharing quarters with the shieldbearers was completely unnecessary to her training and she would have had to be a fool if she didn't realise the risk it posed to her. But she saw it for what it was: one of no doubt many tactics to get her to quit. And she wasn't about to do that.

Another young man entered from a chamber to the right, and Thea realised with a renewed sense of dread that it must be the bathing chambers… Which she needed desperately.

'The guild master asked me to remind everyone about the strict no fraternising rules,' he said loudly.

Thea nearly groaned. Nothing fostered action like prohibition. Her skin crawled as eyes roamed over her.

'What's all the noise about?' a familiar voice sounded. Cal walked in from the bathing room, a towel slung around his waist, his chest bare.

'Look who moved in,' someone pointed at her.

Cal started. 'Thea? Don't tell me.'

'I'm to receive the complete shieldbearer experience, it seems.'

'Fuck.' Cal rubbed the back of his head.

'My thoughts exactly,' she replied.

Thea wanted to ask him where the closest female baths were, but she clamped her mouth shut. Cal, and Kipp, wherever he was, had already stuck their necks out for her at dinner. She couldn't ask them to continue to do so and jeopardise their own positions in the ranks.

Reluctantly, the men went about preparing for bed and Thea was forced to stare out the window into the pitch black beyond to allow them to change in some semblance of privacy, though she got the feeling not all of them would repay the favour. The thought of sliding under her sheets in her filthy travelling clothes made her cringe, so she sat cross-legged atop the thin quilt, training her gaze on the yellow orb of the moon.

Slowly, candles were blown out one by one and Thea found herself grateful for one thing: apparently Sebastos Barlowe did not share this dormitory.

Small mercies, she thought, her fingers moving to toy with her fate stone absent-mindedly.

When the room was all but pitch-black, she heard someone padding towards her and she froze. Not for the first time, she wished she still had her dagger, and she sent a silent curse to the thieving Warsword wherever he was.

'Psst,' a voice said.

'Cal?' she whispered.

He didn't touch her, but she could see his outline nodding in the faint light. 'Kipp said to tell you… Wait til it's late,' he told her. 'Then you can sneak out and use the masters' baths down the hall. It's the last door on the left.'

Thea was glad it was dark, because a surge of tears welled up behind her eyelids. She reached out, aiming to clasp his forearm in gratitude, but instead groped the air beside him. It was probably for the best.

'Thank you,' she said softly. 'Truly.'

'No problem. It looks like we're gonna be spending a fair bit of time with you. Can't have you stinking up the fortress.'

Thea held in a laugh. 'How can I —'

'Shhh… None of that. It's the way of things here. Eventually, everyone finds someone to have their back.'

Thea suppressed the overwhelming urge to embrace the shadowy figure. Perhaps she would survive the dormitories yet.

'Thank you,' she said again.

'You didn't hear it from me, or Kipp. If you're caught.'

'Course not.'

'Then I'll bid you goodnight.'

Thea stopped herself from thanking him a third time and simply watched as his outline disappeared down the room to his own bed.

Then, she began the long wait into the night.

Hours had passed, and the air was thick with snoring of various volumes and other... noises. It was like being housed with a bunch of animals. Thea did her best to tally the distinct sounds to the number of men. When she was almost certain they were asleep, she gathered her things and tiptoed to the door.

She winced as it creaked open and shed a beam of light into the dorm, but she was too far out now. Making quick work of it, she was out in the hallway in under a minute. She paused on the other side, waiting for her inevitable discovery.

Either they were all asleep, or those who weren't didn't care.

Both suited her.

Clutching the sack with her clothes in it, she crept down the passageway, following Cal's instructions to the last door on the left. She held her breath as she pushed it open, praying there would be no one within.

There wasn't, and she almost cried with relief.

It was a far more luxurious bathing room than she was used to. Glowing torchlight illuminated mosaic tiles along the walls, depicting the legendary cyrens from the lands beyond the veil. Beautiful women with waist length hair in clinging wet shifts were detailed amidst the waves. Audra had spoken of their kind before, creatures who with a single song could reduce a man to a pile of bones. Thea had always liked that.

Thea gazed upon the art in wonder, hardly daring to imagine what else lay beyond those towering walls of mist across the seas. She moved further into the bathing quarters to find several large wooden half in-ground tubs dotted around the tiled floor. Cauldrons of simmering water were also placed around the room on small stoves, along with a number of privacy screens.

'Thank the gods,' Thea murmured, moving towards the bath furthest from the door and setting her belongings down on a bench by a stack of clean towels.

She set about preparing the tub, pouring steaming water from a cauldron, and adding several buckets of cold water so she didn't scald herself. There was a little shelf nearby that housed countless bottles and soaps and Thea took her time selecting a scent she liked. She brought it to her nose and inhaled deeply... *Rosewood.* Warmth flooded through her as recent memories came rushing to the surface, her chest fluttering —

'What are you doing?' she muttered to herself, practically throwing the bottle back on the shelf and picking another at random.

This stops now, she decided. She was here for one reason and one reason only. Wilder Hawthorne did not factor into it, nor would he ever.

At last, she dragged a privacy screen in front of her tub and surveyed her handiwork. Ribbons of steam drifted up from the water and the aroma from the soap was near-intoxicating. She couldn't wait any longer. She was dying to feel clean, *properly* clean.

Thea peeled the Warsword's shirt from her body, cursing the fact that she'd have to have it laundered and returned to him. She unbound her braid and made quick work of her boots, trousers and undergarments before approaching the edge of the tub. The only thing she didn't remove was her fate stone. The piece of jade was her constant companion, a permanent reminder that death always walked beside her.

Tentatively, she dipped her toes in the water and let out a soft cry. It was hot, but that was how she liked it. Slowly, she stepped down into the bath, easing her body in and wincing against the initial heat.

At last, she gave a deep, gratifying sigh, and submerged herself.

The warmth soaked into her aching muscles; both the ride and the sparring match had taken a toll on her and she sent silent thanks to Kipp and Cal for telling her about this place. Finally, she could wash the grime from her skin and the dust from her hair; nothing had ever felt so satisfying. She ran the soap through her long tresses, inhaling the rich scent of lilies, though it didn't smell as good as —

She pushed the thought aside in favour of ducking under the water again. She couldn't remember the last time she'd had the luxury of an uninterrupted hour to herself like this, nor the indulgence of a tub this large and water this hot. As Thea floated, the world outside faded and she considered all that had happened over the last week. She had left Thezmarr and seen Harenth and its capital for herself, something few women of the fortress got to experience. She had ridden alongside a Warsword... And met the rulers of the midrealms. She had felt their magic, their power, wrap around her. And she'd *saved King Artos' life...* A fact that seemed so distant now. Only to return to Thezmarr to be runt of the shieldbearers —

'What the fuck are you doing?' a familiar voice cut through the serenity.

Thea's eyes flew open to see Hawthorne looking down at her, his lips parted at the sight of her wet, naked body.

She jolted in the water, scrambling to scoop as many bubbles in front of her as possible. But he'd seen. He'd seen *everything*.

'What the fuck are *you* doing?' she bit back, cheeks flushing. 'It's called a fucking *privacy* screen.'

'I called out. Twice.'

'So?'

His usual brutal glare was hooded as his gaze explored the tub. 'All the masters and commanders are with the Guild Master...' He took a measured breath, his eyes lowering to her lips, her collarbone. 'No one else is supposed to be in here.'

A flush of warmth that had nothing to do with the temperature of the water spread through Thea's body, her skin suddenly sensitive to the cool air that kissed the nape of her neck and her exposed shoulders.

'At least have the decency to turn around,' she snapped, her heart pounding.

'Sorry,' he mumbled and started to move away.

But Thea's whole body had come alive, and his hesitation emboldened her. She knew she hadn't imagined the connection between them on their journey; the lingering looks or the heat in their accidental touches.

A shiver of anticipation rushed through her as she rose above the water level, soap sluicing down her breasts and abdomen, her wet hair plastered to her skin. 'Are you?' she challenged. 'Sorry?'

Hawthorne turned back to face her and this time he openly drank in the sight: her swollen breasts and her nipples hardening under his stare, the curve of her hips and the rest still hidden by the water.

'No,' his deep voice rumbled, sending a rush of longing through her, right to the ache between her legs.

A small sound escaped her as she, too, surveyed him: the hard set of his jaw, the tension in his broad shoulders, the sweep of his chest and lower... the undeniable bulge in his pants.

Beneath the water, Thea's thighs parted, every inch of her singing out to him.

Hawthorne was deadly still, making no move to hide his desire, before at last he spoke again. 'The Furies know I'm not sorry to see you like this,' he said, his hooded gaze travelling up her exposed skin once more to linger on her face. 'But as much as I want...' he trailed off, running a hand through his hair. 'I have to go.'

Thea exhaled shakily, all the tension holding her body taut vanishing as she watched him snatch something from a nearby shelf and go.

With a mortified groan, she wrapped her arms around herself and ducked back under the water, hoping it would wash away the stain of her embarrassment.

WILDER HAWTHORNE

I t took every ounce of willpower for Wilder to force one foot in front of the other and leave the beautiful, naked woman behind. By the Furies, he was in deep shit. Before tonight, he had been torn between throttling her and fucking her, but now... Now there was no question.

He clutched the remedy he'd snatched from the shelves tightly in his clammy palm and made for Malik's rooms. If his brother hadn't been having an episode, nothing would have stopped him tearing his clothes off and taking Althea Zoltaire there and then in that tub.

He could hardly recall what he'd said to her. His cock was still rock hard, straining against the rough fabric of his pants, begging for release – begging for *her*.

'For fuck's sake,' he muttered, scraping his other hand through his hair again and trying to banish the images of her flooding his mind: those celadon eyes brazenly surveying his erection, her round breasts rising as her breathing hitched, the soap suds sliding over her hard nipples...

'Fuck,' Wilder cursed again, hitting the flat of his palm

against a nearby wall and picking up his pace. It had been a long time since he'd been with a woman, since he'd felt the need. He'd seen firsthand what infatuation could do to a Warsword. But the alchemist... She made something inside him blaze to life.

Malik, he commanded himself. *Think about Malik.* Upon his return to Thezmarr, Wilder had sought his brother to return his dagger and try to understand the friendship he'd nurtured with the young alchemist. But when he'd entered the rooms, Malik's giant frame was wedged in the small space between the end of the bed and the wall. He had been sitting with his knees to his chest, his huge hands covering his ears and his eyes screwed shut.

Wilder had backed away, knowing there was nothing he could do in that moment but wait for the worst of it to pass, that his presence might even make matters worse. Instead, he'd decided to get one of Farissa's remedies for when Malik calmed down. It was one they'd used plenty of times before, just a few drops under the tongue seemed to help bring Malik back to the present. The Master Alchemist always kept a full supply of basic medicines in the bathing chamber, but upon seeing Althea... All thoughts had emptied from Wilder's head.

But now, as he reached Malik's room once more, he had gained some measure of control over himself. He knocked gently before letting himself in and was relieved to find his brother in his armchair by the fire, Dax at his feet.

'Good,' Wilder said roughly, closing the door behind him. 'You're alright.'

Malik, who still looked pale, managed a lopsided smile, his hand absentmindedly toying with Dax's matted coat.

Wilder held out the vial of remedy drops, his chest tight. 'Got you these.'

Malik simply blinked slowly and Wilder's heart sank a little, recognising the look of his brother's semi-fugue state.

'Let me help you then,' he mumbled, taking the stopper from the bottle and filling the glass dropper. Ever so gently, he helped Malik tip his head back and open his mouth, administering three drops of Farissa's tonic.

Wilder squeezed his brother's shoulder. 'That should help,' he told him before stoking the fire to life and dragging a spare chair before the hearth. 'I'm bored, so if you're not busy, I might stay awhile.'

Malik didn't reply, but Wilder sat back anyway, stretching his long legs out and crossing them at the ankle, careful not to disturb Dax. He glanced at the dog. 'You get around, don't you?'

Dax ignored him, apparently preferring Malik and the alchemist. Wilder couldn't say he blamed him.

As the fire crackled to life, Wilder looked across at his brother, who stared intently at the flames. He often did that when things got too much for him. Wilder swallowed the lump in his throat, trying to force back the memories of that day in Naarva all those years ago. A day that had looked like night amidst a swarm of shadow wraiths and worse, where Malik and Talemir had fought side-by-side in the stone circles of Islaton.

He realised he was gripping the arms of the chair so tightly his knuckles were burning, and for a moment, his vision blurred. Malik had lost nearly everything that day. Talemir, too. And Wilder hadn't been able to save either of them.

Composing himself, Wilder's hand went to the dagger at his waist.

'Mal,' he said. 'I found this...' He held out the Naarvian blade, not sure what reaction to expect, if a reaction at all.

Slowly, Malik's giant torso turned and his gaze found the weapon offered to him.

Wilder's mouth fell open.

His brother was grinning. And not the dazed grin that so often graced his face, but a grin of recognition and mischief.

'You know what this is, then?' Wilder asked, a strange giddiness fluttering in his stomach as Malik reached for the dagger. Malik had once been the more serious of the two brothers, but his injuries had seen a reversal of their roles. Wilder had become the tense and stoic one, while Malik seemed to find a quiet amusement in unusual aspects of their world.

To Wilder's surprise, Malik did not take the weapon. His brother merely pushed it back to him, his lips moving as though he wanted to say something.

But no words came.

Wilder's heart seized, but Malik was still smiling, and so he decided that was more than enough for him.

'Have it your way.' He resheathed the blade at his belt, wishing he'd asked Althea more about her friendship with his brother. Her very name sent a charged thrill through him.

Gods, what have I got myself into? He got to his feet, feeling weary at the thought of the trek to his cabin outside the fortress grounds. 'I'll leave you to it, Mal,' he said, making a point of leaving Farissa's remedy drops within easy reach.

His brother was still smiling when he left.

As Wilder walked through the torchlit passageways, he

noticed he was not alone. Dax followed at his heels, the giant dog padding along soundlessly. He trailed him through the fortress only to pause outside the shieldbearer dormitories.

The mongrel let out a low growl and Wilder halted, looking from the dog to the door.

Unsure of what possessed him, Wilder reached for the handle and opened it a crack. 'Look out for her, will you?' he told Dax, who slipped through the gap without a backward glance.

CHAPTER EIGHTEEN

Thea had pushed all thoughts of Hawthorne aside, hurrying back to the dormitories, having dressed in tomorrow's fresh shirt and trousers to avoid any awkwardness in the morning. As the minutes passed, she steeled herself once more, determined that she would grit her teeth through the hazing and bullying, that she would prove the bastards wrong. She was going to be the best damn shieldbearer they'd ever seen – and one day, something more, something formidable.

But as she'd crept back into the sleeping quarters after her encounter with Hawthorne, dread had settled in her stomach. If anyone inside was remotely like that prick Seb, there would be unpleasantries ahead.

Inside, a lone candle was still lit. The same man who'd called her 'love' earlier was reading. His eyes roved over her as she made her way to the dark corner where her bed was and Thea's skin crawled. She was more glad than ever she'd dressed in a shirt and pants and not a nightgown.

The man's words returned to her in a chant. *You don't belong here. You don't belong here.*

Her prickling scalp told her there was more than one pair of eyes on her and all that determination and courage she had felt only moments before fell away as she resigned herself to a sleepless night, wishing that she had her dagger with her. Heart hammering in her chest, she reached her bed and pulled back the covers, checking the sheets for any sort of pranks they might have put in place.

There was nothing to be found. But that didn't mean she was out of the woods. The tension in the surrounding air told her that there were several who wished her harm.

Fighting to keep her movements steady, Thea tucked her possessions under the bed and slipped beneath the quilt, suppressing a yelp at the cold sheets, her body tense.

The lone candle blew out.

Pitch-black swallowed the room and Thea's heart pounded.

Would they wait until they thought she'd fallen asleep? What manner of horrors did they have planned? Was it merely hazing? Or something far more sinister…?

The springs of a mattress sounded, and Thea tensed, hearing bare feet slapping against the floor.

So there would be no waiting. They were coming for her now. She balled her fists, ready to swing, vowing that if she made it through the night, she'd steal a weapon from the armoury, or even a knife from the morning meal. She could hear them getting closer.

A menacing growl sounded.

Thea sat bolt upright.

'What the —' a shieldbearer muttered, followed by a shout of terror.

Someone lit a candle, cursing at the noise.

Only to see Dax, Malik's dog at the centre of the room, his huge paw nearly crushing a man's head beneath it.

'Alright, alright,' the man, the one who'd called Thea "love" cried. 'Call off your beast, girl. I meant no harm.'

Heart still hammering, Thea caught her breath, approaching her would-be attacker, who was sweating under Dax's considerable weight.

'Please,' he moaned.

Another growl echoed across the length of the room, low and full of warning.

Thea fixed the man with a dark stare. 'You won't be trying that again, will you?'

'I wasn't, I wasn't going to —'

Dax bared his fangs, spittle dripping onto the man's face.

Thea watched, utterly impassive. She was half tempted to let Dax maul the bastard, but it would hardly make for a positive start as a shieldbearer.

'Dax, come,' she said at last.

The man let out a whimper as Dax removed his giant paw and bounded for her bed.

The shieldbearer scrambled away.

Thea smiled to herself as she slipped between the sheets and watched the massive dog turn in three circles before settling at her feet, his yellow eyes watching the dormitory.

For the first time since she had returned to Thezmarr, Thea felt at ease.

She scratched the giant beast behind the ears. 'Good boy,' she told him.

With Dax guarding her, she curled up in her narrow bed and slept dreamlessly through the night.

· · ·

It wasn't yet dawn when the grumbling of her fellow shieldbearers woke Thea. All around the dormitory they were wrenching on clothes, muttering curses at the cold, flesh bared with no mind for her presence. It was too early for them to care, it seemed.

Thea sympathised. Outside the warmth of the covers, the air and floor were icy, which did nothing for her stiff, sore body. Her numb fingers struggled to pull her woollen socks over her feet.

Dax was nowhere to be seen, though a patch of heat lingered on the end of her bed where he had been curled up.

Thank the gods for that dog, she thought to herself as she laced her boots and tugged on her cloak. With no clue as to what happened next, she sat on the edge of her mattress as she waited for the others to finish dressing, wondering how she might get word to Wren that she was safe and whole.

'Survived the night, I see?' Cal said by way of greeting.

'Apparently.'

'Kipp will be glad to hear it. He seems to think he bested you in sparring yesterday.'

'He did.'

'Has anyone ever told you that you're a terrible liar? Besides, even those of us who love Kipp know he's no swordsman.' Cal tugged on her sleeve. 'Come on, or all the food will be gone.'

Thea followed her new friend down to the Great Hall. The rest of the fortress wasn't awake yet, so the shieldbearers spread out across the tables for morning meal. Thea preferred it this way. She could take what she wanted from the main table and then retreat.

Kipp waved at them happily, a book of maps laid out before him. 'You're alive!' he called.

Thea glanced at Cal suspiciously. 'Did you doubt me?' she asked when they reached Kipp's spot.

'Not for a second,' Kipp replied between mouthfuls of bread.

'Good,' Thea told him, warming her hands around her mug of tea. 'Because I'm here for the long haul.'

'I know,' Kipp said. 'That's why I put three silvers on you.'

Thea baulked. '*You're* placing bets on me?' She didn't know why she was surprised. She had known Kipp and Callahan for exactly one afternoon, they owed her nothing.

'Sure am,' Kipp said proudly. 'Bet Lachin three silvers that you'd pass initiation with flying colours.'

Cal nudged her with his elbow. 'Kipp's betting against the others,' he said. 'He's saying you'll win.'

Thea didn't know if it was the cold or the lack of food in her stomach that was making her obtuse, but the pieces clicked together. 'Oh. Well, I'll aim to make you rich.'

Kipp looked pleased. 'When I've got Lachin's coin, we'll head out to Harenth. I'm dying to return to the Laughing Fox for some of their sour mead.'

'The Laughing Fox?' Thea asked.

'It's this jester's favourite tavern in Harenth, apparently,' Cal supplied, shaking his head. 'Though I suspect he hasn't set foot in any tavern —'

'I've been to loads.'

Thea drizzled honey over her porridge and shovelled it into her mouth, unsure when they'd be able to eat again. 'I didn't realise shieldbearers could leave the territory...'

'Not for free time,' Cal scoffed. 'We're often sent on errands for the Guild Master, the commanders, and the Warswords. Delivering messages, picking up goods and supplies for the fortress and such.'

'And sometimes we might *accidentally* stumble into a tavern on the way...' Kipp added.

Cal rolled his eyes. 'One tavern. One time. Allegedly. And it's all you bloody talk about.'

'It wasn't just —'

Thea sat back and ate her breakfast as they bickered. They reminded her fondly of Sam and Ida, and her and Wren, but she made a vow to herself not to become too reliant on them. They had kindly taken her under their wing for now, but who knew how long it would last? She needed to find her own two feet as a shieldbearer, and she needed to find a way to make the others respect her, or better still – fear her.

Even as she thought such things, the glares she was getting from the other tables bored into her. She had no doubt in her mind that Seb was sowing the seeds of some underhanded mutiny against her. If there was one man in Thezmarr whose masculinity could be threatened by the mere presence of a woman, it was him.

'Who's dog was that on your bed last night?' Cal asked. 'I've seen him round the fortress for years, but he never approaches anyone like he did with you.'

'A friend's,' Thea told him.

'I see...' Cal replied, a suggestive hint in his voice.

'Not that kind of friend,' Thea said quickly, though at the insinuation she couldn't stop the memory of Hawthorne surveying her naked torso flooding back.

Cal raised his hands in surrender. 'No judgement.'

A shadow fell over their table. 'By all means,' Esyllt's voice grated like a rusted blade. 'Let's all gather round the fire and tell our life stories rather than work.'

All three of them scrambled to their feet.

'Courtyard! Now!' The weapons master was apparently already in a foul mood.

They practically fell over themselves to get to the doors.

Someone shoved Thea from behind and she went sprawling across the stone floor, hands stinging.

'Watch where you're going, stray,' Seb snarled, doing his best to step on her as she tried to get up.

Kipp hauled her up, surprisingly strong for such a wiry frame.

Seb had pushed his way ahead, but he called back loudly, 'Heard you even sleep with dogs, stray. Won't be long before they throw you out with the rest of the ferals.'

Thea dusted herself off, nodding her thanks to Kipp before cupping her hands around her mouth. 'How's that rash coming along, Seb?' she said loudly. 'Some of the fortress girls said you were red raw for a week?'

There was a burst of outraged commotion up ahead, but Seb couldn't get back through the doors where the throng of shieldbearers were at a bottleneck.

Both Cal and Kipp looked at her in disbelief, and she gave them a smug smile. 'My sister put him and his lackeys in the infirmary a few weeks ago...'

Kipp's mouth fell open. 'I have to meet her. Immediately.'

Thea laughed. 'If you can tell me the best way to get a message to her, I might just introduce you.'

'Whereas I need no introduction,' Cal declared, resting a hand on his puffed out chest.

Thea suppressed a snort, quietly wondering what Wren would make of the two shieldbearers beside her. But all thoughts emptied out of her head as they stepped out into the chilly courtyard.

Osiris, the Guild Master, stood before the fortress gates,

his glare cold and hard. Esyllt was to his right, flanked by the three Warswords of Thezmarr. Including Hawthorne. Thea's gaze fell to him immediately, her body reacting with a rush of heat. Wearing all black, his swords were strapped to his back, and his hands rested on the hilts of a pair of wicked cutlasses at his belt. He looked as unflinching as always. Gone was the hooded gaze and parted mouth she'd glimpsed the night before. Thea's heart stuttered.

She hoped to catch his eye, but he didn't look at her. He merely scanned the shieldbearers before him and his comrades with a look of contempt. Even Torj, the one who'd seemed the most relaxed to Thea, was taut with tension.

'What's going on?' Kipp whispered.

'Announcement,' someone muttered back.

'They couldn't have made it in the hall where it's warm?' Kipp replied bitterly.

'Shut it,' another man snapped.

Osiris raised a hand, and the crowd of shieldbearers fell silent. 'We have news for you today, recruits,' he began, his voice ringing out across the courtyard. 'Recent years have seen our Warswords travel far and wide in order to protect the midrealms. Though their numbers have dwindled, it is thanks to them that our three kingdoms have remained whole and that the magic of their rulers has endured. But our kings and queens have decided that we need our leaders close, need their wisdom, their expertise to shape the warriors of the future...'

Thea was hardly breathing.

Osiris cleared his throat. 'It has been over a decade since this last occurred... From now on, shieldbearers will be more closely scrutinised than ever.'

All around Thea, the shieldbearers were buzzing with

anticipation. She glanced at Kipp and Cal, but they were transfixed on the Guild Master.

'Look closely at our glorious Warswords, gentlemen. Think of whom you might be proud to serve. For after the initiation test, the Warswords of Thezmarr will each select an apprentice.'

CHAPTER NINETEEN

Thea's gaze darted to Hawthorne and lingered there long enough that eventually those silver eyes raised to hers, his piercing stare sending a thrill through her. He folded his arms over his chest, arms that had shown her how to hold a bow, arms that had held her through the night, arms that could have easily lifted her naked from the bath and —

A muscle twitched in his jaw, a dark gleam to his gaze as though he, too, were recalling those moments between them and what they could mean now in the face of the Guild Master's news.

The Warswords were taking on apprentices... and they did not look happy. All three warriors surveyed the crowd coldly as whispers broke out across the courtyard. The reversal in the policy clearly hadn't been their idea. But it didn't matter to Thea. An *apprenticeship* was on the line. Like everyone else, she knew next to nothing about the Great Rite of the Warswords, but it only stood to reason that those who apprenticed to one had the best chance of passing the harrowing ritual. Her mind raced at the possibility. Three years was all she had left. To become an apprentice could alter the course of her fate, could mean carving her own legend into the realms that much sooner.

She was going to die, yes, but she would die a Warsword's death. Thea had never wanted anything more in her life.

She tore her gaze away from Hawthorne.

Kipp was wide-eyed. 'A Warsword's apprentice. And we can nominate the one we want! Do you —'

Someone nearby snorted. 'You don't seriously think you're in with a chance?' Lachin jeered.

'Anything's possible,' Kipp shrugged. But then to Thea and Cal he said: 'Obviously not, doesn't mean it's not exciting though.'

He seemed much younger in that moment, but Thea found his optimism infectious.

'It would be something...' she murmured, her skin prickling in anticipation.

'Did you two get on? You and Hawthorne?' Cal asked, following her gaze. 'When he escorted you to Hailford? Do you think you've gained some favour with him?'

Thea's face went bright red and she made a poor recovery. 'Uh... Not exactly —"Alchemist.' Thea turned to find the Warsword himself towering at her side, his jaw set, his powerful frame poised for battle, even now.

'A word,' he said.

Thea hated the command in his tone, hated that she was already moving with him, leaving her gobsmacked friends behind. She followed him into the fortress and down an unfamiliar passageway until he pulled her into a hidden alcove.

While Cal and Kipp hadn't pressed her for information

about the journey with the legendary warrior yet, this instance was sure to ignite their curiosities beyond repair.

But all thoughts emptied from her head as Hawthorne leaned against the stone wall and studied her in the same intense way he had when her skin had been bare.

'Well?'

Thea tried to get control over her racing mind and thundering heart. 'Well, what?'

'I'm not the right mentor for you.' His gaze never left hers.

Whatever she'd expected him to say, it hadn't been that. 'I didn't say you were...' she replied slowly, putting the pieces together. 'Did you think after last night I would come begging for a place as your apprentice?'

'Begging? Not for that, no...' His dimple showed.

Outraged, Thea's mouth fell open. 'You prick. I would never —'

'What? *Beg?*'

Fury blazed in her veins. The audacity of this man was unparalleled. 'Let's get one thing clear,' she said through gritted teeth. 'I don't *want you* as a mentor. You're moody, unpredictable and —'

'And what?'

Thea tried not to let herself get carried away. 'Infuriating.'

'That's not what you were going to say.'

'I'm not doing this dance.'

'What dance is that?'

His rosewood soap tickled her nose and the Furies damn him, she almost leaned in. Steeling herself, she ignored his question. Instead, she folded her arms, desperate for any semblance of a barrier between them, desperate to forget that he'd seen her naked. 'So we're in agreement. I won't nominate you as my mentor, happy?'

'Not even close, Alchemist.'

'What then?' she bit back. 'What would make you happy, Hawthorne?'

A charged silence lingered between them for a beat and Thea gazed upon the Warsword, unable to tame her pounding heart or the pulse of desire between her legs.

He seemed to sense it because, for a moment, his eyes dropped to her mouth.

'I don't intend to be a good mentor.' His words only stoked her fury.

'You'd rob a talented shieldbearer of the same opportunity you were given?'

He braced an arm against the wall above her and leaned in. 'I would have been better off.'

'Bullshit.'

'I'd be a bad teacher,' he told her, his face nearing hers. 'I had a terrible example.'

'So you've said,' Thea replied coldly. 'I'll nominate Elderbrock then.'

'He's a good choice.'

Thea glanced down, needing to look anywhere but at him. Why did *she* feel like the fool? She had done nothing to be ashamed of, not truly, and yet her stomach roiled, as though she'd lost something she'd never had. But he'd wanted her too. She'd seen proof of that in the bathhouse. Even now, the tether of tension between them was taut.

Smoothing down her clothes, Thea composed herself as she met his gaze again. 'Is that all?'

Something in Hawthorne's expression softened. 'Alchemist...' His voice was low and gentle this time. He reached for her, his large, warm hand closing gently around her arm. 'Althea...' he murmured, as though there was so much more to say, but that her name alone captured it all.

Despite the words they'd exchanged, despite the tightness in her chest, Thea's body betrayed her yet again, and she found herself arching into his touch, his warmth.

He would have made a lousy mentor, he'd made that much clear, but perhaps... Perhaps if she was apprenticed to another Warsword, it could give them the space to explore whatever this thing was between them. Maybe —

A whistle from the courtyard carved through the tension like a hot blade through butter.

Hawthorne sprung back from her, her arm cold where his hand had been.

'We are in agreement then, Alchemist?'

Thea sucked in a sharp breath. 'Yes,' she told him, chest aching as she spoke the words. 'We're in agreement.'

To Thea's surprise, the shieldbearer cohort was where she had left them.

Thankfully, there was no time for Cal and Kipp's questions.

'Enough gossiping,' Esyllt's commanding tone cut through their chatter. 'You've each been assigned a group, and that group will be led by one of the Warswords. Learn all you can. And don't piss them off with your whinging. You're lucky to have them.'

The message was clear: *they don't want to be here. Don't make it worse.* Thea made a point of looking nowhere near Hawthorne.

The weapons master went on to read out names from a

crinkled piece of parchment, and Thea hated how relieved she was to find herself with Kipp and Cal in her cohort. To her dismay, Seb and Lachin were as well.

'You lot are with Torj,' Esyllt shouted as the shieldbearers sprang into action.

With her friends, Thea pushed her way towards the towering Bear Slayer, his golden hair glinting in the dawn light spilling over the turrets. He eyed them warily.

'Gods…' he muttered, pinching the bridge of his nose.

Thea was used to disdain by now, so she ignored this and instead took the opportunity to survey the warrior before them more closely. He didn't wear his famous war hammer, only a longsword sheathed at his belt. But that mighty weapon was enough to mark him for what he was. She'd know the sheen of Naarvian steel anywhere.

'Get yourselves together,' Torj called. 'We're heading to the Bloodwoods for a training session. It's time for some ranged weapons practice.'

'Finally,' Cal said.

'If you wipe the floor with Seb, I'd be much obliged,' Kipp added.

'I'd pay to see that,' Thea agreed.

Cal gave a mock bow as they made their way past the gatehouse. 'Consider it done.'

Kipp turned to Thea next. 'You going to tell us what all that was about before? Don't tell us the Hand of Death has already chosen you?'

'Not even close,' she said.

The early morning sun barely penetrated the thick canopy of the Bloodwoods and thus, the dense forest was just as cold as the dungeons might have been. Thea cupped her hands together, trying to blow some warmth into her fingers. As they walked, she mulled over the Guild Master's announcement and her mind drifted back to what Hawthorne had told her.

'There are forces at work we do not understand... Things that threaten the peace the three kingdoms have fought so hard for... It creeps across the lands like a poison... A scourge of sorts, breaking through the Veil.'

Was that why the Warswords were remaining at Thezmarr? Was that why they were now suddenly involved in 'shaping the warriors of the future'?

'I feel that the era of peace is once more at an end. Thezmarrians need to be ready.'

Before long, they reached a familiar clearing in the Bloodwoods, but this time, Thea didn't have to hide in the shadows. This time, Thea was one of the shieldbearers. That small victory was not lost on her.

Someone had already set up and for a second, she pitied the poor sod who'd been up even before the shieldbearers. She'd take clean-up duty in the armoury any day over set-up duty before dawn.

Racks of weapons had been laid out along the edges of the clearing. Spears, longbows, crossbows, throwing stars, slings and quivers of arrows stood waiting for them. Pieces of parchment with thick painted targets had been pinned to the trees.

Thea was just as aggressive as Kipp and Cal in shoving her way to the front of the group so she could see everything up close. This was different to being in the armoury or in a sparring session – she was finally going to wield real steel.

Torj the Bear Slayer crossed his arms over his considerably muscled chest, leathers creaking, and waited.

His mere presence was powerful enough to demand silence, his build as imposing as the other Warswords.

His piercing blue gaze skimmed across them, pausing on Thea for a moment with a flash of recognition. He offered her a subtle nod of greeting before focusing back on the group before him.

'Our purpose today is twofold,' he stated without ceremony. 'First, you will learn the nature of the totem you will be instructed to seek in your shieldbearer initiation test.' The golden-haired warrior held one between his fingers.

Thea licked her lips as she studied it: a pair of crossed swords, the emblem that signified the first rank of a Thezmarrian warrior: *Guardian*.

'These are worn by every Guardian in our forces on their right arm. However, those of you who are new to our units may not know that these totems are more than just a symbol of rank within Thezmarr. All are imbued with an echo of ancient magic that allows them to recognise any worthy warrior. During your initiation test, the totems will call to those destined for Thezmarr's guild, emitting a signal to deserving shieldbearers only. Once you have one, it is yours for life. Without one, you are no Guardian of the midrealms, no warrior of Thezmarr. When the time comes for your trial, you will find them in the most unlikely of places, in situations that will challenge you. Fail that challenge, and you no longer belong amidst our ranks.'

The Warsword's words weighed heavy on Thea and she suddenly itched to move, to train. There was no point in standing idle when there was a totem somewhere out there, waiting to test her worth.

Torj cleared his throat. 'So with that said, we are also here today to ensure you find a preferred weapon. For those of you who are already inclined towards something particular, follow your instinct.' His eyes landed on Cal as he said this. 'For those who are less experienced, I urge you to try several and determine what feels most right to you. We have the entire morning at our disposal, so take your time. Thezmarr is not interested in Guardians who rushed through the basics only to discover they can't shoot for shit later.'

One or two shieldbearers laughed.

'Is it true that Warswords are masters of all weaponry?' Thea asked loudly, half expecting to have her head bitten off.

'Yes,' Torj replied.

An awed silence followed.

Until Thea spoke again. 'Will you give us a demonstration?'

'What?'

'A demonstration.'

Torj stared at her, his brow furrowed as he considered her request.

Thea panicked. *Gods, have I insulted him? Asking him to perform like some act in a troupe? I should have kept my big mouth shut. Wren's right. I bring myself nothing but trouble.*

A wide, unexpected grin split across the Warsword's face, the expression almost appearing a little manic with those ice-blue eyes. He strode to one of the racks and slid a spear from its position.

Thea blinked just in time to see a blur of movement streaking through the thicket.

A loud thud sounded.

Thea gazed with the rest of her cohort where the spear was deeply embedded in the target, right on the bullseye, its end still wobbling from the sheer force of Torj's throw.

Mouth hanging open, she turned back to the Warsword, only to find him nocking an arrow to a longbow. Thea was struck by how powerful the warrior looked as he drew the string, his chest expanding as he did; an unwelcome reminder of Hawthorne's prowess, punctuated by gentle touches.

The arrow whistled as it carved through the air.

Another thud sounded as it, too, hit the target.

Someone let out an additional noise of appreciation, and a moment later, Thea saw why. The arrow had shaved off a piece of the spear's timber as it had shot into the target.

Before they could turn back, a trio of throwing stars flew between the trees, whipping so close past a shieldbearer that they sheared several loose threads from his cloak before piercing the mark in a perfect semi-circle around the arrow and spear.

'Is that demonstration enough for you?' Torj asked smugly.

He was met with only awed stares. 'Good,' he said. 'Get to it.'

Thea didn't hesitate. She shoved her way through the crowd, determined to get her hands on a set of throwing stars. At last she could put her Dancing Alchemist skills to the real test. This was the opportunity she had been waiting for. Her body came alive with anticipation; she might not have been as big or as powerful as some of her peers, but Thea was fast and accurate. She had been honing her blade-throwing skills for years and now was her chance to show her potential Warsword mentor exactly what she was capable of.

Ensuring she was in Torj's line of sight, Thea took up a position in the centre of the clearing, and planted her feet apart, facing the target that still bore the proof of the warrior's prowess.

She didn't wait; she threw the stars in quick succession, the small metal points flying with startling precision, burying into the parchment and the tree trunk in three satisfying beats, exactly where she'd intended: a hair's breadth beside those Torj had thrown.

'Whoa,' Cal's voice sounded from behind her.

The rest of the cohort seemed to pause in curiosity as their comrade approached the target, studying her work with a slack jaw.

'You've done that before,' her friend accused.

'No idea what you mean,' Thea replied.

'Oh, come on...'

Thea offered him a conspirator's grin. 'My sister and her friends have this game...'

'Go on.'

'It's called Dancing Alchemists.'

She threw a star that landed between Cal's boots, and he jumped back, swearing.

'What the —'

Another left her hand in a blur and he leapt again with a yelp.

'Now imagine you were an alchemist worker.' Thea grinned and threw a final star, causing Cal to lunge out of its path dramatically.

'See? Dancing Alchemists.'

Cal looked from the stars that had nearly severed his toes to Thea, letting out a surprised laugh. 'Impressive.'

'What would be more impressive...' Torj emerged from the dense undergrowth, his hand on the hilt of his sword. 'Is if my shieldbearers were *actually training* rather than laughing and jumping around like prized fools.' There was an edge to his tone that made Thea's stomach churn. Had he not seen her throws? Had he not noticed the accuracy of her work?

'Whitlock,' he snapped at Cal. 'Longbow, now.'

Cal surged into action, snatching the bow from the rack and shouldering a quiver of arrows. 'Target?' he asked.

Thea watched nervously as Torj considered the shieldbearer before turning his gaze upon the forest, scanning its depths for an undoubtedly impossible mark. Time seemed to slow as he did so, and Thea knew it was now an exercise of humiliation for them both, for appearing to not take their task seriously.

At last, Torj pointed. 'See that little red flag? About a hundred yards or so ahead? Mid way up that big tree.'

A hundred yards away? Thea followed the line of his finger and had to squint in order to see the tiny scrap of red fabric he referred to. *What's that doing up there, anyway?*

'Yes, Sir,' Cal replied, already readying an arrow.

He can't be serious... Thea stared.

But it was the most serious she'd ever seen Callahan Whitlock. He drew the string back expertly, his gaze trained on the target she could barely make out in the dense forest.

The arrow hummed as it soared through the air.

And impaled the flag into the tree.

Slowly, Cal lowered the bow.

Torj clapped him on the shoulder, smiling broadly. 'Just as good as I remembered, Whitlock. Keep it up and you'll be Thezmarr's lead archer in no time.'

Thea was practically gawking. Cal had said his strengths were with long-range weapons, but *this?* He'd just pulled off an impossible shot. And Torj's praise? Did that mean *Cal* had already caught the Warsword's attention as a potential apprentice?

Cal merely shrugged, offering her a sheepish smile. There was a story there, that was for sure.

But apparently Torj hadn't forgotten her role in the laughter and silliness.

'You're up, Althea.' He motioned for her to take the long bow from Cal.

Her hands were trembling as she did, and she knew why. She'd only just earned a scrap of respect from some of the shieldbearers with her throwing star stunt, but it was very possible that she was about to lose it now.

'Target?' she asked, following the example Cal had set.

Torj picked up a spear and sent it hurtling through the forest. 'That.' About fifty yards away, the weapon quivered in a tree trunk from the force of impact.

'Right...' Thea said, gritting her teeth and squaring her shoulders. She centred herself and called the memory of Hawthorne's lesson to the forefront of her mind, allowing his words to wash over her, remembering the guidance of his hands on hers as she gripped the front of the bow and brought it up before her.

She focused on her target, still wobbling in its place, and set an arrow to the string.

Exhaling, she drew her arm back, reminding herself that her muscles needed to burn with the effort if she wanted to loose the arrow with enough force.

Now.

Thea could almost hear Hawthorne's command in her mind, and she released the string.

The arrow sang as it sliced through the air, landing with a thud a few hands north of her mark.

Cal let out a low whistle of appreciation.

And Torj was nodding alongside him. 'Not what I expected...' The golden-haired Warsword studied her curiously. 'Interesting technique.'

Thea looked to her hands, still gripping the longbow, frowning. 'Is it wrong?'

'I didn't say it was wrong. I said it was interesting.'

'Why?'

Torj gave her a look she didn't understand. 'Because there's only one warrior I know who holds a bow like that. And he's not known for sharing his methods.'

'Oh.' Thea's skin prickled.

But Torj didn't look concerned or angry, just a little bewildered as he walked off.

Cal was watching her. 'Who taught you?' he demanded.

Thea fidgeted with the hem of her cloak, instinct demanding that she hold back. Cal had been nothing but kind to her since they'd met. There was an earnestness to him she found endearing, and she *wanted* to trust him and Kipp. She knew her hesitation was borne of confiding in the wrong boy years ago and being singed with regret. But despite knowing all this, the name wouldn't form on her tongue.

Instead, she turned to Cal and blurted: 'Where did you learn to shoot like that?'

Cal's cheeks flushed. 'Uh... Well, my family were hunters. Deer mostly. I was basically born with a bow in my hand. But...' His blush deepened. 'Game in my homeland grew scarcer every year and my parents couldn't afford to keep me, so they sent me here when I was a teenager. I left behind three sisters.'

'I see...' Thea said slowly. She hadn't met many people in

Thezmarr who had grown up outside the guild. Most were infants when they arrived, abandoned like her, sometimes sold with a claim a child had a special gift, sometimes as an offering for the good of the midrealms, all of them passing into the care of the Guild Master. But Cal had known a life outside the fortress, had known a family… and had been ripped away from them.

'I'm sorry,' she told him.

He shrugged. 'It was a long time ago.'

Thea recognised that forced nonchalant tone. She used it often enough herself. 'But you still miss them.'

'Every day,' Cal replied, reaching for the bow.

They practised until noon, and all the while, Thea picked Cal's mind for advice on how to best handle the longbow. She soon discovered that he was also rather proficient with the sling and the spear, and was generous with his knowledge. He patiently walked her through several techniques with both weapons.

'But from what I've seen,' he told her. 'Your strength lies with the throwing stars.'

Thea nodded stiffly.

'That's not what you want to hear?' he asked.

Thea chewed her bottom lip. 'I… I want to be a master of all,' she answered at last. She waited for laughter or mockery, but none came.

Cal simply shrugged. 'Then you're going to need a lot of practice.'

A harsh voice cut through the woods. ' — moron is just as useless with a bow as he is with a sword. Furies know why he's still here.'

Thea's skin crawled at the sound and, instinctually, she knew its target.

With Cal at her side, they searched the Bloodwoods, finding Kipp wedged between two of Seb's lackeys, the point of an arrow held to his throat.

'I've been telling you for years, Sebastos, my talents lie in the War Room,' Kipp said, inching his neck away from the tip, revealing a trickle of blood.

Seb leaned in. 'And I've been telling *you* for years, no one wants a commander who can't swing a sword or throw a spear.'

The creaking sound of a bow being pulled taut sounded.

'Seb!' Cal had drawn to full height, an arrow nocked and ready in his longbow. 'Let him go.'

Thea's heart rate spiked. Things had escalated so quickly. Where was Torj? Surely he should step in.

But Seb turned his sneer towards Cal. 'You, I've never understood. Why you throw yourself in with a bunch of freaks? First this weakling.' He smacked Kipp's face with the flat of the arrowhead before jutting his chin at Thea. 'Then the bitch who thinks she's a man.'

Thea refused to blush. Instead, she clenched her fists and adjusted her stance. If Cal shot, chaos would follow. She only wished she'd pocketed a few of the throwing stars.

Cal's knuckles were white around the bow, but he held steady. 'You want to know why I'm not in with your lot?' He laughed darkly. 'I have no interest in playing errand boy for some entitled prick who uses others to fight his battles for him. You're only here because your uncle is friends with the Guild Master.'

Thea's mouth nearly fell open. *What?*

The tips of Seb's ears reddened. 'That's not true.'

Cal ignored him. 'Let Kipp go.'

'Or what? You'll shoot me?'

Blood roared in Thea's ears and she took a step forward without thinking, something crackling in her chest, a static buzzing at her fingertips. All the fear she had felt fell away and her focus became singular: teach Sebastos Barlowe a lesson. Her whole body coursed with a fierce energy that she knew in her bones could take that bastard down.

'Well?' Seb taunted, digging the tip of the arrow into Kipp's neck.

Their friend winced, a bead of sweat trickling down the side of his face.

Seb was enjoying this. 'You going to shoot me or what?'

Thea took another step forward.

'Maybe he will,' came Torj's deep voice from behind them.

Seb had the good sense to flinch.

Thea froze.

'And from what I've seen, Whitlock doesn't miss,' the Warsword added, moving to Thea's side. His voice was calm, as though he hadn't just found his shieldbearers in a deadly standoff, but his ice-blue eyes betrayed the fury beneath.

'Everyone lower your weapons, now.' Pure command, no room for insubordination.

Immediately, the lackeys released Kipp. Seb dropped the arrow, and Cal lowered his bow. Thea let her fists fall to her sides, but kept them clenched, her tingling fingernails digging into her palms.

Torj surveyed them coldly. 'This can go one of two ways...' he drawled. 'One, I chalk this up to the usual shieldbearer hazing bullshit, and we don't speak of it again. Two... If I *ever* find this happening again... I'll string you up in the mountain cliff caves and let the storms drown you slowly. Is that understood?'

'Yes, Sir.' Came the unified mumble.

'Good.'

After that, he called their training to an official halt. 'Get yourselves back to the hall, eat up. I've got no doubt that this session was a warm-up compared to this afternoon's.'

Thea and Cal waited until the group had dispersed before they rushed to an ashen-faced Kipp.

'I'm fine,' he mumbled, wiping the trail of blood from his neck.

'He's a fucking bastard,' Cal snarled, watching Seb disappear towards the fortress.

'That was never in dispute,' Kipp replied.

Thea looped her arm through his and squeezed his hand. 'You're sure you're alright?'

Kipp gave a resigned smile. 'I can't say that's how I wanted to spend my morning. But yes, I'm fine. Thanks to you and Cal.'

'I didn't do anything,' Thea said truthfully.

'You would have,' Kipp argued. 'You looked... powerful, like you had some secret weapon you were going to bring down on him. I was almost scared myself.'

Charged energy coursed through Thea even now, but she laughed. 'Apparently rage will do that.'

'Apparently...' Kipp echoed, sounding distant.

'What is it?' Cal asked.

Kipp hesitated, visibly swallowing before removing his arm from Thea's, his body caving inward. He didn't look at them when he spoke. 'You both know that I'm more inclined towards military strategy, don't you?'

Thea exchanged a confused glance with Cal and frowned. 'What of it?'

'Well... I just want you to know that I'm good,' he told

them tentatively. '*Really* good. I might be "useless" on the battlefield, but I will always have your backs from the War Room.'

Thea's heart fractured for him. 'We know that, Kipp.'

'Of course we do,' Cal chimed in. 'Everyone has their strengths.'

Kipp forced a smile and tapped his index finger to his head. 'This isn't just for decoration, you know.'

'Thank the Furies for that, cause it ain't pretty.' Cal threw an arm around Kipp's shoulders.

Kipp snorted. 'Can always count on you for a morale boost, can't we, Callahan?'

Thea laughed shakily, the tension ebbing away at last.

As they started back to the fortress, Kipp's hand drifted to where the arrow tip had broken the skin on his neck. Shaking his head, he muttered. 'Fucking Seb Barlowe... He'd never get served at the Fox.'

For once, Thea and Cal didn't comment.

Back at the Great Hall, Thea snatched up what food she could carry and made for the alchemy workshop. Even though her old cohort had every third afternoon free, she knew her sister would be tinkering away at her Ladies' Luncheon Teapot.

Wren was hunched over a workbench, scowling at some part of the porcelain design, when Thea walked in. Ida was seated a few benches over, she glanced up and a slow smile spread across her lips. 'Althea Nine Lives lives to fight another day.'

Thea grinned. 'I'm a shieldbearer...' she ventured,

glancing at her sister to gauge any emotion. Nothing. Wren was absorbed in her work, as usual.

'So we've heard,' Ida replied. 'Everyone's talking about you.'

'Saying what?' Thea hoped her chipper retort would stir some sort of response from Wren.

'Some say you're a brazen fool. Others say you're the fresh blood Thezmarr needs.'

'Interesting.' Thea approached the bench, studying Wren's handiwork and handing her a thick slice of bread.

At last, Wren looked up and took it gratefully.

'How's the design coming?' Thea asked.

'Not quite there yet,' Wren said around a mouthful. 'I'm using dye to colour the water so I can be sure there are no leaks from the different chambers.'

'That could be unfortunate.'

'Exactly. It's taking some tweaking.'

'You'll get there.'

'I know,' Wren replied, taking another enthused bite. 'How is life as a Thezmarrian shieldbearer? Is it everything you always dreamed it would be?'

Thea glanced at Ida, who looked intensely interested in her own potions. It wasn't that Thea kept secrets... not many, anyway. But she didn't talk as openly with the others as she did with Wren. Despite her sister being younger, Wren had mastered wisdom and a cool head – much to Thea's frustration. With Ida distracted, Thea allowed herself to consider Wren's question. She thought of the morning lesson with Torj and the pull of her muscles as she drew the bowstring back. But she also recalled the fear spiking as she entered the dormitories last night, the eyes on her both there and across the dinner table. 'Parts of it,' she said honestly.

Wren nodded.

'You knew it would be like this?' Thea asked.

Wren grimaced. 'I suspected that not everyone would be thrilled about a woman wielding a blade alongside the guild's most prized warriors.'

'I was too wrapped up in getting here, in being able to call myself a shieldbearer.'

'I know,' Wren said again.

Thea hauled herself up to sit on the workbench, her feet dangling beneath her. 'You seem to know a lot these days.'

Wren laughed. 'I'm very all-knowing, all-powerful.'

'Doesn't surprise me.' Thea paused.

Shaking her head, Wren shifted through various sheets of parchment before consulting a sketch. 'I suppose you want to be a Warsword's apprentice? That was the announcement this morning? What you and… Hawthorne were discussing?'

Thea baulked. 'How did you know he and I discussed anything?'

Wren shrugged. 'I saw him approach you in the courtyard,' she said matter-of-factly. 'I don't like the way he was looking at you.'

'What are you talking about?' Thea retorted. Her pink-tipped cheeks did her no favours, though.

Wren gave her a knowing look. 'Wars have been started over looks less heated than that, sister. Is something going on —'

'No,' Thea cut her off. 'He only wanted my word that I wouldn't nominate him as a mentor. Less than nothing there.'

If her sister detected the note of hurt in her voice, she didn't say. Wren only continued looking at her designs. 'I don't think that's the issue, Thee…'

'There's no issue.' Thea sniffed. 'And who wouldn't want to be one of their apprentices?'

Wren scoffed. 'I can think of a few people —'

'I was *made for this*, Wren,' Thea interjected.

Wren's gaze lingered on where Thea's fate stone rested against her skin beneath her shirt. 'I don't doubt it,' she said. 'Just be careful. You're not invincible.'

A flicker of fear from the previous night fluttered to the surface, but Thea didn't want Wren to know the half of it.

So Thea finished her food and brushed the crumbs from her chest.

'Must you?' Wren chastised, motioning to the mess that now littered her workspace.

Thea only grinned. 'So, what else are people saying about Althea Nine Lives?'

Wren gave one of her long suffering sighs that constantly had people assuming she was the older sibling. 'Mostly variations of the two previous notions. You're either an idiot with a death wish, or an enlightened vision of the future.'

Thea snorted. 'And what do you say?'

Wren concentrated on her creation, tinkering with an element that Thea couldn't see. But there was a smile on Wren's lips and the glimmer of pride in her eyes. 'I tell them you're my sister.'

CHAPTER TWENTY

Thea threw herself into the life of a shieldbearer with everything she had, her fate stone a constant reminder of the hourglass draining. When the time came to submit her official nomination for the Warsword she wished to apprentice to, she didn't hesitate as she scrawled Torj Elderbrock's name next to her own. Training with the Bear Slayer was going well, and she found she liked the warrior's openness and sense of humour. He would make a fine mentor, she was sure.

Wilder Hawthorne may have been the youngest warrior to pass the Great Rite, but Torj Elderbrock was going to help her break that record. And so Thea kept her head down, grateful that Seb and his lackeys seemed to have taken Torj's warning seriously, grateful that Dax still guarded her by night, and even more grateful that she'd had no more run-ins with Hawthorne. At long last, she could focus on her goals, with luck on her side.

A week after her return to Thezmarr as a shieldbearer, that luck ran out.

Thea, Cal and Kipp waited with the rest of their cohort in the courtyard one chilly autumn morning. The stable master, Madden, greeted them, and to Thea's mortification, his apprentice Evander, who didn't bother to hide his shock at seeing her there.

Thea looked away immediately, but not before Seb caught the awkward exchange. Thea didn't like the glint of interest in his eyes one bit, but there was nothing she could do about it. Instead, she listened to the stable master.

'I'd like to reinforce the importance of good horsemanship to a shieldbearer of Thezmarr. In your position, you will be expected to assist the guild in any way you can, which can entail anything, including carrying messages, riding into conflict alongside the Guardians and commanders, and attending to them on the battlefield. Should you pass your initiation test, you will be expected to travel swiftly to assist the three kingdoms when called upon. There should be no lack of skills you can offer the guild.' He looked them over, apparently as unimpressed as the Warswords always seemed.

'We'll be taking horses down to the Plains of Orax. There, we'll have you practise riding with weapons, riding as a unit and riding against one another,' he told them.

'Hopefully you're not as pathetic as yesterday's group,' came one of Esyllt's familiar insults. The weapons master was standing at the entrance to the stables. 'The first shieldbearer to fall from their horse will be on clean-up duty at the armoury for the rest of the week. Don't embarrass me in front of Madden.'

They took a shortcut through the Bloodwoods that Thea hadn't known about and just when she thought they were so deep they might never see the sky again, the trees thinned and eventually opened up onto open grassy plains at the tops of the Thezmarrian cliffs. Past their sharp edges, the dark seas beckoned and even further out, the misty Veil towered on the horizon.

She inhaled the briny sea air. Those lone moments beneath the shadows of the jagged mountains and the lightning felt like a lifetime ago. How long had it been since she'd stood up there, clutching her fate stone, desperately wishing for the chance to be more...?

And now here she was. Her hand went absentmindedly to the piece of jade, but she caught herself at the last minute, stuffing her hands into her pockets instead and turning her focus to the training unfolding before her.

Thea watched intently as Madden and Esyllt demonstrated several styles of riding, itching for her turn already. To his credit, Evander had always taught her it was an advantage to have a slight frame when it came to riding quickly, but this was about more than being fast. The two masters heaved their shields and swords up, and Thea knew her muscles were in for another session of torture.

As she waited for her turn, she noticed Seb cornering Evander with a small group of his lackeys. The stable master's apprentice had his hands up in defence and was talking low and fast. Thea felt instantly sick. She didn't know what that bastard was playing at, but she knew no good would come from it. The thought of him having *any* knowledge of her former love life didn't sit well with her. However, intervening was not an option. Her meddling would only spur Seb on, and who knew what horseshit Evander had said already?

Tearing her gaze away from the troubling sight, she fit her foot to the stirrup and mounted the white and grey gelding. He was larger than her mare had been, and far more stubborn, but she reined him in using the techniques Evander had taught her. She was sure to give the unruly beast only one instruction at a time, walking him in a few tight circles to distract him from his willful attitude.

'Good approach, girl,' Madden commented from nearby. 'It's always important not to be impatient or heavy-handed, particularly with the young ones.'

'Thank you, Sir,' Thea replied.

'You'll need to use your knees and heels to guide him,' Madden spoke again, approaching with a training sword held up to her.

Feeling momentarily dazed by the situation, Thea draped the reins over the saddle horn and took the practice weapon wordlessly.

Cal then handed her a shield, smaller and lighter than the one she'd used on her first day.

'A cavalry shield, rather than the infantry style,' he supplied before stepping back.

She strapped the shield to her forearm as she'd seen Esyllt demonstrate earlier and squeezed her gelding's sides with her heels. Suppressing the urge to snatch the reins back, Thea turned him so that he faced the open plains, where she was to canter across, holding shield and sword high, without falling off.

Several other shieldbearers had already succeeded, letting out shouts of victory. From the looks of their efforts, many of them had been training in horsemanship for years. Gripping her shield and sword, Thea couldn't help but glance at Evander, recalling his answers to her many questions so long ago. Even back then, she had dreamed of this moment.

'We don't have all day,' Esyllt barked, almost causing Thea to jump.

But she wasn't the only one hesitating. A fresh group of riders had mounted, shieldbearers far less experienced than those who had come before, she gathered, their hesitation apparent.

Anticipation pulsed not only between the shieldbearers, but the mounts as well. They were growing uneasy, some pawing the ground with their hooves restlessly.

'Gods, don't let me be the one to fall,' Thea muttered.

She didn't let herself falter a moment longer. She squeezed her heels and the gelding lurched forward. He was eager and fell into a canter almost immediately, charging across the grass.

Thea engaged all of her core stomach muscles to remain upright in the saddle, the briny wind suddenly whipping her face. She hung on with sheer will, raising her shield against imaginary opponents, and even daring to take a swing with her sword.

She sucked in a sharp breath as the end of the run came upon them all too suddenly. But she mastered her panic, sitting back in the saddle to signal to the horse it needed to slow its pace. There, she used her feet to steer him around and urge him back into a canter on the return across the field.

As she rode with her weapon raised and the chilled sea air kissed her skin, it felt like victory. It felt like liberation.

She slowed upon approaching the group, a wide grin splitting her face —

'That's not the only thing you've ridden hard, is it, stray?' came Seb's nasty sneer.

All illusions of victory shattered with those words.

'What did you say?' she said between clenched teeth as she dismounted from her horse, taking a step towards the older shieldbearer.

'You heard me.' He gave a pointed look at Evander, who stood alone on the outskirts of the group, his eyes downcast. 'I knew the stable boy liked animals but...'

Lightning coursed through Thea, and her fist went flying. It collided with Seb's left eye.

He staggered back, clutching his face. 'What the —'

Thea stared at him in shock, her knuckles aching.

'Sir!' Seb shouted. 'Did you see —'

'See what?' Esyllt surveyed the shieldbearer with open dislike.

'The bitch hit me!'

Esyllt frowned, not even sparing Thea a glance. 'I have no idea what you're talking about. But if you're insisting that an untrained woman landed a punch on you, then I'd say you're the bitch Sebastos.'

A startled silence fell over the group.

Until Madden burst out laughing, which set off a chain of laughter throughout the entire group of shieldbearers.

Seb's face reddened by the second and he swore, storming off towards the Bloodwoods.

'You'll need to throw a better punch than that if you mean to be a warrior of Thezmarr,' Esyllt murmured in Thea's direction.

She looked up in surprise, but the weapons master was already walking away.

It wasn't long before Cal and Kipp joined her.

'What a prat,' Cal sniffed in Evander's direction. 'No spine on that one, no fucking class, talking about you like that. That'll be a shiner for sure, though.'

Thea's face still burned. It was one thing to have Wren, Sam and Ida know those sorts of details about her life, but another thing entirely to have all the shieldbearers in Thezmarr aware of her past. Unease churned in her gut. What *exactly* had Evander told them? That he'd fucked her in the stables? What she looked like naked? She spent enough nights in the dormitories now to know how the men talked about women...

'I had a girl once,' Kipp said rather dreamily, interrupting her thoughts.

That piqued Thea's and Cal's interest, enough that she momentarily forgot her embarrassment.

'What?' Cal scoffed in disbelief.

'Met her at the Laughing Fox tavern. A real beauty.'

Cal roared laughing. 'You? With a girl? At the Laughing Fox? The place you've been to a single time, if at all?' He was actually clutching his stomach, his head tipped back.

Thea grinned. Far be it from her to judge Kipp, but it *did* seem rather unlikely.

Kipp ignored them. 'Black hair soft as silk,' he continued. 'A dazzling smile and an incredible —' he hesitated for a second, glancing at Thea, who simply raised a brow — 'personality,' he finished.

Cal was now wiping tears from his eyes. 'And this woman... She fancied you?'

'Yes!' Kipp insisted. 'We laughed all night.'

'You sure she wasn't laughing *at* you?'

'Oh, leave him be,' Thea said, smacking Cal on the arm.

'Don't believe me then,' Kipp told them, shaking his head.

'What are you three nattering about now?!' Esyllt bellowed. 'Can't you see half the group's left for their next session? Believe me, it's not one you want to be late for.'

To Thea's shock, he was right. Madden, Evander and the horses were gone, as was most of their group, but for a few stragglers they could see at the edge of the Bloodwoods.

All three of them jumped into action while the weapons master shook his head. 'A more sorry lot of shieldbearers I've never seen. Get moving!'

'Ah, Sir?' Kipp said tentatively.

'What?'

'Where exactly are we going?'

Thea braced herself for more yelling as Esyllt turned to face them, his mouth actually slackening.

'You mean to tell me you've not heard *a single word* I've said for the last ten minutes?'

'Sir, we —'

He raised a hand to silence Kipp.

Besides chores, Thea had no idea what sort of punishments were doled out to the trainees, and she *really* didn't want to find out.

'In all my life...' Esyllt trailed off, running his hand through his thinning hair. He shook his head. 'You're expected at the northern training arena for hand-to-hand combat. A skill which all of you –' he gave Thea a pointed look – 'could sorely use.' He focused on Kipp. 'And *you*... You are, without doubt, the worst shieldbearer I've ever had the misfortune of meeting.'

He heaved an aggravated sigh. 'Get out of my sight.'

The trio were more than eager to oblige, darting for the Bloodwoods at a run.

'Did you hear that?' Kipp panted as they wove through the trees.

'Which part?' Thea asked, still reeling.

Kipp grinned. 'I'm famous.'

'Furies save us,' Cal groaned.

Laughter on their lips, they raced through the Bloodwoods to the northern end of the fortress. Thankfully, Kipp knew where the training ground was, but that was where the joy ended.

The training ground was at the base of the black mountains, not just a clearing, but an arena where all could watch bloody victories and defeats unfold from a vantage point. Bloody, because Thea could actually see dark patches of crimson on the ground.

And at the centre, stood the Warswords of Thezmarr.

Hawthorne at their heart.

CHAPTER TWENTY-ONE

Thea almost stopped in her tracks. She hadn't seen Hawthorne since their tense exchange in the alcove nearly a week ago, her heart lodging in her throat as it echoed in her mind:

'I won't nominate you as my mentor, happy?'

'Not even close, Alchemist...'

The bitterness remained on her tongue even now, but the sight of him... It undid her. He stood straight-backed with his feet apart, the promise of violence in his eyes. He was brutal and terrifying, yes, but something else simmered beneath the surface there. Something she wanted to learn for herself, something that continued to slip through her fingers, each of their stolen moments unfinished.

Cal nudged her to keep moving towards the platform.

Vernich the Bloodletter and Torj the Bear Slayer were shirtless, their enormous frames corded with muscle, while the Hand of Death had simply rolled his sleeves up to the elbow, as though he didn't expect to break a sweat.

Vernich addressed them first. 'You are here to learn hand-to-hand combat,' his voice was gravelly, but it projected to the far reaches of the training ground. 'We'll spar first, so you can see technique at its finest, then you'll pair up and beat each other to a pulp.' There was a note of satisfaction in his words that made Thea flinch.

Hand-to-hand combat was the skill she had the least familiarity with. She hadn't even known this training arena existed before now. To think that in all her years of spying, she'd never managed to see a fighting lesson here. And now... Now she was to be thrown in the deep end, expected to *beat someone to a pulp*. All the while, the Warswords would be watching, considering each of them for the open apprentice positions.

She wasn't the only tense shieldbearer in the crowd, though she took little comfort from that.

'I'll take the Bear Slayer first,' Vernich said, nodding to the golden-haired warrior.

Torj merely grinned. 'As you wish, brother.'

There was a hint of mania to the exchange, and Thea wondered how much blood they'd spilt between them. The men sized each other up in a primal way, taking their places.

Hawthorne gave a subtle shake of his head before striding to the edge of the arena to watch.

Thea swallowed and turned her sole focus to Torj – the Warsword who would hopefully become her mentor, her key to becoming a legend in her own right.

There was no official start, no ceremony. The Warswords simply lifted their fists to protect their faces and circled one another. There was a unified intake of breath as they began. Their Furies-given gifts became apparent in moments – the unnatural speed, strength and agility rolling off them in waves. They stalked each other like prey.

Thea shifted on her toes nervously.

Vernich threw the first punch, which Torj blocked easily enough, taking the chance to make his own swing at his fellow warrior. The sheer power in each blow was enough to make Thea wince – even when one was deflected, it looked painful.

But the Warswords were grinning savagely. Their expressions were wild enough that, not for the first time, Thea imagined how the Great Rite turned men into Warswords, and what exactly they faced in order to be gifted those extraordinary abilities. And then there were the other legends... That some were granted even more, that some were granted... immortality.

The Bear Slayer and the Bloodletter were a blur of fists and kicks, breaking apart only to circle each other once more.

'This makes for poor entertainment,' Hawthorne said drily from the sidelines.

His words seemed to spur Vernich on, for the older Warsword launched into a flurry of jabs, his fists blurring as he moved. Thea tried to focus not only on the punches, but on their footwork as well. It was just as much a dance as swordplay was, and as someone who didn't have the same weight behind her, she knew she had to take advantage of the finesse and precision involved.

The two Warswords fought across the width of the arena, the audience of shieldbearers utterly transfixed on their every move. Jabs, vicious hooks and uppercuts all failing to land. The intensity increased as each warrior fought to gain an advantage. Vernich swept a leg beneath Torj's feet, but the

Bear Slayer leapt above it, then delivered a teeth-rattling blow to the side of the Bloodletter's face. It landed, only riling the older fighter up. He lunged, raining blow upon blow down on Torj, who blocked each one. They sparred back and forth, back and forth.

'I think they get the idea...' Hawthorne called from the edge of the ring.

Torj looked surprised to find him there, as though he'd lost himself to the rhythm of combat.

Vernich seized the opportunity, lifting his opponent clean off the ground and hurling him bodily from the ring.

Torj crashed to the ground, sending a group of shocked shieldbearers scrambling.

The force of it should have broken his back, but the Bear Slayer was on his feet in an instant, grinning sheepishly as he dusted himself off.

'If you're worried about them getting bored,' Vernich snarled at Hawthorne. 'Let's make it interesting.' He went to Seb on the sideline, who was holding his scabbard.

Thea frowned. Since when were they so close? Though it made sense, the two most detestable people in Thezmarr uniting.

The Bloodletter unsheathed a wicked-looking blade.

'If you insist,' Hawthorne sounded bored as he drew his own sword. 'To first blood.'

'Fine.' Vernich stalked to the middle of the arena.

Thea had never seen anything like it. Hawthorne struck first with a brutal swing of his great blade, the sheer strength of him radiating outward. Vernich blocked it and drew a dagger from his boot, palming it menacingly. Hawthorne's expression remained unchanged, but his sword blurred as it carved through the air.

The impact of steel on steel echoed up the arena and Thea was frozen in place as she watched them parry, feint and lunge, each movement more savage than the last, their muscles quivering with the effort.

'Haven't you had enough, old man?' Hawthorne growled.

Vernich spat blood in the dirt. 'Fuck off, Hawthorne.'

Hawthorne fought with his dark hair tied back, his rolled-up sleeves revealing tanned, muscular forearms and the tattoo that extended from his hand. He moved with a brutal efficiency that made Thea both envious and flushed with desire. She recognised several manoeuvres from the morning training she had witnessed. There was great discipline there, so sharply honed that it was now instinct.

Watching him fight, Thea instantly regretted giving him her word that she'd nominate Torj as her mentor. What she'd seen in those mornings on the road, what she'd seen when he'd taught her how to shoot, was nothing compared to this. He was the power of the Furies incarnate, the most skilled Warsword Thezmarr had ever seen.

The Hand of Death.

His sword flashed through the air, drawing a hiss from Vernich.

A thin line of blood trailed from a minor cut on his bicep.

'First blood drawn,' Hawthorne said, lowering his sword.

'Again!' Vernich roared, lunging violently.

Hawthorne batted the blade away, drawing another curse of pain from Vernich.

A matching cut on the other bicep was now bleeding.

Hawthorne waited expectantly, red trickling down the steel of his sword.

For a split second it looked as though Vernich was ready to attack again, his face contorted in a frustrated snarl, but with a grunt, he wiped the blood from both his arms and nodded to Hawthorne, withdrawing from the centre of the arena.

'Pair up,' Hawthorne said. He didn't need to raise his voice, and he didn't need to say it twice. In the wake of his demonstration, the awed shieldbearers flung themselves into action.

Suddenly, Seb was blocking Thea's view. 'I'll take the stray,' he said, a nasty smile spreading across his face. 'It's about time I put her in her place.'

'Absolutely not,' Cal interjected, shoving Seb back.

'Why not?' Thea heard herself say. 'That black eye's looking a little lonely...' Despite her words, fear had seized Thea's heart. She was no fool. She'd got a lucky shot before, but she knew she was no match for Sebastos Barlowe. Not only was he bigger and stronger than her, but he'd been training for years.

'Don't fight foolishly,' a familiar deep voice said in her ear, sending a current of charged energy through her.

Thea was pulled away from the gathering tension to find Hawthorne peering into her face, a flash of frustration in those silver eyes.

'I'm not,' Thea replied stubbornly.

Hawthorne ignored this, his grip still firm on her arm as though he expected her to lunge for Seb.

She wanted to, hatred simmering just below the surface at the bastard who was so intent on humiliating her. She yanked her arm out of Wilder's grip. 'I *will* beat him,' she muttered determinedly.

Hawthorne didn't move from her side. 'Perhaps one day,' he said. 'But not today. Not tomorrow. You know it, and worse, he knows it.'

Thea's throat constricted. 'Why are you here? Talking to me?' she asked quietly. 'You made it clear you wanted nothing to do with me.'

Hawthorne's eyes darkened, and he shook his head in disbelief. 'Is that what you took from that conversation?' His low voice vibrated against her skin and once more Thea became particularly aware of her heart thudding against her chest.

The Warsword considered her for a moment before he wet his lips and rubbed the back of his neck. 'Not here,' he said. He stepped away and pointed to Kipp. 'You!'

Whatever they were doing, it was playing with fire. Still, she tried to hide her disappointment as Kipp approached. She liked her friend a lot, she really did, but he was no born fighter and if she wanted to master her own abilities, she needed stronger opponents.

As though sensing her hesitation, Hawthorne spoke again. 'You do not become a legend overnight,' he told her quietly. 'A legend is forged with blood and steel. It takes time.'

I don't have time, Thea wanted to shout at him, but she clamped her mouth shut and stopped herself from grabbing her fate stone.

'Learn the rules,' he said, his voice low and rumbling. 'Only then can you break them.'

'Any other pearls of wisdom for me?' Thea asked, wishing he'd stay to instruct her and Kipp, but knowing that he wouldn't.

'You *are* in desperate need of wisdom,' he replied wryly. 'But start with this: if you fight like a fool, you'll die like a fool.'

'Great.'

Kipp stood beside her now, shifting from foot to foot, interest bright in his eyes at the presence of the mighty warrior.

Hawthorne waited until the lanky shieldbearer had composed himself and stopped fidgeting. 'One more thing,' he added. 'Always end your opponent when you can. Men are known for playing dead and running away in the night, or coming back to slit your throat in your sleep. But no man or monster can run away with his guts hanging out or with his head detached from his body.'

And on that brutal note, the Warsword left the two shieldbearers to stare after him as he stalked through the sparring pairs.

'Well, that was morose,' Kipp stated, his expression somewhat baffled. 'What else did he tell you?'

'Something about if you fight like a fool, you'll die like a fool?' Thea replied, the hair on the back of her neck rising as her heart pounded wildly.

Kipp huffed a laugh. 'Guess I'm a dead man then.'

With Vernich the Bloodletter yelling orders from the arena, they began their drills.

The rest of the day slipped away from them and by sundown, every muscle in Thea's body was screaming in protest. The week had taken its toll and she could hardly walk the trail back to the fortress without limping. She wasn't the only one suffering. Two recruits left Thezmarr that evening without farewells.

Despite all her prior efforts, Thea was unfit and undisciplined. She was certainly no match for Seb, and if she was no match for the likes of him, then she wasn't worthy of any warrior title. With the apprenticeships for Warswords now in play, she was going to have to push herself harder than ever before.

If you seek power in a world of men and monsters, there is nothing more powerful than knowledge and the ability to wield it.

Filled with a renewed sense of purpose, Thea curled up in her cold narrow bed, Dax once again at her feet and, with no fear for her safety, fell soundly asleep.

She woke long before dawn and slipped from the room to train alone in the dark.

The weeks that followed very much resembled Thea's first as a shieldbearer. Training and sparring, training and sparring, with endurance sessions and shield wall lessons thrown in for good measure. At first, Thea was in perpetual pain, her muscles, her lungs, her bones... Everything hurt from the relentless exertion she put her body through, yet she persisted and, ever so slowly, she felt herself growing stronger, faster. She woke up and trained before the rest every day, no matter the violent storms that seemed to lash Thezmarr in the early hours of the morning.

As Esyllt had predicted, a handful of recruits dropped out, unable to stand the thankless drills and dire warnings of impending doom. Some days they simply found themselves down a person, and no one said anything about it. Kipp and Cal became her constant companions, and though she often missed Wren, Sam and Ida, she was grateful to the young men for their friendship. Without them, the Bloodwoods, the arena and the Great Hall would have been bitter, lonely places. Together, they celebrated their small wins and commiserated with each other over their bruises, cuts and scrapes. Kipp and Cal understood her in a way that her sister and their friends never had. They knew what being a warrior of Thezmarr meant to her.

Thea fell into a steady routine of more training, drills, eating, researching former trials and Warsword history with Malik in the library and passing out in her bed with Dax curled up at her feet. Depending on her level of exhaustion, she switched between using the masters' baths and the women's bathing quarters on the other side of the fortress, not wanting to push her luck.

With each passing day, the urgency and desperation to pass the initiation test grew, as did her burning desire to be named one of the Warsword apprentices. That tension rippled through the entire cohort, the competition amplifying with every lesson, every drill.

Her spying days were not altogether forgotten, and Thea listened for whispers in the fortress, for news of breaches in the Veil and the scourge Hawthorne had mentioned to her. Such secrets were heavily guarded among the higher ranks of the guild, but the unease was palpable nonetheless. Something was coming.

Time slipped by and soon, late autumn was falling around Thezmarr in the orange and golds and reds of the Bloodwoods.

The Warswords and commanders remained unimpressed with them. Cal and Kipp often likened the brutal warriors to caged animals, snarling at the slightest inconvenience or mistake. It was no secret that they did not want to be training the shieldbearers, and it was certainly no secret that none of them wanted to take on an apprentice. Still Thea trained. Hawthorne had been right about her being years behind the rest and so she was determined to work twice – thrice as hard as the rest.

As autumn turned cold and the days grew shorter, Thea, Cal and Kipp drank in everything and anything the masters had to teach them: how to stay upright in the saddle while wielding both blade and shield; how to brace a shield wall against a volley of arrows; how to find north and south by the smattering of the stars in the night's sky and the height of the sun. But the lesson that Thea embraced with every fibre of her being, so much so that it became one with her, was how to wield a blade. She learnt how to swing a sword, how to slice and pierce her mark every time, how to kill her enemies. Rough calluses formed on her hands and fingers, adding to the assortment of burn scars that already marred her skin. She didn't care.

She could feel her progress every day. Could sense it in the lack of mocking comments from the other shieldbearers. Slowly, from an object of ridicule and disdain, she had become a peer, and as more time passed, she was determined that her role would change again – to a threat.

Like the other shieldbearers, Thea practically fell over herself every time there was an opportunity to run an errand for one of the commanders, whether it was delivering messages around the fortress, cleaning weaponry, or tending to horses before a journey. Just like the others, she wanted to prove herself indispensable to Thezmarr. She wanted them to know her name; she wanted their recommendations, their praise, though that was always rare.

There were clear standouts in each cohort and, to her dismay, Sebastos Barlowe was one of them. While she had improved immensely since her first day, she still lingered in the middle of the group in terms of her skills and abilities.

Whenever she dwelled on this, Hawthorne's words echoed in her mind: *'You're already years behind some of them. The next test for warriors will be in three months, then not for another year. You need to be ready.'*

And Althea Nine Lives would be. She had no other choice.

CHAPTER TWENTY-TWO

It had been a month since Thea's first day as a shieldbearer, and with her own training in addition to the required load, she'd hardly seen Wren. But when her sister tracked her down in the hour before dawn in the armoury, she knew something had changed.

'I've been looking all over for you!' Wren practically shouted. Despite the cold and the ungodly hour, she was beaming. 'I've been made Farissa's apprentice! A formal apprentice of the alchemy arts, Thea!'

Thea blinked for a moment and then dropped the blade she was sharpening. She launched herself at her sister. 'That's amazing, Wren. I knew it would be you! You're the best there is.'

'You're truly pleased for me?'

Thea pulled back. 'What? Of course I'm pleased for you. This is your dream.'

'I know, I just...'

'Just what?'

'Well, I wasn't sure you'd be entirely happy.'

'Why in the realms would I not be?'

'I… It doesn't matter.' Wren grinned. 'Come and see my new quarters! I get rooms all to myself, can you believe it?'

Thea hardly had any choice in the matter. Wren was all but dragging her back to the fortress. Somewhat dazed, Thea allowed Wren to pull her through the passageways to the upper levels towards the masters' and commanders' residences.

'You stay up here?'

'I have to be close to Farissa. I have the room next to hers.'

At last they came to her door and Wren opened it, proudly motioning for Thea to step inside.

'How long have you been here?' Thea asked, frowning as she took in the obscene amount of clutter. Her sister had always had a tendency to be messy, but this was a whole new extreme. There were plants on nearly every surface, glass vials balanced precariously on uneven edges.

'Two days.'

Thea baulked. '*Two days?* And it looks like this?'

'It's organised chaos, I'll have you know, Althea. I know where everything is.'

'Gods help anyone *else* who needs to find something, though,' Thea replied with a laugh.

'But no one would,' Wren said gleefully. 'It's *my* room. My very own.'

Thea knew what that meant. In all the years they'd lived at Thezmarr, neither of them had ever had a space of her own. So Thea reached out and squeezed her sister's shoulder. 'Congratulations, Wren. You deserve it.'

'Thank you.'

Thea waited a beat. 'Did they give you a spare key?'

Wren rounded on her. 'Not a chance, Thea. I only just got rid of you.'

Thea laughed. 'I was only joking… Mostly. You try living with twelve men in your room. They're loud. They stink. And they constantly brag about sleeping with women they've clearly never spoken to.'

'Sounds charming.'

'You have no idea.'

'You should come and visit more, Thea,' Wren said suddenly. 'Sam and Ida miss you. And you've missed a lot in our alchemy shifts. They're throwing me a little party this afternoon to celebrate. You should come.'

'I can't.' Thea gave a heavy sigh. 'I don't have time, Wren. Not if I want to be —'

'A Thezmarrian warrior. A Warsword,' Wren cut her off sharply. '*We know*. We know how important it is to you. But it's not the *only* thing that's important.'

Thea's hand flew to her fate stone. 'It is to me —' She regretted her choice of words as soon as they left her mouth, but she couldn't take them back.

Wren's expression hardened. 'When was the last time I asked anything of you, Thea? When was the last time you did anything for someone other than yourself?'

'It's just a party, Wren…'

'But it's *not* just a party. It's about supporting me, *your sister*. It's about acknowledging that I've achieved something I've been aiming for for years. How would you feel if you became a Warsword and no one gave a shit?'

'It's not the same.'

'Not the same? You mean that being an alchemist isn't as worthy as being a Warsword? That your dreams are bigger and better than the rest of ours?'

'I didn't mean —'

'Yes, you did. And it's fine. If you're so determined to become a Warsword, you go do that, Thea. But when you've cheated death and you want someone to cheer for your victories, don't be surprised if you turn around to find yourself alone.'

'Wren...'

'You have *no idea*, Thea. *No idea* what I do for us, for *you*. And here you are, with your Warsword complex, thinking you're so much better. Do you know where you'd be without me? Do you know what would happen —'

'Wren, please.' A sour taste filled Thea's mouth. She had never seen her sister like this: furious to the point of tears, almost unhinged. What was she talking about? Was it that stunt with the Widow's Ash and Seb? Was it about covering for her with Audra and Farissa? Thea's heart was sinking. This was not how this conversation was meant to go. She *wanted* to celebrate Wren's achievements, she just...

Wren was shaking her head, cheeks flushed in anger. 'I can't stand the sight of you,' she spat. 'Get out. I have silly potions and teapots to make.'

'I didn't say —'

'*Out.*'

Head hung, stomach in knots, Thea left Wren's new room to find Dax waiting for her. But not even the dog's stoic presence padding beside her could pull her from her dark mood, for she had the feeling that there was more to the argument than she knew, that there was something Wren wasn't telling her.

. . .

Over the next few days, Thea turned inward. While she and Wren had bickered and argued their entire lives, this was different. A crack had formed between them, a fissure that grew wider with every day they didn't speak.

Thea had tried to explain, had tried to track Wren down the next day and the next, but her sister was suddenly like a shadow that kept slipping between her fingers. And the thought of Wren celebrating her new position without her made Thea's chest ache. She should have been there.

'What's wrong with you lately?' Cal asked over breakfast, his brow furrowed deeply as he studied her.

'Nothing,' Thea mumbled into her porridge.

'Liar,' Kipp interjected. 'You've been moping for days. And you're not a moper. I've seen you get walloped into the ground by a man twice your size and you hardly blink, so there's definitely something wrong.'

They waited expectantly, to the point of irritation.

'I had a fight with Wren, alright?' Thea snapped.

'What about?' Kipp asked.

Thea sighed. 'I don't know. About me only caring about being a Warsword, or something to that effect.'

'You told her that?'

'Accidentally.'

Cal let out a low whistle. 'Brutal.'

'I didn't mean it.'

'Well, you'd best fix it with her soon. You're not gonna win any apprenticeships by being a sad sap, are you?' Kipp told her.

'Helpful, as always,' she said flatly.

'We could request some leave. Take her down to the Laughing Fox.'

'You and the fucking Laughing Fox, Kipp!' Cal nearly

273

upset his breakfast. 'For the love of all the gods, will you shut up about it? And you git, when has anyone in the history of Thezmarr requested "leave"?'

Thea waved him off. 'It's fine, it's fine. He's only trying —'

'To help, I know. Tell me this though, why is his version of help so annoying?'

Thea twisted in her seat, exchanging a surprised glance with Kipp. 'It appears I'm not the only one in a mood this morning...'

'Oh, don't start.'

But to her surprise, Kipp grinned gleefully. 'Who is she?'

'What?' Cal snapped.

'There's only one way to get you in such a strop and it's certainly not my poor attempts at helping Thea. Who is she?' Kipp winked in Thea's direction.

Suddenly fascinated, Thea watched the tips of Cal's cheeks turn pink.

'We're not having this conversation,' he told them firmly, getting to his feet.

'We are *definitely* having that conversation,' Kipp whispered to Thea as they left the breakfast table. 'Skip your reading and have a jug of mead with us tonight. We'll get it out of him. If anything, it'll make you forget about your sister troubles for an hour or so.'

For the first time in days, Thea smiled. 'Alright,' she told him.

Though the nagging guilt persisted at the back of Thea's mind, she felt lighter throughout the day, grateful for Kipp and Cal, despite his bad mood.

The hours passed in a blur. They finished endurance training; they completed a session of archery and they spent an unusual few hours with the Guild Master himself in the library, where he explained several military strategies the warriors had employed over the years. Kipp was the most eager of their cohort, interrupting regularly with questions and comments. Surprisingly, Osiris didn't seem bothered by this, but rather energised to have a keen contributor. Though Kipp had told Thea of his interest in strategy, she had thought little of it until that afternoon, where it became clear that Kipp's mind was a cut above the rest. What he lacked in coordination and strength, he more than made up for in devious tactics and a vast understanding of how an army worked.

When they left the library, Kipp was practically glowing. 'Incredible isn't it?'

'What?' Cal asked sullenly. 'All the ways men and monsters can kill one another?'

'Exactly,' Kipp beamed. 'In all our time here, you'd be forgiven for thinking that fighting is just swinging a blade or brandishing an axe at someone, but this...' he trailed off for a moment in awe. 'This shows a much bigger picture. It shows cunning and brutality in a much more refined way.'

'And that's admirable?' Cal replied, raising a brow in Thea's direction.

'Of course. Certainly no less admirable than what happens on the battlefield, surely?'

'Come on,' Thea urged, tugging Kipp's sleeve. 'We'll be late.'

'Oh gods, it's combat with the Bloodletter, isn't it?' Her friend quickened his pace instantly.

'Yes, and you know how he gets,' Thea muttered. She had only been in a handful of training sessions with the older Warsword, and what she'd seen had not sat right with her. But right or not, they were due back at the training arena within minutes, and she didn't want to risk his wrath.

Thankfully, they made it in time, their cohort only just gathering around the arena. Thea's body was already taut with anticipation. Since that initial demonstration, she had sparred with a range of partners besides Kipp and Cal, and from each of them, she had learned something new. Over the weeks, she had memorised the rules of engagement, and following Hawthorne's advice, had experimented with how to break them. She had noticed a change in herself. Not only was she physically stronger and faster than before, but she was also more confident. That initial fear of being overpowered had faded and while she was what Torj called a 'scrappy' fighter, she could hold her own against most. Thea relished the physicality of close combat, the impact of the blocks and blows, the ringing in her ears from the clash of steel and the weight of a shield on her arm.

And so when Vernich the Bloodletter walked into the arena, she did not fear him.

But she should have.

The older Warsword was in a foul temper already, she could tell by his clenched jaw and the narrowing of his eyes as he surveyed them.

'Pair up,' he barked.

As always, the instruction caused a second of hesitation in their trio, but Thea relented and turned to find herself another partner. Lachin was one of the few shieldbearers left without an opponent and so, reluctantly, Thea approached him.

He looked around in genuine surprise. 'Really?'

'We're both out of options, it seems,' she replied. She hadn't sparred with him before, always lumping him in with

Seb, whom she did her best to avoid. Because of that, she expected some nasty comment or objection, but he merely shrugged and tossed her a training sword.

'Alright then,' he said, planting his feet apart. 'When you're ready.'

'I'm ready,' Thea told him and launched into an attack. She had learned that most of her fellow shieldbearers expected her to hesitate or take her time, and so she did neither of these things. More often than not, she was the first to strike, and typically it was this tactic that caught her opponent off guard.

Not this opponent.

Lachin was ready. He deflected the first thrust of her practice sword and delivered a powerful blow of his own. Thea didn't know how old Lachin was, or how long he'd been training at Thezmarr, but from the way he moved she guessed it was a damn sight longer than her.

But it didn't intimidate her. She was stronger and faster than she'd ever been, and she had an edge that no one knew about - she always fought like her fate depended on it, because it did.

And so she advanced without pause, throwing a high, horizontal cut from her strong side to Lachin's weak side, his wooden blade looping around to meet her own with a strong, two-handed strike. The impact vibrated up Thea's arms and she grinned. She lived for this, for the challenge, for the fight.

Lachin was grinning too. 'You're better than before.'

'I know,' Thea replied, slicing again.

This time, he nearly failed to block – *nearly*, before striking again.

'You didn't want to use a shield?' Lachin joked.

And Thea suddenly realised that he *was* joking, not mocking… Something had shifted in the dynamic.

She flashed him another grin. 'Don't need one with you.'

Lachin snorted and attempted an upward cut with the back edge of his blade, but she deflected it, cutting him off and managing to momentarily hook his blade under hers, drawing it down as she delivered a swift kick to his exposed side.

He grunted at the impact.

Thea drew back and circled him. 'Tired yet?' she teased.

'You're dreaming —'

'*You fucking useless idiot!*' Vernich's bellow echoed across the entire arena, bringing everyone's sparring to a standstill. The sound of a fist cracking bone followed his words.

Thea froze, exchanging a look of alarm with her opponent. Panic latched its claws into her heart as she scanned the shieldbearer pairs, dread sinking in her gut. She spotted the Warsword's hulking frame almost immediately.

He stood towering over Kipp, who was clutching his bleeding face, doubled over.

Thea's throat constricted, and she thought she might choke.

Vernich crowded her friend, his face flushed, his lip curled in a snarl. 'You can barely hold a sword, you pathetic piece of shit.'

Cal took a step forward. 'Sir, it was my —'

But Vernich grabbed the front of his shirt in his fist and threw him backwards with enough force that he barrelled into several shieldbearers behind him.

'Stay out of it,' Vernich growled, advancing once more on Kipp.

Thea's breathing became quick and shallow, her hands

suddenly shaking at her sides. He couldn't do this, could he? None of the other commanders or masters had laid a hand on the shieldbearers.

Vernich struck Kipp again, sending him sprawling in the dirt with a moan.

Thea's feet were moving before she had time to think, blood roaring in her ears, spots floating in her vision.

Sensing her movement, Vernich whirled around, his eyes locking on hers. Thea flinched at the hatred she saw there, fear clenched its fist around her.

'You...' Vernich spat, taking a step towards her, casting his shadow over her. 'You're just as worthless as he is. What were they thinking, letting a *woman* into the guild?'

Behind him, Cal had rushed to Kipp's side, and was struggling to get him to his feet, all the while staring at Thea in horror.

'Let this be a lesson to you all,' Vernich shouted to the rest of them. 'Don't go where you don't belong.'

Thea couldn't feel her fingers or toes, feeling smothered as Vernich closed the gap between them.

'You wanted to be one of us?' he said, quietly this time. 'Then show us how much.'

Thea fought to keep her panic under control again, her chest tightening by the second. She could hear the scrape of Kipp's boots in the dirt as Cal dragged him upright. She could hear the laboured sounds of his breath, could smell the metallic tang of the blood that leaked from his mouth.

She lifted her gaze to Vernich's and waited.

'You are to deliver his punishment,' the Warsword ordered. 'Three blows.'

Thea stared at him, suddenly desperate to believe that someone would step in at any moment.

Vernich gave a nasty smile. 'If the blows aren't enough, the humiliation will be.'

Thea allowed herself a glance at Kipp. He was hanging in Cal's arms, one of his eyes was swollen shut but he still met her gaze and tried to nod, to give her permission for the brutality that was asked of her.

'No.'

Vernich folded his arms over his chest and loomed over her. 'What did you say?'

Thea forced herself to swallow the lump in her throat and lift her chin. 'No,' she repeated.

'I wasn't asking.' Vernich's voice was laced with violence.

Thea unclenched her jaw. 'I said no.'

Vernich's hand flew out, grabbing her by the collar of her shirt and shoving her towards Kipp and Cal.

She stumbled, but kept herself on her feet, despite her knees buckling.

'Then you'll be punished alongside him,' Vernich roared, his face reddening again. He whirled to the crowd and pointed at Sebastos Barlowe. 'You,' he commanded. 'You do it. Three blows a piece. If they're not on the ground crying for their mothers by the end...' He didn't need to finish his threat.

Seb, however, needed no incentive to take part in something so vile. As he stalked towards Thea, the expression splitting his face was one of triumph, of sadistic joy.

Standing before her, Seb cracked his knuckles menacingly, but she refused to flinch.

This is going to hurt, she told herself, *but I won't give him the satisfaction. I will stay on my feet. I will not cry.*

Thea was mid-breath when his fist collided with her gut,

sending her reeling backwards, snatching all the air from her lungs. Pain barrelled into her, her hands clutching her stomach as she gasped desperately. Coughing and spluttering, her eyes streamed, but she forced herself to straighten, meeting Seb's satisfied gaze defiantly. She couldn't speak, but she let her eyes say what she knew would pierce his fragile ego.

Is that the best you've got? she taunted.

Thea saw the second hit coming, but it made no difference. There was no way to brace herself against the impact, no way to lessen the pain or the panic that came with having the air knocked out of her so soon after the first.

She doubled over, a ragged wheeze escaping her as her insides spasmed. Intense pain burst through her midsection, almost forcing her stomach up through her throat. Nausea followed and Thea's legs threatened to give out from under her, but sheer willpower forced her upright once again. Her vision blurred this time and she could feel saliva hanging from her mouth, but she remained unbroken.

The final blow caught her off guard. This time, Seb's fist struck her on the side, the sharp agony sending her sprawling across the dirt. But this pain had been different, not only for its location, but...

Thea's shirt was wet.

Looking down, she saw red leaking from her side.

'You bastard!' someone shouted, and Thea looked up in time to see a flash of silver between Seb's knuckles before it disappeared into his pocket.

'He fucking stabbed her!' cried someone else.

But Thea was too battered to register what he'd done to her. She cared about one thing. It didn't matter that her eyes were streaming, or that she had spit on her chin.

If they're not on the ground crying for their mothers by the end...

With those words ringing in her head, clutching her bleeding side and choking down the need to vomit, Althea Nine Lives got to her feet.

'Can't even beat a girl, Seb,' she wheezed, spitting blood on the ground.

Humiliation and fury blazing in his eyes, he launched himself at her.

Only to be sent flying back into the dirt.

'What in the realms is going on here?' Torj the Bear Slayer bellowed, his gaze shooting to Vernich in disbelief.

The older Warsword eyed him with dislike before he shrugged. 'Usual shieldbearer hazing,' he said before shouting to the rest of them, 'You're all dismissed.'

Like the coward Seb was, he left in the Bloodletter's shadow. Dizzy, Thea gazed after them for a moment.

You're only here because your uncle is friends with the Guild Master,' Cal had said all that time ago in the woods. It suddenly made sense that Seb faced so few consequences for his actions.

Torj turned to Thea, gripping her by the shoulders. 'What happened?' he asked, staring at the blood staining her shirt. Cal was helping Kipp limp to her side.

Thea could feel the rest of the shieldbearers lingering around them, and she knew she had a choice. All that time ago, Cal and Kipp had told her of the code of silence between shieldbearers and she'd be damned if she would be the one to break it. And if Seb truly had an in with the Guild Master, then snitching would do her no good.

Forcing her hand to drop casually from her bleeding side,

she straightened, suppressing a wince. 'Nothing, Sir,' she said.

'Doesn't look like fucking nothing.'

Thea was struggling to remain upright; were it not for the big hands gripping her shoulders, she would have swayed.

'It was nothing,' she repeated, tasting the blood between her teeth.

'Thea's right,' someone called. 'Just some hazing that got out of hand.'

'Yeah, Sir. Barlowe was just being his usual bastard self,' Lachin chimed in. 'Nothing Thea can't handle.'

Was she hearing correctly? Or had the blows to her gut gone to her head? What were they —

'Didn't you see Seb's face, Sir?' Cal chimed in. 'Thea had him.'

Cal's voice in the mix anchored her and fuelled her understanding. The shieldbearers weren't condoning Vernich or Seb's actions. They weren't downplaying her suffering... They were supporting her choice not to say anything. The shieldbearers, including Lachin, of all people, had her back.

Scanning the determined faces around them, Torj released her, and somehow, she managed to stay standing.

'Just a few knocks and scratches, Sir,' she rasped.

The Warsword radiated fury, no doubt recalling the last threats he'd made when he'd discovered the trainees at violent odds with one another, but as no one objected to her story, nor offered the truth of the matter, Torj's hands were tied.

'Fine,' he snapped. 'If you say so.' He turned to the group.

'You're all due back at the fortress. I suggest you make quick work of it.'

When he had gone, it was Lachin who looped his arm through Thea's and helped her towards the gates. 'That was some serious grit back there...' he muttered.

Thea sucked in a painful breath. 'Didn't –' she gasped again – 'think... I had it... in me?'

'I'll never doubt you again.'

'Better... Better have those three silvers...' she trailed off.

'Oh, they're ready and waiting for Kipp. I'd give them to him now if he could walk straight.'

Thea glanced back to see Cal hauling their friend up the grassy knoll. He'd taken head hits from a Warsword. He was likely to have a concussion, or worse.

When they reached the gates, Thea slid her arm from Lachin's. 'Thanks,' she muttered.

'You don't need help...?'

Oh, she needed help alright, but while the shock of it all kept her upright, Thea shook her head. 'Defeats the purpose, doesn't it?'

'I get it,' he said, giving her a nod of understanding before striding off towards the hall.

Thea paused to lean against the doors. Her body had taken a battering unlike anything she'd experienced before and she could still feel the warm trickle of fresh blood flowing from her wound. Despite how she'd left things with Wren, she needed to find her sister. The shock was bound to wear off, and when it did she knew she'd be in trouble.

If she'd attended more healing classes with the girls, she might know how to temporarily treat herself, but aside from staunching the bleeding, she knew little else about combat injuries. Her shieldbearer lessons hadn't covered that topic yet.

She tried to take some small satisfaction in that she'd shown everyone, including Vernich the Bloodletter, that Sebastos Barlowe couldn't bring her down. She had shown them all that she was unbreakable, and that she belonged at Thezmarr. But all of that would be for nothing if she died in the hallway.

Thea winced as she took her first solo steps. 'You can do this,' she muttered. The wound in her side had not stopped bleeding and the light-headedness she was experiencing told her the blood loss was taking its toll.

There was no sign of Cal and Kipp and from that she knew that they'd gone straight to the infirmary, which was where she should be going.

She staggered down the corridor, leaning against the wall for support. *I have to find Wren. I have to find Wren.* The words became a chant in her head as she turned a corner and her breathing became more shallow. She just needed to reach Wren's rooms, then all would be well. Spots swam in her vision as her hand found the cool surface of a door handle and she turned it, stumbling inside.

It was pitch-black and even in her dazed state, Thea knew she was not where she'd intended to be. A rasping wheeze escaped her and she knew she had reached her limit, that she could go no further. Her back hit a cold stone wall, and she leaned her head against it. She just needed to rest for a moment. She just needed to gather her strength. Then she could find Wren. Wren would know what to do. Wren always did.

Thea's knees quivered under her weight and she felt herself sliding —

The door flew open and a huge figure blocked out the light from the corridor.

'Gods,' a deep voice sounded, a melody that skated along her bones.

She knew that voice.

Large but gentle hands were peeling her blood-soaked shirt from her side. A callused finger lifted her chin.

'Who.' Hawthorne demanded. 'Who did this to you?'

CHAPTER TWENTY-THREE

The Warsword caught her as her legs finally gave out and she slid to the floor.

'Who did this?' he demanded again, his firm hands circling her waist. His silver eyes surveyed her with a fiery expression.

His words sent a crackle of fire through Thea, but she gritted her teeth.

Hawthorne's hand brushed her side. 'You truly won't tell me who did that to you?'

Thea's lungs rattled. 'No.' It wasn't his fight, it was hers.

'I could easily find out,' he warned. 'I could punish them in ways you couldn't even imagine.'

For a brief second Thea pictured Seb strung up and bleeding, all manner of horrors inflicted upon him. But she shook her head. 'You could, but you won't,' she replied, her voice raw.

'Won't I?'

'No. You wouldn't take that from me.'

'What is it I wouldn't take?' This time, the question seemed loaded.

But Thea met his stare, coming back to herself. 'Vengeance,' she said.

The Warsword's nostrils flared, but his intense expression softened after a moment. 'No,' he agreed slowly. 'I wouldn't take that from you.'

Thea felt suddenly cold and confused; she became aware of the tiny, cramped space and how close the warrior seemed.

'Where are we?' she managed, her eyes heavy.

'A broom closet,' Hawthorne answered as he tore her shirt down the middle and studied the wound.

Up top, Thea wore a tight band of material around her breasts and her fate stone, but nothing more. She was too dazed to feel embarrassed as he peeled the rest of the fabric away from her battered body.

He swore softly at the state of her. 'It's deep,' he murmured.

Everything was spinning and Thea felt completely untethered from herself. 'Why?' she mumbled.

'Why what?' His hands were hot on her cold, clammy skin as he pressed his fingers around the puncture.

She inhaled sharply through her teeth at the pain. 'Why are we in a broom closet?'

'Don't ask me. I followed the trail of blood here.'

'I... I was trying to find my sister. She... she can help.'

Hawthorne was tearing her shirt into strips now. 'We have to stop the bleeding first.' His fingertips brushed her skin as he wrapped the lengths of linen around her. 'This is going to hurt.'

Thea didn't register what he was doing until the strips

tightened at her middle, crushing her tender abdomen and pressing painfully against her stab wound. Agony lanced through her and a strained gasp escaped, her hand shooting out, gripping his forearm, finding the strength there comforting.

He let her hold on to him as he reached for something with his other hand. From a pouch at his belt, he produced a dried leaf and held it to her mouth. 'Chew on this,' he ordered.

Thea's lips touched his skin as she did as she was told, the plant bitter on her tongue.

'It should make you more alert, keep you from falling unconscious,' he told her, checking the makeshift bandage at her side. 'I need you to stay with me, alright?'

Thea swallowed the herb with a grimace and almost instantly, she felt her senses prickle back to life. The first thing she noticed was that she was still touching Hawthorne, her hand wrapped around the corded bulk of his forearm. The second thing was that his hand was resting against the curve of her bare waist. Warmth radiated from his skin and she had to fight the instinct to lean in and savour his scent.

He went taut, as though he, too, had noticed where their bodies met.

'Whatever it is you're thinking, we can't,' he growled. 'You're half-dead, Alchemist.'

'I didn't say anything.'

'You didn't need to.'

'My mind isn't the only one that went there, Warsword.'

She could see his jaw working where he ground his teeth.

'How did this happen?' he asked instead, motioning to her injuries. 'Can you tell me that at least?'

Thea's side throbbed terribly and an icy shiver raked

across her skin, but neither sensation was enough to distract her from him. 'Training,' she managed.

'You're not using steel yet. How?'

Wincing as she steadied herself, Thea gritted out: 'There were punishments to oversee, apparently.'

Fire blazed in that icy stare; the only sign that he'd heard her. For a moment, he was unnaturally still before he spoke again.

'Do you think you can stand?' he said softly. 'Thea?' he prompted, when she didn't respond straight away.

He'd used her name. Not 'Alchemist', not even Althea, but *Thea*...

She found her voice hoarse when she spoke. 'I think so.'

Slowly, he helped her to her feet, her whole body trembling with the effort. He draped his cloak around her bare shoulders, pulling it closed across her banded chest at the front.

He can probably feel my thundering heart, she thought, glancing down at where his knuckles brushed her skin, where they lingered.

And there, in the dim light of the cramped closet, for a moment she forgot about the pulsing pain at her side and her maimed abdomen, she forgot about Seb and Vernich and their cruelty entirely... Instead, she focused on the subtle hum of Hawthorne's body. Her eyes caught his, and they simply stared at one another before his gaze dropped to her lips.

Am I delirious? she wondered, warmth flooding her.

'You could have died in here,' he said, something unrecognisable in his tone before strained lightness sounded. 'Some legend you would have been then... The alchemist who keeled over in a broom closet.'

Thea's heart raced, her fingers itching to hold her fate stone, to press it into his warm palm and tell him what it meant, what it *truly* meant. Enovius wouldn't take her, not yet.

Instead, she shook her head and stepped away from the Warsword, opening the door. 'No,' she told him. 'I couldn't have.'

Torchlight from the corridor flooded the tiny closet and as soon as she was outside, she inhaled the cold air, instantly missing the closeness of his body, her skin still tingling.

Hawthorne still looked tense. 'If you're going to be a warrior of Thezmarr,' he said. 'You need to learn more than fighting.'

'More wisdom for me today?' She sounded weak.

'You will need friends in this fortress, you will need a team. You need to learn to tend to wounds. You'll have plenty of them. As will your friends. So if not for your own sake, learn for theirs.'

Thea thought of Wren and Ida and Sam, then Cal and Kipp as well. Sometimes she tried to convince herself she didn't need them, that they were better off without her, a young woman with one foot already in her grave...

'I haven't noticed you with any friends.' Thea hadn't meant to say it aloud, but it was too late to take it back.

Hawthorne gave her a piercing look and ignored her comment. 'Every discipline this fortress offers has a vital part to play. You should respect them all. You should master them all. There is more to this guild than blades and fists.'

'So my sister tells me,' Thea heard herself say.

'And you should listen. She knows what she's talking about.'

Hawthorne supported her all the way to Wren's rooms, where the door flew open upon their approach.

Her sister's eyes were wild with panic and she was instantly at Thea's side, looping Thea's arm over her shoulder, taking her weight from Hawthorne.

'I'll take it from here,' Wren told him.

The Warsword hesitated in the doorway.

'Thank you for helping my sister,' she said rather tersely, before closing the door in his face.

Thea was too exhausted to protest her sister's rudeness, or voice that she wanted him to stay.

Wren helped her inside and gently lowered her onto the bed. 'Callahan has all the alchemists out looking for you. He told us what happened. Gods, Thea. Why didn't you send for me? You know I would have —' Her words came out in a terrified flurry and her voice broke at the end. 'No matter what shit was happening between us, *you're my sister.*'

'I know,' Thea managed. 'I was coming to find you.'

'Then where in the midrealms were you?' Wren exclaimed, pulling back the heavy cloak to get a look at the bloodstained linen binding her midsection. Then she froze, noticing the dark wool between her fingers.

'This is the Warsword's cloak,' she said.

Thea gave a nod of confirmation, and she watched her sister stiffen.

'The Hand of Death himself gave you his cloak?' Wren asked. When Thea didn't bother confirming this, she weighed her words, chewing the inside of her cheek before meeting Thea's questioning gaze. 'I...' she struggled. 'I don't like him.'

'Since when do you have strong opinions about any

Warsword?' Her breath whistled between her teeth as Wren examined her injuries.

'I have strong opinions about everyone, thank you very much.' Wren sighed again. 'Since one seems to trail my sister.'

Thea laughed and then gasped at the sharp pain that lanced through her. 'He does not,' she wheezed.

Wren perched on the edge of the bed, no amusement there. 'Stay away from him, Thee... He's the worst one. I know you think they're noble —'

'Some of them,' Thea muttered, clutching her side.

'But the stories I've heard about Wilder Hawthorne...' Wren continued carefully. 'They'd make even your stomach turn. He's dangerous.'

'Of course he's dangerous. He's called the Hand of Death, for fuck's sake. They're all dangerous, that's sort of the point, isn't it?'

Wren was shaking her head. 'People talk, Thea. He's a monster, more so than those he slays. He brings back the hearts of the creatures he kills... Trophies. That's what the fortress staff say.'

'Gossip,' Thea retorted. 'Bored, nosy —'

'Listen to me for once,' Wren hissed. 'I've seen it. I've had to take... supplies to him. I saw those bleeding black hearts for myself.'

Thea's own heart stuttered, a memory suddenly coming back to her. Hadn't she seen Hawthorne enter Thezmarr on the night of his initial return, a sack dripping with blood in his hands?

But Thea shook her head. 'He helped me. He stopped the bleeding. Gave me some leaf to chew.'

Wren looked up, alarmed. 'What was it?'

'Uhhh…'

'Oh, for Furies' sake, Thea. You did alchemy for over a decade, you don't know what he gave you?'

'It was a dried herb,' Thea said defensively. 'Tasted bitter. He told me it would stop me from losing consciousness.'

'Oh,' Wren sighed with relief. 'That's just iruseed.'

'Why the concern?'

'Warswords have all sorts of strange drugs on them. I thought for a moment he'd given you a particular stimulant they use.'

'I was halfway to Enovius, Wren. It wouldn't have mattered what he gave me.'

Her sister snorted, the tension dissipating. 'Here I was thinking you couldn't die… Lie back and stop fidgeting.' Wren carefully removed the bloody linen strips and brewed some sort of terrible smelling tincture as she cleaned the wound thoroughly.

Thea grit her teeth through the pain. The open gash stung terribly through her sister's ministrations. She grimaced. 'Can you open the window? That stuff you're brewing stinks.'

Wren did as she asked and then went to the small cauldron to stir whatever nightmare concoction she was making. Her brow furrowed as she worked, and Thea knew that to mean her mind was on something else entirely.

'Wren?' she said, trying to sit up.

'Don't!' her sister cried. 'You'll open that wound back up. You should have had stitches.'

'I was just going to say… I'm sorry,' Thea told her. 'For the other day. For what I said. It's not what I meant. You know I care —'

'Oh shut up,' Wren cut in, waving her off. 'I know all that.'

'Then what are you thinking?'

A flash of anger crossed Wren's face, her celadon eyes narrowing. 'You were stabbed, Althea...'

'I'm aware.'

'Your way of besting that bastard, Seb Barlowe, was to allow him to beat you half to death and stick a blade between your ribs?' Wren took the cauldron off the small stove and poured the steaming liquid into a bowl.

The smell of it made Thea's eyes water. 'I didn't say it was the perfect plan. But it's about the long game, Wren.'

Wren faced her, her hands on her hips. 'Oh? Since when? I've never known you to strategise past your next meal.'

Thea gave her sister a slow smile. 'Since I realised legends aren't forged overnight.'

Thea spent the night in her sister's rooms, where Wren watched her like a hawk. As the hours passed, her abdomen became a patchwork of purple that Wren insisted on poking and monitoring, going so far as to trace the outline of bruising with ink. Thea was too tired to argue with her and it was a relief to not have to be on her guard. She would have even preferred the broom closet to going through this in her own dormitory, so Wren's cosy quarters were an improvement indeed.

At some point in the night, there was a soft knock at the door and Thea heard low voices outside, but she couldn't focus on what they were saying and soon drifted back to sleep.

Thea dreamt of the seer and the fate stone, the jade as green as ever against the pale skin of her palm.

'*Remember me*,' the words came as they always did, laced

with magic and mystery and the promise of death. She remembered the relief in Hawthorne's voice when she'd told him it didn't belong to her. *What would he say if he knew the truth?* And why, in the name of all the gods, did she care? She'd lived with the knowledge since she was an infant, why the need to share it now?

In the early hours of the morning, Wren woke her to check she was still alive, which seemed ridiculous to Thea. But again, she didn't argue, merely surrendered to her sister's interrogation and examination. She demanded to know about tingling sensations in her hands and feet, or if Thea was experiencing shortness of breath or pain.

All of those things, Thea had muttered.

And Wren had sworn, banging about her room to make more terrible smelling poultices and tonics while Thea sweated through the sheets. Either her sister had a real grasp of the healing art, or she simply enjoyed torturing Thea.

When dawn filtered through the grimy window, Thea opened her eyes a crack to find Wren asleep in the chair beside the bed, a bowl of bloodied fabric at her feet. Her hair was dishevelled, she still wore the same clothes from yesterday, and she had dark smudges of exhaustion beneath her eyes.

Thea hated to wake her, but she knew her sister would murder her if she allowed her to miss one of her beloved shifts.

'You'll hurt your neck like that,' she said quietly.

Wren stirred slowly, her hands moving to rub her temples. 'Gods,' she muttered. 'I feel like I drank a barrel of wine.' She pulled a disgusted face as she wiped her mouth. 'I taste like it too.'

296

'Might have been all those delicious fumes wafting around here last night.'

'That's the thanks I get?' she grumbled, rubbing the back of her neck with a grimace. 'How are you feeling?'

Thea winced as she ever so slowly sat up. 'Like I got pummelled and stabbed by a savage.'

'Good to know he didn't beat the humour out of you.' Wren got to her feet and stretched. 'You can stay here for the day to recover.'

'No, can't do that,' Thea told her.

Wren turned to her, hands on hips. 'Don't you dare, Althea. Not after I've stayed up all night worrying about you and treating you. Don't you dare go back out and get yourself —'

'I thought I'd come with you today.' Thea suppressed a smile. Everyone always thought she was the hot-headed one, but Wren could give her a run for her coin when she wanted to.

'With me?' Wren baulked. 'What? To alchemy? To the healer's studio? To —'

Thea waved her off. 'Yes, yes. To all the above.'

'But…'

'There's more to being a Thezmarrian warrior than fighting,' she said, her cheeks heating at the thought of the Warsword who'd shared that very sentiment with her.

The look of shock on her sister's face told Thea just how single-minded she had been in the past.

No longer, she vowed. If she was going to be a warrior, a legend of the guild, then she needed to get her head out of her arse. She was in no condition to train today and she let go of that furious pride that told her she needed to show her face. Standing around to prove to Seb that he hadn't broken her was not a clever use of her time and with only eight weeks standing between her and the initiation test, she needed to be clever with her time now more than ever.

Wren was standing in the doorway waiting for her. 'You're really coming?'

'Yes.' Slowly drawing her legs over the side of the bed and planting her feet on the ground, Thea tested her ability to hold her own weight.

'You really should rest today,' but Wren had said it weakly, knowing that once her mind was made up, there was no changing it.

'Do you have a staff or... something I can use to support myself?' Thea was wobbly and she was already short of breath, but the last thing she wanted was to delay Wren. She was a master's apprentice now. She had duties and responsibilities beyond showing up for work at the Alchemy workshop.

Wren scanned her cluttered room. 'Will this do?' She pulled several empty pots hanging from a rod by the window and gave it to Thea, who tested it tentatively.

'It's fine, thank you.'

Wren gave her a strange look that Thea couldn't read. Unless... Was it a *surprise*? Had she not voiced her gratitude before? Thea opened her mouth to say more, but her sister was already bustling about the room, collecting things and forcing another horrible tonic down Thea's throat.

Coughing and spluttering, Thea did everything she was told without complaint and when at last they were ready, she followed her into the corridor, shuffling along with her makeshift staff.

'If that wound starts bleeding again, you tell me

immediately,' Wren ordered. 'We will not be testing the fates today.'

Thea gave her a salute and a smile. 'As you say.'

'Why aren't you like this all the time?' Wren muttered as they made their way to the workshop. 'You're far more agreeable.'

'Someone has to keep you on your toes, sister.'

Wren rolled her eyes.

When they entered the Alchemy workshop, the chatter fell silent as all eyes went to Thea.

She spotted Ida and Sam at their usual table, their grins faltering as they took in her staff and sickly pallor. Thea tried to give them a reassuring wave.

'What's this?' Farissa said from the front of the room. 'A lost lamb returned to the herd?'

'Only for a little while, Farissa,' Thea replied. 'If you'll have me.'

The older woman smiled. 'There's always a place for you here, Althea.'

Thea nodded in thanks and shuffled towards her old place at her sister's side. When she reached the workbench, she was drenched in sweat and panting. Thankfully, her sister had procured a stool for her and she sat down with a grateful grimace.

'So,' she rasped. 'How's the Ladies' Luncheon design coming along?'

Wren beamed. 'I'll show you.'

Thea spent the next hour or so listening to her sister intently. She had always known Wren was brilliant, but this... The quaint teapot, complete with its floral embellishments and delicate features, was a weapon. How had it taken Thea so long to realise that Wren was just as much a Thezmarrian warrior as the rest? That she was creating devices to dispatch poison to their enemies, that the guild was relying on her for the subtle art of chemical warfare?

Thea drank in every word and followed every instruction, fascinated by Wren's mind and her cunning nature. Where the Warswords were the face of Thezmarr, the Alchemists were the silent killers, the shadows in the night. Thea's chest swelled with pride; she had no doubt that one day Wren would run this place.

When the shift was finished, she told Wren she wanted to visit Kipp and, to her surprise, her sister insisted on accompanying her.

The infirmary was in the lower levels of the southwest tower and took up an entire floor. Once upon a time it had been used with far more frequency than it was now, when Thezmarr's warriors were returning from battle wounded in droves. Despite her many injuries over the years, the only time Thea had stepped foot in the infirmary was when she had tried to return Malik's dagger to him... As she and Wren passed the rows of empty, narrow beds, she felt a pang at its loss.

'I've only met these men in passing,' Wren was saying. 'It's about time I got to know who's living with my only sister, day in, day out.'

The chuckle on Thea's lips died when they entered the far side of the healer's wing and found Kipp lying in one of the beds. Half his face was swollen beyond recognition.

Thea rushed to his side. 'Gods, Kipp... Look what he did to you...'

He blinked at her with his good eye. 'Fractured cheekbone, fractured eye socket...' he said hoarsely. 'So I'm told. They're keeping me here under observation, lest I have damage to my brain. I told them I'm always like this, though.'

A strangled laugh escaped Thea, though her heart ached for him.

'Worth it,' he told her as he tried to sit up.

Thea gaped at him. 'How so?'

'Well, you brought your lovely sister to sit by my bedside...'

Thea slapped his arm lightly, perching herself on the side of his bed. 'You're shameless.' She beckoned Wren forward. 'Wren, this is my friend Kipp, Kipp, this is my sister Elwren.'

'I'm thrilled to officially meet you, Elwren Zoltaire, sister of the unbreakable Thea,' Kipp said with as much of a grin as his facial swelling would allow. 'I assure you, I'm usually a lot more handsome.'

Wren laughed. 'I saw you before the injuries, Kipp.'

He pressed a hand to his chest in mock offence. 'Brutal as well as beautiful. I like you.'

Thea shook her head, throwing her sister a silent apology for her friend. 'Good to know you're still in there, Kipp.'

'Oh, you know it'd take more than a Warsword's swinging fists to rattle the spark from me. I think he was trying to knock some sense into me, alas, he failed miserably. Did I tell you about the time I got so drunk at the Laughing Fox I tried to arm wrestle a soldier from Battalon?'

Thea snorted. 'Was that before or after the raven-haired beauty?'

'Who could say, Thea? Who could say,' Kipp murmured before surveying her with a critical eye. 'How are you?'

'Better than you, by the look of things.'

'That's debatable.'

'I'm fine.'

She heard Wren's irritated huff before she spoke. 'You're decidedly *not* fine,' her sister snapped. 'You were *stabbed* and you have *internal injuries* to your abdomen. If you weren't such a stubborn fool, you'd be in the bed alongside your friend here.'

Thea gave Kipp a conspirator's grin. 'Unfortunately, just as there's no beating the spark from Kipp, there's no beating the stubborn from me.'

'I know that, or I would have tried already,' Wren told them.

Kipp gave a pained chuckle. 'That I'd pay to see.'

Smiling, Thea squeezed Kipp's hand, finding it cold and clammy. 'Where's Cal?'

'Training,' Kipp replied. 'At least he'd better be. Someone needs to represent our misfit trio.'

Thea didn't miss the wince as he spoke. 'Are you alright?'

His breathing became more laboured. 'The headaches come and go… Some are worse than others.'

Wren stepped in. 'He needs rest, Thea,' she said gently. 'Is there anything we can bring you, Kipp?'

'A growler of sour mead from the Laughing Fox wouldn't go astray…' he replied weakly.

Thea laughed. 'When you're better, we'll get you back there. Maybe even find that girl you're always on about.'

Kipp gave a weary smile before he fell back into his pillow, his good eye closed and his chest rose and fell steadily in sleep.

'Come, Thea,' her sister whispered. 'Let him rest.'

Thea wasn't prepared for the swell of emotion rising in her chest to her throat. 'Do you think he'll be okay?'

'With time,' Wren said, gently pulling her towards the door.

But Thea yanked her out of the way – her wound screaming as two figures staggered into the infirmary.

Esyllt was crumbling beneath the weight of Vernich the Bloodletter, whose face was a patchwork of swelling and bruising, not dissimilar to Kipp's. The two men shoved right past Thea and Wren, deep in conversation.

'The man is unhinged.' Vernich was saying through gritted, blood-streaked teeth.

'Far be it from me to interfere with Warsword business —'

'Then don't.'

'But I've never known Hawthorne to strike without reason.'

Vernich shoved Esyllt away. 'You think this savagery was justified?' Blood sprayed from his mouth.

Esyllt merely shrugged. 'An interesting question coming from you. We all thought you revered lessons instilled with violence.'

'Fuck off, Esyllt.'

'With pleasure,' the weapons master retorted, sweeping from the room without another word, leaving Thea and Wren staring after the bloodied Warsword in shock.

WILDER HAWTHORNE

S omeone had hurt her. *Badly.* Whatever codes of duty and honour Wilder was bound by, they splintered in the face of that.

His hands were still stained with her blood.

That alone was enough to undo him. He wasn't sure when he had crossed the line, or at what point the infuriating alchemist had become someone he'd break rules for...

And break rules for her he had, for it was not just her blood on his hands, not now that he'd delivered swift and brutal justice to Vernich Warner. As his fists had collided with his fellow Warsword's face, splitting skin, fracturing bone, Wilder knew it was reckless, as reckless as the alchemist was... But he didn't care. Vernich deserved what he got.

He scoffed at the notion of that bastard as someone's mentor, then at the image of *himself* as a mentor. It was yet another reason Wilder was against the whole idea of masters and apprentices. Warswords were inherently selfish, the lot of them. And one way or another, they always let you down.

And Althea had been let down in the most violent way.

Though, if the state of Vernich's face was anything to go by, that wouldn't be happening again.

Wilder longed to deliver the same savagery to that prick, Sebastos Barlowe. It had only taken one look at the smug shieldbearer's face to know he'd been responsible for the stab wound to Thea's ribs. And that nepotism alone had allowed him to go unpunished. But she had been right. He wouldn't take her vengeance from her, and her vengeance would come eventually, he'd make sure of it.

With the fire crackling heartily in the living room, Wilder stood at the basin in his cabin, scrubbing the blood from his hands with soapy water. As he worked, he tried not to relive how Thea had fallen into his arms, her face drained of colour, her body limp, almost lifeless. The fear that had gripped him, that still sat like a stone in the pit of his gut, was unlike anything he had felt before; a desperate beast clawing him raw from within.

When he'd treated her wound and given her the dried iruseed, that terror had ebbed away for a moment, replaced by something similarly primal. In the dark recess of that broom cupboard, his body had come alive in her presence, and he'd wanted nothing more than to care for her, to protect her.

Muttering a curse to himself, he took a hard brush to his fingernails, scrubbing roughly to get rid of the blood beneath them, taking no care for his split, bruised knuckles.

A heavy knock sounded at the door, sparing him from his thoughts.

'Heard you gave our Bloodletter a beating and a half,' Torj

Elderbrock said, pushing past Wilder into the cabin and settling into one of the armchairs.

'Make yourself at home,' Wilder muttered, closing the door behind him.

'I come bearing gifts at least,' Torj replied, waving a dark bottle at him from his seat.

Wilder gave a heavy sigh. 'Fine.'

'There's the warm welcome I was after.'

'Perhaps it's time you lowered your expectations.' Wilder fetched two glasses from the cabinet and sank into the armchair beside his comrade. 'What brings you out here, anyway?'

'Came to make sure you weren't in the same state as our esteemed brother in arms.'

Wilder snorted. 'Please. He didn't even land a blow.' He motioned to the bottle in Torj's hand. 'Did you bring it for decoration, or are you actually going to open it?'

'Thirsty are we?' Torj laughed before removing the cork with his teeth and splashing amber liquid into each glass.

Wilder fucking *hated* the fire extract everyone bought from Marise, but knocked it back in a single swig anyway, the liquor burning his throat and warming his belly instantly.

'Looks like you need it, brother.'

'Give me a real pour next time.'

Torj chuckled again and refilled the glass, a more generous dram this time. 'So what was this thing with Vernich about?'

'As if you don't know,' Wilder grunted, nursing his drink. 'Heard you were there at the end.'

'You mean with the shieldbearers? Thought you didn't care about their training?'

'I don't. But it's hardly a good look for the guild when two end up half dead thanks to a Warsword's lessons.'

'No,' Torj agreed, sipping his own drink thoughtfully. 'I tried to intervene, but you know what they're like. That fucking code of theirs doesn't allow for —'

'I don't care what it doesn't allow for.'

'You saying I should have done more? That I should have forced it out of them? Humiliated —'

Wilder made a frustrated noise. 'I don't know.'

Torj let him stew for a moment before he said, 'Attacking Vernich was a mistake.'

'No shit.'

'Now he knows you care for the lady shieldbearer.'

'I don't.'

Torj laughed darkly. 'You can't play that game with me.'

Wilder took a long sip, letting the liquor ease his temper. 'It doesn't matter. She's nominated you to be her mentor after the initiation.'

'Has she now?' Torj raised an eyebrow. 'My popularity never ceases to amaze me.'

'I feel the same way about your idiocy.'

'You say idiocy, I say charm,' Torj replied. 'Why wouldn't you take her on yourself?'

'You know my thoughts about that whole dynamic.'

'I do. Not that it matters. You'll have an apprentice whether you want one or not. Why not choose the one you... like best?'

'It's not that simple.'

'Isn't it? Fuck, Hawthorne... Starling really did a number on you. You ever going to tell me what happened out there? What did he do that was so terrible? I only ever hear good things.'

'He left, Torj,' Wilder snapped. 'That's all you need to know. He fucking left when he shouldn't have. When he'd made vows not to. And for what? Some —'

'He's hardly the first Warsword to leave Thezmarr,' Torj cut in. 'In case you haven't noticed, there's only the bloody three of us left.'

'And look at the state of the realms. All sorts of monsters are slipping through the Veil. Darkness gathering on the horizon... We need Warswords more than ever before.'

Torj topped up their glasses. 'All the more reason to take on an apprentice. And perhaps not beat the current Warswords to a pulp.'

A beat of silence followed. 'He fucking asked for it.'

Torj clinked his glass to Wilder's. 'Of that I have no doubt, brother.'

The fire crackled and the two men stretched their legs out before it, talking of other things for a time. The bottle was soon empty, the warmth and the liquor making Wilder's eyes heavy.

But when Wilder eventually drifted off to sleep still in his armchair, it wasn't monsters and Warswords he dreamed of.

It was Althea Zoltaire, with vows of vengeance on her lips.

CHAPTER TWENTY-FOUR

As the days passed and Thea started down the road to recovery, she found herself in Wren's healing lesson. It was one of the few areas that the guild continued classes in well after the students came of age and specialised in their own fields.

Wren explained that this was because there were always new techniques, new treatments being discovered all the time and that Thezmarr, particularly its alchemists, needed to be at the forefront of these advancements for the sake of its warriors.

So when Farissa ran them through the ingredients for various tinctures and remedies, Thea took out a quill and parchments and made notes. She ignored the ripple of shock across the room and wrote in a hurried scrawl, only pausing to ask Wren about particular spellings.

When Farissa finished demonstrating how to strip Elvan Bark in a way that preserved its healing properties, Thea raised her hand.

Farissa did a double take. 'What is it, Althea?'

'I have a request,' Thea said boldly.

'Oh?'

'I wondered if you might teach us about battlefield healing. You know… the sort of things one might need to know should they need to treat a wound under pressure or with limited supplies. The sort of things that might save a life in the heart of a skirmish.'

The whole room went tense and Ida flashed Thea a worried look from the next table over. While Farissa had said that there was always a place in their ranks for Thea, it was another thing to disrupt her lesson and make requests with her own agenda. There was no official war in the midrealms and no conflict that would see the alchemists of Thezmarr caught in the middle of a fray, and yet…

Farissa smiled slowly. 'I thought you'd never ask, Althea.' She pressed her fingers together and started to pace, her brow furrowed as she considered her next words carefully. After a few moments, she looked up, her eyes bright and eager.

'Battlefield healing is an art like no other…' she began.

For the first time in her twenty-four years, Thea listened to her sister. As much as it destroyed her not to train and spar with the other shieldbearers, she knew her body was not ready. Her abdomen was still tender, her stab wound threatened to tear open with any sudden movements and she was still experiencing fatigue and shortness of breath. Though she desperately wanted to get back to her drills and was increasingly anxious about losing the strength and endurance she'd worked so hard to gain, she knew that to push too soon would see her straight to the infirmary.

Instead, she resumed her old alchemy shifts with a renewed enthusiasm, all the while the Hand of Death's words echoed in her mind.

'If you're going to be a warrior of Thezmarr... You need to learn more than fighting, Alchemist... Every discipline this fortress offers has a vital part to play. You should respect them all. You should master them all. There is more to this guild than blades and fists.'

She took these words to heart, and shared them with anyone who would listen, mainly Kipp and Cal when she sat with them during the midday meal. Kipp was back on his feet sooner than expected. He was restricted to light duties for the meantime and that meant he was all too eager to hear what she'd learned throughout her days, insisting that every aspect of the battlefield, even the clean-up and tending to the wounded could be used in strategy planning.

Thea returned to the shieldbearer dormitories, Dax was there waiting at the foot of her bed on her first night back and ever since. She split her evenings between the library with Malik and the evening meal with her friends and her sister.

As her strength slowly returned, Thea went down to the training arena to watch the combat drills and classes. There, she sat on the outskirts with her crumpled piece of parchment, taking notes on different techniques. She watched the Warswords with an unrelenting intensity, drinking in everything they did, even the sadist Vernich.

Nothing more powerful than knowledge and the ability to wield it...

It wasn't long until Seb spotted her. He strode towards her, swinging his practice sword arrogantly.

'Scribbling away like some school boy won't make you a

warrior.'

'Nor will sticking your big nose in other people's business,' Thea snapped as she finished her note on the best stance for shield walls.

'It's my business when they allow a stray into Thezmarrian ranks. You're —'

Thea sighed, irritated. 'Do I threaten you so much, Barlowe? That you have to stop your own training, your own progress, just to try and belittle me?'

'You? Threaten me?' he barked a nasty laugh.

'Yes,' Thea said simply, trying to peer past him to watch Torj take on one of the older shieldbearers, dual wielding a pair of longswords. 'You're in my way,' she said sharply when Seb insisted on blocking her view.

'I *beat* you,' he blurted. 'Why didn't you leave?'

'I belong here as much as you,' she replied. 'And you didn't *beat* me. Far from it. I withstood two unhindered blows and an underhanded stabbing from you and still I stood, still you couldn't keep me down. I am more warrior than you'll ever be.'

Nearby, some of the shieldbearers paused to listen. But their expressions were no longer those of amusement, but of impatience. They too, it seemed, were fed up with Seb's antics.

Heat flushed his cheeks. 'What do you hope to gain? You'll never be one of us.'

'Wrong, Barlowe. You're wrong. I already am one of you. And I promise you this. When we face each other again, I'll have you on the ground. And unlike me, you won't get back up.'

'Bullshit, you —'

'Shut up, Seb,' Lachin called loudly from a few feet away.

'What did you say?'

'I said *shut up*. You're boring us all to tears with your whinging.'

At Lachin's words, Seb took a step back from Thea, suddenly speechless. His expression soured, and with a final, narrow-eyed glare in her direction, he stalked off.

Thea gave Lachin a nod of thanks. The older shieldbearer merely shrugged and continued his sparring.

Thea trained her gaze on the heart of the arena, where Hawthorne had appeared. As usual, he wore all black, his sleeves rolled up above the elbow, revealing the corded muscle and inked skin there. Like Torj, he gripped two longswords and paced the training ground, every movement thrumming with power and strength.

Thea's whole body responded, tense and tingling. She hadn't seen him since he'd tended to her wound in that cramped broom closet, since he'd saved her life and delivered her to Wren. She'd thought about him though, Furies had she thought about him... and that conflicted expression on his face as Wren had shut him out. Thea had replayed every moment they'd had together in her mind, each time the fire within her burning hotter. The only thing that dampened that fire was the fact that he hadn't sought her out... Hadn't checked on her afterwards. And she didn't know what that meant, or how she should feel. She told herself she should feel nothing but gratitude, but a deeper, darker part of her craved something more from him.

Now, Hawthorne faced his fellow Warsword, challenge gleaming in those silver eyes.

Quill and parchment forgotten, Thea watched, utterly transfixed by the deadly dance unfolding before her. Hawthorne took a long step to the outside of the ring with his leading foot, creating momentum with his hips as he brought his blades down on Torj. The golden-haired warrior took the attack on his own blades, but buckled beneath the impact of Hawthorne's blow.

'It takes great strength to fight in such a way,' a voice sounded from behind Thea.

She twisted to find none other than Audra the librarian at her back. Thea had seen her in passing or from a distance in the Great Hall, but she hadn't spoken to her warden since that day they'd ridden the Mourner's Trail together.

But Audra wasn't looking at her. The older woman was still staring at the duelling Warswords. 'It takes great strength to fight in such a way,' she repeated, sounding distant. 'But sometimes it takes more strength to know when to sit out.'

The bench shifted beneath Thea as Audra took up a place beside her. 'You will come back stronger for it, Althea, I promise you that.'

Together, they watched the legends of Thezmarr train.

Later that evening, confident in her progressing recovery, Thea decided that she'd already waited far too long to run a particular errand, and so after the evening meal, she went to Wren's rooms and, in her absence, helped herself to her sister's mirror and comb. For once, Thea left her bronze tresses unbound and spent a good while untangling the ragged ends. She studied her reflection, grimacing at the sharp lines of her face, wishing there was something else she could do to make herself more... feminine.

The door swung open and Wren didn't look remotely surprised to see her. 'Glad you've made yourself comfortable

—' She cut herself off, pausing as she gave Thea the once-over. 'You look nice...'

'Do I?'

Wren nodded. 'Suspiciously so.'

'Thanks... I think?'

Wren laughed. 'Dare I ask?'

'Probably best you don't.'

'You're still taking the tonic I make?' Wren asked, suddenly serious. 'The one to prevent —'

'Gods.' Thea flushed. 'Yes. I am.'

'Then say no more, sister. But one moment.' Wren reached out and fiddled with her hair, arranging it so that it cascaded down her shoulders in a more elegant wave. 'There.'

'Thanks.'

Wren shooed her to the door. 'As you were.'

Thea wandered the corridors of the commanders' residences, a large clean shirt and cloak tucked under her arm.

It was Esyllt who found her.

'What are you doing loitering around here?' His signature bark was only a few degrees quieter indoors.

'I'm trying to find Warsword Hawthorne,' she replied with more confidence than she felt. She hadn't thought how it might look with her returning a warrior's clothing...

'Hawthorne doesn't live in the fortress,' Esyllt told her, his brow furrowed. 'What'd you want with him?'

Thea squirmed inwardly, wishing she'd thought things through. 'I have some of his belongings he loaned me from our journey to Harenth,' she said. 'I was hoping to return them.'

Esyllt made a noncommittal noise at the back of his

throat. 'Well, he's not here. He's got a cabin on the western foot of the mountains.'

'Right. Can I leave these things with you then, Sir?'

Esyllt's arms folded over his chest and he gave her a hard look. 'I'm no delivery boy, Althea. You've got a task, do it yourself.'

'Yes, Sir. I just... I wasn't sure if it would be... appropriate?'

'Appropriate?' the weapons master scoffed. 'That ship has sailed. What's less appropriate? Returning a Warsword's belongings in a less than timely fashion, or holding onto them for weeks?'

Thea gaped at him.

'I'd run, not walk, if I was you,' he prompted.

'Where —'

'Do I look like a map? Figure it out yourself.' And with that, the tetchy weapons master strode in the opposite direction and into a private residence, slamming the door behind him.

'Gods,' Thea muttered, shaking her head and peering down at the clothes she still held. She went back to the Great Hall where some of her cohort still lingered and she asked around.

'Surely someone here has been there? On an errand? To deliver a message?'

'Nope,' Lachin mumbled around a spoonful of custard, slurping loudly. 'He's private. Doesn't want the likes of us around him at the best of times, let alone after hours, eh?'

Thea ground her teeth. 'That doesn't exactly help me.'

'I can't know what I don't know.' Lachin shrugged, before his spoon stopped midway to his mouth and he stared at her, brow furrowed. 'You look different.'

Thea gestured to her hair casually. 'No braid.'

'Right...' Lachin said, seemingly still perplexed, before he remembered himself. He gave another shrug. 'It's a good different.'

Thea rolled her eyes. 'Gee, thanks.'

Just as she was about to give up and retire to the dormitories, she half-collided with Torj in front of Three Furies.

'What are you up to?' he asked, leaning against the monument.

Thea looked around for the Guild Master, knowing he wouldn't stand for a show of such disrespect, but he was nowhere in sight and Torj was looking down at her expectantly.

'I'm trying to find Warsword Hawthorne, I need to return some things to him.'

'Is that so?' Amusement gleamed in Torj's eyes.

'Yes,' Thea replied, trying not to sound frustrated. 'No one will tell me where his cabin is.'

'I can tell you that,' he informed her smoothly.

Thea blinked. 'I'd appreciate it,' she managed.

'Well, he certainly won't,' Torj said with a laugh, but he leaned in and told her the way.

At last, with Torj's instructions memorised, Thea buttoned up her cloak and lit a torch. Bracing herself against the wind, she went to find the Warsword's cabin.

Taking the hidden trail beyond the training arena, Thea navigated the spindly forest. It was different to the Bloodwoods south of the fortress, many of the trees were already bare for the upcoming winter. In the near distance, the mountains loomed beneath the glowing orb of the moon and soon, she heard the roaring of the falls.

She must have walked through the dark for over half an hour, repeating the directions she'd been given in her head before she saw the soft glow of candlelight up ahead filtering through small, square windows. Tendrils of smoke coiled into the crisp night air from the chimney, drifting dreamily up into the sky as she approached.

Suddenly nervous, Thea stood on the small porch, raising a fist to the door and knocked loudly. She waited, straining to hear any noise from within the cabin.

It was silent.

She knocked again. Her stomach was churning. What if she woke him? What if there was someone in there with him? Or what if he wasn't in? Could she leave his clothes on the front step? She stepped back, trying to decide what to do —

The door flew inward; the frame filled by a huge figure.

Wilder Hawthorne gripped a white towel slung low around his hips, and in the other hand brandished a dagger.

Her dagger, Thea realised, before all the thoughts emptied out of her head.

He was naked, save for the towel, and he was dripping wet.

Water sluiced down his body, following the carved paths of his broad chest, down the ridges of his abdomen, a ragged scar there, and lower, to the V-shaped grooves that disappeared beneath the fabric of his towel. Droplets clung to the dark dusting of hair across his torso and Thea couldn't look away. His body... Well, it had been made by the gods, honed by —

'What are you doing here?' he growled, lowering the weapon.

Thea's mouth had gone dry. She had to clear her throat

before she found her words. 'I came to return your things – your cloak and your shirt. Do you always answer the door like this?'

'Do you always show up to places uninvited?' He made a disgruntled noise. 'How'd you find this cabin?'

'Torj told me how to get here.'

'Of course he did,' Hawthorne scoffed, still holding the towel that hung dangerously low. He didn't exactly invite her in, but he stepped back and left the door ajar, so she entered.

As her shock subsided, she studied the tattoo that she'd glimpsed before, the pattern that trailed from his left hand all the way up his arm and shoulder, and down the same side of his powerfully built back. Upon closer inspection, she saw it was an extensive artwork of black whorls and a language she didn't recognise – except for one section. A line of text that ran parallel to his spine: it was the same text engraved on the blade of her dagger, the dagger now in his possession. It took all of Thea's willpower not to close the gap between them and run her fingers down the words.

'What does it mean?' Her cheeks flamed as she spoke. 'The text on your back, I mean. It's the same as the inscription on my dagger.'

'Still insisting it's your dagger...'

'It is.' Thea waited, watching as Hawthorne faced her again, still in his gods-damned towel, twirling the aforementioned dagger between his fingers. He looked from the steel to her, considering – always considering.

'It means: *Glory in death, immortality in legend.* It's written in the ancient tongue of the Furies – the original Warswords.'

Thea forced herself to swallow the lump in her throat. 'Are you going to get dressed?'

The corner of Hawthorne's mouth tugged upward, showing a hint of that dimple she knew lay beneath his beard. 'Why?' he asked. 'Am I making you uncomfortable?'

'It's...'

'Distracting?' he finished for her.

'Yes,' she said, unamused, only just realising that she'd balled up his freshly laundered cloak and shirt in her hands. She dropped them onto a bench that lined the wall, heat flooding her body. She had to look away from him. She glanced around the inside of the cabin. It was not at all what she expected. Unlike the Warsword himself, it was warm and welcoming. A small fire crackled in the hearth and an array of potted plants were positioned all over the room, adding a pop of colour. A table and chairs were shoved up against the wall beneath one of the windows, and two tattered armchairs sat before the fire.

'Don't even think about making yourself at home,' came that deep, rumbling voice.

Thea nearly jumped.

He re-entered the room still barefoot but wearing loose-fitting pants, an unbuttoned shirt hanging over his chiselled body as he surveyed her.

'You seem to have healed well enough,' he commented.

'Thanks to my sister,' Thea replied. 'And to you,' she said earnestly. 'I'm not sure what would have happened to me if you hadn't helped that day.'

'You would have died in a broom closet.'

'Maybe. Maybe not.'

'Let's see it then.'

Thea baulked, her skin suddenly tingling. 'See what?'

'Your wound. How it's healed.'

'It's fine. My sister —'

'Show me.' It was not a request. Command laced his voice and Thea knew from experience that the Warsword was used to getting his way.

For that fact alone she wanted to be the one to deny him. 'No,' she said.

He was a blur of movement and suddenly she was pinned to the wall; her cloak pushed aside and her shirt untucked and lifted, revealing the bare skin of her side beneath, and the fresh, pink scar that marred it.

'Don't you usually offer your guests a drink before you rip their clothes off?' she muttered, trying to ignore the heat of his body so close to hers.

'Not usually, no.'

But she heard the whistle of air between his teeth as his fingers grazed the newly healed wound. 'He should have been flayed for this.'

Goosebumps rushed across Thea's skin at the contact, and she could have sworn invisible lightning crackled between them.

'He'll get what's coming to him,' Thea vowed.

Hawthorne's fingers lingered on the scar, sending a forceful current racing through her. 'You're going to have to be stronger and faster than this when that day comes.'

Gods, he was close. Thea would only have to lift her head and lean in for his lips to be on hers. Her traitorous body nearly did exactly that as she inhaled that intoxicating rosewood scent, as she felt the heat from his freshly bathed body radiate onto her.

'I will be,' Thea promised, her voice hoarse, her hand reaching for the hem of her shirt to drag it down.

Hawthorne seemed to hesitate, his hand suspended by her hip, as though he wanted to —

He stepped back, and the warmth between their bodies snuffed out. 'You're becoming a constant thorn in my side, Alchemist.'

Momentarily stunned, Thea tucked her shirt back in a tad too vigorously. 'I may be a thorn in your side, but you know well enough by now I'm not an alchemist.'

He moved to the far corner where a small kitchen was tucked away. A goblet sat on the side and he picked it up, taking several long swigs before returning his gaze to her.

Thea stood rigid where he'd left her against the wall, her skin still singing with the echo of his touch. She flexed her fingers at her sides to try and rid herself of the strange sensation. But it remained; she could still feel the imprint of his fingertips on her scar.

He was watching her, his expression unreadable.

Thea folded her arms over her chest, suddenly feeling exposed. 'You hit Vernich,' she said, studying Hawthorne just as intently as he studied her.

'Several times,' he replied, that dark expression still revealing nothing.

'Why?'

'He's a bastard.'

'Is that all?'

A loaded silence followed.

'Is that all?' Thea repeated.

'He deserved it,' Hawthorne said at last. 'For what he did to your friend, to you.'

Thea forced herself to remain still, though her instincts screamed at her to fidget beneath his scrutiny, or go to him –

she didn't know which was more powerful. She sifted through her mind for something to say, but nothing came and she silently cursed him for tangling her thoughts so thoroughly.

That was when her gaze landed on the table beneath the window, and the chain of flowers lying atop. Her breath caught in her throat again. It was the one she'd made on their journey back from Harenth. The one she'd thrown at him... He'd kept it.

Thea gathered her courage as the tension became too much to bear. 'What is this? This thing between us?' she asked at last. All she wanted to do was cross the room and lay her hands, her body, her mouth on him.

'There is nothing between us,' he said.

'Liar.'

That muscle twitched in his jaw but he didn't deny it as *he* closed the gap between them. 'I find you endlessly infuriating,' he ground out. 'And yet...'

'Yet?'

'And yet I can't seem to stay away.' He stood before her once more, mere inches away.

'So don't,' she said boldly. It was the second time she'd taken the risk for him, the second time she'd told him what she wanted. Heart hammering, she reached for him, daring to dip her fingertips between the open folds of his shirt, trailing them across the muscular expanse of his chest, his skin blazing hot beneath her touch.

He didn't move.

'Hawthorne?' her voice trembled, the longing to press her mouth to his, her body to his, was overwhelming.

His hands came up, and she braced herself for that first touch, the touch that would be her undoing.

His fingers brushed a stray strand from her face, tucking it gently behind her ear. 'You changed your hair...'

The whisper of a caress trailed down her tresses, where he twined the ends around his hand and drew her to him. His lips, softer than she imagined, grazed hers, hot and restrained, with the promise of something much deeper, much more intense.

At that alone, Thea nearly moaned, every nerve in her body was alight, every desire she'd ever felt was flooding to the surface. Furies, she wanted him. She wanted to finish what they'd started the moment she'd woken pressed against him in the fields.

And then, his mouth closed over hers in earnest, and he kissed her fiercely.

Thea's lips parted, and his tongue brushed hers, his hand closing around the nape of her neck, drawing her close.

He groaned, the carnal sound vibrating and unfurling the coil of desire within her as she kissed him back, matching his intensity.

It robbed her of breath, and told her that every kiss she'd experienced before had been a lie, a shadow of what it was meant to be. She could only imagine what that said about everything else.

Heart pounding, Thea kissed him harder, losing herself in him, her hands sliding down his torso, revelling in the power there.

His fingers closed around her wrists.

And he withdrew them from his body.

'I'm sorry,' he said roughly. 'We can't. You shouldn't be here, I shouldn't have —'

It was as though a bucket of icy water had been tipped over Thea's head. She pulled back sharply, her stomach hardening, spots flashing in her vision. Twice now, she had made the move, twice now, he'd spurned her. What ever happened to *there's nothing more attractive than a woman who knows what she wants?*

'What twisted game are you playing?' she demanded.

'No game.' His words were pained. 'I have seen what something like this does to people. And you… You've fought so hard to get where you are, I can't be the reason that's taken away. I'm sorry. I shouldn't have done that. I shouldn't have let this happen.'

Thea flinched. 'No, you shouldn't have, if that's how you feel.'

'It… It is.'

'Then I'll go,' she heard herself say. Face aflame, she snatched up her cloak, wrapping it tightly around her and made for the door, taking the torch she'd brought with her.

'Thea…' Her name was a pleading whisper behind her. But it was too late. She was done. Without another word, she left the warmth of the cabin and hurried away into the dark, trying not to choke on her own embarrassment.

But when Thea slipped into bed and Dax settled himself dutifully at her feet, she couldn't sleep. Her body felt too alive, too aware of the sheets against her skin and the low voice that not only now echoed in her mind, but vibrated through her bones. She sighed heavily, trying to push thoughts of the half-naked Warsword, his rippling muscles and heated touch from her head.

Try as she might, there was no erasing his fevered kisses, or the throbbing between her legs.

And so Thea stared up at the ceiling until the watery hours of the early morning before she rose to resume her training.

CHAPTER TWENTY-FIVE

Two weeks had passed since that horrific afternoon with Vernich and Seb, and Thea returned to her shieldbearer duties with a renewed sense of purpose. The days went quickly and quietly, and Thea began to feel stronger; much stronger. Kipp was back as well, though his face looked a little different since his injury.

'It makes me more ruggedly handsome,' he insisted one morning as they scarfed down their breakfast.

'When, in the history of the midrealms, has anyone called you ruggedly handsome?' Cal shook his head.

'Well, if you must know, at the —'

'Don't even say it,' Cal cut him off with a warning glare.

They didn't have time to continue their bickering. The whole cohort was due at the stables and Thea had to practically drag the pair there to avoid being late.

When they got there, Thea's skin crawled at the sight of Vernich, whose face still sported the evidence of Hawthorne's beating. He was in an intense discussion with Esyllt and Torj. The Bear Slayer's presence had her looking for the third, but Hawthorne was nowhere in sight. In fact, she hadn't seen him even in passing since her visit to his cabin, though her thoughts often returned to that night. Her toes curled at the memory of his lips brushing against hers, his smell wrapping around her, her heart fracturing just a little at the thought of that flower braid on his table. But he'd made himself clear.

Beside her, Kipp stiffened at the sight of the Bloodletter and she reached down to squeeze his hand. No matter how brutal Thezmarrian training was supposed to be, what had transpired during that session should never have happened. Neither Kipp nor her spoke of it, but that afternoon had left more than just physical scars on the both of them. The way Cal was grinding his teeth told her the experience had left a mark on him as well, that his guilt for not being able to protect them cut as deep as any wound.

Kipp gave her hand a squeeze back and dropped it before anyone noticed.

Esyllt held up his hand for silence and the cohort fell quiet, eager to discover what madness awaited them next.

'The Guild Master has requested that the shieldbearers undergo a mock skirmish,' he announced. 'Sparring in the arena is one thing, but applying those skills in the midst of battle is another. You are all to gather your shields and weapons and meet us down on the Plains of Orax to await further instruction.'

Excited chatter broke out across the crowd.

'Do not take this exercise lightly,' his voice rang out through the stables. 'We will be watching each and every one of you. If you have a speciality, now's the time to show it.'

That only fuelled the hushed conversations further as the shieldbearers scrambled to get their weapons from the armoury and make their way down to the fields beyond the Bloodwoods.

Unlike Cal and Kipp, Thea didn't have a speciality suitable for the mock battle; she was deadly with her throwing stars, but she could hardly use them without spilling the blood of her fellow shieldbearers.

Throughout their various lessons, she had trained the hardest to dual wield, like Hawthorne and the great Talemir Starling, and so she sheathed two practice swords at her belt.

'Your longbow and cavalry skills are excellent,' Kipp commented, as he chose a lightweight shield for himself. 'That's where I'd put you at the start of a battle, before things get messy.'

Thea nodded her thanks and grabbed a bow and quiver of arrows, strapping them to her back. If the commanders and Warswords were going to watch, then she was going to show them exactly what she was capable of.

'We should work as our own unit,' Kipp said as they walked through the Bloodwoods towards the Plains of Orax, fully armed.

'Well, yeah...' Cal replied. 'Isn't that the idea of a mock skirmish?'

'He means a team within a team, you dolt,' Thea told him. 'Right Kipp?'

'Exactly. We follow the orders of the commander, but we stick together, we have each other's backs. Cal can cover us from long range, Thea, you take the lead in cavalry, and I'll do what I can while assessing the lay of the land.'

Thea waited for Cal to make a sarcastic comment, but his face was serious when he nodded. 'Sounds good.'

Though she knew it was only a mock skirmish, it felt *right* going into battle with her friends at her sides. When they reached the fields with the rest of their unit, Madden and Evander were there with a unit of horses already saddled and waiting.

Evander tried to catch her eye, but Thea turned away – she had more important things to worry about.

'Gather round, gather round,' Esyllt shouted. 'You've been assigned a Warsword to help guide your unit through the skirmish, but you'll be going in alone. We want no dirty fighting, no broken bones or unnecessary blood. But this is a test, this is to show you how chaotic a battleground can be.'

How in the realms are they going to pull this off? But before Thea could think more on it, some of the younger warriors emerged carrying buckets of paint.

'Half of you will be red,' Esyllt called. 'Half of you will be blue. You're to coat your weapons with your colour and you are to mark your enemy as much as possible... Archers, special blunt arrowheads have been created by some clever ladies back at the fortress —'

Thea exchanged a grin with Cal. They had been there when Wren had come up with the idea to cover the points of the heads with a hard sea sponge she'd discovered only a few weeks back. If secured properly, the impact would bruise an opponent, but no arrow would pierce flesh and would mark them with paint.

The cohort was divided in half and Thea was pleased to find Torj at the head of their force; she was even more pleased to discover that Seb and his lackeys were on the enemy team, with Vernich at their helm.

Where's Hawthorne? The thought flashed across her mind like a star streaking across the night's sky and then it was gone.

Torj's voice projected across their group. 'Forget that this is a practice battle,' he commanded, his voice deep and serious. 'Imagine beyond that field is an army of monsters from beyond the Veil, or an army of cursed civilians. *You* are what stands between them and our world, so remember this: being a true Guardian of the midrealms is not about hating the evil before you, but loving the lands and its people behind you. Remember that glory will not be found in failing to fall, but in rising from the chaos when you do. *Do not* let me down.'

A shiver washed over Thea at those words as Torj the Bear Slayer made quick work of splitting them into various units.

'We'll be trying a few standard formations first, and we need a frontline. Who's got the balls to look death straight in the eye?'

Thea was first to step forward. 'I don't have the balls,' she said. 'But I'm always keen to test the fates.'

Teeth flashed in a quick grin. 'Good, you're front and centre, Althea. They won't expect that. Now, who's directing this attack?'

Everyone blinked at Torj for a moment before Cal shouted, 'Kipp!'

Thea shoved their friend forward. 'Yes, Kipp should strategise!'

The Warsword turned to Kipp, who was blushing furiously. 'Are you up to the task then, Snowden?'

'Yes, Sir. Absolutely,' Kipp blurted.

'Then talk to me. What do you see?'

Kipp didn't hesitate. 'The terrain,' he said. 'It may look flat enough, but there are dips and crests in the plains as much as anywhere else. We need our force to take advantage of these.'

Thea scanned the field before them. He was right, at a glance, the grassy plain looked almost level, but when she focused, she could see exactly what the warrior referred to.

'Exactly,' Torj agreed. 'That's your first tactic.'

True to their word, the trio stuck together, the anticipation buzzing between them as they gathered in their first formation. Kipp spoke in hurried tones about how they could use the terrain against their opponents. Thea could only imagine how the feeling compared to being on the precipice of a real battle.

'Remember,' Torj called. 'This is the first of several attacks, fight smart and do not let me down!' He turned to Kipp. 'It's all yours, Kipp.'

Kipp gave a sombre nod before facing their unit. 'Weapons at the ready,' he called, his voice suddenly loud and authoritative.

The force did as he commanded.

'On my mark,' he shouted. 'Charge!'

Thea sprung into action with the rest, sprinting over the plains, brandishing her shield and wooden practice sword.

The two forces clashed messily together, a blur of coloured paints and flailing limbs, shouts filling the air.

And yet no one landed a single blow against her.

She whirled across the battlefield, light on her feet, darting away from attacks and delivering faux slices and thrusts to the opposition, streaking several shieldbearers with blue paint.

But there was something laughable about it all. Wasn't battle supposed to be more sophisticated than this? To Thea, it felt like a bunch of idiotic children trying to mimic something they did not understand.

'Enough!' roared Vernich over the clamour. 'Pathetic! I'd sooner die than fight alongside —'

'You've made your point, Vernich,' Torj snapped. 'My unit, with me. We go again.'

Once they had trudged back to their side of the plains, Torj surveyed them. 'This exercise develops tactical, strategic and disciplined habits... As loath as I am to agree with the Bloodletter – I saw nothing of the sort.'

Torj paced before them, swinging his war hammer and shaking his head furiously. 'When you're out on a real battlefield, it will not be so luxurious. Start taking this seriously. Their paint means death. *Do you want to die today?*'

'No, Sir!' came the unified reply.

'I said, *do you want to die today?*'

'No, Sir!'

'Then get —'

'Sir?' Kipp called out.

Torj raised his brows. 'You're interrupting a Warsword in the middle of —'

'Yes, Sir!' Kipp replied. 'Only because you told me to strategise...'

'And?'

'This is a full-scale field exercise, Sir... And no one is utilising that crest up there,' Kipp pointed to a rise in the land to the north. 'We could send a small unit of archers. Taking the high ground is the backbone of a million military strategies, Sir.'

A slow smile spread across Torj's face. 'And who taught you that, Kipp?'

'You did, Sir.'

Pride swelled in Thea's chest. Kipp might have been a

poor swordsman, but true to his word, he was a killer strategist through and through.

'You're damn right I did.' The Warsword addressed the shieldbearer on Kipp's left. 'Cal, take ten of our best archers and attack from that rise.'

Cal instantly turned to Thea.

'Althea stays front and centre. She volunteered, that's her position for the rest of the battle.'

Disappointment bloomed in Thea's gut, but she obeyed, twirling her sword at the ready. She had a point to prove.

At Torj's command, Thea led the next charge across the plain, while Cal rained arrows down upon the enemy and Kipp directed from the rear of the force. Shouts sounded from the other side, and Thea saw a flurry of blue somewhere ahead. It was going well.

Until the counter.

A unit of spear throwers burst through the enemy's ranks —

'Shield wall!' Thea heard herself shout over the chaos, skidding to a stop and bracing herself against the back of her shield. 'Shield wall!'

She waited for the shields to slide into place alongside hers, but there was nothing. Her unit kept charging, right into the blunt spears tipped with red paint.

'Shield wall!' she tried a final time.

But none listened.

'Pull back!' Kipp's voice cut through the pandemonium. 'Pull back!'

Thea heeded her friend's order, retreating with the rest of her unit, fury coursing through her veins.

'You had the right idea,' Torj said, as they gathered for the next strategy.

'Doesn't matter when no one listens.'

'No,' he agreed. 'It doesn't.'

That did little to quell Thea's rage.

The mock battle went on for another hour, maybe more – Thea couldn't tell. Her anger had ebbed away, replaced by exhaustion as they carried out formation after formation, until at last, Torj and Vernich called an end to it.

Begrudgingly, the Warswords shook hands, declaring Torj's force had secured the victory.

Despite her failed attempt at a shield wall, Thea cheered with the others and clapped her friends on the back with the rest. Though disappointment curdled in her gut at the lack of her own contribution, she was truly happy for Cal and Kipp, who had been the undeniable standouts in the exercise.

'A shield wall was the right move,' Kipp told her amidst the noise.

'I thought so,' Thea replied. 'But no one listened —'

'Why would anyone listen to you?' came the voice of one of Seb's lackeys. 'You're not a commander, you're not a warrior, you're not even a man, try as you might.'

Blood roared in Thea's ears and she clenched her fists ready to take a swing.

But Kipp shoved him. 'Oh, piss off you prick. I saw you lingering at the back out of harm's way. Thea's ten times the warrior you'll ever be.'

The shieldbearer lunged for Kipp, but Torj cleared his throat pointedly. 'Victory will not be so sweet in real life,' he reminded them, his face contemplative as he surveyed his unit. 'Look at how many of your men are streaked with paint. Many would be dead, far more injured beyond repair. And look across the field. You would see a pile of carcasses for the crows, and a carpet of warriors moaning in agony, some begging to be put out of their misery…'

Quiet fell and the Warsword continued. 'While this battle was short, even by my standards it was messy. And you want to avoid a messy battle at all costs. A true warrior of Thezmarr is brutal, yes, but efficient – quick, merciful. We do not draw out the suffering of our fellow man,' he said, 'or woman,' he added with a glance at Thea. 'You'll all do well to remember that.'

Torj's words settled over the group, quelling the excitement and turning things reflective. Thea appreciated the dose of reality, realising how easy it was to get caught up in the celebrations and tales of personal victory when they had not been confronted with the cold, harsh truths of war.

'Do you think we impressed them?' Cal asked quietly, nodding in the direction of the commanders and warriors.

'You certainly did,' Kipp replied. 'How many did you take down?'

'I'm not sure.'

'At least fifteen,' Thea said.

'I wasn't counting.'

'Horseshit,' Kipp scoffed.

Cal laughed. 'Alright, it was twenty-two.'

Thea elbowed Kipp. 'You did well too. A king of tactics, aren't you?'

'I've been telling you that for ages.'

Even though Torj's sombre words had doused the high of victory, nothing could quell their laughter at the sight of Seb, who was covered in blue paint from head to toe. Thea surveyed her long-time adversary, her shoulders shaking as uncontained glee flooded her.

'Looks like he didn't survive the practice battle...' Kipp said loudly.

Even Torj laughed at that.

Seb was seething as he stalked off into the Bloodwoods, his wooden sword limp in his hands.

Thea threw her arms around her friends, letting herself revel in the pride swelling in her chest. They had come a long way, the three misfits of Thezmarr.

But before the trio could start back towards the fortress, Esyllt strode forward, calling out to them. 'You three!'

Thea froze. That phrase was only ever reserved for them and it was usually a bad thing. She mentally readied herself for the prospect of dealing with the armoury, knowing it would be ten times worse than usual to clean up with all the paint.

'Yes, Sir?' Cal asked as they approached the weapons master tentatively.

'Both Vernich and I have correspondence that needs immediate delivery to Hailford,' he said. 'Given your impressive feats today, the Warswords and I have agreed to delegate this task to the three of you.'

'You want us to go to Hailford, Sir?' Kipp asked.

Esyllt barely suppressed his groan of frustration. 'Don't make me regret this, Snowden. *Yes,* you are to go to Hailford to deliver a number of messages across the capital.'

Thea thought she'd seen Kipp happy before, but those times were nothing compared to the broad, dopey grin now plastered on his face. 'Yes, Sir! It would be an honour.'

The weapons master was already shaking his head. 'Go to the kitchens. Cook has prepared supplies for your journey, then you're to take fresh horses from the stables. We will have our letters for you by then. You leave within the hour.'

A fresh wave of excitement washed over the trio. Though they were exhausted from the mock battle, the promise of adventure away from Thezmarr re-energised them and they rushed back to the fortress to follow Esyllt's instructions.

'The Laughing Fox awaits, my friends!' Kipp shouted eagerly as they thanked the cook.

Cal offered Thea a pained look before turning to their friend. 'Don't you think you should drop it now, Kipp?'

'Drop what?'

An exasperated sigh followed. 'The whole tavern thing. You don't have to lie.'

'I'm not! In a few days' time, we'll be dining like kings and drinking like fish!'

Cal rolled his eyes. 'If you say so.'

The weapons master was waiting for them in the stables, tapping his foot impatiently, three horses tacked and saddled behind him.

'You are to take the Wesford Road to Harenth and its capital with no detours,' he told them sternly. 'The journey will take you three days each way, one night's accommodation has been procured for you in the city.'

Stay in Harenth? In Hailford? Thea was practically giddy and she could almost feel the excitement radiating from her friends as well.

The weapons master handed out a series of letters. 'Callahan, you are to deliver this to Nobleman Briar. Kipp, this is for Councilman Henriksson. Ask the guards for directions and you'll find their residences easily enough.'

Esyllt pressed a sealed letter into Thea's hands. 'This is to be delivered to King Artos. It's my understanding His Majesty is already familiar with you, Althea.'

She felt the shocked gazes of Kipp and Cal fall to her.

Ignoring them, she replied: 'Yes, Sir,' and pocketed the letter.

'I trust that I do not need to remind you that the correspondence you hold is confidential? Should those seals be broken upon arrival, you will be whipped or worse for your disobedience. What are you waiting for?' he said sharply. 'Get moving!'

The trio burst into action, stuffing their saddlebags with their supplies and mounting their horses. Without another glance back at Esyllt, Thea took the lead and led her friends from the stables and onto the Mourner's Trail.

Having already travelled it twice recently, Thea didn't pause to marvel at its eeriness. She set the pace hard, so Cal and Kipp could not interrogate her about her familiarity with the king until they reached the Wesford Road. But as soon as they turned onto the wide dirt road that linked the kingdoms of the midrealms, the questions came.

'What did Esyllt mean about you and King Artos?' Kipp said immediately. 'I mean, I know you petitioned the rulers, but...'

'That's what I want to know,' Cal added.

'If you'd shut up, I can tell you,' she said.

And she did. She told them of the journey with the Warsword and how they hadn't used the main road. She told them of nearly missing her audience with the rulers of the midrealms and their initial rejection of her. When she got to the part about the feast and the poison, both young men were gaping at her from their horses.

'You *saved the king?*' Kipp's mouth hung open.

'That's what I said isn't it?'

'But... You... Saved him? *From certain death?*'

'Yes - from Naarvian Nightshade. It would have been a nasty death too. The poor cupbearer showed us that. I'd never seen the effects in action before.'

'He died right in front of you?' Cal asked.

Thea nodded, the memory making her shudder.

'But you saved the king...' Kipp repeated, in awe. 'That's how you got his approval to train with us...?'

'Yes. He convinced the other rulers to let me.'

'What happened after that?'

'We left.'

Kipp's brows furrowed. 'What do you mean, you left?'

Thea shrugged. 'Hawthorne said we had to leave, so we did.'

'He left a king's feast midway through? After you'd just been granted the very thing you'd travelled all that way for?' Cal asked.

Thea shrugged again, squeezing her horse's sides and urging it into a canter. 'Warswords belong to no territory but Thezmarr,' she called back to her friends as she left them in the dust in her wake.

The three days ride passed quickly, full of the unbridled joy and freedom of travelling with friends. As ordered, they travelled by the Wesford Road by day, stopping at dusk to hunt. With his family background, it was no surprise that Cal excelled at finding the best small game for them to cook over the fire each evening. He shared his hunting techniques with Thea who was eager to learn, while Kipp fantasised aloud about the roast boar at the Laughing Fox as he tended to the horses.

Though Thea worried a little about the training she was missing back at the fortress, from her travels with Hawthorne and now the days spent with her friends, she had come to understand that the lessons on the road were just as important.

As another dusk settled, they set up camp by a river flowing south, intending to fish for their evening meal. With the horses already settled and grazing, they soon realised that for whatever reason, the fish were keeping to the far riverbank, out of reach.

Spurred on by a flagon of ale, Kipp invented a game that had them launching themselves across the river on sticks. It involved selecting a stick that would bear their weight, taking a massive run-up to the river's edge and planting the stick in the ground at just the right moment before using it to propel themselves over the body of water. Thea had never laughed so hard, particularly when Kipp ended up waist-deep in the icy current after his stick snapped.

That evening, the trio debated the contents of the letters in their charge, but not once did anyone suggest breaking the wax seals and taking a look for themselves. No matter how curious they were, not for one moment did they think Esyllt's threats were idle.

In the dark hours of the night, Thea's mind turned to Hawthorne and the journey they had shared together – the start of something that would never come to pass now. She tried to understand the hurt she carried in her chest, but could make no sense of it. Instead, she resolved to harden herself, to lock those thoughts of him away at the back of her mind.

It was late afternoon when the capital city of Hailford appeared on the horizon and Thea could hardly believe how quickly time had passed. She had so lost herself in the conversation and the companionship that the days had melted away, but now as the city gates came into view, anticipation buzzed between them. They were to have a night in the city to themselves and the joy of this temporary freedom was not lost on them.

Once they had passed through the gates, Thea turned to her friends. 'I suggest we get these letters delivered as fast as possible,' she said. 'And then we'll meet at this Laughing Fox tavern Kipp is always on about.'

'Sounds like an excellent plan!' Cal said with a wry smile.

Thea turned to Kipp, but he was already riding away.

Giving Cal a wave, she urged her horse forward; she needed no directions to the Heart of Harenth and she wouldn't keep King Artos waiting.

CHAPTER TWENTY-SIX

The palace guards were expecting her and Thea was shown to the throne room. There, King Artos sat with Princess Jasira at his side, deep in conversation. Steeling her nerves, Thea strode in and bowed low before them both. Here was the ruler who had turned the tides of her fate – the ruler who had earned her unwavering loyalty.

Once again, Thea found herself momentarily stunned by the magic that reached out to her, exploring the air around her as though it wanted to play. It was more distinct without the powers of the other royals alongside it, almost stronger on its own.

Something within her shifted in answer, in recognition, causing her to start. It was a curious sensation, but she couldn't forget herself.

'Your Majesty. Your Highness,' she greeted them.

'Ah! Althea Zoltaire!' King Artos said warmly. 'Rise, child. Rise!'

Thea did as he bid, returning his welcoming smile, pride

swelling in her chest. 'I have some correspondence from the Guild Master, Your Majesty,' she told him.

The king waved to a servant, who offered an empty silver platter for her to place the sealed envelope on. She did so and the letter was taken to the king, who slid it into an inner pocket of his doublet.

'The shieldbearer life seems to suit you, Althea,' King Artos commented as he surveyed her sun-kissed skin and Thezmarrian uniform. The surrounding magic seemed to pulse with warmth, as though it reflected his good nature.

'It does indeed, Your Majesty. All thanks to you.'

'I merely gave my approval. The rest has been up to you,' he said kindly.

Thea flushed with pleasure. 'Thank you, Sire.'

'Are you enjoying your training?' he asked.

Thea's stomach fluttered, utterly moved that the King of Harenth was showing such interest in her. Suddenly, she felt the overwhelming need to please him. 'Yes, Your Majesty. I feel as though I was born for it.'

'I'm happy to hear it,' he replied. 'Not long ago, I heard that you were injured. Is that true?'

'How —' she stopped herself immediately. It was not her place to question how King Artos had known about her wounds. 'Only a little, Sire,' she answered, not wanting him to think less of her. 'I was back on my feet in no time.'

'Well, I'm glad you have recovered, Althea. I must admit, I feel invested in your journey, having been there at its inception. Though I probably shouldn't tell you that. After all, the kingdoms are supposed to be completely separate from the guild.'

'I'm honoured, Your Majesty,' she said, blushing again.

For the king to take a special interest in her was incredibly flattering.

Thea looked up, realising that Princess Jasira hadn't spoken a word since her arrival. 'Are you well, Highness?' she asked, hoping she hadn't come across as impolite.

'Quite well,' the princess replied.

A strange silence lingered for a moment.

'I do hope you can enjoy the city this time, Althea,' the king said. 'I know last time you were whisked away by Warsword Hawthorne before you could see the sights. You also left before I could give you something.'

'You have given me all I could ever hope for, Your Majesty.' Thea bowed low.

'Nonsense,' King Artos waved his hand and a servant came forward again, a palm outstretched to her. 'You saved my life, Althea Zoltaire. I wish to bestow a small token of my gratitude.'

Curiosity burning, Thea peered into the servant's palm. It was a small silver coin, not any currency she recognised.

'It's my own personal token,' the king explained. 'Take this coin anywhere in the midrealms and the bill will be sent to my treasury.'

Thea baulked. 'Your Majesty, I can't accept —'

'You must!' he argued. 'Hailford is beautiful at night. I suggest you start there.'

'That's too generous, Your Majesty.' Thea stammered.

'I will hear no more of it. You saved my life. And while I cannot interfere with guild business at Thezmarr, I can treat you as an honoured guest in my kingdom and wherever I have influence across the realms. Take the coin and use it as often as you like.'

Thea couldn't believe her ears. She took the token with trembling hands. 'Thank you, truly, Sire. You are too kind.'

King Artos waved her off. 'I'll let you get on with your exploring. And please, I shall be insulted if I receive no bills.'

The magic that she had almost grown used to humming around her retreated and, bowing low once more, Thea spluttered her thanks again and left the throne room.

Outside the palace gates and atop her mare again, Thea couldn't believe her luck. Not only did she have an entire evening to herself in Hailford, but she also had *coin to spend?*

Asking a passerby for directions to the Laughing Fox, Thea started the descent through the residences and into the city. She couldn't take in the sights fast enough - the beautiful townhouses, the stalls and shops. While there was no longer a formal celebration in full swing, Hailford was just as prosperous, just as lively as it had been during her first visit.

After several wrong turns and a set of new directions, Thea at last spotted the wooden sign swinging from the side of a building. It was indeed a laughing fox, its bushy tail curled around its body with a flourish. There was no sign of Cal and Kipp's horses outside, but she dismounted anyway, and led her mare to the trough, roping her reins to the post there.

She had never been inside a tavern before, so she didn't know what to expect when she entered. Raucous chatter and music greeted her, and she spotted a pair of fiddlers atop a small stage on the far end. The bar was in the centre of the vast room and there were booths and tables all over, not a single one vacant.

Suddenly unsure of herself, Thea did a lap, taking in the merry banter, the delicious smell of roast meat wafting in from the kitchens, and the handful of couples dancing to the festive notes of the fiddles. She was just about to start a second lap when the doors burst open with a bang and Kipp strode in, Cal in tow.

'You!' A burly man behind the bar shouted, pointing.

Cal flinched and Thea's blood went cold as Kipp froze in the doorway.

The whole tavern fell silent, even the fiddlers.

The half-door creaked loudly as the huge bartender came through it, tossing a cloth over his shoulder. With a slow, lumbering gait, he approached the lanky shieldbearer, surveying him critically.

Suddenly, he threw his arms out and enveloped Kipp in a bear-like embrace. 'The son of the fox returns!' he shouted, laughing joyously and ruffling Kipp's auburn hair. 'Clear Kipp's booth!'

Thea's legs buckled in relief.

Across the crowd, Cal's mouth fell open in disbelief.

'Make way, make way!' The barman called, shooing patrons from his and Kipp's path.

Thea made her own way towards them, meeting Cal at the foot of Kipp's freshly vacated booth. They stared at him, gobsmacked.

Kipp grinned. 'Didn't I tell you?' he laughed. 'I was born here.'

Thea nearly choked as she slid into the booth beside him. 'What?'

'Yep, right over there in the kitchen.' Kipp pointed to the door near the bar.

Cal slammed his hand down on the table, with more force than he intended by the looks of things. 'In all your ridiculous stories, you never *once* mentioned that.'

'Didn't seem important.'

'Didn't seem important?!' Cal echoed. 'All this time, I thought you were making this place up.'

'Why would I do that?'

'For a laugh? To annoy me? To prove you knew Harenth better than the rest of us?' Cal reeled off the list of possible reasons, Kipp looking more and more baffled with each one.

'Sorry to disappoint you, nothing like that.'

'Well, I know that *now!*'

Thea was sinking further into the cushioned booth, her shoulders shaking as she laughed silently.

'Are your parents still here?' Cal asked, scanning the busy tavern as though he might stumble upon Kipp's mother or father.

'No, long gone. Ma worked in the kitchens for a time, then I was born. I don't know anything about my father. But the chef here, she knows me, looks after me when I visit and all that.'

The hulking barman cleared his throat. 'First round's on me, Kipp, but born here or not, son, after that you'll still need your own coin.'

Kipp grimaced. 'Ahh, about that Albert, any chance you could —'

The man groaned. 'Don't tell me you came here with an empty purse again? You've still got an unpaid tab from last time!'

'Uh... I may be able to help with that,' Thea said, sliding the king's coin across the table.

The man stared at the small disc of silver. 'Holy shit... The coin of the king. I've never seen one in the flesh.' Blinking slowly, Albert picked it up and turned it over between his thick fingers before letting out a low whistle.

'You're her then? The lass from Thezmarr who saved his life?'

Thea blushed furiously. 'Yes.'

Beside her, Kipp beamed and clapped her heartily on the back. 'Of course she is! Albert, this is the incomparable Althea Zoltaire! Thezmarrian shieldbearer and hero to the king!'

Thea elbowed him to stop, her face still burning.

'And that's Cal,' she pointed to their other friend.

But Kipp was swept up in the occasion. 'Albert, we'll have the boar! And three growlers of your sour mead. And roast potatoes. And some of Malva's sticky toffee pudding and —'

'Kipp...' Thea warned. 'Be sensible.'

'That *is* sensible, my friend! Or do you think we should get two boars?' He got to his feet and chased after Albert. 'Albert, make it two boars!'

Thea shook her head in disbelief and Cal laughed.

'You shouldn't have shown him that,' he said, nodding to the coin Albert had handed back to her.

Before long, the trio sat with the largest tankards Thea had ever seen and filled to the brim with fresh, foaming mead, awaiting what was surely enough food to feed an army.

Kipp raised his drink. 'To Althea Zoltaire, the shieldbearer who saved the most powerful empath in history and shared her good fortune with her friends.'

Cal snorted. 'You hardly gave her a choice in the matter.'

Thea blinked. 'I didn't realise King Artos held that title. I mean, I knew he was an empath, but... The most powerful?'

Kipp nodded enthusiastically. 'Oh definitely. Much of the lasting peace in the midrealms is attributed to him.'

'Truly?'

'Cross my heart.'

'And I saved his life...' Thea said in wonder.

Kipp clapped her on the back, her mead sloshing onto the table. 'That's what I'm told!'

Cal was shaking his head at their friend, looking around at the tavern, bewildered. 'Now we've got that out of the way. Are you going to tell us how in the realms you've been able to frequent this place so often?'

'Are you forgetting that I've been a shieldbearer for... Well, a while... Who do you think the commanders use to deliver messages when the rest of the cohort can't possibly be dragged away from training?'

Thea chimed in. 'How long's a while?'

'Long enough to know all the toasts, all the staff and all the beautiful women,' he replied with a wink.

Thea took her tankard back and took a deep draught. The liquor was cold and crisp on her tongue. 'Tell us a toast then.'

'I need another drink to toast, or it's bad luck.'

'You've hardly made a dent in that one!' Cal argued incredulously.

Kipp seemed offended by the accusation and promptly drained his tankard, a good portion of it slopping down his front.

With a roll of her eyes, Thea went to the bar and refreshed both her friends' drinks, vowing that her next would be her last. She wanted to actually *remember* her time here, after all.

Sliding the fresh tankards in front of Cal and Kipp, she waited.

Looking suddenly very serious, Kipp got to his feet, swaying slightly as he took up his drink using two hands.

His eyes met Thea's and then moved to Cal as he bumped his tankard against each of theirs.

'May you walk amidst the gardens of the afterlife a whole half hour, before Enovius reads your ledger of deeds.'

Then, with utter seriousness, he tipped his head back and downed the entire tankard again, mead sloshing down his front and onto the table, before he dropped into the booth dramatically.

Thea and Cal locked eyes and roared with laughter.

'What?' Kipp shouted.

Thea's face was aching from smiling so much. 'Well, that was a toast alright.'

A moment later, several servers emerged from the crowd, their arms laden with trays of food.

Thea gaped at the sight of it. 'Kipp, you can't be serious. We can't eat all of this!'

Kipp had a pork knuckle in his hands before the plates had even touched the table. 'Watch me.'

The food was some of the best Thea had ever eaten. The roast boar was succulent and rich in flavour, the potatoes were delectably crisp on the outside and fluffy on the inside, while the sticky toffee pudding was made by the gods themselves.

When at last Thea couldn't eat another bite, she rested her hand on her now swollen belly with a contented sigh. She turned to Kipp, who was miraculously pouring another pot of gravy over his plate.

'You're going to make yourself sick,' she told him.

Kipp merely laughed and replied between mouthfuls. 'Thea, my friend, it's not my first time at the Fox.'

Cal rubbed his gut with a grimace before surveying the

tavern again. 'So, the Laughing Fox is real, the food is real...
What about these so-called beautiful —'

As the words left his lips, a stunning raven-haired
woman carved through the crowd and made a beeline for
Kipp. She closed the gap between them and planted her
hands on the table either side of the shieldbearer as Thea
and Cal watched on in amazement.

'Kristopher Snowden, you told me you would write,' she
declared, her face close to his.

Thea whirled round to face Cal. *'Kristopher?'* she
mouthed, eyes wide with disbelief.

But Cal was too busy half shoving his fist in his mouth to
keep from laughing.

Kipp's hands went to hers smoothly. 'I'm so sorry, Milla.
You know how unpredictable the life of a Thezmarrian
shieldbearer can be. I was injured in combat —'

'You were injured?' her lovely face softened at once.
'What happened?'

'Oh, it was nothing,' he replied. 'And it's no excuse for not
writing. How can I make it up to you?'

Milla was already dragging Kipp away from their booth.
'I can think of a few things,' she told him, her voice sultry.

'I'm at your disposal.' Kipp gave a wolfish grin.

Thea watched them go, Kipp's long arms snaking around
the woman's waist and ample curves.

'I don't believe it,' Cal said as the pair disappeared up a
spiral staircase. 'He was telling the truth... About
everything.'

Thea was shaking her head. 'Did you know his name was
Kristopher?'

'Apparently, I knew *nothing* about him at all.' Cal took a
long drink.

While Kipp was occupied with his friend, Thea and Cal drank their mead and listened to the musicians. She told him about her meeting with the king, while he filled her in on how Nobleman Briar threatened to cut off his balls for looking in his daughter's direction.

'I mean, you would have looked at her, too. She had a giant wart on her nose,' he explained helplessly.

Thea laughed so hard that her drink came out her nostrils. Wiping the tears from her eyes, she noticed Cal's arm rested on the back of the booth behind her, his sleeve brushing her neck. They'd been moving closer together as the music had grown louder and louder, but now his leg was pressed against hers and he was looking at her... *differently*, his gaze hooded.

'Cal...' she said slowly. He was close enough that his warm breath tickled her face, and she could faintly smell the mead they'd been drinking all night.

'Thea...' he replied, his voice playful, but her name slightly slurred. Brazenly, he put his arm around her fully now, giving her a gentle squeeze. 'Don't you want to see what's upstairs? I could be at *your* disposal, if you wished it...'

Cal was a handsome man, there was no denying that, and for a brief moment, she let her gaze fall to his mouth, wondering what it would be like to kiss him, to have the stubble of his beard graze her skin. But all the free mead in the midrealms couldn't get her to risk the friendship they had built over the last few months. And it wasn't just that... She felt nothing. Her body didn't sing in his presence. It wasn't Cal she wanted to kiss; it wasn't Cal's hands she wanted exploring beneath her clothes.

Slowly, Thea pushed him back. 'Bad idea, Cal,' she said as

gently as she could. She braced herself for anger, that was her general experience with men when they didn't get what they wanted.

But with a sheepish grin on his face, Cal let her push him away. 'Ah, it was worth a shot, wasn't it?'

'You're an idiot,' she told him, instantly relieved that things weren't strained between them.

'True.'

'Do we leave Kipp to his own devices? Will he find the inn alright?'

Cal laughed. 'I don't think he'll be joining us.' He got to his feet clumsily and steadied himself against the table. 'Let's go sleep this off and pray we're not hungover for the journey back. He'll find us in the morning.'

Arm in arm, Thea and Cal stumbled to the nearby inn, falling into their separate beds, Cal snoring a moment later.

The morning was not Thea's friend. Her head felt swollen, her mouth tasted like sawdust and the thought of being jolted around in a saddle all day had her grimacing before she'd even tugged on her boots.

Much to her and Cal's annoyance, Kipp was waiting for them, fresh and bright-eyed in the stables.

'Didn't know when to stop, did you?' he said. 'You probably didn't eat enough. Rookie mistake.'

'Didn't eat enough? You must be joking,' Cal groaned.

'Do you have to be so loud, *Kristopher?*' Thea added, adjusting the length of her stirrups.

Kipp gave her a maddening grin. 'I'm speaking at a normal volume.'

'Horseshit,' Cal muttered as he led his horse from its stall.

'You're louder than a bloody mountain drake. And must you be so bloody cheerful? You of all people know that a hangover likes miserable company.'

'Don't know what you're talking about. And how can you be miserable? It's going to be a *glorious* day.'

As the sun inched its way into the pink and purple sky, with Thea and Cal a little worse for wear, and Kipp in incredibly high spirits, the trio left the city of Hailford behind them.

Throughout the journey back to Thezmarr, Thea and Cal questioned Kipp relentlessly about his relationship with the dark-haired beauty Milla, and Kipp turned the questioning on Cal, insisting that he had a woman somewhere he wasn't telling them about.

'Remember that morning you were in that foul mood? I was sure something was going on then,' Kipp insisted. 'But then Thea and I got beaten to pulps, and I was so concussed I forgot to ask.'

But Cal refused to divulge any information, claiming that Kipp had only recently deigned to share his real name, so the details of Cal's love life, or lack thereof, were none of his business.

'What about you, Thea?' Kipp asked good-naturedly. 'We know you were seeing that stable boy —'

'Apprentice,' Thea corrected with a groan. 'He was the stable master's *apprentice*.'

'Right. Apprentice... I got the impression that was over? Is there anyone else —'

Thea shook her head. 'No,' she told him firmly. 'There's no one.'

. . .

Just as they had on the outward journey, the days passed quickly as they headed home to the fortress. They saw no one but the odd merchant on the road and, while the nights had grown cold, the impending winter storms were somehow held at bay.

The trip had been good for Thea. She hadn't once dreamt of her fate stone or the seer who'd given it to her, she hadn't obsessed over the handful of years she had until her death came to pass, or how many months or weeks were left until the initiation test. She'd lived in the moment with her friends, something that she'd never allowed herself to do before.

But her feeling of contentment did not last long.

As the edge of Thezmarrian territory came into view in the fading afternoon light, a sound echoed across the land.

Bells.

Warning bells tolling from watchtowers.

Thea's skin crawled, her stomach roiling with dread.

A lifetime at the fortress had ingrained the meaning of those particular bells – a threat had breached the Veil.

And the Thezmarrians had been called to greet it.

CHAPTER TWENTY-SEVEN

The fortress courtyard was chaos. All the shieldbearer cohorts were assembling, with the masters of every discipline shouting over the noise while the stable master and his assistants brought dozens of horses out, saddled and ready to ride. The Warswords were there as well, wearing sleek, black armour and armed to the teeth.

Thea's gaze went straight to Hawthorne, who was surveying the madness from the outskirts, an impatient scowl on his handsome, rugged face.

'What's happened?' Thea asked the nearest shieldbearer as she jumped down from her mare's back.

'Scouts saw creatures come through the Veil to the north. They've since found their way to the Ruins of Delmira.'

Thea's insides squirmed. Was this what Hawthorne had told her about? Was this the beginning? The scourge breaking through the Veil?

The era of peace is once more at an end. Thezmarrians need to be ready.'

'That's not far from here,' Kipp cut in.

'No shit.' The shieldbearer nodded. 'The Guild Master is to send the Warswords and a small force to intercept them before they can reach Harenth or any of the outlying towns.'

'Cal!' Torj the Bear Slayer shouted.

Cal threw himself forward. 'Here, Sir!'

'Good, you're back. You're with me. Grab your bow.' The Warsword then caught sight of Thea and Kipp and paused. 'You two as well.'

'Torj,' Esyllt interjected, shoving his way through the crowd. 'They've only just returned from Harenth. They haven't been training for six days.'

'Then this will truly test them, won't it?'

Thea had never heard Torj snap at the weapons master, so it showed how high tensions were running.

'You heard the man,' Esyllt pushed them. 'Get yourself armed. Real blades. And find some fresh horses.'

Heart hammering and spurred into action, Thea checked the stable stalls for an unclaimed horse. It was no surprise that all the war horses and stallions had been taken, but a young gelding remained, and she set about saddling him. When she fumbled for a third time with the bridle, she realised she was trembling, and when it took her four tries to buckle the girth beneath the horse's belly, she drew back and stared, watching her fingers quiver.

A shadow fell across the hay at her feet. 'You're nervous,' the familiar deep voice said.

Hawthorne stood in the doorway, his eyes on her shaking hands.

'I'm not nervous,' she argued, gripping the reins to hide her tremors.

'Yes, you are, and you'd be a fool not to be.'

Clenching her jaw, Thea did a final check of the tack and made to lead the gelding from the stall.

Hawthorne blocked the way, towering over her. 'Last I saw you, you had a stab wound that was barely healed. You shouldn't be on this ride.'

Thea's stomach dipped at the mention of her visit to his cabin, where his fingers had grazed her scarred skin, where she'd traced the muscles of his chest and had felt the heated brush of his lips against hers. Where he'd left her wanting and alone, *again*. But she didn't yield a single step. Instead, she squared her shoulders and lifted her chin in defiance.

'No one, not even you, is going to stop me from riding out with my fellow shieldbearers. Thezmarr has been called upon, and I intend to answer.'

'Is that so?'

'Yes.'

He seemed to consider her. 'Are you healed?'

'Are you going to paw at my clothes again to check?' she snapped.

Hawthorne's lips parted, as though he were considering exactly that. 'I wasn't the only one doing the pawing, Alchemist.'

Thea refused to blush. 'Perhaps not,' she allowed. 'But I was nothing but clear about what I wanted, you... You, however, did not afford me the same respect.' The words came out as sharp as the hurt she felt, the hurt she thought she had buried well.

He took a step forward. 'Th — Alchemist,' it was a plea, regret flickering behind those silver eyes.

Thea's blood heated, and she yearned to know exactly what words he thought might make a dent in her armour now.

The pandemonium outside grew louder, more demanding, and after a moment's hesitation Hawthorne broke away from her, stepping out of her path.

'You'd best be ready.'

And Thea didn't know if he meant for the battle, or for him.

Back in the courtyard, the other Warswords directed their force with brutal efficiency. It was decided that they would lead an entire unit of warriors comprised of both guardians and shieldbearers to the ruins of Delmira.

Thea got swept up in the madness. Packages of rations and canteens of water were passed around and stuffed into saddlebags. Shieldbearers were arguing over who got to accompany the guardians; commanders were strategising by the gates and the masters were rushing around like headless chickens.

It was Hawthorne's deep voice that carved through the turmoil. 'If you have not been selected for this assignment, get the fuck out of the way. We move out in five minutes. This threat will not wait for us.' There was no room for questions, it was pure command, pure power.

The tension was palpable and Thea grew impatient to leave. She fit her foot to the stirrup and mounted her gelding, ignoring the ache in her lower back.

'Thea!' shouted a familiar voice through the crowd. 'Thea, wait!'

Wren tore through the cluster of remaining shieldbearers, not even wearing a cloak against the chilled air. In one hand she had a fistful of her skirts so she didn't trip and in the other, a small satchel which she held up to Thea when she reached her at the gates.

'I knew you'd be going,' her sister panted, shoving the bag towards her.

'What's this?' Thea asked.

'Supplies.'

'Like what?'

Wren gripped her ankle, eyes wide as she stared up at her. 'Tell me you were listening, when you came back to our shifts with Farissa?'

Thea tensed at the desperation lacing her sister's words. 'I was listening —'

'Move out!' Torj the Bear Slayer bellowed across the courtyard.

Wren was already breaking away from her. 'Then you'll know what to do,' she called, darting towards the fortress before she was trampled.

'Thea,' Cal called from nearby. 'Move!'

Shoving the satchel in one of her saddlebags, Thea snatched up her reins and squeezed her horse's sides, already part of the force that was sweeping through the gatehouse.

It seemed that no sooner had Thea and her friends arrived back in Thezmarr than they were riding out again. As they cantered along the Mourner's Trail with the thunderous sound of two hundred horses echoing between the trees, the weary exhaustion in Thea's bones lifted, replaced by the quiet thrum of anticipation. And fear.

Hawthorne was right: she'd be a fool not to fear what lay ahead. No one spoke more of the threat, or what might await them in the ruins, but Thea had sense enough to know this was no training exercise.

Time blurred, as did the Bloodwoods surrounding them as they rode. When they reached the end of Thezmarrian territory, Hawthorne led them north, atop his black stallion and flanked by his fellow Warswords. As the night deepened, they turned left onto the fork in the Wesford Road that had once connected the fallen kingdom of Delmira with the rest of the midrealms.

Thea had never travelled north before, nor did she know how long it would take for them to reach the ruins. Over the years, she had learnt some geography and history about the territory... The terrain inclined steadily all the way to Delmira, which had countless hills and valleys. She knew a great lake rested between the ruins and Harenth, though she couldn't remember its name.

Perhaps it no longer matters, she reflected.

Books had told her that Delmira itself, or what was left of it, was situated on a plateau of land beyond ancient cliffs. Over the many years since its demise, farmers had tried to settle on the empty land, but misfortune had befallen each and every one of them, leading the entire midrealms to believe that the kingdom and its lands were cursed.

It was these thoughts that filled Thea's buzzing mind as they rode into the night. All the while, she wished she could see the landmarks; wished she knew the terrain as well as the Warswords.

One day, she vowed. *One day I'll know the midrealms so well I could ride with my eyes closed.*

In the blanket of darkness around her, she could make out the outline of her friends riding beside her. Neither had spoken since they'd left Thezmarr. In fact, no one had spoken except the Warswords; the low sounds of their voices carried to the back of the unit. Doing her best to signal her intentions to Cal and Kipp, Thea urged her horse into a quicker pace, squeezing her way to the front of the unit.

There, the Warswords' words were clearer.

'Any idea how many?' Torj was saying.

Vernich grunted. 'Scout reported at least two, maybe more. They said the darkness that followed was worse than ever.'

'That doesn't surprise me,' Hawthorne allowed. 'I've seen it countless times in my recent travels. Night ripples from the shadow wraiths. They can create it, manipulate it in every way. It can take the form of whips, lashing their victims bloody, or manifest as their darkest traumas. And that's just the start. They can swallow you whole with it.'

A bead of sweat trickled beneath Thea's shoulder blades and an icy shiver ran down her spine.

There was a heavy pause before Torj spoke again. 'You think they're like the ones we fought in Naarva?'

'Exactly like those,' Hawthorne replied.

Tremors wracked Thea's whole body as she listened.

'You have truly been hunting shadow wraiths all this time, haven't you?'

'You knew this, Torj. Among other filth that claws its way through the Veil.'

'We knew you were hunting monsters,' Vernich interjected. 'No thanks to your non-existent correspondence, mind you. But we didn't know what monsters or where.'

'Nor did I, until I was facing them.'

'Do we have enough men?' Torj asked quietly.

Another silence hung between them, and Thea thought for a moment that Hawthorne might not answer at all.

'I hope so,' he said at last.

. . .

The company rode for several hours along the old, unused trail, the yellow moon and glittering stars barely illuminating the path before them. The impending winter's bite was sharp. Thea was close enough to Cal and Kipp that she could hear their teeth chattering, and if she looked up into the night sky, she could see her breath clouding before her face.

It seemed tradition for the men to share stories from other realms as they rode – a distraction from what lay ahead. They spoke of sea drakes and teerah panthers, of strange flesh-eating moths and water horses called backahasts, of reef dwellers and all-powerful tyrants, but not a single creature sounded as harrowing as the ones Hawthorne had described.

If the Hand of Death was wary, so too should they all be.

The conversation then changed to deadly locations. One soldier had escorted prisoners to the Scarlet Tower off the coast of Naarva, a place he claimed had nearly sucked away his will to live. Another had navigated a barge through the Broken Isles, where he swore he blocked his ears against the deathsongs of ancient cyrens. One of the commanders contributed his story about being half frozen to death on the way to Aveum. Each story was presented as a badge of honour, proof that the warrior belonged amongst the rest and had earned the right to fight the darkness that threatened the realm.

At the sound of the next voice, Thea groaned inwardly. She could easily discern Seb Barlowe's haughty tone cutting through the whispers.

'In my first year at Thezmarr,' he was saying. 'I discovered a series of caves in the black mountains that flood every winter during the storms. Lightning isn't supposed to strike the same place twice, but those caves... Lightning strikes there every season, in exactly the same spot.'

'Oh, for fuck's sake.' Thea couldn't help the scoff that escaped her. Everyone else had spoken of their adventures beyond the fortress, of deadly curses, harrowing terrain and ancient evil creatures... While in Seb's pitiful story, he hadn't even left the nest.

But Seb had heard her. 'There are dozens of skeletons up there,' he continued, his voice low and full of menace. 'According to legend, it's where the Thezmarrian warriors tied up the whores they no longer wanted. They left them to drown when the caves flooded during the storms. A sacrifice to whatever gods haunt the seas. Even Elderbrock mentioned them, remember?'

Anger warmed Thea from the inside, and her fingers itched to wrap around the bastard's throat.

'Ignore him,' Kipp murmured.

'It's hard to ignore him when I want to kill him.'

Kipp made a sound that might have been a choked laugh. 'You know what the cook at the Laughing Fox used to tell me when I got picked on as a boy?'

'What?'

'She used to say, Kristopher...'

Thea snorted at the use of his given name.

'*Kristopher*, she'd say,' he continued, changing the pitch of his voice slightly. '*It doesn't matter who stands against you... What matters most is who stands with you.*'

'Oh.'

'I've been living by that token ever since. There will always be people who bet against you, Thea. But the ones you stand with shoulder to shoulder when you face an enemy are the ones who count the most.'

Thea let her friend's words wash over her. As they sank in, she locked them away in the corner of her mind where she kept precious things, and turned her gaze ahead.

The Warswords set a gruelling pace, and the company rode into the day and the following night, with only a handful of brief stops to rest and water the horses. As they drew closer to their destination, the conversation grew thin and eventually only the Warswords spoke.

A palpable tension had settled over the Thezmarrian force, especially amongst the shieldbearers. The reality had sunk in that this was no mock battle they approached, but a real one that might see some of them irrevocably changed, or lost to Enovius.

Thea's own body was taut in the saddle as they rode, her hand absentmindedly reaching for her fate stone. The jade was warm from being pressed against her skin. Faced with such darkness, she didn't know if its presence comforted or terrified her. While it promised she wouldn't meet her end amidst the ruins of Delmira, it offered no other assurances. No matter how many hours and minutes she borrowed and stole from other facets of life, it wouldn't be enough. Not unless... Unless she became a Warsword's apprentice.

Audra's words were a whisper in her mind. *'Most things to be feared exist in life, not in death.'*

Thea traced the number carved into the stone with the pad of her thumb. All her life she had been called reckless, all her life she'd been accused of having a death wish, all the while wanting nothing more than to simply *live*.

A unified gasp snatched Thea from her thoughts.

Ahead, the golden light of dawn revealed a field carpeted in heather, and in the distance stood the Ruins of Delmira. She could make out collapsed watch towers and crumbling walls, and grounds that appeared scorched.

The sun rose higher as the Thezmarrian company rode towards the fallen kingdom's heart.

The earthy scent of heather tickled Thea's nose, an aroma that nudged something at the back of her mind, something she could not place. Her hands grew clammy around the reins and her shoulders were tight with tension, the hair on her arms standing up.

Suddenly, she saw why.

An unnatural darkness gathered on the horizon, sapping the sky of the dawn light. Thea's heart hammered as she counted five distinct shapes...

'Fuck,' Hawthorne muttered, echoing her thoughts exactly.

He signalled for the company to halt and unsheathed both his longswords.

Torj took up his famous war hammer. 'So there's more of them. We can handle them, can't we?'

'It's not just that there are more...' Hawthorne turned his horse to face his fellow warrior. 'Those are no ordinary shadow wraiths... Those are *rheguld reapers*, the kings of the wraiths – a much deeper evil. They're larger and stronger, more evolved. And they are far more intent on spreading their darkness than their spawn. While like regular shadow wraiths, they're attracted to power, they also seek hosts for the curse they wish to disperse. Reapers want to make more monsters, not just maim and kill. We have to change our strategy at once. Our broader forces *cannot* engage.'

Hawthorne didn't take his eyes off the creatures in the near distance. 'There is something strange at work here and beyond the Veil... But the time for speculation isn't now. What matters is that they can only be killed a certain way.'

'Which is?' Vernich glowered.

'Their hearts must be carved from their bodies,' Hawthorne stated, no emotion in his voice. 'They will be drawn to our power. Only we stand a chance against them.'

'Tell us what we need to do,' Torj said.

A muscle twitched in Hawthorne's jaw, but he nodded.

Thea clung to every horrific word the Warsword spoke, and when he was done, she felt sick.

'So we draw them out with our forces, surround them,' Vernich repeated. 'But only the Warswords attack?'

Thea's skin crawled at the sight of the sprawling darkness amidst the ruins of the fallen kingdom.

'That's it,' Hawthorne confirmed.

Vernich looked resentful. 'You're bad news, Hawthorne. Always have been. Nothing but chaos follows you across the midrealms.'

'Then you'd best hope it follows me into battle too and sends this filth back where it came from.'

'Enough,' Torj cut in. 'We need to brief the others.'

An eerie calmness settled around the Warswords as they went to work explaining the tactics to the commanders, who, in turn, rallied their units to them.

Thea, Cal, Kipp and about two dozen Thezmarrian warriors were under Esyllt's direction and Thea had never been more grateful for the weapons master's brusque nature. He spoke to them in the same manner he did back at the fortress, managing to ground them, despite the looming danger.

'We are to act as a diversion, to give our Warswords the best shot of doing what they do best. This is no game. There are no prizes for being heroes. You follow orders. You do only as I do! You do as I *command*,' he shouted. 'When I tell you to charge, you charge. When I tell you to bear right, you bear right, and when I tell you to halt, you gods-damn better halt. I'll have no dead warriors on my watch, you hear?'

The silence that greeted him was stunned, but Esyllt was clearly having none of it.

'I said, *do you hear?!*'

'Yes, Sir!' the answer echoed back.

With the voices of her comrades around her, Thea steeled herself, for it was not nerves that raced through her now, but bright, unadulterated terror.

Esyllt looked to the Warswords and gave them a nod; his task was done, they had been briefed, though Thea doubted anything he said could prepare them for the horrors ahead.

Still in his saddle, Torj reached across and clapped Hawthorne on the shoulder. 'We have an army to address. Or rather, you do. You know what we're facing better than anyone.'

'Fine,' Hawthorne muttered.

All units looked to him, leaning in.

Thea's heart pounded painfully as she took in the sight of him. The hardened Warsword closed his eyes and inhaled deeply through his nose, as though fortifying himself against what was to come. Emotion crackled deep within Thea as she watched him: a mighty warrior, a defender of the midrealms.

He turned his horse in a circle to face the swell of fighters before him, and Thea couldn't tear her eyes off him. He cut a commanding figure against the backdrop of the end of the world as they knew it. The black amour he wore fitted his broad shoulders and muscled chest like a second skin. He sat upright in his saddle, the reins looped around the horn as he struck his two longswords above his head to silence the company, the black tattoo on his hand stark in the fading light.

Quiet fell like a heavy blanket over the squadron, and Hawthorne's silver eyes were fierce as he fixed them upon the crowd.

'What awaits us in the ruins are creatures unlike you've ever known.' His voice projected to the furthest shieldbearer. 'Not only are these beasts capable of ripping a man in two, but they leak shadow and darkness. They can reach into a man's soul and infect it with the same curse they bear...'

Thea's stomach turned to iron.

'These are *rheguld reapers*, ancient monsters, kings of the shadow wraiths. In my time at Naarva, I discovered that to kill one is to kill those wraiths it sired, but a reaper can only be destroyed in one way. Today, that task falls to me and my brothers alone. But we did not bring you all this way to sit idle. Your commanders have their orders. Yours are to follow them.'

Thea swore his gaze lingered on her.

'Warriors of Thezmarr,' he yelled. 'Will you ride into battle with us? Will you fracture the enemy's focus with your war cries and your courage?'

Torj beat his hammer against his shield.

'Will you follow us into the very heart of evil and help us drive it back into the black fissure from which it came?'

All around Thea, men struck their shields with their weapons, the beat strong and steady; the rhythm of a war drum. The sound found its way into her blood, moving in time with her pulse and feeding the crackling energy in her veins.

'Warriors of Thezmarr,' Hawthorne called again. 'The destiny that awaits us amidst the rubble is one of glory, should you want it enough. Rage with me, rage against the darkness and emerge victorious protectors of the midrealms once more.'

The war drum beat on, building and building with each powerful word. Thea hadn't realised she'd been clutching her fate stone so hard her fingernails had cut into her palm. She tucked it into her shirt and unsheathed her own blade, the steel gleaming in the little remaining light as she struck it against her shield.

'And so we test the fates again,' she murmured.

Hawthorne's horse reared onto its hind legs and the Warsword thrust his swords into the sky. His command barrelled into their forces like a breaking wave.

'Charge!'

CHAPTER TWENTY-EIGHT

Thea's horse surged forward with the rest, all thoughts emptying from her head as she was swept up in the sea of warriors charging towards the darkness.

The hooves of two hundred horses trampled the heather in a thunderous assault. For a second, Thea forgot about the hierarchy of warriors and her fate. Instead, her chest swelled with a mixture of fear and pride. *This* was the spirit of Thezmarr, *this* was what it meant to be part of the guild, and there was no denying she was a part of it now.

Her shouts were swallowed by the rest as they galloped in a frenzy towards the ruins, the three mighty Warswords as the vanguard.

But as their forces closed the gap between them and the enemy, Thea could not only see the ribbons of shadow, but finally the creatures from which they rippled...

Her heart seized.

Cloaked in black mist, the beings were not of this world. Once, they might have been men, but no longer... Their bodies had been elongated; each figure towering to what she could only guess to be eight to ten feet in the air. They had strange, sinewy frames, with claws for hands and curled, antler-like horns protruding from their heads.

'Bear right!' Esyllt's voice cut through the horror. 'Bear right, now!'

Thea and the rest of her unit did, splitting off from the other half of their forces and charging around the outskirts of the ruins to circle their prey.

The *rheguld reapers* shrieked at the diversion, and at the Warswords, who broke away from the main force and charged straight for them. There was no mistaking the twin blades raised at the front.

Darkness now flowed freely from all five of the creatures. Thea could feel its iciness and malice from several yards away.

'Halt!' Esyllt's cry sounded as their forces met on the other side.

Thea's body went taut as she drew her reins up short with clammy hands. The Thezmarrian cavalry surrounded the ruins, where the capital's city walls had fallen long ago, watching on as the Warswords leapt from their horses and launched into their attack.

It was three against five.

The *rheguld reapers* moved as shadows. One moment there, a hair's breadth away from the kiss of a blade, the next they were somewhere else; a whisper of what once had been, darkness lashing out like a whip.

Thea could taste their insatiable thirst for blood and destruction.

'Firebearers! Archers!' Esyllt called. 'At the ready!'

Thea surveyed their forces as burning arrows were nocked and bowstrings creaked.

'For the love of the Furies don't hit our own!' the weapons master bellowed. 'Loose!'

Arrows of fire rained down on the monsters, coaxing outraged shrieks from their withered throats, splitting their focus, distracting them from the main attack.

Why are the rest of us just standing here? Thea's mind screamed desperately. Her ribs were too tight and her insides felt hollowed out. There was nothing she could do from here, nothing but watch as the Warswords flung themselves at the unworldly creatures.

Time slowed.

A ragged gasp lodged in her windpipe as Hawthorne, wielding his twin blades, stalked towards the largest monster. He moved with the power of the Furies, their gifts of speed, strength and agility thrumming from him. Springing into an attack, his swords were nothing but blurs of silver against the black power raining down on him. The Warsword blocked the lashing darkness and rolled beneath the creature, slicing the backs of its legs.

The reaper shrieked, lunging for Hawthorne, incensed.

But the warrior struck again, this time launching himself from Torj's braced shield and leaping into the air. He brought both blades down into the beast's abdomen, its scream piercing through the noise of combat around them.

Another volley of flaming arrows flew through the air.

A wave of darkness crashed into one of the Thezmarrian units.

Thea didn't know where to look. To Hawthorne's right, Vernich was battling two of the horrid things, and on the other side of him, Torj duelled with another...

Then... where is the fifth? Thea thought with a start, scanning the ruins.

'Gods,' the word escaped her lips as she spotted it stalking the perimeter around the Warswords. Without thinking, Thea urged her horse forward —

A sword flung out, stopping right before her chest.

'Don't even think about it,' Esyllt snarled.

Where did he come from?

'We can't just leave them to fight alone.'

'Your only role here is to follow my orders. Are you questioning those orders?'

Thea faltered. 'No, Sir, I —'

'The answer is "No, Sir" and that's it.' The weapon master's eyes locked onto hers, drawing her attention away from the battle unfolding before them. His gaze was brimming with fury, with warning. 'There is nothing we can do. Only a Warsword can kill a creature like that,' he added. 'Our forces are doing all they can to assist.'

'If you told us how, we could —'

'Not another word,' he glowered. 'If you question my authority again, I'll string you up and feed you to one of those things myself. You are a shieldbearer. There is much you do not know about the realms. If you want to survive to one day fight yourself, you'll shut up and follow my orders.'

Thea struggled to swallow the lump in her throat. 'Yes, Sir.'

She tore her gaze away from Esyllt as he moved to the front of the unit once more, to find Hawthorne pinning a reaper to the ground, one of his blades slicing through its chest. The creature's high-pitched screams echoed across the ruins as the Warsword carved into its flesh. Hawthorne stabbed his other sword into the soft earth and crushed the reaper's throat, muffling its shrieks beneath his boot before reaching into its ribcage with his bare hand.

If it hadn't been strapped to her forearm, Thea would have dropped her shield.

There was a sickening, wet sound as Hawthorne ripped its heart from its chest cavity.

A strange cry made Thea's blood run cold.

Another was lunging for Hawthorne.

'Archers, loose!' Esyllt's order carried across the battlefield.

But the arrows did little against the leathered skin of the monsters.

Torj flew into action, leaping in front of his fellow Warsword and taking the attack on his shield.

Gasps sounded from the cavalry as they watched Torj and Hawthorne take on two of the creatures, Hawthorne's blades now aflame.

A few yards away, there was an earsplitting cry.

Vernich tore the heart from a reaper with a roar of his own, throwing it aside with a thud, red blood streaked with black rushing down his arm.

It was three against three now.

Thea's eyes were watering, she'd forgotten to blink, her knuckles white as she gripped her horse's reins in a death grip. She couldn't look away, unable to believe what she was seeing, unable to stand her own lack of action.

The Warswords moved like gods, tearing through the darkness, wielding their weapons as extensions of their own bodies. *Winning.*

What had seemed impossible only moments before was now unfolding before their very eyes. The Warswords of Thezmarr had taken on the masters of shadow and were emerging victorious.

No sooner had the thought fluttered into Thea's mind, something changed.

The black ribbons leaking from the *rheguld reapers* multiplied and not only did they hit the frontlines of their forces in a punishing blow, but they struck out like vicious vipers, wrapping around the Warswords' legs, coiling around their wrists —

'*No,*' Thea gasped.

Two of the creatures held the three warriors in their claws, toying with them cruelly as they fought off the lashings of darkness, while the third reaper sized up the force surrounding the ruins. In the overwhelming presence of a giant wraith, two hundred men seemed like no men at all.

With the Warswords occupied, the third creature paced the perimeter, drinking in the sight of the cavalry with huge, clouded blue eyes. Some of them were already disbanded, bleeding on the ground from the previous attacks. The rest trembled in its presence. Shadows seeped from its long body, coiling towards shieldbearers and warriors alike, while the monster emitted a strange hissing sound that made the hair on the back of Thea's neck stand up.

Despite all their training, the horses panicked, pawing the ground with their hooves and whinnying in distress.

'Hold the line!' Esyllt yelled, holding a fist up as the creature approached their unit. 'Don't you bastards dare move, I said, *hold!*'

The reaper sniffed the air, as though it could smell their fear, as though it were savouring it like the aroma of a fine wine. It slinked towards them, shadows dancing.

Thea drew a trembling breath.

The creature's head snapped straight to her, piercing her with its eerie gaze.

'Hold!' Esyllt's voice boomed again.

Was he waiting for the Warswords? Because they seemed to have their hands full —

The creature surged towards the unit.

Someone screamed and Esyllt went flying from his horse, his body hitting the ground with a hard thud.

In a panic, his horse bolted, as did a dozen others, their riders either falling from their saddles or barely hanging on as their mounts fled from the chaos.

The line broke.

The hissing sound was even closer this time.

The reaper towered before them, brandishing its claws with the promise of violence and death, black mist rippling from its being. It surveyed them with those unsettling eyes, its gaze seeming to search, landing again on Thea.

She gave a strangled cry as a current of something powerful shuddered through her, her body trembling.

'Seb, no!' someone screamed.

Sebastos Barlowe was on the ground, brandishing his sword at the monster, one of his lackeys at his side. The two young men advanced on the creature, wielding their blades but failing to land a hit.

Black energy struck out, throwing Seb's friend across the ruins, battering his body into the stone rubble with a sickening crack. The reaper turned back to Seb, advancing with another hiss and another crack of its dark whips.

And Thea leapt through the air, landing in a crouch in front of Seb, dragging him down behind the wall of her shield.

The impact of the reaper's magic nearly split her shield in

two. It shuddered through the timber and into her bones, which came alive at the touch of power. Together, she and Seb braced themselves behind the barrier as the creature struck repeatedly.

'Shield wall!' she heard herself shout, as the dark sorcery recoiled, readying to attack again. 'Shield wall!' She didn't know if anyone would hear or if anyone would listen. The calamity across the ruins was no longer contained to the creatures of power and the best of the Thezmarrians.

Heart in her throat, she readied herself for another blow, not sure the shield could withstand the continued assault.

But suddenly there were bodies around hers, shields thudding into place alongside hers.

A shriek in the distance told her the Warswords had overpowered their opponent.

'Drive it back,' Thea bellowed. 'Drive it back to the Warswords. They can finish it off. They can carve out its black heart!'

Shoulder to shoulder with her fellow Thezmarrians, their shields overlapping, Thea led the formation forward, forcing the creature back, its attacks growing weaker against their braced armour.

Beyond their formation, the Warswords at last escaped the poisonous tendrils, brandishing their blades.

More and more shieldbearers and warriors joined Thea's wall, shields slotting into place, their strength growing as they advanced inch by inch, pushing the —

A spray of hot liquid rained down upon them, and even in the dim light, Thea saw the black-streaked red. *A reaper's blood.* A trickle of it ran down her face and her nostrils were filled with the scent of burnt hair.

She peered through a crack in the wall as they pushed

onward, to see Torj brutally bringing his hammer down on the creature's head, and Hawthorne, covered in blood, holding a wet mass in his clenched fist - another heart.

'Forward!' she yelled, putting her whole weight into the shield.

Together, they drove the monster back.

A victorious shout echoed across the ruins and something thudded on the ground, rolling towards Thea's boots. Slowly, she lowered her shield.

The head of the reaper lay there. Its clouded blue eyes now blank, staring up at the sky.

The remaining darkness ebbed away and Thea's unit gradually broke apart, a wet sucking sound filling the silence as Torj used a dagger to cut out the creature's heart.

Nearby, someone threw up into the dirt.

The morning light that had been swallowed by the creatures of darkness slowly returned, illuminating the aftermath of the battle in horrifying clarity.

Thea had been so caught up in what was happening with her own unit, she hadn't seen what had happened to the others. Men lay sprawled across the ruins, some bleeding profusely, some with limbs sticking out at strange angles. Then she remembered —

'Esyllt!' Dropping her sword and shield, Thea threw herself to where she'd seen the weapons master thrown from his horse. She felt Kipp beside her as they rushed to what remained of the city walls, finding Esyllt amidst the rubble, his back against a half crumbling stone pillar. His grey hair was matted with blood – his own.

Thea skidded to her knees beside him. 'Esyllt, can you hear me?'

The weapons master groaned, his chin clumsily lifting from his chest. 'Yes, unfortunately I can...' he muttered.

Thea sighed with relief, sitting back on her heels while Kipp examined his head wound.

'You'll need several stitches, Sir.'

'Not by your hand, boy,' Esyllt growled, wincing beneath Kipp's touch.

'I wouldn't dream of it, Sir. Only the best for you.'

Esyllt scoffed, causing a line of blood to leak from his mouth.

'Kipp,' Thea said, suddenly remembering. 'Get the black satchel from my saddlebag. I might have something.'

Kipp was already on his feet.

'Where's Vernich?' Hawthorne's voice boomed.

Waiting for Kipp, Thea peered across the carnage, searching the grounds for the older warrior.

'There!' someone shouted after a moment, pointing to a limping figure approaching them from the northern ruins.

As the older Warsword drew closer, Thea could see that under the grime and blood, he was pale. The fabric around his left leg was split open, as was the flesh beneath it, fresh blood pulsing from the wound.

'Torj!' Hawthorne shouted as he rushed forward, catching Vernich as he stumbled.

'What happened?' Torj demanded, joining his fellow warriors and peering down at the grotesque state of Vernich's leg.

'Cursed thing got away,' Vernich answered through gritted teeth. 'It clawed the shit out of my leg and then... It exploded. I thought it had blasted itself into nothing, but... when my senses returned, I saw it, a black shadow drifting out to sea, towards the Veil.'

'Fuck,' Hawthorne cursed.

'Here Thea.' Kipp's voice called Thea back to poor Esyllt. She just hoped she'd been right about what Wren had packed for her...

'Esyllt,' she said gently. 'Who in our forces is trained in battlefield healing? Did we bring healers' kits?'

The weapons master groaned as she helped him sit upright.

'Esyllt?' she prompted.

'The Warswords,' he said. 'But by the looks of things, they'll need to tend to their own. Some of the commanders —' he grimaced as she parted his matted hair around his wound.

Thea looked up at Kipp. 'Go speak to them, see who among them can take care of the wounded.' She peered into the satchel and heaved a sigh of relief. 'Tell them I have some supplies.'

Kipp was about to launch himself towards the commanders.

'Kipp?' she called out, and he stopped instantly, turning back.

'Find Cal, will you? Make sure he's alright.'

'On it,' he told her with a salute.

Along with several others, Thea worked into the midmorning tending to the wounded shieldbearers of Thezmarr. While she knew she'd never be as skilled as Farissa or Wren, she was grateful for the lessons she'd insisted upon, for the tasks keeping her hands steady in the aftermath of all that had come to pass amidst the ruins of Delmira.

She saw numerous shieldbearers displaying signs of shock. Farissa had warned her about that, and she knew were it not for keeping busy, she would likely be experiencing the same. Thea was careful to distribute the contents of Wren's satchel herself, because her sister had not only packed a range of healing supplies, but poisons as well.

Wren's nothing if not prepared...

Thea lost herself in the work, wrapping gashes with clean linen bandages, sure to tell every 'patient' that she wasn't a real healer and they'd need to visit the infirmary upon their return to Thezmarr. None of them seemed bothered by her proclamations, merely thankful for her treatments that she hoped would keep any infection at bay.

'Thea?' Kipp said softly.

Thea whipped around. 'Is it Cal? Have you —'

'Cal's fine. A few scratches, stinks like a foul chamber pot, but fine.'

Thea's whole body sagged with relief. 'What is it then?'

Kipp's face fell. 'It's Lachin.'

'What about him?'

'I thought you should know. He's... He's dead.'

Thea blinked, the words refusing to settle. 'Dead?'

Kipp nodded.

Thea's hands fell away from the shieldbearer she was treating and she sat back on the damp earth, covering her mouth with a trembling hand. 'He's...' but she couldn't form the sentence.

'Here.' Kipp pressed something cool into her palms. 'Drink that. You haven't stopped since...'

Numb, Thea lifted the canteen to her lips, only to find the burning liquid wasn't water and for that, she was grateful. She hadn't realised how cold she'd become.

'How? How did Lachin die?' she eventually managed.

Kipp grimaced. 'One of those things near sliced him in two...'

Thea forced down the bile that had risen in her throat and tried not to picture their comrade. 'Gods.'

A shadow fell over them as Hawthorne appeared at Thea's side. The Warsword surveyed the line of warriors, all bearing marks of her treatment, and offered her his hand. 'I think you've done all you can here.'

Thea took it, warmth flooding through her as he helped her to her feet.

'You're unharmed?' he asked softly.

'Yes. Unharmed.' She scanned his body, noting the countless gashes, the mottled bruising already forming across his skin.

He followed her gaze. 'I've had much worse than this,' he murmured.

Thea reached for her satchel. 'Let me help —'

Hawthorne shook his head and stilled her hands, swallowing them with his. 'Rest now.'

Then, he was walking away.

They were always leaving one another, it seemed.

It was some time before Thea registered Cal had joined her and Kipp, sporting a gash to the collarbone, but otherwise unharmed.

'I thought you told us there was "no one" in the picture, huh?' Kipp said, following her gaze trailing Hawthorne across the ruins.

Thea ignored him. Her own shock had sunk in as she walked, wandering the rubble aimlessly, waiting for orders. She forced herself to take deep breaths of the crisp morning air, ignoring the metallic tang, and took comfort in the presence of her friends on either side of her. In the midday light, she could see the blood, both human and wraith, staining the earth.

At the centre of the ruins, the Warswords convened.

Vernich's leg had been sewn up rather gruesomely, but he stood as straight as the others, arms folded over his chest as they considered the heap of gore at their boots.

'We should burn them,' Torj was saying.

'And toss the ashes out to sea,' Vernich added in agreement.

But it was Hawthorne, covered in blood and filth, who shook his head. 'We take the hearts,' he stated. 'We take them back to Thezmarr.'

And so, with the hearts of monsters in blood-soaked sacks, and the bodies of fallen comrades fastened to riderless horses, the Warswords mounted their stallions once more to lead the warriors of Thezmarr home.

WILDER HAWTHORNE

As they journeyed back to Thezmarr, Wilder rode ahead of the company. He needed to distance himself from his Warsword brothers, from the commanders, from everyone and everything, including the terror that had gripped his heart when the reaper had clapped eyes on Thea.

A *rheguld reaper...* A creature of unending darkness, a monster who could *reach into a man's soul and infect it with the same dark curse they bear.* It had been drawn to *her.*

His shirt grew damp with sweat beneath his armour. The shadow wraiths and their masters didn't belong in the midrealms, they never had, and yet here they were, stalking the kingdoms freely, seeking power to feed off. That was what they thirsted for the most, more than blood, more than death.

Power. They could sense it, sniff it out amongst a crowd...

And one had found it in Thea.

From the heart of the fray, Wilder had watched the creature pause mid-kill, its attention snapping to her, as though someone had lifted a cover from its eyes and at long last it could see the very thing it had always wanted.

The attacks had continued to evolve since he'd first learnt of them, since he'd dealt with the monsters firsthand himself. For them to send in five reapers was unusual, given that their deaths ensured the demise of those they had sired. To Wilder, it meant there must be more of them than they knew, that their numbers must be great enough that losing entire units was of no concern. That the reapers were getting arrogant. Both thoughts were terrifying.

Wilder's chest burned as it grew tighter. He pushed the loose hair from his brow and reached for his flask, taking a much needed draught of the fiery liquid within.

Dratos' message had mentioned wraiths, not reapers. But five of them had got through... Five.

The Veil grows more unstable each day. Our rangers have reported sounds echoing from beyond its mist, and tremors wracking the outskirts of our lands.

So there was a tear in the Veil to the south of Naarva, and now another to the north of Delmira. One threat after another, there was no limit to the horrors that could be unleashed upon the midrealms. And not enough Warswords in the realms to protect the people of the three remaining kingdoms.

The wraith hearts knocked against the side of his saddle, the putrid stench of burnt hair leaking from the blood-soaked bags. As always, he'd hand them over to Farissa to see if anything could be learnt about the creatures' make-up and weaknesses.

Pain tugged at the flesh between his shoulder and his chest as he rode. There was a deep gash there. Not for the first time, he cursed his unfortunate timing of undertaking the Great Rite when Delmira had already fallen and their supplies of Warsword armour had been used. Where his shitty imitation armour left him vulnerable, one of the creatures had got a decent swipe in, it seemed.

He glanced down, the wound hot with a looming infection. Reluctantly, he poured some of his liquor on the cut, swearing as his skin blazed. This was exactly the sort of injury one might use their vial of springwater from Aveum on. It was the purest of all the lands, boasting healing properties lusted after by many. But Wilder had suffered wounds far worse than this, never deeming them worthy of the vial's use. No, he'd manage just fine, as he had all the times before.

Both Talemir and Malik had used their vials too soon, so that when the dire hours came, they had nothing left. And by the time Wilder had got to them, it had been too late for him to use his. He wouldn't make their mistake. He'd save his until the most grim circumstances gave him no other choice.

A scratch wasn't reason enough. He only wished they'd slain that final piece of filth before it escaped out to sea. Who knew how many wraiths would have disintegrated upon their sire's death? It had been a missed opportunity.

He took another drink of fire extract and winced as the movement pulled at the gash. Still, he could not let go of the nagging sensation. A *rheguld reaper* had singled Thea out.

Ignoring the pain, Wilder urged his stallion into a gallop. He needed to get back to the fortress. He needed answers.

CHAPTER TWENTY-NINE

Hollow cheers sounded upon their return. Caked in
blood and dirt, with the bodies of their fallen in tow,
the Thezmarrian forces felt anything but victorious. They
entered the courtyard, a heavy sombreness cloaking them as
they went about returning their horses to the stables, many
of them dazed. The horror they'd witnessed was unequalled
in scale and violence, and of the two hundred Thezmarrians
who fought amidst the ruins of Delmira, six had lost their
lives. Including Lachin.

None, however, had been claimed by the dark curse the
rheguld reapers bore. None had been turned into monsters of
shadow. That was a small comfort.

A deep sense of unease still permeated throughout the
cohort.

'They kept the hearts...' Kipp ventured slowly as they
entered the Great Hall.

Cal rubbed his temples, looking as weary as Thea felt.
'What are they going to do with them? They hold dark

magic… There's a reason they didn't burn them and cast them into the seas.'

'They bloody should have,' an older warrior muttered behind them. 'Bad luck to keep cursed things like that.'

Cal and Kipp murmured their agreement.

But Thea stayed silent. As the shieldbearers trudged numbly to their quarters and bathing chambers, she peeled away from the group. Ignoring the exhaustion screaming in her bones, and the filth that covered her, she shouldered Wren's near-empty satchel and trekked up the endless stairs, to the only place that might hold answers for her.

A crackling fire blazed in the hearth and a familiar form took up the entirety of one of the armchairs, a furry mass at his feet.

'Malik,' Thea sighed. She was glad he was there.

Slowly, he turned in his seat, for once not transfixed by the flickering flames. Upon seeing her, he was on his feet faster than Thea had ever seen him move. Dax let out a bark for being disturbed.

But Malik's grey eyes were filled with alarm and at the sight of his concern, Thea was suddenly raw, fragile even, something she hadn't felt or allowed herself to feel in a long time.

Malik froze in place.

'I'm alright,' she croaked. 'I'm not hurt.'

But her voice broke as she spoke the words. All at once, it was too much. She didn't even know what she was looking for; she didn't know where to start. The thought of searching the shelves for a clue to something she was well beyond understanding was overwhelming in the face of all that had happened at the Ruins of Delmira, and soon, her gasps were coming in hard and fast. She couldn't get enough air —

A large, gentle hand closed over her arm.

Disorientated, she allowed Malik to lead her to the spare armchair, which he carefully pushed her down into.

Thea couldn't remember the last time she'd sat in something other than a saddle. Her chest caught with emotion as she leaned back into the cushions.

'I'm alright,' she told him, told *herself*. 'I'm alright.'

He clearly didn't believe it, and Thea couldn't blame him for that. She could only imagine what she looked like; the chaotic, bloody state of her.

But Malik didn't step away. He waited.

She rested her hands on her knees and leaned forward, trying to quell that restless sensation shooting through her veins.

Malik took up his usual place once more, leaning back in the tattered armchair and stretching his long legs out before him. He patted her hand in comfort and Dax resumed his position at his master's feet in front of the fire, huffing, as though being interrupted had been a big inconvenience to him.

'Thank you, my friends,' she said quietly.

They stayed like that in companionable silence for a time, both Malik and Dax giving her the space she needed, but waiting to offer support should she need it.

Dax's ears pricked up and Thea leapt to her feet as Hawthorne entered the library. While he no longer wore his armour, there was still blood coating his skin from the battle.

'You,' he said, taking a step towards her. 'What are you

doing here?' His gaze travelled from her filthy appearance to Malik and Dax, who didn't rise in his presence.

'Reading,' Thea replied finally, reaching for the nearest book.

Hawthorne's gaze lingered on the former Warsword in the armchair. 'Leave,' Hawthorne commanded her.

'I —'

'It wasn't a request, Alchemist.'

But then Thea noticed a wound, still bleeding, just beneath his collarbone. 'You're hurt.'

'Hardly.'

'I can help.'

'I don't want your help.'

That was the final straw for Thea. She stormed right up to him, her rage as fair a match as any for his towering frame and battle experience. 'I don't care what you want,' she snapped. 'Sit down. Shut up. And let me treat that wound before it worsens.'

She hadn't realised her hands were on her hips, but they were. With fury in her veins, she let it blaze in her eyes as she stared the Warsword down.

Stunned, he took a step back.

'Now,' she practically growled.

Surprisingly, after a moment's pause, the Warsword did as she bid, seating himself in the armchair she'd vacated.

'Shirt,' she ordered, picking up Wren's satchel and digging through the remaining supplies.

A loud rip sounded, and Thea looked up to see Hawthorne tearing through the fabric.

'Was that necessary?' She swiped the last clean bandages from the bag.

'It was ruined anyway.'

Shaking her head, Thea went to him.

Even seated before her, he was enormous. It was a funny sight – a mighty warrior squeezed into a green velvet armchair. She kept that thought to herself as she studied the gash.

It was deep and ragged, the surrounding skin hot and irritated. She couldn't help but click her tongue in annoyance. 'You should have let me tend to this in the field.'

'You'd done enough.'

'That's not really your call to make,' Thea replied, cleaning the wound with the last of Wren's paste.

He gave a hiss of pain.

'I don't have a gentle healer's touch, I'm afraid,' she said as she worked. 'The creature's talons pierced your armour?'

The Warsword made a noise of confirmation. 'My breastplate is a piece of shit.'

'Isn't it supposed to be impenetrable? You get special armour from Delmira, don't you?'

'Every Warsword before me did,' he supplied with a grimace. 'By the time I completed the Great Rite, Delmira had fallen and its supplies had been exhausted. I got stuck with a poor imitation from Harenth.'

'Oh.'

Hawthorne gave Malik a pointed look. 'If he wasn't such a great hulking giant, I could have borrowed his.'

Malik seemed pleased by the jab.

'What of your vial from Aveum? It has healing properties, doesn't it? That could have cured this...' Thea ventured.

'I'm saving it.'

'For what?'

'Something worse than a scratch, Alchemist.'

'Gods, you're stubborn.' Thea wiped her hands on her

own filthy shirt and returned the tin to her satchel. 'But this should help stave off that looming infection before you go to the infirmary.'

'The infirmary is full. I don't need —'

'Yes, you do.' Thea didn't know where all this command in her voice had come from, but she liked it. She especially liked it when he didn't argue back.

Slowly, she placed a patch of gauze over the wound and started bandaging him. All the while, she could feel Malik's eyes on her, on *them*...

'So you took my advice...' Wilder ventured.

'What advice?'

'The bit about knowing how to treat wounds.'

'Perhaps you should have taken it yourself.'

'I know plenty.'

'This wound begs to differ...' Thea scoffed. 'But yes. I asked Farissa to teach us, me and the other alchemists. Figured it wasn't an entirely useless suggestion. Besides,' she added, stepping back and surveying her handiwork, while also trying to ignore the sculpted grooves of his torso. 'Now we're even.'

Hawthorne drew his lower lip between his teeth as his gaze travelled over her. 'I suppose we are.'

Suddenly self-conscious, Thea packed away Wren's dwindling supplies, fiddling unnecessarily with the cork of one of the vials to distract herself from the weighted silence between them.

Hawthorne was the first to break it, clearing his throat. 'Now you can leave.'

Thea's brows shot up. 'That's not much of a thank you.'

The Warsword shrugged. 'Like you said, now we're even.'

'Glad to see you're back to your usual self,' Thea snapped. But then she eyed Malik, who seemed a little unsettled.

Hawthorne noted her hesitation. 'I'll keep him company. I like that he doesn't talk.'

Thea could have sworn she saw amusement in Malik's eyes.

The Warsword motioned to the door. 'Go on, get out. For once, I need some peace without you.'

'Bastard,' she muttered and went to the exit. Gods, she was done with his moods. But something made her linger in the doorway, a strange tingling at the base of her neck, and she glanced over her shoulder.

The Warsword sighed heavily, resting his head against the back of the armchair before giving Malik, who was *grinning*, a long look. 'Oh, shut up,' he muttered, and then reached down to scratch Dax behind the ears.

With her brow furrowed, Thea tiptoed out the door into the corridor beyond and ran straight into Audra.

The librarian took one look at her filthy clothes and said: 'You'd best not be bleeding on my books.'

After assuring Audra that she had done no such thing, Thea threw caution to the wind and headed for the master bathing chambers. Though she suspected that no amount of time in a tub would erase the filthy feeling from her skin or fill the gaping chasm in her chest.

CHAPTER THIRTY

Thezmarr went into mourning for those lost on the battlefield. Atop the cliffs where not so long ago they had held the mock battle, now six funeral pyres burned for the fallen warriors.

They gathered around in silence, and Thea noted that the eyes of those who'd been there that day were haunted. Throughout the night, the shieldbearers had murmured in their sleep and she didn't need to be in their dreams to know that reapers stalked there, casting their shadows across minds when they were most vulnerable. Thea had dreamt of them too, and the seer and the fate stone, as though all their destinies were entwined.

Now, as the flames licked the sky, the first snow of winter began to fall.

Thea lifted her face to the clouds, closing her eyes against the icy flakes that kissed her skin and thinking of the shieldbearer they had lost amidst the ruins. She had despised Lachin at first, considering him just another mindless lackey following Seb around. But as the weeks had worn on, he'd changed. He'd become more than that... He'd become an ally. And had the forces of darkness not snatched him from the midrealms so soon, he might have one day become her friend.

The tightness in Thea's chest did not abate.

Her cohort had lost one of its own. And a good one at that.

With the cold numbing her face and making her nose stream, she stood shoulder to shoulder with Cal and Kipp, saying her silent farewell to Lachin. And when the fires had burned out and they returned to the fortress, they watched as the Guild Master carved Lachin's name, along with those of five others, into the stone swords in the great hall, acknowledging their sacrifice to the midrealms.

The following days saw a change in Thezmarr and its guild. A looming sense of danger spurred them on through their drills and sparring matches. They had seen what enemies could do with a single swipe of their claws and the fact that one of the *rheguld reapers* had escaped was not lost on them.

With only a handful of weeks until their initiation test and the rancid scent of burnt hair still lingering in her nostrils, Thea pushed herself harder than ever. Despite the winter storms that constantly lashed Thezmarr, she rose before the others every day to perform her own set of weapon and strength drills as well as endurance training, and she retired long after her peers, determined to prepare her mind as thoroughly as her body for whatever came next.

It had been one thing to hear Hawthorne's words of warning about the scourge, another entirely to see the festering shadows for herself. Everyone was on edge, everyone was waiting.

'This is not the last we have seen of their black hearts and foul curses,' Cal murmured as they trekked through the Bloodwoods back to the fortress one afternoon. 'The midrealms have been darkening for years... And now, every day is worse than before.'

'But no one talks about it. Not even to us,' Kipp replied. 'It's not a good sign, is it?'

Thea couldn't shake the feeling that she had been marked in some way. She still flinched at the memory of the warm splatter of blood that had hit her face. She had scrubbed her skin raw multiple times, and yet the stain remained, lingering on the surface.

But she steeled herself. 'I don't know what to make of it. All I know is that the Warswords prevailed that day in Delmira. They'll continue to do so.'

'You saw Vernich's leg. Not even the Warswords are invincible,' Kipp said.

Silence settled between the friends as the fortress came into view.

Thea knew something was different as soon as they passed through the gatehouse. Several gleaming thoroughbred horses were being tended to in the courtyard and half a dozen guards bearing the Harenth sigil were stationed at the entrance.

'What's going on?' Cal murmured beside her.

Unease coiled in Thea's gut. 'King Artos is here.'

'What?' Kipp said. 'None of the royals ever visit Thezmarr.'

Thea was already making her way up the stone steps. 'They do now, apparently.'

There were more guards inside the fortress, but no sign of the king or the Guild Master. It was Esyllt who Thea spotted on his way to the Great Hall, and she made a beeline for him.

'What's all this about, Sir?' she asked when she caught up with him.

The weapons master looked older to her all of a sudden. He was thinner and new lines around his face made his demeanour even more stern. But oddly, his expression softened upon seeing her. Perhaps it had to do with her tending to his wound on the battlefield.

'There is to be a feast tonight,' he told her, glancing at Cal and Kipp, who fell into place behind her.

'What for?'

Esyllt seemed to hesitate a moment before answering tersely. 'King Artos wished to celebrate the victory at Delmira.'

The trio stilled.

Celebrate? Thea thought. While they had defeated most of the reapers, not only had one escaped, but they'd returned to Thezmarr to burn funeral pyres. How could they think to celebrate in the face of that loss?

The thoughts must have been plain on her face, for the weapons master cleared his throat. 'The king also wishes to honour the dead and their sacrifice for the midrealms,' he told them stiffly. 'His Majesty has generously brought all the supplies for the feast, along with his household staff to tend to the tasks at hand.'

'That's a lot of people...' Cal murmured.

Esyllt nodded. 'King Artos intends to reward all of Thezmarr. You'd best get back to your quarters and clean yourselves up. Everyone is to be presentable, dressed in their best for our royal guests.'

The three friends did as their weapons master bid and rushed off to their rooms.

The fortress was buzzing and those who hadn't been at Delmira were downright excited. Thezmarr had never played host to a royal feast before, and that King Artos had brought the palace chefs with him was all anyone could talk about. But to Thea, it seemed wrong. The embers in the pyres were barely cold. A reaper was free somewhere out there, and there had been a moment each day where she could still feel the trickle of fresh blood down her face.

But there was nothing for it. Thea made quick work of changing into a clean shirt, wondering if Wren and the others would don their best dresses. Sam and Ida had always dreamed of attending a ball, and Thea supposed this was the closest they might ever come to a formal occasion.

In the rush to the Great Hall, Thea got separated from Cal and Kipp, bodies pressed all around her as they shoved their way through the corridors, everyone eager to get a good seat where they might glimpse upon the king – or better still, the beautiful young princess.

Thea was forced onto a bench with shieldbearers whose faces she recognised but names she didn't know. She craned her neck, looking for Cal and Kipp, but the tables were more crowded than normal and she couldn't spot them amidst the fortress staff and warriors. Instead, she turned her attention to the head table, where the Guild Master had offered his usual place to the king.

King Artos of Harenth sat in the high-backed chair, his gilded crown gleaming atop his head, his daughter, Princess Jasira to his right and Osiris to his left. The Warswords were at their regular seats, whereas people like Audra and Esyllt had been moved to another table entirely.

Thea's breath caught as Hawthorne's eyes met hers for the briefest of moments. He wore the same mask of unbroken violence as always, but the twitch in his jaw told Thea that something was amiss.

She trained her gaze elsewhere.

Even from a distance, Thea could sense the magic rolling off the king, and for a brief moment, she wondered what he felt from them all. He was an empath, not a mind whisperer, but what did that entail? Was it merely a matter of feeling emotion from others or was it more than that? Could he influence it? Manipulate it? Kipp had said he was the most powerful in the Fairmoore family in centuries...

Servants from the palace came forward with silver trays of food, the aroma of roasted meat making Thea's mouth water. Great dishes of baked potatoes, honeyed carrots and buttered greens were placed all down the middle of their table, along with freshly baked bread, jugs of rich gravy and decanters of fine wine. It was a display of decadence that Thezmarr had never seen before.

When what seemed to be the entire population of the fortress had been seated, King Artos raised his palm in a wordless command for silence.

Quiet fell, and the king got to his feet, goblet in hand.

'Greetings, people of Thezmarr,' he said, his voice projecting to the far corners of the Great Hall. 'First, thank you for hosting myself and my household in your wondrous fortress. After the events that transpired at the ruins of Delmira last week, both myself and my fellow rulers of the midrealms felt it was important to show our gratitude and unity in a tangible way. I am here as a representative of not only my kingdom, Harenth, but Tver and Aveum as well. The feast we have tonight is to honour the great work you do here and across the lands to protect us and our people.'

He paused a moment, allowing his words to settle over the hall.

'Last week, the midrealms experienced a furious assault, an assault that threatened the very fabric of the peace we have worked so hard for. But our warriors of Thezmarr, our Warswords, liberated our lands from the darkness. Tonight we celebrate that liberation.'

Thea shifted in her seat, feeling a tightness in her gut. Around her, several others were fidgeting as well. Again she tried to search the tables for her friends, wishing they were at her sides to exchange glances with. She couldn't see her sister's bronze top knot either, the hall was simply too full.

'Of course, we wish to honour those who lost their lives,' the king was saying, his voice sombre. He listed the six names one by one. Thea's hand clenched around her goblet and she couldn't help but look to the giant swords where only days ago they had carved their comrade's name. Who else's name would she see marked there before she met her own end?

King Artos raised his drink. 'To the fallen!' he called.

'To the fallen!' the hall echoed back, raising their own goblets and tankards and drinking deeply.

The king, however, was not finished. 'The events at Delmira and the loss of such promising warriors have forced our hand,' he told them.

At those words, Thea's skin prickled and she watched as the unease washed across her cohort. She sought Hawthorne's gaze again, but he didn't look at her. His eyes were on the king.

King Artos addressed Osiris. 'Guild Master, shall I share the news?'

Osiris stiffened in his seat and Thea got the impression that sharing whatever news it was had not been the original plan. But the Guild Master had no choice but to clasp his fingers together on the table and nod.

King Artos cleared his throat again. 'I shall stay on in Thezmarr for another week. Due to the looming threat of these creatures from beyond the veil and the darkening days, your Guild Master, along with the rulers of the midrealms have agreed that we need more warriors in our midst... Which is why we have decided that the pending shieldbearer initiation test shall be moved up.'

There was an audible gasp from all around Thea, whereas Thea herself wasn't actually sure the air was reaching her lungs.

Moved up? She twisted in her seat again. *Where in the realms were Cal and Kipp?*

'The trial will take place in two days' time.'

The hall erupted.

CHAPTER THIRTY-ONE

T *wo days.*

Two days until the test that would determine if Thea and her friends were worthy of the Thezmarrian warrior title.

Thea used the pandemonium that had broken out across the hall to slip away from her table. Standing on the outskirts of the chaos, she scanned the sea of shieldbearers and fortress staff for Cal and Kipp. They should have all been together for the news, and they needed to be together now, to process it, to come up with some sort of plan of attack. Kipp would no doubt have a strategy. They had to be ready. They would leave no man – or woman – behind.

So where are they?

Then it hit her: they had thought the same thing and had snuck away to meet her. Relief surging through her, Thea ducked from the hall, glad to escape the chaos. She made for the dormitories, imagining Kipp and Cal waiting to dissect the news with her.

Together they had taken on the most demanding training

programs in the midrealms, they had faced down the cruelty of Vernich the Bloodletter and they had braced their shields against the attack of a *rheguld reaper*, a master – a king – of shadow wraiths... A trial would be easy, wouldn't it?

Thea burst into the dormitories, her pep talk at the ready, determination gleaming in her eyes —

The room was empty.

There was no sign of Cal or Kipp.

Rubbing the back of her neck, Thea paced. Had she misjudged things? She checked the other rooms – also empty. Was there a place she'd forgotten about? Perhaps the armoury? She hadn't considered it initially because in the middle of winter, the armoury was freezing. But if they weren't here... She snatched up her thicker fur cloak and made for the door, a roiling sensation churning her stomach.

Dismissing the feeling as nerves for the impending trial, Thea hurried along the corridor, her sense of urgency growing with every step. But upon hearing voices around the next corner, she slowed to a halt just before the bend.

' — idea of a sick prank, apparently...' It was Torj, his voice lowered. 'But with what we've seen lately... We need to get them back. They're our responsibility.'

'We never asked for that responsibility,' came Hawthorne's harsh response.

Thea steadied herself against the cold stone wall, her heart racing as she crept forward.

'It comes with the territory,' Torj snapped back. 'We are protectors of the midrealms, *all of the midrealms*, including Thezmarr. We cannot just leave —'

'Have the offenders go find them.'

'They're denying all involvement.'

Thea's skin was crawling, blood rushing to her ears as

suspicion took hold. There was only one bastard that came to mind.

'Of course they are. Throw them to Vernich. He'll beat it out of them.'

'You and I don't work like that, Wilder. And Vernich has his favourites.'

'You know *nothing* of how I work, Torj, besides that I work alone. And this is why. You cannot trust anyone. Nor can you rely on anyone.'

Torj's next words were quieter, so much so that Thea had to creep even closer to the corner of the corridor to hear them.

When she did, she wished she hadn't.

'It's Callahan Whitlock and Kristopher Snowden...' Torj said.

Thea's knees buckled, her hand flying to her chest that suddenly felt too tight.

A heavy silence followed and Thea dug her fingertips into the wall, desperate to latch onto something that would keep her upright.

At last, Hawthorne spoke. 'How do you know?'

'Someone reported it. One of the younger shieldbearers broke the code. He said it was going too far, that it went beyond the usual shieldbearer hazing.'

'And yet he couldn't say where they've been taken?'

'No. The others sensed his hesitation. They knocked him out cold. I only found him in the stables just now.'

Hawthorne swore viciously.

'It sounds bad,' Torj said. 'But I haven't the faintest idea where to start.'

Thea swallowed the lump in her throat and stepped

around the corner, coming face to face with both Warswords. 'I do.'

Hawthorne swore again, pinching the bridge of his nose and pacing a few steps away, but Torj turned to her.

'Do you have something to do with this?'

'You think I would ever hurt Cal and Kipp?' The words flew out of her mouth in anger before she realised who she was speaking to.

But Torj was shaking his head. 'No, no, I don't... But you know where they are?'

As she'd been eavesdropping, Seb Barlowe's face kept flashing before her. He was the main offender for everything, and he had apparent immunity because of his uncle's relationship with the Guild Master. She had hardly seen him since their return, chalking it up to a silent truce between them. After all, she had saved his life from the reaper, some naïve part of her had thought he was exercising some humility. But she should have known that humility was not, and would never be, in Seb Barlowe's nature. Instead, he had seen her actions as a form of humiliation, a questioning of his own warrior prowess... and had been biding his time ever since.

His words echoed in her mind now: *A series of caves in the black mountains that flood every winter with the storms. Lightning isn't supposed to strike the same place twice, but those caves... Lightning strikes there every season, in exactly the same place... There are dozens of skeletons up there... It's where the Thezmarrian warriors tied up the whores they no longer wanted.'*

And that was exactly the sort of location he'd take any captives; a place he deemed an embarrassment, a place of death for lowly women and whores, not men. For whatever reason, Seb had been unable to get to her, so he had gone for the next best thing.

That bastard, she cursed. *I should have let the reaper have him, I should have let him die.* If her friends were hurt, that would be the fate that awaited him.

'Althea?' Torj prompted.

'It's a guess,' she admitted. 'But I think Seb took them to the caves in the black mountains, the ones that flood every —'

'Winter storm,' Hawthorne finished for her. He was already moving, Torj right alongside him.

Thea darted after them.

'Gods,' Torj muttered as they ran towards the stables. 'It was me who gave them the fucking idea.' He shook his head. 'There's two trails up to the caves. They could have taken either.'

Hawthorne nodded. 'We split up. I'll take the northern path, you take the southern and we meet at the caves.'

'I'll tell the Guild Master —'

'No time,' Hawthorne snapped. 'Plus, the king is here. We don't want him involved.'

Thea's blood went cold as she chased after them. When she had first met Kipp, she had thought he would be her downfall, but it was she who would be the end of him if she didn't get to those caves. It was hard to run with the world suddenly closing in around her, as every moment where she had antagonised Seb flashed before her eyes. This was her fault. Her friends could die because of her. And she could not, *would not,* allow that to happen.

She charged into the stables, close on the heels of the Warswords, only to be wrenched from the ground and slammed into the wall.

'What in the name of all the gods do you think you're doing?' Hawthorne snarled, the front of her shirt curled in his fist.

Thea threw herself into action, disengaging his grip on her and shoving him back.

He looked almost surprised.

'I'm going with you,' Thea said fiercely.

'Not a chance, Alchemist.'

But Thea was done with listening, was done with men underestimating her and telling her what to do. She squared up and took a step towards the Warsword, nothing but fire in her eyes. 'Try and stop me.'

'Hawthorne?' Torj peered out from one of the stalls, his brows raising in surprise at the sight of her. 'What are you doing here, Althea?'

'I'm getting my friends back.'

Fury blazed in Hawthorne's silver eyes. 'I'm not letting some reckless shieldbearer accompany me to the Black fucking Mountains —'

Thea whirled to face him, fury of her own crackling in her veins. 'You told me to find friends in this fortress, to get myself a team,' she snarled. 'And I did that. Cal and Kipp are it. They're the people I trust more than anyone in this godsforsaken place. And I'm going to get them back, with or without you.'

'Alchemist...' Hawthorne warned, his voice low.

'My name is *Thea*,' she interjected angrily, 'whether or not you have the balls to say it. And answer me this: haven't you ever wanted to protect someone?' she argued. 'Would you deny me that?'

Torj watched on, his horse forgotten. 'I'd wager he's trying to protect someone right now...' he murmured.

But Thea ignored the Bear Slayer and focused solely on the Warsword whose path seemed entwined with her own.

His expression darkened for a moment, a muscle flickering in his jaw.

Thea held her breath as the Warsword closed the last few inches of space between them.

He leaned in, closer and closer to her —

The slide of steel sounded.

He drew a sword from the rack on the wall behind her and pressed it into her hands.

'You tell no one what happens here,' he said quietly.

'No one,' she agreed, her fingers curling around the hilt.

Torj cleared his throat loudly as he mounted his horse. 'Right. Now that's settled...'

Thea and Hawthorne sprung apart.

The golden-haired warrior eyed them warily as he strapped his war hammer across his back. 'I'll meet you at the caves.' And with that, he nudged his stallion towards the gates and left them to it.

Together, Warsword and shieldbearer saddled their horses in silence, strapped on their weapons, and rode quietly into the night.

Even in the moonlight, Thea recognised the path almost at once. It was the one she had so often climbed to the cliffs, before Hawthorne had caught her with her dagger, before everything had changed. It led to the spot from which she had watched Hawthorne's return to Thezmarr, and imagined herself the stuff of legends.

On horseback, they covered the forest portion of the trail quickly and the hair on the back of Thea's neck prickled. The terrain inclined and grew rockier, the winter winds snarled around the mountains and the cliffs, cutting through every layer of clothing Thea wore. She grit her teeth and cursed silently as the skies opened up, sending down a steady sheet of icy rain.

'They'll die if we don't find them,' she heard herself say.

'We'll find them,' came Hawthorne's reply. 'We'll get them back.'

Warsword and shieldbearer continued up the mountains in the dark, passing the cliff where Hawthorne had first caught her spying. Thick black clouds covered the moon and there was not a star in sight, but Thea could hear the roar of the waves, unable to stop the shudder that wracked her body as she recalled how high they could soar before they crashed. With her reins clutched tightly in one hand, Thea used the other to rummage through her cloak for her fate stone. The piece of jade, smaller than the head of a teaspoon, offered both curse and comfort.

The horses took them higher still. Up on the edges of the mountains, the wind was so sharp it cut like glass, and one wrong step would spell doom. She held the stone tighter. That would not be her destiny. Not today.

The sound of the waves grew louder and, having seen them touch the clouds before, Thea pictured them barrelling into the side of the mountain, flooding whatever cave her friends had been abandoned in. With another shiver, she urged her horse to quicken the pace as much as the perilous terrain would allow.

The steady sheet of rain hammered down on them with renewed vigour, now torrential. Lightning lit up the sky, shooting a jagged bolt into the raging black currents that surged at the base of the cliffs and lapped at the mountainside.

The spray of the sea hit Thea and she tasted salt on her

lips, panic gripping her heart in an iron fist. How flooded was the cave already? How long had Kipp and Cal been subjected to its torture?

'There!' Hawthorne shouted above the howling wind.

Thea squinted through the downpour and the dark, only just able to make out a narrow fissure on the cliff's side.

'We have to leave the horses,' he called, swinging himself down from his stallion.

'They'll run!'

'Here!' His hands reached up, encircling her waist, helping her down as more lightning flashed around them, followed by the near-deafening crack of thunder. Once her feet were planted on the wet rock path, he took her reins.

He loosely tied the horses to an overhanging branch. 'If they're spooked, it's best they break free rather than hurt themselves,' he told her.

The beasts were frightened, but at Hawthorne's touch, they seemed to understand it was safest to stay put.

Thea was already heading towards the cave. Water poured down either side, a river flowing into the darkness beyond.

'Cal!' she shouted. 'Kipp?'

There was no answer.

Hawthorne was beside her in a second, striking a flint to a torch. Without another word, she took it from him and lunged for the entrance —

His hand wrapped around her arm, water sluicing down his face. 'Are you mad?' he yelled. 'Are you so desperate to throw yourself in harm's way?' He pushed her aside and reclaimed the torch, entering the cave first.

Swearing, Thea followed closely behind, and let out a

sharp breath when she found herself thigh-deep in an icy swell as they descended into the hollow.

Even in the cave's shelter, the noise from the storm outside rattled her teeth, the thunder echoing off the wet walls.

'Cal? Kipp?' she shouted again, her voice hoarse.

All manner of filth floated around them, but Thea kept her focus forward, scanning the strange grotto for any sign of her friends. Hawthorne's torch illuminated stalactites hanging like daggers from the ceiling and a series of what looked to be claw marks on the walls.

They rounded a bend, the water climbing up their bodies at an alarming rate. It now reached Thea's waist —

A strangled gasp escaped her.

Ahead, two limp bodies swung suspended by their wrists over a hollow. Their heads hung to their chests.

Thea heard the scream, the sound echoing through the cavern, but she didn't register that it had come for her own mouth as she rushed towards her friends, water swelling around her.

Where they were hung, the water was up to their shoulders, but their hair was drenched, which meant the flood had been hammering them for some time.

'No, no, no,' she murmured, now swimming out to them.

The surge beside her told her that Hawthorne was with her, the glow of the torch left somewhere behind, but she ploughed ahead, desperate to reach her friends.

She wasn't the strongest swimmer and the weight of her clothes and the sword at her back dragged her down, but the terror that gripped Thea by the throat was unlike anything she had ever experienced and it fed strength to every part of her, fuelling her as she carved through the water.

With a sob, at last she closed her hand around Cal's leg beneath the surface and Hawthorne reached Kipp beside her.

'Cal,' she spluttered. 'Cal, look at me, please.'

His eyes remained closed.

Thea looked around desperately. Neither she nor Hawthorne could reach their binds from below, but there had to be a way —

'There!' she shouted.

A ledge in the rocky walls stood out to her, and she swam to it. It took every ounce of strength to haul herself up, water pouring from her clothes, threatening to pull her back into the swell. But Thea dug her fingers into the rock, finding purchase with her wet boots as well. Pressing herself against the jagged surface, she inched towards the ledge, heart in her throat. She didn't take her eyes off her friends. How long had they been here? How much suffering had they endured? Thea pushed the thoughts from her mind. Her sole purpose was to get them out of this torture chamber – to make sure they survived.

Unsheathing her sword, she crept along the shelf, realising too late that the ropes were too far out for her to reach.

'You'll have to jump,' Hawthorne called. 'And fast - the water's getting higher!'

Both ropes that held her friends hung a few feet out from the ledge. She would have to slice through Kipp's rope and then Cal's on the way down.

One shot, she realised. *That's all I have. If I miss, the cave might be flooded by the time I get back up here again.*

A vision of Cal and Kipp's drowned bodies drifting beneath the water flashed before her.

'You can do this,' came Hawthorne's voice, strong and sturdy.

Thea shoved the fear down and eyed the two lengths of taut rope before her, gripping her sword.

One shot, she told herself, backing up a few paces.

She ran and leapt.

Time slowed as her feet left solid ground, her sword slicing through the air with her. For a moment it felt as though she wasn't falling, instead suspended above her dying friends, her weapon poised to strike —

But suddenly wind rushed beneath her and her blade carved through one rope, then two, and she was plunging back towards the water below.

She heard two distinct splashes before she hit the surface.

Thea went under.

Icy water swallowed her, dragging her down. She hadn't realised how deep it was, her feet yet to touch the bottom. Still gripping her sword, she kicked and kicked hard. Cal and Kipp were up there. She had to see them home, see them safe and well. Her lungs were burning as she fought her way to the top, at last breaking through with a ragged gasp.

In the lone torchlight, she could see Hawthorne hauling her friends from the water with his formidable strength, neither of them conscious. When her boots met the rising incline, she staggered towards them, her waterlogged clothes weighing her down with every step.

'Alchemist,' Hawthorne's voice commanded, and her head whipped around to face him.

'It's getting worse,' he told her, motioning to the water still rising at their feet and the roar of the waves outside. 'We have to get out of here before we all go under.'

As if in response, a brilliant flash of light lit up the cave and the rumble of the storm outside shook the walls.

Hawthorne hauled Cal over his shoulder and supported Kipp as Thea looped his limp arm around her, struggling beneath his tall frame.

'Hurry.'

Together, Thea and Hawthorne carried the shieldbearers from the depths of the flooded cave, water sloshing at their knees, hiding the obstacles in the terrain until they were stumbling over them.

Every muscle in Thea's body burned as she helped drag Kipp through the cavern, his soaked, unconscious body heavier with each desperate step.

'Come on, Kipp,' she muttered. 'I've got you. We're gonna get out of here.'

A wave surged into the cave, nearly knocking Thea off her feet, but Hawthorne braced himself behind her, preventing her from being swept away. She steeled herself against the impact, as hard as any blow, salt water stinging her eyes and filling her nose and mouth.

Coughing and spluttering, she gritted her teeth and took another step forward. 'We've got you, Kipp,' she rasped as Hawthorne took more of his weight.

At last, the entrance came into view, and Thea prayed the horses were still there. If they weren't… If they weren't, Cal and Kipp were done for.

Hawthorne waited for her to right herself; with Cal draped over his shoulder, his feet dangling and Kipp braced against his other side, the Warsword was the image of strength and endurance.

'Horses?' Thea gasped, scanning the dark cliffs wildly. 'Are the —'

A bolt of lightning split the black sky in two, shooting down to the storm-ravaged earth, to Thea.

Shoving Kipp into Hawthorne, she had no time to leap from its path, not even a second to shield her eyes from the blazing light and force of it. She only threw her hands up instinctually, as though that could somehow save her.

All she saw was white, blindingly bright.

The impact didn't hurt.

Its current shuddered through the mountain at her feet, *through her* —

And her whole body sang *in recognition*.

Thea staggered beneath the weight of it. She *knew* this feeling, knew this *power*... She fell to her knees.

Suddenly, thunder clapped in the strike's wake, echoing deep in Thea's bones, and she gasped for air.

The tempest raged around them, the wind lashing like a whip, the rain as sharp as shards of glass. Thea's whole being surged as another streak of brilliant white light cut a pathway through the sky, a jagged, forked network of power that suspended the chaos surging over the seas.

And then, the entire storm retreated, leaving the glowing orb of the moon and the stars illuminating the now quiet, rocky mountain.

In a heap, Thea panted, her ears ringing as she saw where the lightning had struck, finding a black scorch mark visible even on the wet stone at her knees. She shuddered and lifted her gaze to find silver eyes upon her.

With Cal still hanging limply over his shoulder and Kipp clutched to his side, Hawthorne took a step towards her, peering into her face as though he were seeing her for the first time.

'You should be dead,' he murmured.

Thea's heart was hammering so hard she thought it might break through her chest and she tried to ignore the strange, flickering sensation in her veins. 'I... I know,' she said, out to the glass-like surface of the sea.

But Hawthorne hadn't taken his eyes off her. 'What are — Who... *Who* are you?'

CHAPTER THIRTY-TWO

'I think you might be needing these?' From a narrow path in the rock, Torj Elderbrock appeared atop his stallion with Thea and Hawthorne's horses in tow.

Leaving Hawthorne to his staring, Thea darted forward.

'Thank the gods,' she said.

'I'd prefer it if you thanked me,' Torj retorted, jumping down from his saddle to help Hawthorne with Kipp, pressing a hand to her friend's icy skin. 'We need to get them to shelter, and fast,' he said, glancing at the Warsword, who still peered out from the cliff's edge. 'What's with him?'

'No idea.' Thea shrugged, mounting her horse.

'Wilder!' Torj commanded, wrapping Kipp in his cloak and hauling him up into the saddle in front of him. 'We have to get them tended to. They won't last much longer out here.'

Those words sent a chill rattling through Thea's bones.

Hawthorne moved, mounting his own stallion, holding Cal to his front with one arm and gripping the reins with the other.

To Thea's horror, thick black clouds were rolling in from

the seas once more and thunder rumbled somewhere in the distance.

'To my cabin, Torj,' Hawthorne ordered. 'We won't make it back to the fortress before the next storm breaks.'

'Got it.'

Thea gripped her reins hard as the horses lurched into action, navigating the narrow, winding path of the mountains. She locked her gaze on the backs of the Warswords in front of her, the lives of her friends hanging in the balance.

They have to be alright; she chanted to herself. *They have to be alright.*

The storm broke anew, the clouds once more swallowing the moon, sending rain pelting down at them, the wind howling through the fissures in the mountains and the thunder cracking in the distance.

As they rounded another bend in the trail, Thea glanced out to the thrashing seas and the unimaginable power that gathered there. The very same power that had struck her, that had coursed through her. Were it not for the buzzing in her bones, she wouldn't have believed it. But there was no time for questions now. She tore her gaze away from the rolling waves and focused once more on the path ahead.

At last they reached Hawthorne's cabin, the warriors leaping from their stallions and carrying the shieldbearers inside. Making quick work of tending to the poor horses, Thea rushed inside after them.

A fire had been lit in the hearth, as had several candles, and in the glowing warm light Thea could finally see just how bad both Cal and Kipp looked. They were laid out on a huge bed, deathly pale, with deep rope burns around their wrists.

'Get their clothes off,' she heard herself say. 'We need to get them warm and fast.'

She left the Warswords to undress her friends, while she gathered blankets and heated water over the fire. The tasks kept trembling hands busy, but not her mind.

Will they live? If they live, will they be the same? Will they recover in time for the test in two days? Do they even know it's in two days? All that time she had sat in the warmth of the Great Hall listening to King Artos, they had been suffering. And it was all her fault. It was *she* who Seb truly hated. He had done this to hurt *her.*

Her friends could have died because of it, because of her. *They might yet still.*

Sitting at their bedside, Thea started to unravel. She had saved Seb's arse during the battle at the ruins, and this was the consequence. Who was she to think she could have ever been a shieldbearer, let alone a warrior or Warsword of Thezmarr? The only thing she would ever be was inadequate.

'Whatever you're thinking,' Hawthorne's voice growled. 'Don't.'

The pain in Thea's chest wouldn't abate. 'You don't understand...'

'I do. Better than you know,' came the reply. 'I sent Torj to get a healer. They'll get through this.'

'How do you know...' Thea's voice broke.

'They're strong and stubborn,' he said. 'Just like you. Now come and get dry by the fire. They won't wake for a while yet.'

Thea let the Warsword lead her from the bedroom to the hearth in the main room of the cabin. She hadn't realised how weak she felt until he guided her to a chair before the flames. Gently, he pushed her down into its cushions and handed her a steaming mug.

'Drink that.'

Thea didn't even bother to ask what it was; it was easier to follow directions than anything else. So she raised the mug to her lips and drank.

Peppermint tea, she realised as the steam carried the aroma to her nose. *He remembered...* The hot liquid heated her from the inside out and only then did she realise how cold she'd been. She was soaked through, had been for hours —

A heavy blanket fell around her shoulders.

'It's not your fault,' Hawthorne said softly.

Thea pulled the blanket tighter and stared into the flames. 'It is. Seb – the person who did this... It was because of me.'

'His actions are his own and he will answer for them.'

'I'll make sure that he does,' Thea whispered, already imagining Seb's face as she carved her blades through his flesh.

'I have no doubt.'

Thea looked up, surprised. 'Why are you being kind to me? I thought you didn't want —'

Hawthorne sighed. 'Because I have felt the burden of guilt and would wish it upon no one. Not even a maddening shieldbearer with a death wish.'

'I don't have a death wish.'

'No? Then why is it every time I see you, you're flinging yourself into danger?' Another sigh. 'Get some rest.'

. . .

Thea woke sometime later. She rushed to Cal and Kipp, who were both still sleeping. Some colour had returned to their faces and their brows were warm when she pressed her hand to them.

The relief surging through her chest threatened to overwhelm her, so she stepped back, and left them to rest. She found Hawthorne on the porch, leaning against the wall, staring out into the dark early hours of the morning, the rain still hammering atop the cabin's roof.

'No sign of Torj?' she asked.

He didn't so much as flinch at the sudden intrusion – he'd known she was there. 'No, but he shouldn't be long now. It'll take time to find the right people, the right supplies and ready fresh horses.'

Thea nodded. 'Cal and Kipp are looking a bit better,' she ventured.

Hawthorne nodded. 'I managed to get them to take a bit of broth each.'

'They were awake? Why didn't you —'

'Because you needed rest too. I didn't want another half dead shieldbearer on my hands.'

Thea's gut lurched. 'Did they say anything?'

'Didn't do much talking.'

'But... You think they'll make a full recovery?'

'That's not for me to judge,' he said, tearing his gaze away from the woods and looking at her, studying her intently.

'What?' she snapped, suddenly self-conscious.

'Are we going to talk about it?' he asked quietly, turning to face her fully.

'Talk about what?'

'What you did out there on the cliffs.'

Thea went still.

'Your *magic*, Alchemist.'

Thea stared at him, stunned. The word was like a whisper against her skin, calling her back out into the storms... a sudden buzzing filled her head, like a swarm of bees, the sound vibrating through her whole body.

'You have *magic*.' Hawthorne folded his arms over his chest. 'That was *magic* back there.'

Magic. Thea hid her trembling hands. She hardly understood it herself and she certainly wasn't going to discuss it with *him* of all people. Not to mention if the guild got word she possessed some inkling of power, her place would be jeopardised, there would be questions, interrogations, even.

No, she wouldn't entertain such notions, not with him, not so close to the initiation.

'That?' Thea scoffed. 'That was the Furies trying to smite our sorry arses on the mountain, and it was sheer, dumb *luck* that they didn't.'

'I know what I saw,' he told her, his voice low.

'Horseshit. Perhaps you've taken a few too many blows to the head, or the lightning momentarily blinded you. There was nothing to see.' The words flew from her mouth and her hand went to her fate stone, running her thumb over the carving as she always did. Magic or not, she'd escaped death again, not because she had secret powers, but because now was not her time.

But Hawthorne didn't need to know that.

'Where are you from, Alchemist?' he asked, taking her by surprise with the change of tact.

'Thezmarr.'

He made an impatient noise. 'You are not *from* Thezmarr.' He was still leaning against the wall, his arms crossed over that broad chest, but he watched her with an intensity that caused her toes to curl in her damp boots.

The flickering sensation in her veins was back, and he tensed, as though he could feel it too.

'I know what I saw,' he repeated. 'I know what I felt out there.'

'So you've said.' Thea scoffed. 'Do you really think...'

His eyes narrowed and he pushed off from the wall, closing the gap between them in a single step. 'You want to know what I think? I think —' He took a deep, measured breath, his whole body rising and falling.

'What?' she baited him, feeling her own temper rise to his. 'I desperately need to know what deep thoughts bounce around in that thick skull of yours. Go on, tell me.'

'I think that I have never known someone to be so *infuriating*... Someone who makes my blood boil in such a way that I want to kill you and kiss you all at once.'

Thea's heart stuttered, her skin tingling as she realised just how close he was. 'You'll no doubt fuck it up either way,' she taunted, recalling how he'd drawn her in before, only to leave her wanting. 'But go on,' she challenged. 'Do it.'

His gaze darkened. 'Kill you or kiss you?'

Despite all logic, she leaned in. She wanted this, wanted *him*, even though she shouldn't. Even though she knew better. Even though it put everything she'd worked for at risk. Even though he was *Wilder Hawthorne* and he had spurned her twice before.

Thea lifted her chin. 'Take your pick, Warsword.'

Then, his hands swept around her waist, pulling her to him, and he kissed her.

It was hard and brutal, nothing like the kiss they'd shared in his cabin before, as though even in the action itself he warred within, just as she did. Her lips parted under his, his rough stubble grazing her chin. The taste of him was peppermint on her tongue, the scent of rosewood soap and leather engulfing her senses, her legs turning to liquid beneath her.

She met his kisses fiercely, losing herself in the taste and feel of him, intoxicated, a storm in her chest begging to be unleashed.

His arms encircled her waist fully, and he turned them around, half carrying her to the wall, pushing her against it so her body was flush against his, the warmth of him encompassing her.

He deepened the kiss, scorching and bruising, demanding...

Thea arched her back and moaned against his lips, kissing him just as savagely, feeling his heart beat madly against hers. She traced his muscular torso, revelling in the strength and power of him beneath her touch, running her hands over his chest freely as she'd wanted to do for so long, his shirt still damp from the rain, his nipples hard through the soft material.

His fingers curled roughly in her hair and he claimed her mouth with his, catching her lower lip between his teeth, stealing the air from her lungs before he broke away, pulling back to gaze upon her.

The heat in his stare had her fingers at the buttons of his pants.

'What are you doing to me, Thea?' he murmured, his soft lips finding the column of her throat.

Desire pulsed all over, an insatiable need coursing through Thea. She slid one knee between his legs.

And Hawthorne made a sound deep in his throat that was her undoing.

She kissed him again, her tongue brushing his as his fingers trailed her nape, then her collarbone and the soft skin below, where her fate stone rested.

More, she wanted to cry out. *More.*

And he gave it to her, coaxing spirals of pleasure from her with every little touch, so that her whole body ached for him. Was it possible to die from need?

He kissed her neck, where her pulse fluttered wildly, and his hands sought the hem of her shirt, slipping beneath. Calluses met her bare skin, mapping her ribs and the curve of her breasts before dipping to cup her between her legs, rubbing her through the fabric.

Thea gasped.

'Is this where you want me?' Wilder asked, the rich timbre of his voice promising all manner of dark pleasure.

'Yes,' she breathed.

We're going to do this, here, *on the porch, out in the open.* The thought echoed pointlessly in her mind. Pointlessly because she didn't care where she was, all she knew was that she wanted the layers between them gone, she wanted his hands on her, his cock inside her. She wanted to feel every part of him. At last the buttons of his pants came undone and his breathing hitched.

Her own chest heaved, need coursing like a blazing fire – she was utterly lost in him. And she knew that would be their downfall, knew this would change everything.

The same hands that had taken the hearts of monsters now traced her skin, dangerously close to her own heart. Would he rip it from her chest as well? Would it matter?

'Wilder,' she whispered, his name like a prayer on her lips.

Suddenly he was pulling away.

'Someone's coming —' he murmured, starting towards the door, leaving her alone and panting.

A moment later, footsteps sounded on the porch, followed by someone clearing their throat.

Torj was there, Farissa and Wren close behind him.

CHAPTER THIRTY-THREE

It was as though Wilder had stolen all the breath from her lungs. Without him pressed against her, she was suddenly cold. Thea had to stop herself from touching her fingers to her lips, instead she masked her expression and greeted Farissa and Wren.

'I'm so glad you're here,' she said, pulling her sister into a hard embrace.

If either alchemist had an inkling as to what they'd just interrupted, they didn't let on. Wren simply squeezed her back, enough for Thea to know that Torj had filled them in on the events of the evening.

Thea showed them inside, where Torj and Hawthorne were waiting.

'Through here,' Hawthorne said, leading them through his cabin into the bedroom.

To Thea's relief, both shieldbearers were awake, albeit weak. 'You're alive.' She rushed to the bedside.

'Just,' Kipp managed with a wince as he tried to sit up.

Guilt lanced through Thea. Not only was it her fault that

her friends had endured such suffering, but while they'd been lying in their sickbed, she'd been outside pawing at a Warsword.

Her face must have visibly fallen because Kipp reached for her hand and squeezed it. 'We're alright,' he told her. 'Or at least, we will be.'

Cal, however, said nothing.

Farissa and Wren stood in the corner of the room rummaging through a large bag for various tinctures, and Thea couldn't help but look at the horrible marks on his wrists again. She forced herself to nod and blink back the tears that stung her eyes. 'What happened?' she asked. 'How did he get you?'

Kipp's cheeks reddened. 'In plain sight. As we were coming out of the dormitories, someone grabbed us, put a cloth over our mouths that was soaked in some sweet smelling poison —'

'What exactly did it smell like?' Farissa interjected. 'If we can identify it, we can make a tonic to counter any remaining adverse effects,' she explained kindly.

'Uhhh... Cal?' Kipp asked. 'What do you reckon?'

'I don't know,' Cal said.

'Right... Well, I guess to me...' Kipp paused, frowning. 'It smelt... sickly sweet, I... I can't remember it now.'

'That's alright, lad,' Farissa assured him. 'What happened when you inhaled it?'

'Everything slowed down, didn't it, Cal?'

Cal didn't reply, so Kipp forged on. 'I got all dizzy and then everything went black. Woke up in that cave hanging from my wrists...'

Tears stung Thea's eyes. It had been one of the worst moments of her life, seeing them like that.

Farissa was nodding to herself. 'Ah, I think I know what they used then.' Without another word, she returned to the corner to confer with Wren.

Seeing Wren, Kipp brightened. 'Elwren, come to visit me at another sickbed. We should really stop meeting like this.'

Wren snorted. 'Perhaps you shouldn't get yourself into so much trouble.'

'It's all worth it if it brings you closer to me,' he told her brazenly.

If Thea hadn't been so close to tears, she would have laughed.

'Do you ever let up?' Cal gave a weak chuckle, seeming to come back to himself. 'What of the lovely Milla at the Laughing Fox?'

'And what does a shieldbearer know of the Laughing Fox?' Torj commented from the doorway.

'Uh... Nothing, Sir. Nothing at all,' Kipp stammered.

The Warsword snorted. 'A likely story. Glad you're both still alive. The fortress would be a dull place without you.'

'Thank you, Sir.'

Thea sought Hawthorne's gaze, but he was no longer there.

The longest night of Thea's life at last bled into day and she stayed by her friends' sides, helping Wren and Farissa where she could. They treated the rope burns with a healing salve and monitored them closely for fever and signs of internal injury.

Farissa had questioned them about how long they thought they had hung there, but neither shieldbearer could tell. Kipp was almost his usual self, but Cal... Cal seemed distant to Thea, but she said nothing in front of the others.

She would wait until the three of them were alone, and then she'd beg for their forgiveness.

In the meantime, she was determined to talk to her sister and when both Cal and Kipp had drifted off to sleep again, she got her chance. With Farissa in deep conversation with Torj and Hawthorne nowhere to be found, Thea pulled Wren outside.

Even in the midst of day, the sun didn't pierce the grey clouds that loomed overhead. A thin mist had settled at the foot of the trees and everything was damp and icy in the winter chill.

Thea didn't let Wren go until they were well out of earshot.

'What is it?' Wren folded her arms over her chest against the cold. 'What's got into you?'

They stood on the porch, where only hours before she had been tangled in Hawthorne's arms... Thea shoved the thought from her head.

'I wanted to ask you something...' she ventured slowly, suddenly not sure where to start, and not wanting to ambush her sister.

'Is it something to do with why you looked so... flustered... when we arrived?'

Thea flushed. 'No.'

Wren smirked. 'You're not half as sly as you think you are, Althea Nine Lives. And how typical. I tell you to stay away from someone and you go and —'

'I don't think I'm sly,' Thea cut her off, cheeks heating.

Wren paused and took in her worried expression. 'What is it then?'

You have magic,' came the echo in her mind.

'I...' Thea stammered, searching for the right words, but

there were no right words for this. It was plain and simple. 'What do you remember, from before Thezmarr?'

Whatever Wren had been expecting her to ask, it clearly wasn't that. 'Before our parents left us here?'

Thea nodded.

'Why?' Wren demanded.

Thea pushed the loose hair from her face and sat on the top step of the porch, chewing the inside of her cheek. Wren sat next to her, trying to peer into her eyes, into her soul. She always knew when Thea was holding something back, it was an infuriating trait.

Thea rubbed her aching temples. 'Please, Wren.'

Her sister's brows crinkled in surprise. 'I don't remember the last time you said "please"...'

Thea gave her a warning look.

'I've told you before, I don't remember much...' Wren started with a shrug. 'Sounds, colours... And even those I'm not sure if they're memories or figments of my imagination, based on what Audra told us later on. All I know is what we were told: that we were left at the fortress gates, bundled in a couple of blankets and not much more. No sign of where we'd come from, no note, nothing.' She seemed to mull over her next words, chewing on her lower lip. 'When we were younger and in lessons, sometimes I'd get a strange eerie feeling wash over me, like I'd heard a particular fact or phrase before, or when some piece of imagery looked familiar. Or I'd smell something and a surreal recognition would surface... But it's all so blurry, Thea. I was an infant. We both were. How can we remember anything from back then?'

'I don't know,' Thea admitted. 'My sole memory is the seer giving me this.' She drew her fate stone from beneath her shirt. 'And even that... It's distant, you know? When I dream of her, she has no face, no discernible words beyond "Remember me" – as if I could forget the woman who told me my life would be cut short.'

Wren reached across and took the fate stone between her fingers, her brows furrowing as she studied it. 'What is this really about, Thea?'

The ache behind Thea's eyes was growing worse and a pit of dread yawned inside her. The shieldbearer initiation test was the day after next. Her friends were still recovering and had no idea, she'd had little to no sleep and her body was taut with tension. Who knew what sort of drills and training they were all missing out on today that might better prepare them for the trial? Did she really need to be having this discussion with Wren now? Could it not wait until she faced the bigger, more immediate hurdles?

'You have magic,' Hawthorne's genuine shock was what resonated most as his voice whispered against her mind again.

The scorch mark on the rock flashed before her, the deafening waves receding with the storm, the flash of recognition within...

Wren was still staring her down while she continued to grip Thea's piece of jade between her thumb and forefinger. 'Tell me.'

'It's probably nothing.'

'Tell me anyway.'

Thea opened and closed her mouth several times as she tried to decide where to start and how much to divulge. 'Something strange happened when we got Cal and Kipp out of the cave...' she started slowly.

Wren simply waited for her to continue.

'The storm... Well, it was really intense. The waves were crashing against the side of the mountain, and then the lightning —'

An odd expression flitted across Wren's face.

Thea paused, thinking her sister might say something, but she didn't.

'The lightning, it hit me.'

Wren's whole body was tense. She was so still Thea wasn't sure she was breathing.

'Wren?' she asked, tugging her fate stone from her sister's frozen grip and tucking it back inside the front of her shirt.

Her sister visibly swallowed. 'Gods, were you hurt? Are you sure it actually hit you? Because —'

'I know how it sounds. Insane. But no, I wasn't hurt.'

'Well, then what happened?'

Frowning, Thea went on. 'It was like the storm hesitated for a moment and then... it retreated.'

'Retreated?'

Thea nodded. 'Yes... It seemed to pause, then the whole chaotic mass of it pulled back and drifted off, until the seas were still.'

'Right... And what is it that you're asking me?'

Thea rubbed her temples again, trying to blink away any exhaustion and delirium. 'Hawthorne... He said it was magic.'

'You can't be serious.'

'That's what he said. He sounded certain.'

A moment passed, and a grin split across Wren's face. 'Magic?' she laughed. 'Can you imagine?'

Thea hesitated, suddenly unsure of herself, unsure what she'd been expecting from Wren... Not this.

Wren slung an arm over her shoulder, still laughing

quietly. 'Sounds like the gods were looking down on you to me.'

The tension gripping Thea's body slowly ebbed away and relief found her. 'I said something to that effect.'

'Oh?' Wren grinned slyly. 'And was that before or after you nearly tore his clothes off on this very porch?'

Thea stiffened. 'You saw?'

'Didn't have to.' Wren winked. 'A sister always knows. Besides, you forget I was the one to discover you and Evander rolling around in the hay that time. I recognised that guilty look on your face.'

'I didn't have —'

'Here I was thinking you shieldbearers would have to be better at masking your emotions.'

Thea rested her heavy head in her hands. 'You'd think...' she murmured, her heart sinking.

Wren's tone was much gentler when she spoke again. 'You know it can't continue, don't you, Thee?'

Thee... Wren rarely ever called her that.

And although she knew the truth to her sister's words, it didn't make them hurt any less.

'I know.'

'It's for the best.' Wren moved closer, so her body blocked out the cold on Thea's right side. 'Some people's paths aren't meant to be entwined for long. They can meet for the briefest of moments, dovetailing together and then parting ways once again. But that doesn't make it without meaning,' she said, her voice soft.

Thea sniffed. 'How does my little sister know of such things?'

'I'm not so little anymore.'

Thea smiled sadly. 'I'm well aware...'

Wren reached out and fixed her braid. 'Nothing would jeopardise your position here more than him, you know that...' she murmured. 'Screwing *anyone* of a higher rank could sully the reputation you've fought so hard for.'

'I know.'

'He's a *Warsword*.'

For the first time in a long while, Thea leaned into her sister's embrace and rested her head on her shoulder, hating that she felt so small, so weak. '*I know*.'

Wren kissed her brow. 'You're nearly there, Thea. The day after tomorrow, you'll be a warrior of Thezmarr and all of this... All of this will seem like nothing in the face of that.'

Thea didn't reply. She only hoped her sister was right.

Wren shifted, hugging Thea closer to her and squeezing her shoulder. 'So he thought you had magic, huh?'

'Yes.' Thea could still feel the echo of power at her fingertips, but swallowing the lump in her throat, she pressed the issue no further.

Wren huffed another disbelieving laugh. 'Can you imagine? After all these years working at Thezmarr finding out you were some long lost magical heir?'

The words clanged through Thea, jarring for a moment. Amidst everything, she'd forgotten that only the royal families of the midrealms had magic.

'Imagine.'

And there the two sisters stayed for a time, before the icy winter air chased them inside once more.

Later, when Farissa and Wren had returned to the fortress, voices dragged Thea from sleep. Drowsy, she found she was back in one of the armchairs by the fire, the living room of the cabin otherwise empty.

' — was never this bad before,' Cal was saying.

The bedroom door was ajar, and Thea couldn't help but pause at the threshold.

'Something about Thea enrages him...'

'Cal, if it wasn't Thea, it would be someone else,' Kipp countered.

'Would it? There are no other women shieldbearers...'

'So it's a problem with women, not Thea. Thea just happens to be a woman. She can't help that, nor can she help how much it seems to threaten that piece of shit. Seb is just an all-round bastard. It's just who he is. Entitled, violent, and obnoxious. All the ingredients for the worst Thezmarrian warrior.'

Cal made a frustrated noise. 'You heard what Farissa said. The initiation test is the day after next —'

So they knew.

' — and *look at us*. How are we supposed to...' he trailed off. 'After everything we've been through... We're here because Seb has it in for Thea, not us.'

His words cut deeper than any blade. Every dark thought she had had about herself, they thought, too. She was their curse. And they had finally realised it.

'She nearly died rescuing you,' came a deep voice from within the room. 'If you're looking for someone to blame, blame the bastard who bound you and left you there to drown. Don't you dare lay the blame at a friend's feet.'

Hawthorne.

'Where —' Cal spluttered. 'Where did you come from? Er, Sir.'

'This is *my* house,' Hawthorne snapped.

440

'Right, sorry, Sir.'

Thea heard Hawthorne's measured intake of breath. 'Had she not been there with me, saving your sorry arses, you would have died. Plain and simple.'

'He didn't mean —' Kipp started.

'I have been a tolerant man, more so than usual lately...' Hawthorne said slowly, as though he were struggling to rein in his temper, his control. 'But I will not tolerate disloyalty.'

Thea's heart fractured.

'We're not disloyal, she's one of us, she's our friend.' Kipp argued.

The Warsword's final words had a dangerous edge to them. 'Then fucking act like it.'

There was the slam of a door and the heavy silence that followed told Thea Hawthorne had left the room by another exit.

'He's right...' Kipp said eventually.

There was a long sigh. 'I know, believe me, Kipp, I know it. But I... I can't help what I feel, I can't help this... anger.'

Eyes burning, Thea took a step back, her knees buckling beneath her, the cabin suddenly too small for them all.

Her chest was tight, pressure building within, threatening to break through. The walls seemed closer than before, the air thinner. She scrambled for the door.

And when the icy winter gale hit her face, she didn't stop.

She ran from the cabin and kept running.

WILDER HAWTHORNE

Althea Zoltaire had stolen all the air from his lungs and lit him ablaze. Wilder couldn't speak, couldn't think of anything other than her; her body against his, her heated skin beneath his touch.

Gods, there had been far too many clothes. How he'd longed to peel away those layers of fabric, to put his hands – his mouth to those curves, to touch and taste every glorious inch of her.

Even now, hours later, he was in knots, unable to stand the feverish feeling of his own skin without her on him. The moment he'd kissed her, the rest of the world had fallen away – there was only her, only Thea.

He had denied it for months, how much he wanted her, how thoughts of her consumed him. And now... *Fuck, what now?* Now his heart pounded at the mere memory of her; her soft mouth, her hands at his belt, her waist and hips and the heave of her breasts against him. At his name on her lips, gasping and wanting.

Desire made his cock throb, and he swore quietly, pacing his now empty cabin, wishing she were back here, wishing they could finish what they'd started. He'd waited for the chance to talk to her, to explain that were it not for the others' arrival, a mountain drake couldn't have stopped him taking her against that porch wall...

But she'd gone, without saying goodbye, leaving him to help Farissa tend to the two shieldbearers and send them back to the fortress. He couldn't blame her for that. He'd fucked it up twice before.

Alone once more, he stewed in his thoughts, trying to focus on something other than the need for her, which only seemed to intensify.

Instead, he forced himself to think back to what he'd witnessed on the clifftops. That brilliant bolt of lightning carving through the night's sky had hit Thea... Or nearly hit her...?

She had denied having magic, but he'd seen it. Or was he simply so exhausted from the battle at the Ruins of Delmira and rescuing the shieldbearers that he'd conjured up some falsity? It wasn't unheard of.

He'd been so sure just before their kiss, but now...

Fuck, I'm a wreck, he thought, still pacing the living room of his cabin, the fire burning low. For the first time in a long while, he longed for Talemir Starling's counsel. His mentor had faced such perils himself. But even were Talemir here, Wilder wasn't sure he would be ready to confide in him, not about Thea. There were still too many pieces of the puzzle missing.

But the things that had occurred with the reapers and on the cliffs made one thing clear: there was something special about Althea Zoltaire, something powerful, even if she wouldn't admit it herself.

Darkness in its many forms was looming.

Wilder ran his fingers through his hair with a quiet curse.

The beautiful alchemist would be his beginning – and his end.

CHAPTER THIRTY-FOUR

I t was the day before the initiation test, and Thea was already in the training arena. She whirled her two practice swords through the air, hoping to keep the fear at bay. Kipp and Cal had been taken to the fortress infirmary for a final night of observation. Wren had informed her that they both looked well, that they were expected to make a full recovery. But her sister's words of reassurance couldn't drive the images of them hanging from the ceiling in that cave, their bodies battered by the storm.

Hawthorne had told her that in order to survive Thezmarr, she needed friends – but they didn't need her. All knowing her had done for them was nearly get them killed.

Maybe this was the reality check I needed, Thea thought as she danced her way through a parry and strike combination Lachin had taught her before he'd died. She didn't go to the Great Hall for first meal. She stayed to train alone in the arena, and when the other shieldbearers appeared for their last training session, she fell to the back, distancing herself from the rest.

But when she saw Seb amidst the crowd, not a glimmer of remorse on his face, nor sporting any evidence of punishment, she felt that strange surging sensation from within. It went deeper than rage and it coursed through her like a burning current. Her fingernails cut into her palms and it took every ounce of willpower to keep her boots planted to the spot.

The bastard had seen her though, had seen the look on her face that told him she would end his miserable existence here and now if —

'What are you looking at, stray?' he sneered, taking a step towards her.

Thea exhaled through her nose, fists still clenched at her sides, still as death as he approached her.

'I heard about that mishap with your little friends,' he said.

Thea did not speak.

Her silence seemed to only spur him on and he drew closer, close enough that Thea could feel his hot breath on her face. She did not yield a single step.

'Why don't you draw that toy sword of yours and see what it's like to fight a real —'

'Barlowe!' Torj bellowed.

Seb had the good sense to flinch at the tone.

'If you're challenging Althea to a duel, I suggest you do it *after* the test tomorrow,' the Warsword said coldly. 'Now stop wasting everyone's time and get back to your training.'

Seb's narrowed eyes slid back to Thea. 'How many Warswords *are* you fucking? They're constantly saving your hide,' he hissed. 'But they won't always be around…'

Thea blinked slowly. There was no need to respond to that. She had made her vow to Seb weeks – months – ago now, when Lachin had still been alive. She had made her promise loud enough for him to hear, for all the shieldbearers to hear.

When we face each other again, I'll have you on the ground. And unlike me, you won't get back up.

It was those words she clung to now, allowing them to anchor her fury, in her outrage at the injustice of it all. She would hone that rage and that strange energy that coursed through her very being. She would sharpen it to the point of a blade and use it to carve her way through the initiation test that awaited her.

The rest of the day was a blur and suddenly night was upon her. Thea was more on edge than ever, and the final drills and warnings weren't the only reason. Though she hadn't seen Hawthorne since, he was never far from thought, stoking that fire within and she was worried it might consume her, might distract her from the task at hand.

King Artos had indeed extended his stay in Thezmarr to oversee the outcome of the initiation test, a decision that had many of the older warriors whispering amongst themselves.

At the evening meal on the eve of the trial, King Artos once more sat in the Guild Master's seat, while Osiris made his formal address from the chair to the king's left.

'My good shieldbearers of Thezmarr,' Osiris called, raising his hands for silence.

Thea shifted in her seat, focusing her gaze on the Guild Master and ignoring the glances Kipp was shooting her way. She'd kept her distance from both him and Cal since they'd been discharged from the infirmary. Kipp had been trying to get her alone ever since, Cal less so. But she didn't know what she'd say to them, didn't know how to tell them how sorry she was.

Quiet settled across the hall and Osiris spoke. 'Though it may be hard to believe...' he started. 'I was once where you now stand; a young man on the edge of becoming a true member of the guild. I know the fear, the excitement, the trepidation that courses through you now, and I know how hard you have worked to get here. This past season has been harrowing. And it would be remiss of me not to acknowledge those we have lost along the way.' He gave a nod to the Three Furies.

A wave of sadness rushed through Thea, and she felt a stab of pity for poor Lachin and the future he would never have.

'With you at the helm of our army, their sacrifices will not be in vain,' Osiris called. 'Through blood and sweat you have trained, you have fought to become part of this great force, the most noble part to play any of us can hope for in this adventure we call life. Tomorrow, you will make your commanders, your masters and our Warswords proud and come the night, we shall celebrate your victories.'

Osiris paused, scanning the faces before him, letting his words sink into the impressionable masses below. He cleared his throat and clasped his hands together. 'Sometimes it can be easy, amidst the drills, amidst the exhaustion and the pain, to forget what it is we truly do here at Thezmarr. But our purpose is always worth remembering: we protect the midrealms at all costs. And at dawn tomorrow, our test will beg the question: are you worthy of it? Are you up to the task?'

Goosebumps rushed across Thea's skin, and all around

her, her fellow shieldbearers burst into cheers and applause, the sound thunderous.

As her cohort toasted to their imminent success, Thea slipped away from the Great Hall and went to find her sister.

Wren, Sam and Ida were in Wren's rooms waiting for her. On the eve of what would become the next phase of her life, it felt only right to spend it with those who had been there from the beginning, those who had never wavered.

Wren had sweet-talked the cook into giving them a handful of desserts, which the women devoured as they sat cross-legged on Wren's bed, quietly talking about what the trial might entail tomorrow. Thea knew they could never guess what awaited her, but their presence meant the world.

'Have those two idiots come to their senses yet?' Ida asked, stuffing an entire sugared pastry into her mouth.

Thea had confided in Wren about what she'd overheard Cal and Kipp talking about back at Hawthorne's cabin, so it was no surprise to her that the others knew as well. However, she found it didn't bother her. She knew her secrets were safe here.

She leaned against the wall, picking at her own dessert. 'For what it's worth, I think it was mainly Cal who had his doubts about me.'

'The handsome one?' Sam asked.

'Yes, the handsome one.' Thea smiled sadly.

Sam made a noise of displeasure. 'That's the problem with the pretty men, there's not usually much going on up there.' She tapped her head with a knowing look.

Ida snorted. 'I didn't realise you were all that interested in their minds, Sam.'

Sam shrugged. 'If I were, I'd know to expect disappointment.'

Wren shook her head in amusement before growing serious. 'I'm not saying this to excuse what Cal said, but... I think he's in shock. He suffered a trauma and he's trying to process it. Don't take it personally, Thea. He'll come around.'

That image of him and Kipp strung up in the cave flooded Thea's mind anew and she had to swallow the lump in her throat before she spoke again, her voice small. 'But he was right...'

'No, Thea,' Wren said firmly. 'He wasn't.'

'Seconded,' Ida agreed.

Sam drained her cup of wine. 'Thirded.'

'No woman is responsible for the weak acts of a man who's had his masculinity so easily threatened,' Wren stated, the strength of her words commanding them all. 'A true man would be proud to fight at your side. He would recognise that you are a force to be reckoned with, Althea Nine Lives.'

Thea's eyes burned as emotion swelled in her throat. These women had been here all along, quietly supporting her through it all.

Wren raised her cup. 'You are infinitely more capable than you could ever dream, Thea, and tomorrow you'll show them all.'

'To Thea,' Ida declared, 'and her many lives.'

Thea tapped her cup against her sister's and her friends', and revelled in the determination that settled deep in her bones.

It was still dark outside when Thea left Wren's rooms, the others snoring soundly. Tightening her cloak, she braced herself against the icy winter air and made for the Bloodwoods.

At the edge of the small clearing, where his arrow remained stuck in the tree, Wilder Hawthorne waited for her in the dappled moonlight.

'You shouldn't be out here,' he said, his voice low. He cut a striking figure and, dressed in black leathers with a fur cloak draped across his broad shoulders, he looked more imposing than ever.

Yet all Thea wanted to do was touch him.

When she reached him, she kept a few feet of distance between them. 'I had to see you, had to talk to you before... Before everything changes.'

Those silver eyes pierced hers as he stepped closer. 'We have unfinished business, you and I.'

Warmth pooled low in Thea's body. 'We do.'

'I need you to know,' he said, voice rough. 'That the other night... I didn't want to leave you. I have never wanted to leave you.'

And then his lips were on hers, hard and demanding. His tongue brushed against hers, sending a rush of lightning through her veins. Thea arched into him, savouring the weight of his hands at her waist, at her lower back, pressing her to him in a quiet hunger. More than anything, she longed to feel his blazing skin against hers, to shed the final layers between them.

But she broke away, her chest heaving, his shirt balled in her fists. 'Show me,' she said, unable to stand it any longer, the ache for him was all-consuming. 'I need you to show me you want this, that you want *me*.'

Wilder searched her face, his intense gaze softening.

Thea stared back, determined, her whole body singing out for him.

His throat bobbed as he glanced around the dark forest. 'You're sure?'

'I'm sure.' The words came out low and husky, and Thea's heart pounded mercilessly, for she had wanted him from the first moment she'd seen him. She undid the clasp of her cloak and let it fall from her shoulders into a puddle on the ground.

'Thea...' Wilder said quietly, his fingers finding the buttons of her shirt, the first coming undone. 'It won't be gentle.'

Another button. 'I don't want it to be.'

'You're certain?' He leaned in, the question tickled the crook of her neck as the rest of her shirt came apart. The night air was crisp against her skin and she gasped as Wilder tore through the band of fabric that covered her breasts, exposing her to him.

He gazed upon her hungrily, his silver eyes hooded, his huge body tense.

'Yes,' Thea told him.

Whatever restraint he'd shown so far snapped, and he shoved her back into a tree, trapping her beneath his powerful torso.

Thea's hand reached up, gripping the shaft of the arrow he'd once shot at her.

His mouth claimed hers again, hot and insistent, his tongue exploring her as his rough palms closed over her bare breasts.

Thea pushed herself into his touch, demanding more, moaning at the contact she'd been craving for so long, her nipples hard and wanting. But it wasn't enough. It was merely the surface of what she needed so deeply, and she had never needed like this before, never been so insatiable.

She fumbled with his cloak, discarding it without a thought. Then, his shirt. He pulled back, only to yank it over his head impatiently, throwing it aside.

Thea's mouth watered. Gods, she had seen enough before to know that he was glorious and littered with scars. But up close, when she could run her hands over his naked sculpted chest and the rippling plane of his abdomen, his skin hot beneath her touch, Thea swore he was carved by the Furies themselves. The moonlight revealed the whorls of black ink trailing from his hand to the right side of his torso and lower, the V-shaped groove that pointed to exactly what she wanted.

'Did you come here just to look?' he murmured.

'No.' Thea palmed the hard length of him straining against his pants.

'Fuck,' he barked, before brutally taking her once again with his lips and tongue.

Thea smiled against his mouth and went for his belt.

They were ravenous, hands stripping away clothing in a frenzy, fabric tearing, buttons popping and still it wasn't fast enough. Thea needed to feel him against her, needed the weight of his body on her.

Thea's mouth went dry, and every thought emptied from her head as Wilder's cock sprung free, his pants bunched around his knees.

She reached for him, but he caught her by the wrists and pinned them above her against the tree. 'I'm not done with you yet,' he growled.

Warmth spread from Thea's spine in a wave through her whole body, her heart hammering in her throat as Wilder held her in place with one hand, and peeled her undergarments down her legs.

Then she was naked, completely bare before him, her skin flushed and aching, her legs spread of their own accord. Wilder used his knee to part them further, not taking his eyes off her as he ran his fingers down between her swollen breasts, past her navel, lower. She writhed beneath his touch, almost panting with need.

A heady moan escaped her as he splayed her wide, circling the wet heat of her with his fingertips. A rush of pleasure pulsed through her, the crisp night air forgotten, the initiation test forgotten. There was only Wilder, his hand, his mouth, his cock.

His lips closed around her nipple, teeth scraping and she bucked from the tree as he worked her still, heat slick between her thighs.

Wilder's finger slid inside her and she cried out, pushing against him. It wasn't enough. She *needed* him.

He drew away to survey her writhing body, his gaze lingering where his fingers now filled her. He seemed to hold himself in check, drinking in the sight of her and the pleasure that rippled through her.

Pressure built and built, and he pulled out, only to circle that sensitive spot, nearly sending her over the edge.

'Wilder,' Thea gasped. 'This isn't what I want.'

He stopped at once. 'No?'

'No,' she panted. 'I want *you*. All of you. Now.'

His gaze travelled over her wet and wanting body, her cheeks flushed, her legs still spread.

'Then you'll have me,' he said.

He released her wrists, only to pin Thea with his whole frame, the rough bark of the tree biting into her back. He positioned his cock where his fingers had been moments before and looked at her, waiting.

Thea wrapped her legs around his waist and pulled him to her.

The hot crown of his cock nudged against her and then he moved, sliding deep inside her.

Thea's head tipped back, knocking against the tree, but she didn't care. All she cared about was this, *him*.

Wilder swore against her mouth and fucked her hard and deep, sinking in to the hilt, his fingers digging into her hips.

The storm within her surged and Thea moaned as he pulled out slowly, torturously, before slamming fully into her again, filling every inch.

Wilder was exactly as she had imagined. Better. Rough and raw and intense, and she met every thrust eagerly, matched every bruising kiss with one of her own. She clawed at the taut muscles of his back, riding every movement with him, their bodies slick with sweat.

'Furies, what are you doing to me,' Wilder murmured as he wrapped her messy braid around his fist and pulled.

The sharp pain only amplified every other intoxicating sensation and Thea gasped as the wave of pleasure that had been building took hold.

'Wilder, I —'

'Come for me, Thea.'

Thea gripped him harder with her legs, clenching around him, wanting him melded to her. 'Come *with* me,' she said breathlessly; she refused to go over the edge without him.

Those silver eyes fixed upon her, and he thrust into her with a renewed ferocity. 'Thea...' he groaned.

At her name on his lips, she came undone. Her climax erupted in tidal waves crashing through her whole body, pleasure shuddering through every part of her as she stifled her cries against Wilder's shoulder. He swore as he found his own release, slowing his thrusts as though drawing out the last ripples of their pleasure together.

For a moment, time wavered, and they remained joined and panting against one another.

Wilder rested his brow against hers and inhaled, as though he wanted to soak up every second.

Thea's heart pounded, an ache already settling there at the thought of having to part from him.

Then, he kissed her, slowly and deeply, like he needed to savour the taste of her, commit her to memory.

Thea laced her fingers through his hair and she kissed him back, taking her time because she knew they had very little left before dawn was upon them, before reality came crashing down.

Too soon, Wilder broke away and lifted her from him, placing her gently on the ground.

Her legs buckled, but he caught her, his eyes lingering on her once again as he tore a scrap of fabric from his shirt and handed it to her.

Thea cleaned herself up as best she could, her body still trembling.

They were quiet as they found their clothes and dressed, ignoring the rips and missing buttons. Wilder helped her tie the band he'd torn back around her breasts, his fingers lingering on the soft skin there.

Already Thea craved his touch again.

Wilder seemed to sense it, or perhaps he felt it too, for he wrapped his arms around her, the weight of them warm and reassuring.

'Are you alright?'

Thea nodded, not trusting herself to speak just yet, still processing what had happened between them and how she felt.

Wilder tucked a loose strand of hair behind her ear before gently gripping her chin, tilting her face to his. 'This thing between us...' he said slowly, cautiously. 'It's real... Isn't it?'

'Yes,' Thea whispered, the ache for him already sparking anew.

'I didn't want it to be,' Wilder admitted, still gazing into her eyes.

'Nor did I. Not at first,' Thea told him. 'What about now? What do you want?' she asked.

'I want you.'

'You've had me.'

His mouth grazed hers and he took her bottom lip between his teeth before flicking his tongue across the small hurt. 'Once was not enough, Thea...' he groaned. 'Not nearly enough.'

His words, her name, the timbre of his voice, sent a lick of longing to her core, but Thea needed to know. 'So, what now?'

Wilder drew back, heat radiating from him. 'If you pass your initiation test and are apprenticed to another Warsword... We'll have the freedom to... explore what this is,' he said quietly.

'Explore?'

'Yes.' He kissed her again, already hard and grinding against her in a way that relit the fire of white-hot need within her. 'I've denied myself for long enough. I want to be with you, Thea.'

Thea returned his kiss fiercely, her fingers tangling in his hair. 'The initiation test...' she murmured against his lips. 'I have to go.'

'So go,' he replied, his hands tracing her curves. 'And when you come back to me...'

'We'll do this again?'

'And again, and again,' he said, a wicked smile revealing his dimple.

With that promise lingering between them, Thea tore herself away from her warrior and made for the armoury.

She needed a shield and a sword.

WILDER HAWTHORNE

Desire still blazed like an inferno as Wilder watched her go, his gaze following the determined set of her slight shoulders and then the curve of her backside. All these months of denying himself had been painful, but now that he'd had Althea Zoltaire, every second without her seemed an agonising waste.

Show me, she'd said. And that had been the beginning and the end of him. Every kiss, every touch, every second spent inside her had been intoxicating, all-consuming. Even now, as the Mourner's Trail came into view and the distant glow of dawn lightened the edge of the sky, he wanted her beyond reason.

He should have known that she was inevitable from the moment his eyes had locked on hers and every moment after. He headed for the fortress, his blood still running hot. He wished they'd had more time, even just an hour more, so he could have wrung every last ounce of pleasure from her writhing body. But with the shieldbearer initiation...

At the thought of it, Wilder went cold. He'd been so

caught up in the ecstasy of her that the harsh reality of what she had left him to face hadn't fully registered. Until now. Thea was about to undertake one of the most harrowing experiences of her life, where every skill, every lesson she'd learnt would be put to the test.

Though he doubted she needed, or wanted, his protection, the thought of her facing anything alone made him want to slam his fist into the nearest tree. He couldn't stand it.

Wilder's chest was tight as he reached the portcullis, and he found himself wandering the familiar passageway to his brother's rooms. He needed to think of anything other than the commotion filling Thezmarr as the shieldbearers readied themselves for their initiation. Thea was somewhere out there, strapping armour and weapons to a body he hadn't nearly finished worshipping.

Malik wasn't in his rooms. The bed was neatly made and the fire had long since burned out. There was no sign of Dax, either. Their absence only fuelled Wilder's agitation. He charged through the fortress, snarling at anyone who half looked in his direction.

Where in the name of the Furies is Malik? Wilder knew he wasn't thinking straight, he knew he was behaving like some feral beast on the loose, but he didn't care. Only the gods knew why, but he needed to find his brother.

He barged through the kitchens, causing the cook to shriek as he upset a pot of stew and sent a basket of bread flying. The Great Hall was mostly empty, but for a few commanders placing bets on the shieldbearers. Wilder put a stop to that with a single, searing look that sent them scurrying in the opposite direction. A group of alchemists gathered outside the workshop and he turned on his heel immediately, the sight of them making his chest ache.

Has she finished arming herself? he wondered. *Has Osiris given them the instructions yet?*

Thea was all he could think about, her and the dangers she would face...

At last, Wilder found Malik and Dax in the library. As the Warsword burst into the quiet room, cursing himself for not looking there first, Malik looked up from the belt he was braiding, that grey-eyed gaze meeting his expectantly.

'Mal,' Wilder managed, his chest heaving as he paced the worn carpet before the hearth. 'I...'

His brother's hands stilled between the strands of leather and he surveyed Wilder's dishevelled and torn clothes without surprise or concern, waiting patiently.

Wilder ran his hands through his hair, through his beard, the words suddenly stuck, his ears ringing. The strange sensation that time had slowed washed over him and his throat constricted as he tried to articulate the warring emotions within. He glanced at the empty armchair beside Mal, but he couldn't sit. He needed to move, needed to rid himself of the fear that was coursing through his veins.

What was he supposed to say? That after all this time and all his attempts at keeping himself in check, he'd... That now the woman he cared for was undertaking the shieldbearer test? That she might not walk out of it the same person? Furies knew he hadn't meant for any of it to happen; he had battled with every fibre of his being to keep himself in control, but... the alchemist had become so much more. How could he have denied her?

Despite his closeness to the fire and his constant

movement, Wilder was cold and jittery. Until a warm, large hand fell gently on his shoulder.

Wilder turned to find his brother on his feet, towering over even him. To his surprise, Malik drew him into a quiet embrace.

Wilder couldn't remember the last time anyone had comforted him, held him like this, and for the first time in a long while, Wilder accepted the support gratefully. For so long he had felt like the older brother, but in this moment, Malik was just as he remembered: sturdy and strong, a shelter amidst a storm.

'Thank you, brother,' Wilder managed, at last pulling away. 'I don't know what came over me.'

Malik pierced him with a knowing look, as if to say, *yes, you do.*

Wilder ran his fingers through his beard again and loosed a dark laugh. 'Fine, perhaps I do,' he allowed.

At that, Mal smiled. Then he reached for a book resting on the side table by his chair. He held it out to Wilder, as though it would solve all his problems.

Humouring him, Wilder took it with a glance at the title.

A Study of Royal Lineage Throughout the Midrealms.

'Is this to help me sleep?' He frowned at the faded leather cover.

Malik made a noise that could have been a snort and forced the pages apart, pointing to the text.

But Wilder's eyes wouldn't focus. He felt the weight of it all on his shoulders, in his gut. 'Brother, tell me she'll make it through.'

'Thea will make it,' came a voice from the door.

Audra, the warrior-turned-librarian, entered, straight-backed and severe as ever.

Wilder didn't deny who he meant. It was written so plainly all over his face. 'How can you be sure?'

The older woman's gaze was piercing. 'Because I raised her.'

Suddenly, Dax shot to his feet with a sharp bark and bolted to the window. There, he jumped up so that his front paws rested on the sill and he looked out, a growl sounding.

Frowning, Wilder, Malik and now Audra followed.

Outside, Terrence the hawk was circling, another scroll dangling from his leg.

'Fuck,' Wilder muttered, opening the window for him. It was unusual to hear back from Dratos so soon.

'What is this about?' Audra's voice was icy.

As soon as Terrence was inside, Wilder opened the scroll, not bothering to shield it from the librarian.

'Another tear in the Veil,' he told her and Malik quietly, his chest tight. 'More monsters getting through.'

'How many does that make now?' Audra asked, her expression hard. 'And don't give me that shit about being a civilian, Hawthorne. I fought beside your brother before you could swing a training sword.'

In response, Malik looked at her fondly.

Wilder passed her the letter. 'Three,' he told her. 'Three tears that we know of.'

'And no doubt there will be more to come.'

'Yes,' Wilder said. 'There will be more.'

The warrior brothers and the librarian peered to the north of Thezmarr, where unnatural darkness gathered beyond the jagged mountains.

Wilder's scalp prickled and a chill washed over him, his hand shifting to the hilt of the dagger at his belt.

His first thought was of Thea. He wished he had said

something more to her, something that did the roiling tempest within him justice. Fighting down the fear for her, he told himself that when he next saw her, when she undoubtedly made it through the initiation test, he'd take her in his arms and wouldn't let go.

CHAPTER THIRTY-FIVE

Thea's last dawn as a shieldbearer bled into the sky quietly, marred by ominous clouds rolling in from the north. At last, armed with a sword of steel and a sturdy shield, she locked all thoughts of Wilder away and waited with her cohort by the Plains of Orax, as the Guild Master had instructed. There, she steeled herself against what was to come.

She didn't like being out in the open like this, vulnerable and unprepared, but she gathered that was how they were meant to feel: on the precipice of panic before the trial even began. In the distance, she could see the dark seas roiling beyond the scattered islands, and she prayed that whatever chaos loomed there would hold at bay until their test had been completed.

Kipp and Cal shoved their way through the ranks to stand beside her, both trying to catch her eye, but Osiris, joined by King Artos, the masters and commanders, beat a spear on the face of his shield, demanding silence, demanding undivided attention.

'The initiation test is simple,' his voice called out across the freezing fields. 'You are to retrieve a Guardian totem from the Chained Islands.'

Thea felt the tension grow taut around her, felt her own body seize up at the thought. No one had ventured onto the Chained Islands in decades.

Until now, she thought as she turned her focus to the lands just off the coast of Thezmarr. Whoever had named the islands had been literal, for the Chained Islands were exactly that: a small archipelago that had been physically linked by thick chains. There were at least seven that Thea could see, towering high above the crashing waves below, their white cliff faces cold and taunting —

'There are fifty of you in this initiation test and only thirty totems. Those who fail to retrieve a totem and those who fail to return in the allotted time will be dismissed from our fighting ranks. Should those poor bastards wish to remain at Thezmarr, they will be no more than staff: cooks, stablehands, launderers and the like. When it comes to this guild, I will make it plain: there is no room here for anything less than a warrior. If you have not learnt our ways by now, you never will. You have until sundown.'

That was it.

Within seconds, two shieldbearers threw their weapons down on the grass and turned on their heels back to the fortress, apparently deciding then and there that nothing was worth the dangers ahead.

For a moment, the rest of them stood in a daze, letting the reality of the Guild Master's words sink in, until Esyllt barked, 'What are you waiting for?'

Thea lurched into action, starting down the hill,

following the Bloodwoods towards the sharp drop of the bluffs, two familiar figures falling in step beside her.

'Thea, please, look at us,' Kipp said.

'This is not the time or place,' she muttered, gripping her sword as the edge of the cliffs came into view, the dark swell of the water surging below.

'It's the only time and place,' Cal countered, resting a hand on her shoulder. 'I know you heard me. I said things I didn't mean, some stupid things in the aftermath of what happened.'

'I'm aware,' Thea replied, still charging forward, the rest of the shieldbearers jostling alongside them.

'But I didn't mean them!' Cal argued.

'You did,' Thea snapped. 'And to be honest, I don't blame you. What you went through that night... It was horrific. I saw you there, both of you, strung up to die —'

Cal took both her shoulders and stopped her mid-stride. 'It wasn't your fault. I know that now.'

'I always knew it,' Kipp offered.

'I was being a fool. The shock got to me. Please, Thea,' Cal said, ignoring him. 'I cannot go into this test without you by my side. The three of us, we are stronger together. We're a team, a unit of our own, remember?'

Thea *did* remember. She remembered them working as a single force throughout the mock battle, she remembered how they'd had each other's backs during the battle amidst the ruins of Delmira.

'Holy gods,' someone shouted ahead of them.

Their conversation forgotten, Thea, Cal and Kipp craned their necks to see what was happening.

Thea's breath whistled between her teeth as she saw it with her own eyes.

There was no bridge to the closest isle of the Chained Islands; no rope; no path down... Only a death drop into the sea and jagged rocks below.

'Shit...' Cal murmured from beside her.

If Thea wasn't so terrified, she would have laughed. 'Perhaps it's best we stick together, just for this round...'

Kipp's mouth was hanging open as he stared at the death-defying leap they were expected to make. 'I'll take all the help I can get.'

For a moment, they watched as some of their peers tried to foolishly tackle the jump. The isle was slightly lower than the cliff upon which they stood, but that gave Thea little comfort. She didn't know the first to fall, nor the second, but the third she recognised from the countless meals they'd eaten together. All three lives now at the mercy of the waves and rocks below.

Thea looked around desperately, anxious that they'd encountered an obstacle of this magnitude before they had truly started. She eyed the bow and quiver at Cal's back.

'You could shoot a rope across?' she ventured. 'Secure it on the isle, and secure it to one of the trees in the Bloodwoods...? We could climb across that way?'

'I don't trust those on either end...' he said slowly. 'Not after everything. There are some who would cut the rope and let us fall to our deaths.'

Thea's heart sank. He was right. Of the three of them, it was possible that Kipp, with his long limbs, could make the jump without aid, but Thea was too short and though Cal was lean and tall, she wasn't sure it would be enough for him either.

Kipp, however, had not for a moment considered leaving them behind.

'Remember on the way to Harenth...' he started, the crease between his brows deep as he looked from the Isle to the Bloodwoods.

'You'll have to be more specific, *Kristopher*,' Cal said.

'Remember when we crossed that river? Using those branches as aids to vault ourselves across?'

Thea groaned. 'I don't like where this is going...'

'Nor do I,' Kipp admitted. 'Especially considering I was the one who ended up in the river. But I don't see another way.' He paused, something grabbing his attention before he pointed. 'Look! There are already some trying the technique you suggested, Thea. And there! A handful who are scaling down the cliffs trying to find a safer path...'

Thea felt sick to the stomach. Was this truly their best option? Some evolution of a stupid game they'd made up on the road to get to a better fishing spot?

Apparently it was. Kipp was already heading into the Bloodwoods.

Her heart in her throat, Thea followed, scouring the forest floor for a decent branch. It had to be strong, but pliable, one that could launch her across.

Gods, was she really going to do this? She had her fate stone; she knew she would not be greeted by Enovius today – but she couldn't say the same of her friends.

Far sooner than she would have liked, each of them held a long branch in their hands, their weapons firmly secured to their bodies.

'I can't watch you go,' Thea croaked, her heart hammering in her throat.

'Ladies first then,' Kipp gave a mock bow, though he looked as terrified as she felt.

'You've got this, Thea,' Cal said. 'Think of it as just a really big river.'

'Thanks,' she muttered, taking a few steps back and lining herself up with the target on the other side. She secured the satchel Wren had refilled over her shoulder, so it rested against her back.

Taking a deep breath, she closed her eyes, pushing aside the fear, pushing aside the urgency and the image of the waves breaking upon the jagged rocks below.

'I do not die today,' she muttered to herself, tensing in anticipation. Another minute and she'd lose her nerve. Thea opened her eyes, and gripping her branch in both hands, she sprinted for the edge of the cliff.

Planting her branch in the earth, Althea Nine Lives launched herself up and suddenly, she was soaring through the air —

For the briefest of seconds, time stopped and Thea was weightless above the roaring sea. Then, she felt the kiss of the wind on her back and the icy salt spray of the waves as they broke upon the rocks below.

She braced her whole body as she carved through the wind, the other side of the isle drawing closer and closer as she leapt – as she fell.

Thea released the branch from her grasp. It had served its purpose. Heart still in her throat, she landed deftly on solid ground, gravel crunching comfortingly beneath her boots, and when she looked up, she saw chaos.

She hadn't realised how many other shieldbearers had actually made it across. Drawing her sword, Thea crouched behind a boulder and motioned to the others, who were still on Thezmarrian soil, to hurry.

The clang of steel and angry shouts sounded from nearby

and Thea peered from behind her cover to see that fighting had broken out...

'There are fifty of you and only thirty totems...'

It appeared that some had felt the call, and those who had not were sabotaging their peers.

Kipp landed a few feet away from her with a grunt, dropping his branch alongside him.

'Over here.'

He darted towards her, his face horror-stricken at what he, too, now saw.

'Gods, it's chaos.' He crouched beside her, unsheathing his own blade.

But Thea was watching Cal size up the gap between the cliff and the isle on the other side.

'Come on, Cal...' she muttered, gripping the hilt of her sword so tightly that her hand ached.

He took a run-up, just as she and Kipp had done, his long legs pounding the grassy earth. Burying his branch in place just shy of the edge, he leapt, suddenly soaring towards them —

The branch snapped.

Cal's arms and legs flailed, his scream silent as his body pitched through the air.

His momentum faltered, and Thea's cry lodged in her throat.

Dropping her sword, she snatched the bough that Kipp had dropped and sprinted for the edge of the isle. Barely registering Kipp latching onto her legs, she slid it out into the gap between their isle and the Thezmarrian cliffs, praying that it would hold, that it would take his weight and the sudden impact.

Cal fell towards them, his eyes narrowing as he spotted

the branch and —

He caught it, right under the arms with a groan.

The timber bowed beneath his weight, springing up and down, Cal's legs dangling uselessly beneath him.

Together, Thea and Kipp dragged the branch inward, towards safety, and as soon as Cal was close enough, he scrambled for the ledge. He reached for them and they hauled him up, all three of them panting.

Thea's chest was so tight she thought it might implode. She didn't let go of Cal, worried that if she did, he'd tumble right back over into the seas below.

His hand gripped hers back, solid and safe.

'Holy Furies,' he croaked. 'I'm never doing that again.'

'Just as well,' Kipp said between ragged gasps, resting his hands on his knees. 'You're awful at it.'

Cal gave a strained laugh, and Thea felt her own face split into a manic grin, but the shouts from nearby snatched the moment of victory from them. Thea yanked both her friends behind cover to survey the situation at hand.

'From what I can tell, there were a handful of totems left in plain sight, which Seb and his lackeys are scrapping for.' She watched as Seb struck down a fellow shieldbearer and reached for something on the ground.

'That bastard hasn't got a fucking drop of honour, has he...?' Kipp murmured, watching their common adversary dish out orders to his comrades. 'So much for being worthy.'

'We knew that already,' Cal replied quietly.

Thea heard Kipp swallow beside her.

'This...' he started. 'This isn't what I thought it would be... How does this make us better protectors of the realm? Stealing totems from one another? Turning on each other like this?'

'I suppose they think it makes us stronger,' Thea said, not taking her eyes off Seb and one of his companions who had discovered another totem. 'It's supposed to weed out the weak, show people's true colours.'

'All it does is make people desperate and unpredictable,' Cal muttered. 'All the shieldbearers should be working as a team. Surely that's the point?'

'Not if there are only thirty totems and fifty shieldbearers.' Thea countered. 'Come on, we need to make a move.'

Kipp's brows shot up. 'You want to fight Seb?'

Thea watched the way the bastard strode about the clifftop, like he had nothing to fear, like he had a right to be there.

'I do,' she said at last. 'But not today...' She turned away from the carnage at Seb's feet and pointed to the other isles. 'We should head to the other islands, where the others haven't been. There are bound to be totems hidden all around.'

'Would have been nice just to pick the first ones up we saw...' Kipp muttered.

The islands were scattered down the coast of Thezmarr, the howling winter winds whipping between them. Thick chains linked them, allowing her and her friends to climb across to the next island. They were keen to put as much distance between them and Seb as possible. No good came from having that bastard on their heels.

The second island was far larger than the first, more than just a column of rock amidst the waves. Thea found herself taking the lead as they took in their surroundings. Jagged white boulders lined the ground, but as they moved further inland, the terrain opened up, revealing a descending valley, framed by unusual thin trees with an array of large emerald green leaves shooting from their tops.

'I've never seen anything like this...' Thea murmured.

But Kipp was already moving towards the strange gorge, his boots sliding over loose scree. 'There's a totem down there.' Kipp said. 'I can feel it.'

A thrill raced through Thea. While they had been told about the magic of the totems, she wasn't sure what to expect, or how much to believe from the stories. But the excited gleam in her friend's eyes told her that it was true, that the totems had a presence, that they had power enough to call to a worthy warrior of Thezmarr.

'It's like... It's like a cyren song,' Kipp murmured, fascinated.

Soon, Thea felt it too: a soft melody, beckoning them towards it. Cal's expression revealed he was experiencing the same pull.

Icy wind whipped through the gorge, cold enough to sting Thea's face and hands, but she gritted her teeth and forged on, desperate to obtain a totem for each of them. Then, they could celebrate in the Great Hall.

'There!' Kipp shouted, darting forward to a plinth-like rockform where the chasm opened up.

Thea spotted the gleam of iron atop its craggy ledge.

Thea's scalp prickled. It couldn't be that easy.

The sound of something snapping, the twang echoing through the canyon. Thea whirled around. Was it an arrow being loosed? Was it a —

Something nearby gave a loud groan.

A huge boulder at the top of the valley was suddenly moving, rolling towards them and gaining speed. It took up the entire breadth of the gorge, designed to flatten everything in its path.

Thea's gaze darted to Kipp, where at his feet lay a broken cord. 'It was a trip wire!' she shouted. 'Grab the totem and *run!*'

The boulder hurtled right for them, demolishing everything at a terrifying speed. There was no way they would be fast enough to outrun it.

'Kipp, *move!*'

Kipp snatched the totem from the plinth and looked to Thea and Cal in panic. Thea was already scrambling towards the side of the valley, which rose up from the ground into a rocky overhang.

'Up there!' She grabbed Kipp's arm and shoved him to the face of the gorge. 'Climb!'

The three of them clambered up the rock, struggling to find purchase.

'It'll crush us!' Cal yelled.

'Get to the overhang,' Thea cried, her muscles trembling with the effort. If they could reach it, the boulder would pass beneath them. 'Hurry!'

Thea was first and she swung herself out across the valley, her legs dangling below as she watched the rounded mass of stone pelt towards them, her friends still in its path. She hung there uselessly, biting down on her shouts of panic – they would not help Cal and Kipp now.

Cal was suddenly hanging by her side, his cheeks red, sweat running down the side of his face.

'Now, Kipp!' he bellowed.

Kipp jumped —

Long limbs flailing, Kipp latched onto the overhang with a yelp.

A roar below sounded as the boulder crashed through the gorge beneath them, crushing the strange trees and grass, scraping the sides of the valley, causing rock to crumble.

Thea watched in horror, imagining the bloody pulp they would have become if they had remained in its path. The three of them dangled there in shock for a moment, as the boulder at last collided with the end of the gorge, splintering to pieces upon impact.

When Thea was sure there wasn't another boulder to follow, she let go, swinging down from the overhang and landing deftly on the ground below.

'Holy gods...' Kipp muttered as he landed less gracefully beside her.

Cal followed. 'We would have been dead without you, Thea,' he said, clapping her on the shoulder.

But Thea's attention was on the totem in Kipp's hands. 'Let's see it then.'

Kipp held it out on his palm. Secured to a black band of fabric, there it was: a pair of crossed swords, a true Guardian's totem. 'How do we decide whose it is?' he asked quietly. 'We all felt it. We're all worthy.'

Thea tore her gaze away from the totem and dusted her hands off on her pants. 'You take that one, Kipp,' she said. 'You felt it first, you got to it first.'

'But without you —'

Cal waved him off. 'One down. Two to go.'

Relief bloomed in Thea's chest. 'Let's get out of here, then. I'd rather not risk getting crushed to death again.'

'Can't say I fancy it much either,' Cal replied, eyeing the gorge. 'Up or down?'

'Up,' Thea decided. 'We keep an eye on the Thezmarrian coast, we can see the lay of the islands better. Agreed?'

'Agreed,' Kipp said, securing his totem to his arm. 'Who would have thought useless little old me would be the first?'

'Oh fuck off, Kipp, without Thea you would have been a splat on the rocks beside that thing.'

Thea laughed shakily as they started back up the valley. 'One down. Two to go.'

By the time the trio reached the top of the gorge once more, the midday sun was surprisingly harsh despite the chill of winter. There was no sign of the other shieldbearers, which made Thea uneasy. Either everyone was leagues ahead of them and totems were sparse, or a terrifying number of her peers had succumbed to the cliffs or their fellow shieldbearers. She didn't know which was worse.

Keeping the coastline of Thezmarr in sight, they made their way to the next island. It was a wider gap than the previous, but they used the thick, rusted chain to climb across with relative ease. From the other side, Kipp gripped Thea's arms firmly and helped her with the final few links, Cal following close behind.

It was little more than a spit of land and in only moments, they were crossing a small chained bridge onto another. This next island was larger, the trees and bushes here denser than before, blocking the sun from view as the canopy closed in around them.

Thea's skin prickled. At first, she thought it might be a totem calling out to her, the beginnings of that cyren song as Kipp had described it. But no – it wasn't that. It was the sensation of the hair on the back of her neck standing up, the sensation that usually occurred when someone was watching.

'Kipp, Cal,' she called.

Both young men paused, turning back to her, their brows furrowed in concern.

'Can you feel something?' Cal asked.

Thea shook her head. 'I think someone's following us,' she told them as quietly as she could, unsheathing her sword once more. 'Be on your guard.'

Cal clenched his jaw and nodded, adjusting his grip on his own blade.

Together, they crept through the strange, jungle-like foliage of the third island, poised for attack, but no one announced themselves, no one leapt from the bushes. And yet Thea's skin still prickled. She didn't lower her guard; she had learned long ago to trust her instincts.

They kept to the edge of the undergrowth, careful to keep Thezmarr in sight at all times. They had already faced a death-defying leap, the backstabbing nature of their own kind and a giant pulverising boulder… Who knew what else was out here to jeopardise their mission, their lives?

'Wait,' Cal whispered suddenly, holding up a closed fist, signalling for them to stop. His head lifted to the canopy, his whole body was taut and leaning forward.

Then Thea felt it, too. That same pulling sensation from before.

Cal pointed to the leaves above. 'It's up there.'

Thea followed the line of his finger to what looked to be a bird's nest in the fork of a tree. The tugging sensation grew stronger. He was right.

Kipp groaned. 'Not more climbing…'

'No one asked you to climb,' Cal replied. 'Flip you for it?' he said to Thea.

But Thea shook her head. 'You take it. I'll get the next one.'

Cal hesitated for a moment before shucking off his shield and passing his bow and quiver to her.

There was nothing for Thea and Kipp to do except watch as their friend started up the tree. Thea bit back the urge to tell him to be careful, assuming that would be the default for all of them from here on out. The hair on the back of her neck still prickled, and she couldn't shake the feeling...

Unease churned low in her gut as she watched Cal scale the trunk, nearly at the top —

'Is it there?' Kipp shouted from beside her.

'It has to be, I can feel it,' came the reply as he neared the nest.

The silence that followed made Thea's skin crawl. She could see Cal's lower body, but not what he was doing in the fork of the tree.

'Got it!' he called triumphantly.

But that triumph was chased by a scream.

CHAPTER THIRTY-SIX

Suddenly, Cal was crashing back down toward them, hitting several branches and bushes on the way down.

Dozens of huge black birds burst from the canopy, flapping and squawking loudly. There were so many of them for a moment they blocked out the light streaming through.

Thea felt another magical pull, forcing her attention skyward.

But Cal was falling. It seemed endless as he bounced between trees, his shouts muffled by the impact.

He hit the ground with a thud. His eyes were screwed shut in pain. In one hand he clutched his totem, but the other hand was streaked with blood, a thrashing brown viper latched to the skin between his thumb and forefinger.

The possible call of another totem forgotten, Thea skidded to her knees beside her friend, her heart racing. Prising the snake's jaw from him without a moment's hesitation, Thea flung it over the side off the cliff.

'Got me,' Cal wheezed, writhing in agony. 'There were three of them.'

Sure enough, it wasn't just the one bite on his hand. Thea turned his arm over, finding two more puncture wounds already swelling.

'Fuck,' she said. 'Kipp, give me my satchel and that canteen of water.'

'I'm guessing it was venomous?' Cal panted through gritted teeth.

'Fraid so,' Thea replied, recognising the brown scales from an experiment Farissa had coordinated a few years ago. 'But stay calm.'

'Easy for you to say,' Cal bit out.

Kipp was at Thea's side, handing her the things she'd asked for. 'Should I suck the venom out?'

Cal gave a moan of pain. 'You're not sucking anything of mine, Kristopher —'

Thea's hands worked quickly to unscrew the top of the canteen. 'That's a myth,' she said, trying to keep the fear from her voice. 'Keep your arm low, Cal. It slows the venom going to your heart.'

'Comforting.' Sweat beaded on his brow.

Thea washed the wounds with water and then rummaged in the satchel Wren had packed for her. There had to be something in there. Salve for burns. Bandages. Dried iruseed – *might need that later*, she thought, forcing herself to think logically. Soot root powder. Lavender tincture for pain —

'Yes!' she half-shouted, ripping a tiny vial of brown liquid from one of the inner pockets and pulling the cork from the top with her teeth. Wren thought of everything. 'This will stop the poison.'

She thrust a small stick at Cal. 'Bite down on this,' she told him, placing it between his teeth. 'Kipp, hold him down.'

His eyes went wide and Kipp grimaced as he placed his hands on their friend's shoulders, murmuring apologies.

Thea didn't waste another moment, she poured the liquid on each of the bites.

Cal thrashed beneath Kipp's hold, his screams muted around the stick in his mouth.

'Anti-venom,' she told him, trying to soothe him as the waves of pain took hold and he convulsed beneath their grip. 'I'm sorry. I'm sorry,' she said.

When she was done, she took the clean linen strips from the satchel and wrapped each of his wounds tightly.

Cal lay at Kipp's knees, drenched in sweat, panting, a slight green sheen to his skin.

Kipp helped him into a sitting position. 'Will he be alright?' he asked her.

Thea wiped her friend's brow and put the canteen of water to his lips, forcing him to drink. 'I think so. Thanks to Wren,' she said, patting the satchel at her side.

'And you,' Cal wheezed.

'You can thank me later.' She turned her back to them so she could gather herself. That was twice now she'd nearly lost him.

But when she faced him again, Cal was grinning weakly. 'Two down…' He held up his totem.

Thea's heart sank, remembering the tug she'd felt towards the flock of birds as they'd broken through the canopy. 'About that…' she said quietly. 'I think there was one with those birds.'

Cal stared at her. 'What?'

'I felt it, just before you fell.'

Cal nudged Kipp to help him to his feet. 'So we'd best get moving. Let's get you a totem.' He was unsteady at first, but as they gathered their weapons, he seemed to find his footing.

They were a little slower now, but they made their way to the edge of the island just the same. Only to stop abruptly.

The gap between their island and the next was far bigger than even the first had been. What awaited them was a horizontal ladder made of thin, rusted chains bridging the two land masses together, the waves churning and foaming against the sharp rocks beneath.

Thea rubbed her temples as she surveyed the obstacle. 'We have to pull ourselves across below. Or climb over the top...' she murmured. The back of her neck prickled again and she turned back, scanning the fringe of the jungle they'd just left. There was no one in sight. Turning back to the bridge of bars, she made up her mind. 'We've all trained, we've got the strength... Don't we?'

Cal nodded. 'I'll manage.'

They strapped their weapons to their bodies securely and, not for the first time, Thea wondered where the rest of the shieldbearers had ended up. She pushed the thought from her head as she squared her shoulders to face the next obstacle. She could see no mechanism or tricks in place... but her skin still prickled, something behind them pulling at her attention. There was nothing there.

'You two first,' she said.

Cal opted to climb above the bars so he didn't have to bear the full weight of his body on his injured arm. Meanwhile, Kipp swung from bar to bar below, like some kind of jungle animal.

In the distance, just beyond them, Thea's heart soared. The flock of black birds circled above the island. She could feel the totem pulsing among them. She just had to get across this ladder of chains…

Thea opted for Kipp's method and fit her hands to the metal bars, checking one last time that her sword, shield and satchel were firmly strapped in place. Then she started across. She marvelled at how strong she'd grown over the months, supporting her whole body weight with ease as she swung herself from one linked chain to the next. Before she knew it, she was halfway across, ignoring the roar of the waves below and reaching for —

That was when the first arrow whistled through the air.

The tip grazed her upper arm and she nearly let go from the shock, a startled yelp escaping her.

'Thea!' Kipp shouted from the other side, his voice pitched with panic.

Another arrow whirred close to her dangling legs and she cursed loudly, flinging herself to the next bar. She could see Cal nocking an arrow to his own bow in her defence.

As arrows shot across the chasm, Thea put one hand in front of the other, using all her upper body strength, desperate to get across without a dozen holes through her body.

'Cal!' she yelled, suddenly thinking of the cursed winged creature who held her totem somewhere nearby. 'I'm going to need some of those arrows to shoot the bird down!'

'But –'

'Don't you dare use another one!' she commanded.

She was two-thirds across, she could make it, she could —

Another arrow kissed her side, pain searing as it grazed her skin, only just missing her middle.

Swearing and sweating, Thea hung by one hand and

reached for her satchel, her teeth clenched with the effort. Fumbling blindly inside the bag, her fingers closed around the jar she wanted and, still hanging on for dear life, she threw it back at her attackers with all her might.

Thick smoke exploded as the glass shattered on the surrounding stones. Shouts of alarm and cries of pain echoed down the chasm.

'I get some credit for that one, Wren,' she muttered to herself as she swung across the final bars to safety.

Cal and Kipp surged for her, pulling her into a near-smothering embrace.

Cal was shaking his head in disbelief. 'What in the name of all the gods was that?'

'Soot root powder,' she replied. 'I've been harvesting those roots since I could hold a trowel. Nice to see the product in action for a change.' She lifted her shirt to examine the damage. A decent gash ran parallel to the scar Seb had given her. Though it wasn't as deep as the stab wound had been, it burned something fierce.

'Are you alright?' Kipp asked, catching her grimace and trying to peer over her shoulder at the wound.

'Just a scratch,' she assured him, tucking her shirt back into the waist of her pants and scanning the terrain ahead for the birds. 'There!' she shouted, surging forward, her pain and her attackers forgotten as the flock circled nearby. The pulse of power called to her again.

'It's close,' Cal murmured. 'I can feel it humming.'

Ahead, the huge black birds gathered on the rocks, some flitting back to the sky.

Thea held up her fist to signal the others to halt, crouching behind a thorny bush for cover.

Then she saw it. The totem, glinting in a pair of claws amidst a blur of feathers, skybound.

'Cal, your bow,' she said, holding out her hand.

'Do you want me to shoot?' he offered.

Thea hesitated.

'It would be my honour, Thea. You saved my life. Twice now. Let me do this for you,' he urged her, hand on heart.

There was no denying that Cal was the better archer, his skills were next to none with a bow, she'd seen him defy the odds, seen him make countless impossible shots, but...

Althea Nine Lives was not without her own abilities, and she knew that to own that totem with pride, she had to win it herself. 'Thank you,' she told Cal. 'But I can make it.'

Nodding, he handed her the bow.

Hardly taking her eyes from her target, the glint of metal still glimmering in the sun above, Thea gripped the weapon, fitting an arrow to the bowstring and taking aim.

She centred herself.

One shot, that was all she'd have.

You could have Cal do it, the little voice said at the back of her mind, but she pushed it aside and drew her arm back.

Another voice filled her head then. *'You need to give it more power than that...'* Wilder whispered in the shell of her ear.

Thea did, her arms, her shoulders, her back straining as she drew the arrow further back, her gaze narrowing in on that single black bird who held her totem.

'*Now.*' She whispered the word as Hawthorne had said it to her, and she released the bowstring.

The arrow sliced through the air, a perfect line.

A shriek sounded.

Then, the bird was falling from the sky.

It hit the ground with a thud a few yards away and Thea ran to it.

Dropping to her knees, she extricated the totem from the dead bird's claws, holding it between her fingers, unable to quite believe she'd finally done it.

'That was some shot,' Cal said from behind her.

Thea looked up at her two friends, both now wearing their totems on their arms. 'We did it...' she whispered.

Both young men knelt beside her, arms wrapping around her.

'We did,' Kipp said, grinning.

They stayed there for a moment, as though they needed a minute to let the reality sink in. Thea felt emotion thick in her throat and she scolded herself, now was not the time for tears.

'We're all okay,' Kipp was muttering. 'We've all got totems...'

At last, they broke apart.

'Good,' Thea laughed, strapping her warrior totem to her arm. 'Now let's get the fuck back to Thezmarr.'

The trio gathered themselves and went to the edge of the isle to survey their options. They had travelled several islands out and the distance between them and the Bloodwoods on the other side was now considerable.

'How do we want to do this?' Thea yearned to be back on Thezmarrian soil, longed for their victory to be solidified before the Guild Master.

Kipp grimaced as he peered over the ledge. 'Well, we could go down and find a way across the rocks below...? It's low tide now, the waves aren't hitting as hard.'

Thea didn't overly like the sound of that. Low tide or not,

the seas beyond were unpredictable, they'd seen as much themselves only a few nights before.

'You don't want to risk it?' Kipp guessed.

'Not if we can help it,' Thea admitted. 'You didn't see how quickly the storm changed the other night. We were lucky it retreated, but it could just as easily send a storm in to shatter us upon the rocks. Plus, I'm worried about time, it might take too long.'

'What about Thea's idea from before?' Cal said suddenly, his eyes narrowing as he tried to make something on the other side.

Thea blinked. 'Which was…?'

'I could shoot a rope across and get back that way. This time there's not a waiting mob who might cut us down. Anyone over there has already made it, they already have their totems and they're likely already drunk in the Great Hall.'

'I… I'm not sure I've got the upper body strength to climb across another obstacle.' Thea admitted. The gash in her side was throbbing, as was the cut where the first arrow had nicked her and her arms were aching from the bow and previous climb.

'Nor I,' Cal replied, motioning to his bandaged viper bites.

'But we won't have to,' Kipp said, his eyes brightening.

Thea could see his brilliant mind piecing the parts of his strategy together.

'*This* particular island is higher than Thezmarr. If you shoot the rope to that ledge down there…' Kipp pointed. 'Then we can use our belts as hooks across the line and our weight to pull us down and across. Should take less than a minute each…?'

Cal seized Kipp around the neck and kissed the top of his head. 'You're a *wonder*, Kristopher,' he declared.

'I'm taken,' Kipp said pointedly, wrenching himself from his friend's grasp.

Between the three of them, their high spirits were utterly infectious. Unable to stop the wide grin spreading across her face, Thea turned to Cal. 'Well, if you'd do the honours.'

Cal gave a mock bow. 'It would be my pleasure.'

Heat radiated from Thea's chest. She felt light as a feather, as though she could drift off into the air. They had done it, they had truly done it; they were Guardians of Thezmarr.

Kipp tied one end of the length of rope to one of the sturdier trees nearby and Thea checked his knot several times while Cal secured the other end to his arrow.

'You saw the ledge I meant?' Kipp asked.

'You think that's better than a tree in the Bloodwoods?'

Kipp nodded enthusiastically. 'Those trees on the outskirts are Carraway Barks. It's incredibly soft wood and its outer layers peel away and disintegrate. I'd be concerned it might not hold our weight. Plus, the ledge there, it'll make the downward momentum easier. It's a simple climb from there to the top. See?'

'I do indeed,' Cal said, nocking his arrow to his bow.

Thea had to marvel at the strength that rippled through her friend as he drew the string back with keen precision.

He let the arrow fly.

The three of them watched as it soared across the void between island and mainland.

The rope trailed after it and went suddenly taut.

Cal heaved on it, testing its hold. It hardly moved. He turned to them and grinned. 'Who's first?'

'You're sure it's strong enough?' Thea ventured, giving the cable a hearty wrench herself. It *felt* solidly in place.

'Well,' Kipp said, puffing his chest out. 'I'll take one for the team and go first. So long as you promise to tell Milla about this.'

'Does that mean you'll actually introduce us to her next time?' Thea laughed.

Kipp checked his weapons and shield were secure and double checked the totem strapped to his arm before facing her. 'No promises, Althea. Time is of the essence when the opportunity presents itself.'

Her friend undid his belt, and looping it over the rope, gave them a salute. 'See you on the other side.'

Then he was soaring across the gorge, a shout of glee echoing in his wake.

There was a stunned silence before Cal shook his head.

'Do you ever wonder if he's a touch mad?' he asked Thea, staring after Kipp, who was growing smaller in the distance.

'Only every so often...'

Cal laughed, then, seeing Kipp was safely across and already climbing to the top, he motioned to Thea. 'Ladies first.'

With trembling fingers, Thea unbuckled her belt, abstractly hoping her pants didn't fall down halfway across the chasm and fitted it to the rope, yanking down to once again test her weight.

With a final glance at the totem that now gleamed at her right bicep, she launched herself from the cliff.

The icy wind shocked her as it tangled in her braid and whipped her skin, but as Thea soared over the rocks and sea below, her eyes streamed with joy. Gripping her belt with all her might, she let out a wild laugh at the absurdity of it all.

She could hardly believe it. This was freedom. This was *victory*.

The ledge came into clear view and she braced herself to slow before she crashed into the cliff face. Her boots skidded across the stone and she dug her heels in, bringing herself to an abrupt stop. She'd made it.

Looking back across to the Chained Islands, she could make out Cal's figure. She gave him a wave with both hands before threading her belt back through the waist of her pants and starting up to the top of the cliff. It only took a few manoeuvres and then she was scrambling over the edge, Kipp's firm hands hauling her up.

Together, they watched as Cal followed in their wake, soaring across the rope as well. Shortly after, he joined them on Thezmarrian soil and as the sun began to dip, the three of them looked out to what they had conquered; the Chained Islands, the initiation test… Ceremony or not, they were all Guardians of the guild now, protectors of the midrealms —

A shout sounded from below.

They had their weapons drawn in an instant, Cal with his bow and arrow, Kipp and Thea with their swords.

They inched towards the edge of the cliff, to see none other than Sebastos Barlowe on the ledge beneath.

Cal aimed his arrow at his face.

Seb visibly paled, looking around wildly for somewhere to take cover.

There was nowhere. He was exposed and at their mercy.

Thea glanced at Cal's face and the rage that simmered there.

'Cal…' she said quietly.

She didn't recognise the voice her friend used, dark and

full of hatred. 'Give me one reason why I shouldn't shoot this through the bastard's eye.'

'Maybe you should,' Kipp said, sword still raised. 'He deserves it.'

Seb panted hard and fast, his hands were raised in surrender, his eyes squeezed shut. 'Please...' It came out a whisper.

'If you don't kill him, I will,' Kipp growled.

Thea threw herself between her friends and the ledge. 'Don't,' she heard herself say.

Cal baulked. 'You know what he did, Thea... You saw us, what he —'

'I know,' she said, her whole body wrought with tension as she held out her hands to implore them both. 'He hurt me, too. But this isn't you...'

'Suits me just fine,' Cal replied, fury still surging in his gaze, his hands trembling around his bow.

'No, it doesn't,' Thea told him, sheathing her sword. 'This isn't you, and you both know it.'

A beat of silence followed.

And then Kipp gave a heavy sigh. 'She's right, Cal...'

Below, Seb was still frozen in place, his wide eyes now watching them, suddenly calculating.

'Cal...' Thea said gently, reaching for him.

With a rage-filled roar, Cal shifted his bow and shot his arrow clean through Seb's shoulder.

Falling to his knees, Seb screamed, the sound echoing off the cliffs as blood seeped from the wound.

'You deserved a fate far more gruesome than that.' Cal swore viciously and stormed off.

Kipp gave Thea a pained look and went after him.

But Thea lingered at the edge of the Thezmarrian cliff

and crouched there, taking in the sight of Seb, who was clutching his bleeding shoulder, whimpering in pain.

'Do not mistake our mercy for weakness,' she told him, her voice cold. 'When we beat you, everyone will be there to see you fall,' she promised. 'And that's two life debts you now owe me.'

With that, she walked into the Bloodwoods to find her friends.

As the trees closed in around her, an icy shiver washed down her spine. It was enough to make her draw her sword again.

'Cal?' she called out. 'Kipp?' They couldn't have gotten far.

She trekked deeper into the forest, sure she would hear their voices up ahead at any moment.

'Cal? Kipp?' she shouted again, her voice a little higher this time. 'It's not funny —'

No sooner than the words had left her lips, black shadows swept in and suddenly it was almost pitch-black.

A strange, guttural hiss pierced the silence and Thea leapt back, recognising the sound as the one that stalked her nightmares and the scent of burnt hair filled her nostrils.

She felt movement nearby, the hiss close enough to vibrate against her skin. Shaking, Thea inched forward.

Blood sprayed.

Her blood.

CHAPTER THIRTY-SEVEN

A*rheguld reaper* was here.

Claws tore through Thea's shoulder and she screamed as she was sent hurtling through the air, colliding with a tree and sliding to the forest floor with a muffled cry. But she had seen what happened to those who didn't move fast enough. Biting back a yelp of pain, she sprung to her feet, ripping the shield from her back and bracing it in front of her, scanning the darkening forest.

Where are you? Pain blazed at her open wound, hot blood gushing down her arm, but she staggered forward, clutching her sword, trying to peer through the black shadows that swam around her.

How it had gotten to Thezmarr undetected didn't matter right now. She just had to survive. She had to find Cal and Kipp and escape —

A roar rattled the forest, loud enough that she felt it in her bones.

And there, the reaper appeared, towering amongst the trees, making the earth beneath her boots quiver.

Fuck, fuck, fuck. How in the realms was she going to manage this? She'd seen what they were capable of in Delmira. She'd seen what they'd done to Lachin and the others...

Keep a cool head, she told herself, pressing her back to a nearby tree and ignoring the searing agony at her shoulder. Was there more than one? Had they already attacked her friends? The fortress? *Wren?* She pushed the barrage of questions from her mind and adjusted her grip on her sword, the blood trailing down her arm making her hands slippery.

Focus, she commanded.

There was a flash of white and suddenly Thea's blade was sliding down a long, sharp claw, blocking it from slicing into her face. Gasping, Thea parried with it, using her shield to trap the attacking limb. She whirled away, avoiding the rapid slash of the creature's other claw, already gleaming with her blood.

She could do this. She had trained for this. She silenced her thoughts, slowed the thundering of her heart. She knew she had to find that place, deep inside herself, that pocket of calm before the kill.

Her eyes flew open and Thea jumped aside, dodging the whip of a shadow lashing at her. The tip of it kissed her forearm and she screamed, her vision blurring with tears.

It was the agony of a blade red hot from a forge fire, searing her flesh at the slightest touch.

The creature paused, sniffing the air as though savouring the heavy scent of her suffering. It tilted its horned head, studying her, its ribbons of darkness curling, violently curious. The thing stalked towards her, its power seeking her out.

Thea shifted one foot behind the other, not taking her eyes off the reaper as they circled one another in the forest.

It was toying with her, taking its time, revelling in the hunt, the game.

But Thea could hunt, too. She twirled her sword menacingly. If it was blood the shadow wraith wanted, it was blood it would get.

She deflected another slash of its gruesome claws and took the impact of its darkness on her shield with a grunt, the force of it driving her boots into the damp earth, the power of it vibrating through her bones.

Feinting right, Thea delivered a hard thrust of her blade to the creature's sinewy leg.

It shrieked, the ear-piercing sound echoing through the trees.

She lunged again, trying to push her advantage.

But the reaper was clever, experienced in slaying fighters far greater than her, and its patience was suddenly wearing thin. It wanted its prey.

Darting away from another attack, Thea wracked her brain for how the Warswords had done it in Delmira. But they had worked in a team to bring the creatures down and they had Naarvian steel to carve out those dark hearts...

And with her friends nowhere in sight, more than likely dead somewhere nearby.

Here, there was only her. And she could not hold it off forever, she could not bring it down on her own.

Maybe if she'd had some rope, or Cal's bow, she could delay it enough for her to run, but she had neither of those things.

It lunged for her with claws and shadows, ribbons of black whipping at her, coiling past the barrier of her shield, slashing at her legs. Thea scrambled back through the blood-soaked leaves, chest heaving with the effort. She had completed her initiation test with all its dangers and obstacles, only to walk straight into a reaper's trap. Her limbs were burning, her muscles screaming with every movement, and yet she didn't stop.

She threw herself forward with a yell, blade slashing at the creature's exposed limbs. No matter how tired she was, she would fight to the end. She was a Thezmarrian warrior through and through —

Thea went flying, and she slammed into another tree, her teeth singing at the impact, the shock jarring her whole body.

But no, this wouldn't be the end of her. It couldn't be. Unless she wasn't to die, but become one of those monsters... She lurched forward, vision blurring —

A shout carried through the air.

Not her own.

And suddenly, the blaze of flaming twin blades lit up the darkness.

Wilder Hawthorne landed in between her and the reaper.

Thea let out a strangled gasp, her knees buckling at the sight.

But the creature wasn't deterred. It hissed at its new target and the Warsword twirled his fiery swords in invitation.

The reaper gave an enraged shriek as it lunged for Wilder. The predator was a blur of slashing claws and lashes of darkness, but the Warsword knew this deadly dance. He ducked and withdrew from the advance, before attacking in a flurry of slices and strikes to its torso.

'Thea?' Wilder called.

She was half-collapsed against the tree behind her, panting through the reprieve the warrior had given her. Forcing down a breath of air, Thea pushed off from the trunk and raised her own sword.

'To your right.' She lifted her shield up to block a thrashing whip of darkness, and gripping her weapon determinedly, she sliced through the shadows, fighting her way to the exposed side of the creature, where she delivered a hard thrust with her blade.

The reaper shrieked in pain and Thea twisted her sword, wringing out every drop of agony that she could.

'Block!' Wilder shouted.

Thea's shield arm came up again instinctively, just in time to deflect a deadly blow of those razor-sharp claws.

Her strength wavered beneath the crushing force of the reaper's power and she stumbled, her body suddenly feeling every slice, every bruise. Thea remained crouched behind her shield, wheezing as she tried to gather herself.

The monster seemed to sense her weakening resolve and it struck out more savagely than ever, its ribbons of onyx magic coming for her in a relentless wave of attacks. She couldn't block them all, she took one on her shield, and slashed another away with her sword, but the third... The third lash struck her across the top of her chest and she screamed and darkness carved into her, her vision going black and then —

The scorched courtyard smelt of blood and heather.

Bodies lay lifeless on the cobbles; seeping crimson into the ground while the wheels on an upturned cart still spun, mead flowing from broken barrels.

Fresh claw marks ravaged the high walls, carving through the tiny flowers which sprouted even in deep winter, the echoes of ear-piercing shrieks still vibrated through the stone there. Tangled scents of iron and earth drifted up into the night's air, dancing with the shadows, remnants from the wraiths that retreated into the roiling storm above.

Darkness had descended upon Thezmarr, and at its heart was a copper-haired little girl, no older than six, clutching a necklace of dried flowers and a small scythe of Naarvian steel to her pounding chest.

The last of the onyx power left the blade in curling tendrils, wisps of magic swallowed by rolling thunder that seemed to call her name.

Anya.

With a quiet cry, Anya dropped the scythe, the steel singing as it hit the stone, as it fell amidst the rivers of blood that trickled towards her slippered feet.

Time hung suspended for a moment, and there was nothing. No other noise, no other movement. Everything was still and silent.

'You condemn her to death?' said a voice.

Death. *Anya had never fully understood this word. Her mother had tried to explain it to her once...* What was once here is no longer. It has moved on to another world, guarded by the great god, Enovius. *But it had made no sense then and it made no sense now.*

'She is a daughter of darkness, a monster. She needs to be dealt with before she unleashes more madness upon us all,' another voice replied. 'She has brought the truth of the prophecy to our very doorstep...'

'Guild Master, you can't mean —'

'In the shadow of a fallen kingdom, in the eye of the storm

A daughter of darkness will wield a blade in one hand

And rule death with the other
When the skies are blackened, in the end of days
The Veil will fall.
The tide will turn when her blade is drawn.
A dawn of fire and blood.'

Then Anya was somewhere else. A stony shore beneath her feet.

'I'm sorry, lass,' a man murmured. 'There was no convincing him... If Starling was at Thezmarr, it might have been different. He can always get through to the Guild Master. But... I don't know where he is, lass. Nowhere close enough to help you now.' He sighed heavily. 'I don't know how you did what you did, but... though you don't look it, you're dangerous.'

Anya was tired and hungry and scared. Dazed, she let him take her in his arms. He carried her for some time beneath the waning moonlight and she slept against his shoulder, for in sleep, he could have been her father, sturdy and strong.

Only when they came to a stop much later did the little girl wake fully, the fear setting in.

'I want to go home,' she cried. 'I want Mama and Papa.'

The warrior wore a pained expression as he set her down in front of the mouth of a dark cave. 'It'll all be over soon,' he told her, smoothing her hair from her eyes. 'Your parents, they're in there, waiting.' He pointed inside the cave.

In the distance, thunder clapped.

A lie, a soft voice told her.

The little girl knew what a lie was. She had learnt to tell them herself not all that long ago... But this lie was different... Like the shadows that had whipped through the fortress courtyard; the promise of something sinister.

And yet, the cave called to her... A song of recognition, of welcome.

Anya, it called.

She took an unsteady step forward, the warmth of the man leaving her.

His words followed her in a broken whisper, 'May your death be swift and painless. May you rest well with Enovius, little one.'

They faded away along with the man behind her, her feet moving, one after the other, as though in a trance. Anya walked into the cave, deeper and deeper, until she was alone.

For a moment, the pitch-black swallowed her.

There was no swift and painless death waiting for her. There was no death at all.

A breath rattled from within – not her own.

But Anya was not afraid.

For she knew the darkness, and the darkness knew her.

Thea felt untethered from herself as the strange image faded before her and the rest of the world fell away like flecks of ash from a fire. She was dying, she realised, her fate stone had met its match in the black lashings of the shadow wraith. Pain wrapped around every part of her, a searing brand of torment.

Thea rasped for air, choking on the scent of burnt hair once more.

Claws assaulted her and there was no time to think on what she'd seen. She could only think of the agony as she braced herself behind her shield. Unimaginable power knocked her back, stealing the air from her lungs. She tasted iron on her tongue as blood filled her mouth.

The darkness came for her.

And Thea let it take her. She had tried; she had tried *so hard* to leave her mark on this world, but Wren had been right. She was not invincible, and even destiny was no contest to the dark forces sent from beyond the Veil —

'Don't you dare give up now,' came Wilder's deep voice, shattering the rapture of impending death.

The sound brought her back from the brink and stirred something within. Coming back to herself, Thea ignored the pain as a familiar pressure began to build from the centre of her. Something ancient coursed through her veins and she tipped her head to the darkened sky, dropping her weapons. Her hands unfurled at her sides, power pulsing at her palms.

White lightning split the sky and Althea Zoltaire claimed it as her own.

Magic danced at her fingertips and without thinking, she brought its force down upon the shadow wraith.

The creature's scream broke her trance.

The bolt of power vanished, but Thea wouldn't waste this chance. She snatched up her blade and was on her feet again in a second, her whole body charged with surging strength. She advanced on the wraith where it scrambled upright, its skin smouldering where the lightning had struck.

Thea grit her teeth against the beat of lingering pain. Her hand was slick with blood and sweat around her sword, but it didn't stop her from throwing an upward cut with the back edge.

Black and red blood rained.

'To me!' Thea shouted to her fellow warrior, seeing their opening.

Wilder was at her side in an instant, and together, they

forced the weakened creature back, brandishing fire and steel against its shadows.

Side by side, they fought. Thea could feel the searing heat of the Warsword's blazing weapons as he broke away from the clash of claws, only to wield them with even more power, throwing high horizontal cuts to the wraith's torso.

The creature screamed again; the sound vibrating through the entire forest, the entire realm.

Thea threw her shield aside and sprinted for the beast, launching herself into the air. She looped her blade around as she'd seen the Warsword himself do, and with all her remaining strength, she delivered a two-handed thrust to the demon's chest.

Her sword broke through leathered skin, cartilage, muscle and bone.

Suddenly she was falling with the reaper.

Beside her, Wilder had also leapt —

They crashed into the monster, Wilder landing right on top of it, pinning it to the forest floor with each flaming blade embedded in the creature's biceps.

The thing screeched and thrashed in agony, but couldn't dislodge itself.

Wilder's face slick with gore and sweat, he reached for his belt, where he unsheathed Malik's dagger.

Thea didn't take her eyes off him as he held it out to her, grip first, his silver eyes ablaze with determination. His voice was hoarse as he said, 'You're forged with blood and steel now.'

Thea didn't hesitate, her hand was steady as she took the blade and carved into its chest. Black and red blood oozed from the incision site, as well as dozens of other wounds while Thea worked, cutting through foul tissue and tendons.

Its screams weakened and its whole body heaved a strangled wheeze before it fell silent beneath her blade.

Thea slid the dagger deeper, and Wilder's gaze never left her as she took the reaper's heart.

CHAPTER THIRTY-EIGHT

Upon the reaper's death, the shadow and darkness swallowing the Bloodwoods retreated, revealing a sun-dappled canopy and the usual stillness of the forest.

Panting, Wilder dropped his swords and rushed over, his hands closing gently around her, drawing her to him as he examined her amidst the mess of the leaf litter. Panic was bright in his silver eyes, following the indiscernible blood spatters across her shredded clothes, his gaze falling to the hot, wet mass of the wraith's heart heavy in her hand.

'Are you hurt?' he asked quietly. He looked as bad as she felt. Clothes ripped, covered in blood and muck from head to toe, and sporting several nasty bruises and gashes.

'I'll live,' she replied at last, her voice raw.

But his concern only deepened as he peeled her shirt away from her skin, where webs of black veins stood out around a jagged slash at the top of her breasts.

Thea stared at it, too. The skin there seemed to fester before their eyes.

Wilder pushed something into her hand. 'Drink this.'

It was his vial from the Aveum springs.

'I can't, that's yours —'

'Thea, please.' He uncorked it and pushed it towards her mouth.

She looked around the carnage for her satchel. 'I've got iruseed somewhere, that will keep me awake until I can get to the —'

'Thea... Iruseed will do nothing. This is no ordinary wound. I knew someone who was shadow touched... They became part wraith. It's no life I would wish upon anyone, especially you. I've saved the vial all this time, for a wound like this.'

'But —'

'Furies save me, just drink it.'

He was already tipping the vial to her lips.

The trickle of water was sweet, crisp, and fresh on her parched tongue. Her whole body tingled as its magical properties surged through her.

The deepest of her wounds knitted together, leaving only faint pink scars behind. And the network of black veins across her skin retreated, disappearing entirely within mere moments.

'Thank the gods,' Wilder murmured, tracing her healed skin in awe. 'I've seen what a reaper's touch can do. But it worked, you're still... You're still you.'

Thea blinked at him in shock. 'You used your vial on me.'

'I told you I was saving it for something worse.'

'Thank you,' she croaked, her throat thick with emotion. Her hand trembled as she reached out to him, needing to know that he was alright. 'What about you?'

He leaned in, resting his forehead against hers and closing his eyes for a moment. 'I'll live.'

'Good,' Thea managed.

At that, Wilder smiled. 'I'm glad you think so.'

Thea rose up on her knees, an arm snaking around the Warsword's neck and kissed him deeply, needing the reassurance, needing his heat to banish the cold from her bones. 'We survived,' she whispered against his lips.

'Thanks to you.' He drew back to gaze upon her again, awed. 'That was some lightning...'

Thea blinked, the memory of the current coursing through her causing a shudder. 'That was me...' she said slowly, her skin tingling. 'I...'

'Have magic.' Wilder finished for her.

Thea felt dizzy and small. Her voice cracked when she spoke. 'I don't understand how it's possible.'

'Nor do I.' Wilder drew her close. 'But we can figure it out, together.'

Thea's shoulders sagged as she allowed herself a moment to rest against him, to take from his strength and revel in the way that, even now, her body responded to him. But above, the light was fading.

'Magic will have to wait,' she said, gathering herself and breaking the tender moment. 'I need to be at the fortress by sundown.'

Thea suddenly remembered what she'd dropped in the blood-stained dirt. It took a minute for her to find it, but when she did, she held the dagger of Naarvian steel out to Wilder. 'Here.'

But the Warsword shook his head. 'It belongs to you.'

They were quiet as they moved through the Bloodwoods,

though Thea kept catching Wilder stealing awed glances at her, and she, at him. Amidst her varying degrees of disbelief about all that had occurred, one thought echoed intensely as she gazed upon the man who walked beside her.

It was Wren's words from long ago. *A true man will help sharpen your sword, guard your back and fight at your side, in the face of whatever darkness comes...*

There was no sign of Cal or Kipp as they trekked back, no sign of a struggle, or evidence that there had been other reapers or wraiths. Questions peppered Thea's fragile mind, but she fought them back. *Later,* she promised herself as the gates came into view and the sun threatened to dip below the horizon.

When they reached the Great Hall, Wilder pushed the doors open, and they flew inward with a loud bang, startling those within.

Together, Thea and her Warsword entered, faced with the stunned crowd within. As they walked the long stretch to the head table, the silence was so resounding that all Thea could hear was the *drip, drip, drip* of blood leaking from the black heart still clenched in her fist.

The Guild Master leapt to his feet, looking madly from Thea to Wilder, gobsmacked at the state of them. Beside him, King Artos, the other Warswords and commanders, bore similar expressions.

'Somehow, a *rheguld* appeared in the Bloodwoods this afternoon.' Wilder's deep voice carried to the far reaches of the Great Hall.

Despite the sight before him, Osiris braced himself on his knuckles. 'Impossible.'

Another stunned silence thrummed before Thea threw

the black heart at Osiris' feet, blood spattering over the stone floor.

'Is this proof enough?' she said.

Stillness settled across the hall as torchlight flickered, illuminating the gore of the carved heart.

'I was separated from my friends on the way back to the fortress,' Thea explained. 'That thing attacked me in the Bloodwoods.'

It was King Artos who spoke next. 'What in all the realms was a *reaper* doing in Thezmarr?' he demanded. 'Let alone in the midrealms at all?' He wielded his questions with as much force as he would a blade at the Guild Master, who blanched in the face of it.

'We informed the rulers that one of the monsters escaped our clutches at the ruins of Delmira.'

An odd sensation clanged through Thea like a warning bell and the image of that small girl in the scorched courtyard came flooding back to her. *Anya*, the girl who'd set in motion the biggest changes in Thezmarr's history. Why had Thea seen her amidst the black lashings of the shadow wraith?

'Am I to understand that the situation was not rectified?' King Artos asked. 'The people of the midrealms entrust their safety to the Guardians. Are you telling me that you failed in this endeavour?'

'Majesty, I assure you —'

King Artos raised a hand. 'It sounds to me that Thezmarr and the midrealms owe Miss Zoltaire a great debt.'

Osiris' face had reddened, his eyes slid to Thea and then to Wilder. 'You mean to tell me that this girl slayed the reaper?'

Tension rolled off the Warsword in waves. 'Yes. It was Thea who carved out its heart.'

Osiris blinked. 'A mere shieldbearer?'

Thea squared her shoulders and pulled her totem into view. 'I'm not a shieldbearer anymore. I am a Guardian of the midrealms.'

King Artos clapped Osiris on the shoulder. 'Now Guild Master, if *this* is the calibre of warrior you are honing at Thezmarr, we have no issues whatsoever.'

Osiris continued to stare at Thea until, eventually, he nodded. 'Very well. Congratulations Miss Zoltaire. We will certainly need to debrief on the situation further, but for now we must continue with the Guardian Ceremony and the announcement of the Warsword apprenticeships.'

Thea's stomach fluttered at the very word, but she let Wilder pull her to the side of the hall so the proceedings could go on. Dazed, she watched on as her peers' totems were verified by the Guild Master.

Her heart leapt as she saw Cal and Kipp approach the table, relief surging through her, releasing knots of tension in her body.

'They're safe,' she whispered to Wilder. 'How, I have no idea...'

'I think the reaper was lying in wait for you,' he replied quietly, watching as her friends shook hands with Osiris. 'It had no interest in Snowden and Whitlock. It was *your* power it hungered after.'

A chill raked down Thea's spine, causing her knees to knock. But the conversation was cut short as Osiris finished congratulating the new Guardians and welcoming them officially into the ranks of Thezmarr's warriors.

'Now for what we've all been waiting for,' he declared,

arms outstretched. 'Announcing the Warsword's new apprentices. Your Majesty, if you'd do the honours?'

Beaming, King Artos clasped his hands together. 'With pleasure, Guild Master. Good people of Thezmarr,' he began. 'On behalf of Harenth, Aveum and Tver, congratulations to all of those who made it through the initiation test. The midrealms welcomes your service and your protection.'

Thea could feel the restlessness of the surrounding crowd. The shuffling of feet, the fiddling with cutlery and the barely audible whispers of impatience.

'The Warsword apprentices have been chosen as follows...' King Artos gave a long, dramatic pause. 'Apprentice to Vernich Warner, is Sebastos Barlowe.'

Thea's blood ran cold. 'No,' it came out a broken whisper.

There was a smattering of applause from behind her, but Thea didn't dare turn back, didn't dare face Cal and Kipp, whose vengeance she had stolen, only to be faced with this horrific reality.

Seb, his injured shoulder bandaged, his face slick with sweat, came forward.

But the king gave them no time to process such things. 'Apprentice to Torj Elderbrock,' King Artos called above the noise.

Thea's heart stuttered. This was it. This was the moment she'd been working towards for months. Her palms grew clammy and she imagined the sound of her name being called —

'Is Callahan Whitlock.'

Thea didn't know where to look, certainly not at Cal, who was now striding proudly towards the Warsword, his hand outstretched.

Thea forced her own hands together, clapping with the

rest of them, though her face heated against her will at the humiliation. The applause that followed Cal's name was much more enthused.

Torj Elderbrock had chosen Cal.

And much to her dismay, Thea understood why. But it didn't dull the hurt, nor the pang of envy she felt knowing Wilder's apprentice was next to be announced.

At last, she glanced up at the head table, only to find Osiris' eyes on her again, wide in outrage. He flung up a hand. 'Hold on, Majesty,' he half-shouted, his chair scraping as he left the table and stormed towards Thea.

Thea fought the urge to step back. *What now?*

'Tell me that's not what I think it is,' he glowered when he reached her, pointing at her hip.

Frowning, Thea looked down.

There, Malik's dagger hung from her belt.

'Tell me that's not Naarvian steel, that it's not the dagger that got you into this mess in the first place,' the Guild Master demanded.

Thea recoiled but did not yield a step, her heart hammering. 'I can't tell you that, Sir...'

Spit gathered at the corners of Osiris' mouth, his nostrils flaring. 'The last time a female touched a sacred blade, chaos rained down on Thezmar,' he raved. 'Naarvian steel in the hands of women *calls the darkness*. How do we know it wasn't *you* who lured the wraith from the Veil?'

Wilder stepped forward. 'Because I gave the dagger to her,' he growled. 'I watched as she carved out the monster's fucking heart. '

'Then she is *your* responsibility, Hawthorne. You're the Warsword who placed a Naarvian blade in the hand of a woman. *The tide will turn when her blade is drawn. A dawn of fire and blood.* You alone will be held accountable.'

'So be it,' Wilder said. 'I vouch for her.'

A look of triumph spread across the Guild Master's face.

'Good,' he said. 'Then I hereby announce Althea Zoltaire as Wilder Hawthorne's apprentice.'

WILDER HAWTHORNE

W ilder dragged Thea from the Great Hall, desperate for somewhere to talk to her in private. He settled for the broom closet he'd found her in weeks ago, half bleeding to death. With a shudder, he realised that her blood still stained the stone floor.

'Wilder?' Thea stared up at him in confusion as he shut the door behind them.

He was being irrational, hauling her away like this, but he had to talk to her. If they could just get on the same page, everything could still work out for them, the magic, the apprenticeship - it could all be dealt with.

Ignoring the damp smell of the closet, he gripped her arms gently. 'If we both reject your appointment as my apprentice, there's nothing they can do. They can't force us,' he told her, pulse racing. All his senses seemed heightened in her presence, his insides vibrating. They could still be together, things between them could still work, just not as master and apprentice, for with how he felt about her, he couldn't be the master she needed.

His thoughts slowed as he took in her expression. Thea's eyes were downcast, her dark brows furrowed as she fingered that piece of jade around her neck.

'What is it?' he asked.

'I don't want to reject the appointment.'

Wilder stared at her, suddenly light-headed. 'What?'

'This is my last chance,' she said, a pleading note in her voice. 'My last chance to become a Warsword. You're it.'

'But we agreed —'

'That I would nominate Torj as my mentor, which I did. But now... It's you or no mentor at all. I only have three years to make my mark. Less.'

Wilder's hands fell away from her. 'Three years? What are you talking about?'

Thea's bottom lip quivered as she placed the piece of jade, the fate stone, in his palm. 'I'm talking about this.'

Wilder stared at the marked gem. When he had first seen it, his heart had nearly fallen through his stomach, but when he'd asked...

'You told me this wasn't yours...' he said slowly, rolling it between his fingers.

Twenty-seven, the stone read, the number sending goosebumps rushing across his skin in a cold sweat.

'I lied.'

His eyes locked to hers, pulse spiking. 'You lied?'

Thea nodded, her eyes lined with tears. 'I didn't want you to pity me... I didn't want you to think it was a waste to train me.'

Wilder flinched, dropping the stone. It fell back to Thea, landing between her breasts, hanging from its leather string, taunting him. She truly thought he was so cold?

His eyes burned, and his throat constricted. He wasn't

sure he could muster the courage to ask what needed to be asked.

Twenty-seven, the number echoed in his mind.

Thea answered anyway, her voice soft. 'It's the age I'll be when I die.'

Suddenly, the broom closet was too fucking small, and Wilder couldn't breathe. His chest heaved, his heart heavy. Thea would die at the age of *twenty-seven.* Three years from now... The future he hadn't even realised he'd been imagining flashed before him cruelly, a beautiful unfolding of events that would never come to pass.

Thea, *his* Thea, wanted something more from the little life she had left. And Wilder knew he could not give that to her if he was both lover and mentor. Their brief time together had branded him in a way that terrified him. Already he could think of nothing else and he knew that there was no way he could teach her, could train her if they were together... If they were together, he knew he wouldn't push her the way she would need to be, because what she wanted was to become a Warsword of Thezmarr, and a Warsword needed to be pushed to breaking point.

'Please, Wilder,' Thea choked. 'I need this. More than anything.'

More than anything... More than you.

'So you insist on honouring the Guild Master's decision?' he asked. He wanted to scream, he wanted to rage at the Furies themselves for a gift that was all too fleeting.

Thea met his stare, her eyes red-rimmed but determined. 'I do.'

He and Thea... They had started something in the Bloodwoods, and long before that, but this... This changed everything. This was her life, her choice. And he would always put her first. If she was to attempt the Great Rite, then he was going to give her the best fucking chance he could. That meant being Warsword Hawthorne, her mentor and master, not Wilder, her lover. There could be no room for confusion, no room for interpretation. He had to end it. Despite what he felt for her, he couldn't save her by being with her. He could only do that by being the hardest, fiercest mentor to ever walk the midrealms.

Shoving his trembling hands into his pockets, he fixed her with a cold, hard stare. 'You lied to me.'

She reached for him. 'I'm sorry, I —'

'Don't bother. It makes things simple,' he said, words harsh as he pushed her hands away, something within fracturing.

'Wilder —'

'If you insist on this stupid arrangement, then so be it. We will be mentor and apprentice, nothing more.'

Thea's eyes went wide. 'But what about —'

He drew himself up to full height and reached for the door, his expression pure wrath. 'What happened in the Bloodwoods was a mistake. It won't ever happen again, Alchemist.'

He couldn't stand the pressure building in his chest any longer.

Wilder fled the broom closet, leaving the fortress and his new apprentice behind.

CHAPTER THIRTY-NINE

W hen he was gone, a ragged gasp escaped Thea, and she doubled over, clutching her middle. The pain had struck at her heart first, but now... Now she hurt all over. In the privacy of the shitty broom closet, she allowed herself a minute, just one, to absorb the ache in her chest, the punch to the gut, to exhale through the agony.

For a brief moment, the events of the past twenty-four hours threatened to overwhelm her, hitting her hard and fast, but she clung to one feeling in particular, one that numbed her and fuelled the fire within: rage.

Thea was no longer an alchemist, no longer a shieldbearer: she was a *Guardian of the midrealms* and apprentice to the most infamous Warsword in history. She would not break, not over this.

Who the fuck was Hawthorne to be angry at *her*? *She* was the one who was dying. *She* was the one who raced against the hourglass of fate.

Her fingertips tingled, answering the terror tempest that whirled in her chest. The part of her that had slept dormant within for so long now had both eyes open and it wanted to be unleashed.

And she knew exactly where to direct it.

Wren was alone in the alchemy workshop and she took one look at Thea's blood-streaked, ragged appearance and burst into tears, throwing herself at Thea despite her apparent injuries, hugging her tight. While Wilder's vial had taken care of the worst of her injuries, Thea still felt tender.

'Gods, Thee… What happened to you?' Wren asked, her voice breaking, her tears wetting Thea's neck. 'I tried to get word of you, but they said you hadn't returned.'

A flood of memories and emotions came rushing back to Thea, so intense she had to steady herself on the edge of the table.

'I need to talk to you,' Thea said quietly.

Wren stepped back, suddenly silent.

Is that realisation dawning there? Thea wondered, staring at her sister, numbness spreading from her chest outwards. Wren had always been her first confidant, she knew everything there was to know about Thea, the good, the bad, the death looming over her. And yet… She suddenly felt as though she didn't know Wren at all.

'Is there something you want to tell me?' Thea asked softly.

Wren turned to busy herself again with her tinctures, her hands flitting about the range of glass vials. 'That I'm glad you're alive? That I'm wondering what in the realms went on out there?!'

But Thea's mind was spinning. *'You have no idea… No idea what I have done for us,'* her sister had yelled not all that long ago. And Thea had never thought to ask what *exactly* Wren had done for them. Until now.

'No... None of that,' she replied.

'Then what?'

'You know what...' It was taking all of Thea's strength to remain upright, exhaustion and pain threatening to sweep her away. But she would *not* have this conversation from a sickbed. 'You lied to me.'

It wasn't lost on her that her words echoed those Wilder had spoken to her mere moments ago.

But Wren didn't flinch. 'I did? About what?'

'Magic.'

Thea stared at her sister, waiting for the cries of denial, waiting for the show of shock and the claims of ignorance.

But none came.

When her sister turned to face her, her stare was as defiant as ever. 'Yes,' Wren said at last, with not a trace of regret. 'I lied.'

Thea's legs did buckle then and she caught herself on the edge of the table, her sister making no move to assist her.

'Why...' she managed, ears ringing. 'Why would you lie about that?'

Wren crossed the small space between them and standing right in front of Thea, reached for the fate stone at her breast. The cause of so much pain and suffering already. It was stained with blood and muck, but the jade colour gleamed through.

'I did more than lie about it,' Wren said slowly, turning the stone over in her fingers. 'I suppressed it.'

'*What?*' Thea couldn't believe what she was hearing from her own sister's mouth.

Wren tapped the fate stone with her dirt-lined fingernail. 'When was the last time you took this off?'

'I... What does that...' but Thea trailed off, the weight on her chest threatening to crush her.

Gently, Wren pushed her down to sit on a nearby stool. 'I've been coating that stone with a powerful suppressant for years.'

Thea could only gape at her, her stomach knotted.

Wren watched her sadly. 'I felt mine when I was much younger —'

Thea's head snapped to hers. 'Yours?'

'Yes. I have the same magic as you. I suspect you managed to keep yours at bay with all your physical activity. You were always running off somewhere, always trying to scrap with the fortress boys, always demanding that we play Dancing Alchemists... I was more sedentary. I think that meant it settled in me sooner.'

'This... It's impossible, Wren.'

'Tell that to the lightning coursing through our veins.'

Thea's hands were shaking. 'Wren.'

But her sister wasn't done. 'I created the suppressant when I was fourteen and felt the first crackle of power at my fingertips. You showed no signs, but I knew it was only a matter of time. Then, six years ago, when you were crying on the clifftops about that stupid stablehand, I felt it ripple in you as well. So I stole your fate stone and treated it with the same suppressant I had been using for years. You've been none the wiser all this time.'

'But I asked you, that night Cal and Kipp were hurt. I asked you and you laughed in my face. You made me sound insane —'

'You weren't ready. And you were so easily deterred, even though you'd felt the power yourself. You dismissed it. You let a few words deny the fabric of your very being.'

Thea stared at her hands, for the first time noticing the blackened marks at her fingertips. 'Until today,' she croaked. 'When I used lightning against a *rheguld reaper*.'

Wren jolted, failing to hide her shock. 'Yes, well... Magic can overpower even the strongest of alchemies in the most desperate of situations.'

'How... How do you know so much? Does anyone else know?'

'I'm a scholar,' Wren replied matter-of-factly. 'As soon as I started showing... symptoms of magic, I started my research. But no, no one else knows, though I think that Warsword of yours suspects.'

'He's not my Warsword.' Thea felt sick. 'But if we have magic, that means... This can't be, Wren. We're just orphans abandoned to Thezmarr, nobodies.'

Wren was watching her carefully, monitoring her response. 'Nobodies don't have magic, Thea.'

Suddenly, it was all too much. Thea felt none of her lingering pain, none of her exhaustion as she lurched to her feet, heart hammering wildly, breaths coming in short and shallow.

'Thea, I did it to protect us, to protect you.'

'No.' Thea backed away from her sister.

Wren reached for her. 'How many lives do you think you have left, Thee?'

But Thea could take no more. That pit of power inside her yawned wider, a chasm of magic within sending a blazing current through her veins, demanding to be freed. Pushing aside her injuries, the bloodshed and the black marks at her fingertips, she left the fortress, and for the first time in their lives, Wren did not follow.

. . .

Althea Zoltaire found herself atop the jagged black mountain cliffs of Thezmarr, looking out onto the darkening horizon. The sun was long gone and the swollen clouds loomed heavy over the churning seas below.

'You have magic,' Hawthorne had declared on his porch, what felt like a lifetime ago.

And her sister had laughed when she'd repeated those words. 'Can you imagine?'

All her life, that crackling in her veins, that strange sensation creeping across her skin, that restlessness… Pieces of a long unsolved puzzle started to fit into place.

And then there had been the reaper, struck by the lightning at her hand, its shriek still ringing in Thea's ears, its blood still coating her skin.

Thea's fingers went to her fate stone, her curse.

Wren had used her obsession with it against her so cunningly.

Liar, the voice in her head hissed. Her sister had betrayed her.

With a strangled sob, Thea ripped the leather string from her neck and, with all her remaining strength, threw the piece of jade over the edge of the cliff with a scream.

Without its weight, without it suppressing all that came naturally to her, she was knocked back.

Power barrelled into her, lightning crackling at her fingertips, stealing the breath from her lungs. Rasping for air, she staggered forward, something calling to her out on the horizon.

She didn't know what she was reaching for, but when she did, her arm outstretched, her finger pointing to where the sky met the sea —

Three thick bolts of lightning carved through the realms,

brighter and stronger than any she'd ever seen, threatening to split the world apart as if in retribution for her turmoil.

And Thea felt it in her bones, in her heart, in her soul.

The lightning belonged to her, and she, to it.

Magic surged, vibrant bolts dancing at her fingertips. Above, black clouds gathered and thunder clapped, raging with her.

Behind her, a twig snapped, and she whirled around, eyes wide.

Wilder Hawthorne emerged from the jagged rocks. His gaze locked on her, locked on the power radiating from her.

'I've asked you this before and I'll ask once more,' he said, his deep voice adding further charge to her magic as he took a step towards her.

'*Who are you?*'

EPILOGUE

WILDER HAWTHORNE

'*ho are you?*' Wilder demanded, staring at the woman whose name, whose voice, whose touch had set his body alight and nearly destroyed him. Even now, as a black tempest gathered around her and waves crashed violently below, he felt utterly anchored in the moment, to *her*.

Thea whirled around, shock rippling off her, lightning dancing at her fingertips. He could feel her power thrumming in his chest, could feel its untapped potential tangled in her confusion, her rage.

He took a step towards her —

'Don't!' she shouted, her eyes wide. 'I... I don't know how to control it,' she said. 'I didn't know...'

How is that possible? He had seen her summon that power and spear the reaper with it. He stared at her, taking in every little detail – the lack of the fate stone at her breast, her torn, blood-soaked clothes and the utter terror lacing her words.

She was vulnerable in an entirely different way to how she had been in the broom closet. There, she had feared the pain of losing him and losing her future, here... Here she feared herself and what she might unleash upon the world.

A daughter of darkness. The words echoed in his chest.

'It's alright,' he told her.

More lightning split the sky over the thrashing seas, the bolts at her fingertips growing brighter as if in answer. Her magic was immense, chaotic and beautiful, just like her.

She stared at it in wonder, in horror. 'How can this be?'

In this moment, his harsh words were forgotten and he watched as she blinked several times, as though hoping that upon opening her eyes again, the evidence would be gone and she could convince herself it had never been there.

Wilder took another step towards her, to do what, he didn't know. He just needed to be closer to her.

'I don't want to hurt you,' she said.

'You won't,' he told her, meeting her gaze, trying to offer some semblance of reassurance.

'How did this happen?' she asked, voice trembling.

He stood beside her now, careful not to touch her. 'Why don't you tell me that, Alchemist?'

At the title, Thea's whole body shuddered, her magic crackling around them. 'Wren...' she croaked. 'She lied to me. She... did something to my fate stone.'

Ah. So the sister is involved in this. Of course... The master alchemist.

'We'll figure it out.' He didn't take his eyes off the lightning dancing between her fingertips. It glowed an other-wordly blue, a jagged network of forks flickering at her command.

'We?' she asked weakly.

'Yes, *we*,' Wilder replied firmly. 'You're my apprentice, after all.'

Thea's shoulders sagged, and with a final flash, the lightning vanished. Overhead, the black clouds retreated, rolling out to sea with a thunderous roar.

Body tense, Wilder closed his hands around hers, finding a soft energy that hummed there.

At his touch, Thea swayed, her lips parting as if in surprise.

When she fell, he caught her just in time.

The Warsword carried his apprentice back to his cabin, his mind churning with all that he'd seen and all that he was yet to understand. Thea's body was limp in his arms. Despite the healing properties of the Aveum springwater, she was utterly spent from the trial, the battle with the monster, and her discovery of magic.

Magic. He'd suspected since that unfortunate night with her friends on the cliffs. He'd sensed it then: the lightning bowing to her silent order.

And yet, she hadn't known. She truly thought she was an orphan from Thezmarr and nothing more...

Wilder kicked open the door to his cabin. This was *not* how he'd imagined the day unfolding. The devastating sex, the high of claiming her as his, the utter terror when he'd felt the reaper hungering for power – *her* power.

When he'd seen the darkness lashing at her, he'd lost all semblance of control. Fear unlike anything he had ever known had gripped his heart in its claws and refused to let go. Only the rhythm of his blades swinging and Thea's presence fighting beside him had guided him through.

He faltered at the thought of everything that had come after. Her brush with the cursed reaper's claws at her chest;

the Guild Master's manipulation of them both; her confession about the fate stone and his dismissal of her.

After their wretched conversation in the broom closet... He'd planned to leave his newly announced apprentice behind to travel to Harenth and get roaring drunk with Marise. It was the only way he knew how to deal with a fraction of what had transpired between them.

But as he'd saddled his stallion with trembling hands, he'd seen the lightning carve through the skies and he'd known. Her power had called to his. She needed him.

Wilder hadn't thought twice, he'd moved. The climb up the cliffs had been a blur.

Now, swallowing the thick lump in his throat, he placed her on his bed, still unconscious, mercifully lost to the world around her.

Understanding that he was in shock himself, he paced the cabin, toying with the necklace of flowers Thea had braided all those months ago, something he couldn't bear to throw away. Jaw set, shoulders tense, he watched over her, counting the rise and fall of her chest before his eyes landed on the volume Malik had given him in the library.

A Study of Royal Lineage Throughout the Midrealms.

Wilder's scalp prickled as he traced the title, remembering how his brother had tried to show him something, but his distress and Audra's appearance had brought that to a halt. Now, he let the book fall open on the table before him. His heart leapt at the messy scrawl he recognised as Malik's. His brother had drawn a star next to a long list of royals.

Wilder read on, a wave of goosebumps spreading over his arms, his stomach hardening. He read the text over and over, his thoughts swirling so quickly it was hard to follow them.

But follow he did, for the book confirmed the very thing he had suspected since they'd rescued the shieldbearers from the mountain caves.

Malik had known all along. His final spoken words to Thea when he'd been in the infirmary after the wraith battle had been, *Beware the fury of a patient Delmirian.*

He had known.

At last, Wilder set the heavy tome aside to wait.

It was a long while before Thea came to, but when she did, she stared up at him, those celadon eyes brimming with an unbroken tempest.

He swore quietly as all he had guessed rang true.

He now knew three things…

First; Althea Zoltaire was a *storm wielder*. The magic she possessed made her not only one of the *lost royal heirs* of the midrealms, but a princess of none other than the kingdom of Delmira.

Second; Althea Zoltaire had been forged with blood and steel, and was now, against his wishes, his apprentice.

And third… Despite the harsh words he had spoken and the vows he had taken, Wilder Hawthorne, the Hand of Death, a Warsword of Thezmarr, was irrevocably in love with her.

ACKNOWLEDGEMENTS

I'll be the first to admit that writing this book scared me. Be it the shift in subgenre, the more adult content, or the scope of the adventure I wanted to embark on, there were times when *Blood & Steel* felt beyond challenging. However, through it all, was an incredible support network of beautiful people.

First, to Gary... Another dedication to your name, and with good reason. Thank you for encouraging me to take the leap with this new series, for the seemingly endless brainstorming sessions and the weekends spent going over feedback. In particular, thank you for your suggestions about the prophecy, as well as Kipp and the Laughing Fox. His return to the tavern will always remind me of what it's like to walk into a bar with you in Queenstown. In the broader life sense, thank you for being the most supportive partner an author could ask for.

To the rebel queen, Sacha, I'm probably sending you a voice memo as you read this. Thank you for your wisdom and your endless encouragement. I'm sure I've said it before and I'll say it again: I honestly don't know how I got through this whole author thing before you came along.

Aleesha, thank you, as always, for your insightful feedback and pushing me to be a better writer, even when I can't stand the sight of the book anymore.

To my fellow author friends, Clare Sager and Sylvia Mercedes, thank you for helping me understand this subgenre a little better, for answering my questions and for your encouragement.

Thank you to Anne, a very special reader and friend from across the pond. Your beautiful messages and gifts have meant the world to me, and your typo-hunting skills are next to none, thank you.

To my amazing patrons, thank you so much for your patience with me as I disappear into my writing cave, and for your support with all my updates. A special thank you to whoever suggested the name 'Audra' when I was at my wit's end for naming characters. Though I can't find the thread, I'm sure it was one of you!

To the Scheuerer clan back in Sydney... It's been nearly four years since we've last seen each other, but as always, thank you for your love and support from afar.

Thank you to my wonderful friends who show their ongoing support in a myriad of ways: Lisy, Eva, Fay, Natalia, Claire, Hannah, Ben, Erin, Danielle, Phoebe, Maria, Bethany, Podge, Joe, Annie, Chloe and Nattie.

More special thank yous to these incredible bookstagram friends: literarycollectors, itsmejayse, bookbookowl, bookscandlescats, bookishbron, leezland, just_perfiction, queenof_midnight, bookbriefs, balancingbooksandcoffee, joyfulreader, linathebookaddict, labsandliterature, leezland, clareapediabooks, coffeebooksandmagic and devoured_pages.

And as always, last, but never least... Thank YOU, dear reader, for choosing this book, for joining me on another adventure. Here's to the next one!

ABOUT THE AUTHOR

Helen Scheuerer is the fantasy author of the bestselling trilogy, *The Oremere Chronicles,* and the *Curse of the Cyren Queen* quartet. Often likened to the popular series *Throne of Glass* and *Game of Thrones,* her work has been highly praised for its strong, flawed female characters and its action-packed plots.

Helen's love of writing and books led her to pursue a creative writing degree and a Masters of Publishing. Now a full-time author, Helen lives amidst the mountains in New Zealand and is constantly dreaming up new stories. You can find out more via her website: www.helenscheuerer.com

ALSO BY HELEN SCHEUERER

Made in the USA
Monee, IL
10 August 2023